# ABSOLUTION CREEK

Also by Nicole Alexander

*The Bark Cutters*
*A Changing Land*
*Divertissements: Love, War, Society – Selected Poems*

# NICOLE ALEXANDER

## ABSOLUTION CREEK

BANTAM

SYDNEY  AUCKLAND  TORONTO  NEW YORK  LONDON

A Bantam book
Published by Random House Australia Pty Ltd
Level 3, 100 Pacific Highway, North Sydney NSW 2060
www.randomhouse.com.au

First published by Bantam in 2012
This edition published by Bantam in 2013

Addresses for companies within the Random House Group can be found at
www.randomhouse.com.au/offices

National Library of Australia
Cataloguing-in-Publication entry

Alexander, Nicole L.
Absolution creek/Nicole Alexander.

ISBN 978 1 86471 282 7 (pbk.)

A823.4

Front cover photograph of horses by Sylvain Cordier, courtesy of Getty Images
Front cover photograph of woman courtesy of Image Source/Corbis
Back cover photograph by Kevin McGrath, courtesy of Wildlight
Cover design by Blue Cork
Internal design by Midland Typesetters, Australia
Typeset in Fairfield Light by Midland Typesetters, Australia
Printed in Australia by Griffin Press, an accredited ISO AS/NZS 14001:2004
Environmental Management System printer

Random House Australia uses papers that are natural, renewable and recyclable
products and made from wood grown in sustainable forests. The logging and
manufacturing processes are expected to conform to the environmental regulations
of the country of origin.

*For those who are lost, who would be found.*

**absolution** *n.* 1. the act of absolving; release from consequences, obligations, or penalties

## ⋘ Chapter 1 ⋙

## North Sydney, 1923

The jolt of knuckle on flesh pushed Jack backwards. He felt his lip swelling and in retaliation aimed a punch directly at Mills McCoy's freckled nose. His next blow winded the Irish hooligan so that he doubled up in pain. Jack wanted to put the boot into the man, however his father had always encouraged him to fight fair, even when his opponent possessed more underhand tactics than the rats running wild in the Rocks.

Mills wiped his bloody nose and spat on the road. 'You always did have a sneaky jab, Jack,' he complained, his breathing ragged. 'Ever since you were ten and I stole that bit of bread from you.'

Jack held out a dinner-plate-sized hand and Mills tossed him the shilling coin. 'That was eight years ago, Mills, and you're still picking on youngsters.' Jack turned to a boy who was standing behind him with a loaf of bread and a string of sausages under his arm, and dropped the coin into the lad's palm. 'Next time your ma asks you to fetch the bread, do it right quick.' The sandy-haired kid nodded his head furiously and ran off.

1

'You turned into one of those do-gooders, Jack Manning?' Mills asked. Having caught his breath he was ready for another round. He lifted his fists; moved his feet from left to right.

Jack rolled his shoulders in anticipation. 'Don't you ever get sick of acting the school bully?'

'Not with you, Jack. You've only bested me once.'

'If you don't count outing with Mandy Wade. She never did take to you, eh Mills?'

Mills swung a meaty punch, which glanced off Jack's shoulder. They circled each other slowly.

'What're you doing over here, anyway? Are the pickings getting too slight in your neighbourhood?' Jack nodded towards the expanse of Sydney Harbour and the Rocks area, which straddled the fore-shore beyond. They were standing on the corner of Blue and Miller Streets, a layer of cold glazing the terrace houses and shops that stretched down the hill to the water's edge. Bunting still hung from the fronts of some buildings following the first turning of the sod for the Sydney Harbour Bridge only a few days prior.

Mills threw a punch that would have floored a bullock had Jack not ducked and landed a swift uppercut to Mills's cheek. The Irishman staggered. He spat another wad of blood onto the footpath. 'I've a mind to finish you, Manning.'

'What, without your pack to back you up?' Jack gave Mills a spiky jab to the forearm.

Mills wiggled his nose with obvious pain as a shiny black police wagon crawled the length of the street to park a few hundred yards away. 'You're always saved from a sound thrashing, Manning.' Mills gestured towards the coppers with his thumb and, searching for tobacco, nonchalantly began rolling a smoke.

'They'll be parked down there for a while, you know,' Jack informed him.

'I've got time.' Mills lit his smoke and nodded at the bunting. 'This bridge'll mean the ruination of the Rocks.'

2

'You've been listening to the scandalmongers. I was in the crowd not two days ago. Saw John Bradfield himself, I did. Hundreds of people, there were. There was a band and we all sang "Advance Australia Fair".'

'We don't mean nothing to them toffs. They need a road to get to this here bridge they're talking about, and my pa reckons it'll go straight over the likes of us. They're talking a new railway line and the resumption of houses.'

Jack knew the talk. They too were near the path of the bridge on the northern side. 'Nothing's been decided,' he answered cautiously, glancing down the street towards the coppers who were now chatting to Father Patrick. He was a crafty one, Mills. 'Why are you over here?'

'Thought I'd go aways a bit and find work in one of the northern suburbs. Maybe wood chopping, timber carting, that sort of thing.' He snorted once, twice; the mucus landed glistening at Jack's feet. 'Why wait for the rest of the family to be turned out with this bridge debacle? That's not for me. Figured I'd try my luck without the rest of them riding my heels.' Mills rubbed his hands together; cracked his knuckles one by one.

Jack could just imagine Mills doffing his cap, a load of firewood under his arm at the door of some gentlewoman in the leafy northern suburbs. He was a heavyset, ungainly man, with a fighter's busted nose and a face like a partially stretched concertina. Such looks would hardly endear him to the gentrified. 'Well, good luck.' Jack gestured over his shoulder.

The constables were out of the van and stretching their legs. The priest could be heard laughing.

Mills's eyes clouded. 'We'll leave it for another time then, Manning?'

'Right you are,' he replied as they parted company. Although not averse to the odd round of fisticuffs, today Jack's mind remained fixed on a rendezvous of a far more pleasant kind.

Jack dabbed at his cut lip with a handkerchief before checking that his shirt, waistcoat and suit coat were presentable. He glanced down the street in both directions. Their meeting place was a shady tree a good block from Olive's parents' home. Rubbing his hands against the cold he tried to calm down a little. He wasn't a kid peering through a lolly-shop window any more.

Olive was waiting for him, wearing a drop-waisted beige dress and long coat. A green clouche hat sat low over her eyebrows. Jack was fascinated by her shapely ankles, and silently blessed the new fashion for shorter skirts. 'Buy you a soda down at the arcade,' he said, trying not to stare too admiringly.

Olive slipped her arm through his. 'What happened to your lip?'

Jack feigned ignorance. 'Oh, that. Knocked it at the store. It's nothing.'

'Hmm. Well, I've news. I'm to start at Jessop's Hairdressing next week. I'm to be a trainee.'

'You? Working for Mrs Jessop?'

'Jack Manning, women have been working in earnest since the war began, and they've kept on working.'

'I didn't mean that. I meant your parents.'

'Oh, I'll tell them and they won't like it,' Olive replied firmly. 'They don't want me to work. However, everyone is out doing something and I am nearly seventeen.'

'Your sister isn't working,' Jack pointed out. Still, he admired Olive's determination to be like everybody else. She'd read Latin and studied home sciences at a private girls' school, yet here she was by his side talking about getting a job.

'What they won't like is my employer. Mrs Jessop runs a boarding house in Blue Street as well as her hairdressing business.' Olive pinched her nostrils together and crossed both her eyes as she looked down the bridge of her nose. 'So lower class,' she mimicked her mother.

'Olive Peters, I'm shocked.'

They walked briskly across to Alfred Street, careful of the tram rushing down to the Milsons Point ferry terminal and wary of the horse-drawn carts, cars and light trucks heading in a myriad of directions. Olive stared at the large terraces with their twenty-foot frontages, and smiled at a uniformed maid sneaking a quick puff of a cigarette outside. There were children returning from school in straw boaters, with long socks and school satchels; and the odd dray and horseman trundling slowly uphill, having recently disembarked from a punt. The hot-food shops began soon after. Jack felt his stomach rumble as he smelt pies and toffees and fish and chips.

'No you don't,' Olive cautioned when his feet strayed towards a vendor spruiking the catch of the day.

They tarried outside shop fronts as Olive admired hats and stockings, blouses and dresses. 'There always seems to be a lot of beige,' Jack remarked as she marvelled at a white silk clouche hat for sale at over one pound.

'They say that there is so much khaki dye left from the war that we'll be wearing beige until the thirties. Don't laugh, it's true.'

Jack looked pointedly at her ankles. 'War shortages and oversupply, eh? Well, I'm happy with that.'

Olive tugged on his arm. 'Scallywag.'

He wrenched her away from a window display of flesh-coloured stockings.

'Why, I do believe you're blushing!' she teased.

'That's a bit modern.' It was one thing to show a little leg when covered in black, tan or white, but flesh-coloured? He wasn't a wowser or a moralist, however it made him uncomfortable to think that the likes of Mills McCoy could glimpse his girl's ankles. 'Come on.'

Together they walked downhill, the winter cold seeping up from the cement beneath. A clear view of the harbour lay before them, the water gleaming grey in the late afternoon light. Across its surface the wakes from the many craft crisscrossed each other like streamers. Jack tried counting the vessels on the busy waterway but gave up at thirty-five. There were numerous ferries, punts and barges, small boats and the Union Steamship Mail Boat. Puffs of black smoke trailed the larger vessels, ruining what was otherwise considered a fine view.

'Imagine being able to cross a bridge to the other side, Jack. Why, we'll be able to walk straight across to Circular Quay.'

'It's a mighty endeavour,' Jack agreed. 'It'll bring changes, though.'

'Father says it's all for the good. The harbour is an accident waiting to happen, what with the number of craft. It's bad enough during the day, let alone when a fog comes in. Then the only things people have to rely on for guidance are fog horns and bells.'

Jack had heard the benefits of the bridge orated by a master. Mr Bradfield possessed an uncanny ability to glorify his proposed engineering marvel so that many Sydneysiders thought it to be a wonder of the modern world. 'Sydney has always been like two distinct towns,' he reminded her. 'Here in the north it's quieter, safer. In the still of night you can hear the animals at Taronga Zoo. It's like a frontier.'

Olive's neat eyebrows knitted together. 'Who wants to live in a frontier country? We're city people, and soon we'll be living in the most wonderful city in the world with the most marvellous bridge spanning the harbour like a rainbow.'

Jack rolled his eyes. 'We already have five bridges.' He counted them off. 'Pyrmont, Glebe Island, Iron Cove, Gladesville and Fig Tree.'

'Yes, but we don't have one here,' Olive reminded him.

Ahead lay Milsons Point wharf. There were ferries ploughing across the harbour, and in the distance a steam train snaked towards them from Lavender Bay. They walked through a queue of cars and drays waiting for the next punt, as a tram left the open terminus and shuddered past them uphill. At the soda bar Jack found a little wooden cubicle near the front of the shop. Patrons were lined up along the shiny black counter on tall stools, each slurping the latest drink from America. The soda pumps buzzed noisily. There was the clink of glass and the friendly hum of conversation.

'What you be having then, lovey?' The waitress was poised before them with pen to paper.

'I'll have a Delmonico Banana Sundae,' Olive replied.

The waitress looked at Jack, scratching her hairline with the stub of her pencil.

'To share,' he replied, patting the coin in his pocket. It was an expensive business this outing with a girl. 'What's in that?' he asked as the waitress departed.

Olive ran her finger down the menu. 'A split banana on a lettuce leaf with two serves of ice cream atop it. One side of the ice cream has crushed maraschino cherries over it, the other crushed raspberries. It's finished with whipped cream, chopped nuts and a cherry. It's delicious, Jack. I had one with my sister only last week.'

'Trust the Americans to ruin a good ice cream.'

Olive's foot jabbed Jack's ankle.

When the concoction arrived Jack dived in, shovelling spoonfuls of the sickly cold mess into his mouth. Soon his stomach began complaining and he let Olive finish the dish.

'You know Mrs Jessop promises to train me quickly.' Olive licked her spoon. 'She says that at the rate women's fashions are evolving there will be a totally new hairstyle next year.'

Jack edged a little closer to her on the bench seat. He made a show of stretching and then rested his arm behind her. The crowds began to rush past the shop's entrance: labourers, office clerks and secretaries all hurrying through the terminus. Ever since Bradfield's announcement, Jack's own view of the world had changed. It was as if, having picked up on all the excitement that such a grand scheme offered, his options now appeared limitless. The war was a distant memory and this new world was transforming every day.

Olive settled back into the seat, dabbing at her mouth with a napkin. 'It's getting cold.'

He slid his outstretched hand along the top of the bench seat, his fingertips touching her shoulders. He wasn't much for public displays and he knew his mother, bless her memory, would be appalled at such conduct. Unfortunately, although public desire was socially unacceptable, today it would fall prey to uncontrollable need. Jack's thoughts were fixated on a kiss. Indeed he'd been thinking about Olive's fleshy pink lips for nearly a month since his last attempt whilst picnicking at Lavender Bay. In hindsight that Lavender Bay effort was poorly timed, coming only a week after their meeting, so he couldn't blame Olive for being shocked. Still, he believed if they kissed again, properly, some of what he was feeling would seep into Olive's heart. Surely she felt the same way. Otherwise, why else would she be spending time with him?

Her wide grey eyes were fixed on the harbour beyond. 'We never would have met if you had not been on Alfred Street that day, Jack.'

'Saving women from ill-tempered Clydesdales is my specialty.' He leant towards her, tentatively.

'Really?' Olive teased.

*You can do this,* Jack told himself silently. He ran his forefinger across the smooth arc of Olive's cheek, touched the blue vein throbbing rapidly at her throat. Olive retreated ever so slightly. Sensing her reluctance, yet committed to action, Jack took her hand. His feelings for her went beyond class and common sense. Despite the people milling about them he hugged her close to his chest, his mouth finally touching hers. The pain of his cut lip sealed the moment. This then was their bridging.

When he finally released her, Jack searched for a few words, his brain as capable of sense as the melted remains of the banana sundae sitting before him. Olive looked stunned. A crack of thunder sounded and the sky deepened to a nasty blue. Through the soda bar's window a bank of angry cloud signalled a squall. Lost for words and with an equally silent companion, Jack scattered some coins on the table and laced his fingers through Olive's. Now, he decided, was the time for a suitably appropriate comment. 'Come on, let's get you home.'

Jack ran the last block to Manning's Grocers just as it began to sprinkle with rain. The sandstone edifice of the post office with its imposing clock tower rose grandly on the corner. He ducked across the three-way intersection of Mount, Miller and Lane Cove Road. The wide street was an obstacle course of slippery tram lines, drays and T-Model Fords. Overhead, cables crisscrossed the street in a mess of wires. The bottom end of Miller Street, however, was nearly deserted as the familiar green awnings of the shopfronts came into view. Outside Mr Farley's shop, Mr Farley was hurriedly packing up a display table of pre-loved books as thunder sounded.

'Hi, Mr Farley.' Jack carried the foldable table into the dimly lit interior of Mr Farley's book-binding business. 'Any deliveries for the morning?'

The older man patted his greying moustache and stared at Jack's cut lip. 'Looks like a bit of trouble may have found you.' He pointed to the end of a wooden work bench where two book-laden crates stood ready for delivery. Jack checked the address details. Anything within three or four blocks, Jack delivered for free. The arrangement had begun when Mr Farley injured his back some five years ago and had continued purely because it got Jack away from the family business next door.

Mr Farley wrapped up a parcel of books, wound string around the newspaper packaging and sat the parcel on the last crate. 'I wish you'd let me pay you.'

'Nonsense,' Jack replied.

'Here then, take this.' Mr Farley placed a slim volume on the stack. 'One of the crop of romantic writers. A Mrs Campbell Praed. You give it to that girl of yours.'

Mr Farley was the only one who knew of his aspirations towards Olive Peters, and if he considered Jack's aim a little high he was polite enough not to say so.

'What do you think about this bridge business then, Mr Farley?'

'My opinion hasn't changed, Jack. It's a great thing for Sydney, however you and I know that there's going to be a cost, especially for those of us who have the misfortune of being in its path.' He looked towards the shop door and, satisfied they were alone, leant forward. 'Businesses will have to close and homes will be destroyed to make way for the approaches. Be ready is my advice, Jack. After all the hoopla of the sod turning, the pageantry, brass bands and bunting, well, it's like that old saying: after the Lord Mayor's carriage comes the night cart.'

Jack nodded. 'You're ready, aren't you, Mr Farley?'

'Yes, I believe I am.' He followed Jack to the door. 'Thank you, lad.'

The rain had stopped. Jack stepped under the green awning that advertised Manning's Grocers in bold white lettering next door. Although past closing hour, displays of fruit and vegetables waited to be taken inside.

'So, right on closing you return.' Jack's younger brother, Thomas, wiped the counter in a circular motion. His sister, May, tilted her head in shared accusation. Behind them tins of foodstuffs lined the wooden shelves, while castor oil, Epsom salts, Beecham's pills and a sure-fire laxative were arranged near the till with a discreet sign: *Life's Necessities*.

May Manning fluffed her short brown curls. 'What happened to you?' She examined his cut lip, and prodded at the swelling.

'Mills McCoy.'

Thomas looked up. 'What? That hooligan from the Rocks?'

May wiped her hands on the corner of Thomas's apron. 'Not again?'

Jack nodded. 'Reckons he's moving north for a better life.'

Thomas appeared hopeful. 'Did you get him this time, Jack?'

May crossed her arms. 'You're meant to be setting an example, Jack. You're the eldest.'

Jack winked at his brother, younger by two years, as together they carried in the wooden boxes from outside and sat the displays of fruit and vegetables on the shop floor. Despite the cold, tomorrow they would have to pick out the soft ones and basket them up separately to be sold at a reduced price. 'No doubt that will be the highlight of the day,' Jack mumbled as Thomas drew the bolt on the shop door and May counted the till and wrote down the takings, depositing them into a strong box. Once behind the counter all three closed the door on another day.

Beyond was their timber-walled kitchen and living area. May placed the tin box in the centre of the wooden dining table, and they scraped back their chairs to sit down. The room was hot from the wood stove, and their breakfast of eggs and bacon still hung stubbornly in the air. The scents mixed with whiffs of escaping smoke, and not for the first time Jack wished for clean fresh air. He'd grown up in this house, with its crowded kitchen and cramped adjoining lounge room. Sometimes he wondered how he'd managed not to be stunted himself. From the rear of their dwelling they listened as their neighbour Mrs Farley berated her husband.

'Yesterday it was the beans she complained about,' May revealed, 'now her cabbages are yellowing.' She hung her long woollen jumper over the back of the chair. 'There they are rambling about in that terrace, just the two of them, and here we are like a tin of sardines.

And you –' she pointed at Jack '– delivering his books for free. Why, I've a mind –'

'Here.' Jack passed his sister Mrs Praed's novel. 'Mr Farley said it was for you.'

May narrowed her eyes.

'It's a romance.'

'Really, Jack Manning, and when did you start having romantic inclinations?' she enquired, reaching for the novel.

Thomas snatched the copy from his sister's fingers. 'When he started pining for Olive Peters.'

May seized the book back. 'And how does Mrs Peters feel about you outing with her daughter? You've nothing to offer the likes of her.'

'Olive isn't one for being told what to do,' Jack retaliated. He could always rely on May to destroy any modicum of confidence he had, no matter the subject.

May poured water from a ceramic jug and took a long drink. 'She isn't one of us, Jack. Don't be thinking she could be.' With practised efficiency she gathered cups and saucers from the hardwood cupboard and sat them on the table with plates and cutlery.

Thomas cleared his throat and asked after his sister's day.

'I wasn't born to be a seamstress,' she complained, sucking on the fleshy pad of her thumb. 'Why every thrifty woman in Sydney must live on this side of the harbour is beyond me. I wonder if the Farleys would take me on. I could do bookbinding, have a bigger room and share in their vegetable garden.'

Jack cut a wedge of bread from the half-loaf on the table. 'You're lucky to have the job you've got,' he reminded her. 'Things are tough.' He bit into the day-old bread, wishing there was a little jam to sweeten it up. He'd always found it a mighty temptation having a selection of produce only a wall's width away.

'Where's father?' he asked when the stillness of the kitchen reinforced the man's absence.

Thomas untied his filthy apron. 'He went to deliver Mrs Davies's order.'

'Why didn't you go, May?' Jack asked.

His sister smoothed her skirts over her knees. 'I wasn't here, was I? I already have a job, plus minding the house for you lot.' She pointed to the laundry basket on the floor, the saucepan simmering on its blackened cook top and a pile of partially peeled potatoes. 'I'm always busy, and I'll not be cajoled into helping in the shop. My sewing money's far better than the measly pittance Father could offer.' She gave a haughty stare.

Jack glanced at Thomas, acknowledging that their argument was lost. At seventeen, May had quickly assumed the role their dear departed mother left void last year. He opened a tin of tobacco and placed moist shreds into his palm, rolling a cigarette first for Thomas, then himself. They sat companionably, puffing rings of smoke into the warm kitchen air. May walked out to the lean-to where the Coolgardie food safe competed for space with the dishevelled bed Jack insisted on occupying, even in winter, and returned with dripping and sausages.

'Father's here,' she hissed.

Jack and Thomas moved as one. The window was open and the smokes disposed of in seconds.

'Wipe up that lip of yours.' May nodded towards the washstand and threw Jack the towel strung over her shoulder. She placed the kettle on the wood-burning stove.

'You've been gone half the work day, Jack,' Nicholas Manning admonished as he came in and sat down wearily. Once, he'd out-stripped Jack in height, but age was now shrinking him in both directions. 'There's a lot of talk going on about Mr Bradfield's bridge scheme, none of it good.' He lay a piece of paper on the table. 'We may have been a little premature in our celebrations.'

'Last I heard, there was to be a tunnel. A train would go straight to the water's edge and then . . . plop.' May dropped a wedge of potato onto a plate. 'The next thing I'm waving a banner with Brad-field himself talking about a bridge.'

There was a hollow look in his father's eyes. Jack reached for the slip of paper. It was a listing of buildings to be resumed in Blue Street, North Sydney.

'Everyone was so excited when the Bridge Bill was passed. I for one stood in this very kitchen last year with my own departed wife, your dear mother, and saluted the great Mr Bradfield. The man's smart, I'll give him that. The introduction of the land tax before the closing of tenders meant we would be assured of a bridge. No politician would ever renege with taxpayers already footing the bill.' Nicholas cupped the steaming tea offered by his daughter. 'Well, now it's coming and some of us have been paying for our own demise.'

'Mrs Jessop's boarding house,' Jack said, reading from the list. His thoughts went immediately to her two boys and then Olive.

May slumped down in the chair beside her father and took his hand. She brushed a finger across his blotchy skin.

'They're posting notices on all the buildings.' Jack flicked the paper. 'Anything that's in the way will be knocked down. Blue Street will be nearly demolished. Schools, churches, houses . . .'

Nicholas looked at his children. 'I'm glad your mother's not here to see this.'

Jack crumpled the list in his hand. They were only one street away from the planned carnage. 'You can be sure they won't pay us much,' he said angrily.

'They'll be blasting the rock for the North Sydney rail line next week,' Nicholas advised.

'I don't understand,' May said. 'Jack, you yourself said it was the most marvellous thing. That it was an incredible engineering feat, that –'

Nicholas silenced his daughter with a raised finger. 'Unless, my dear girl, you happen to be in its way.'

'Everyone's been too preoccupied with what it would look like,' Jack reminded her. *So much for Olive's rainbow.*

'We're being sacrificed for the benefit of everyone else,' Thomas said, stunned.

Nicholas rattled the few items on the wooden table as he leant heavily on it. 'Mark my words, this project is going to cost the government a fortune. There'll be no money spent on getting rid of the likes of us. Well, we'll have to make plans. Even if this building isn't resumed I'd imagine that the disruption to our business will be substantial. The majority of our clients are in Blue Street and its surrounds; so, no more credit and no sales to any customer who hasn't paid his account in full.' He turned to his eldest. 'And you'll have to pull your weight, Jack.'

'I'm not afraid of work, Father, it's the type I dislike.' He helped himself to the bowl of dripping on the table, smearing it thickly on a slice of bread.

Nicholas frowned. 'It's good honest work. My father raised his family on it, as I have you and your brother and sister.'

'And I'm betting Thomas will be content to do the same,' Jack countered, glancing at his brother. 'Anyway, by the looks of it we may all be out of a job.' He didn't mean to sound flippant, however if Manning's Grocers ceased business tomorrow he would be free.

'That's what I'm afraid of.' Nicholas stared at the grainy black-and-white photograph of his wife. It sat next to her favourite spot in the kitchen: a horsehair-covered armchair. 'If we lose the shop, our home, if the worst happens, then it will fall to you to provide for the family, Jack. I'm too old to start anew.'

The kitchen was deathly quiet. It was as if his mother stood before them, reproaching Jack with her pale eyes, her fingers flicking at her rosary beads, reminding him of what it meant to be the eldest. The small carriage clock on the cupboard struck six. Sleety rain began to pepper the window. Suddenly the kitchen, the house, the family business suffocated him.

'Jack?'

It was his father again. Waiting for his question to be answered; waiting for the demands of the parent to be accepted by the child. Jack saw his life spread out before him: one in which he would never be his own person. He could feel the weight of responsibility like a large rock on his chest.

'Jack?' May touched his shoulder.

He looked at Thomas, at the wooden crucifix hanging on the wall.

'May, fetch the Bible from my night stand,' Nicholas commanded his daughter. 'I believe we need to pray.'

## ∝ Chapter 2 ≫

# North Sydney,
# Two Days Later

Olive left the house early. Her siblings were still breakfasting on fruit, eggs and freshly baked bread, the household having long ago forgone the staple of eggs and bacon. 'Too working class,' their mother declared. Fresh fruit was the chosen food for those who could afford it.

As the front door clicked shut behind her, and no querying voice followed, Olive felt relief. She was yet to inform her family of her new employment. It was only her third day at Mrs Jessop's salon yet her excitement was already diminished by the shock rippling through the suburb. This morning Olive was torn between visiting Manning's Grocers for the first time to see exactly where Jack lived, and detouring via Blue Street to see if the rumours were true about houses being auctioned. Morbid curiosity, however, won over romantic love, despite Jack being the most handsome boy – in a roughish sort of way – she'd laid eyes on.

At the corner of Blue and Walker Street a crowd gathered in front of a boarding house. The harried occupant, who was no doubt a war widow like many landladies in North Sydney, was carrying a suitcase from the building. This she piled precariously atop an upturned four-poster bed and mattress. The bearer of her possessions – including wooden crates with protruding saucepans, blankets and a large dresser – was a dray pulled by a spotted horse. The animal's head hung despondently and each of its legs lifted in turn as it shifted its weight. Olive puffed her cheeks out against the cold. Why, she wondered, when everyone in Sydney wanted a bridge, did this seem so wrong? She hugged her arms around her body to ward off the morning chill, doing her best to isolate herself from the bystanders huddled together. There was much shaking of heads and pointing. For the first time in her life Olive was afraid for these people, who were being forced from their lives in the name of progress, and afraid of her own place in the world.

The houses in Blue Street that were already sold were in the process of either being demolished or dismantled and carted away. Olive watched this gradual unravelling as those uprooted packed belongings into cars, trucks or drays, some residents crying openly in the street. The dust and grit in the air stung her eyes and throat and she clasped a lace-edged handkerchief to her nose. There was nothing to be done but to ask Mrs Jessop what the future held. She turned and walked the two blocks to the hairdressing salon, as trams buzzed by and taxis hooted.

Now that Mrs Jessop's boarding house was being resumed, Olive wondered where her employer would relocate. Maybe Olive would be placed in charge of opening the salon, for she lived the closest of any of the staff members. Such a responsibility, she reasoned, would have to be worth a few more shillings which, when added to her weekly allowance, would make her purchase of a white silk clouche hat and pair of flesh-coloured silk stockings seem hardly outrageous. Olive imagined Jack's face when she displayed her new hose. At the thought she gave a little giggle. Oh, she did like Jack, really.

It was late by the time she arrived at the salon, but Mrs Jessop said nothing about her tardiness. Olive immediately set about attending to her duties. As the street outside filled with shoppers and commuters, she made tea for a customer.

By noon she had washed five heads of hair and swept the linoleum floor eight times. Susan, a blowsy woman with a knowledge of cutting, deigned to give her a fleeting smile. They were short of a staff member thanks to the 'kerfuffle outside', as Susan termed it, and a willing worker capable of taking up the slack was a boon to any business.

When there was a break in the morning rush, Olive watched Mrs Jessop curl Mrs Whitney's blonde hair with hot tongs. One of the North Shore Establishment, with more money than common sense, Mrs Whitney visited the salon twice weekly and was by far the most fashionable client.

'And so I said to my husband, "Mr Whitney, you cannot possibly expect me to wear the same diamond ring for another year." Of course he appeared quite affronted, with the ring having been handed down on his grandfather's side –' Mrs Whitney held up her right hand for inspection.

'It's a lovely ring, Mrs Whitney,' Mrs Jessop enthused, teasing a reluctant curl around her finger.

'Oh, I don't expect you trade people to understand. Look.' Her wedding finger, which had recently discarded the family heirloom, was now graced with a large square diamond surrounded by two rows of sparkling counterparts.

Olive's employer gave compliments worthy of the Crown Jewels as Mrs Whitney's attention turned to her own reflection in the mirror of a gold compact. The woman gave a tilt of her head, obviously pleased at what she saw.

'Mrs Jessop,' Olive interrupted politely, ignoring the two ugly frown lines forming an *M* on Mrs Whitney's brow. 'Have you found another place to live?'

'Good heavens.' Mrs Whitney snapped her powder compact shut. 'How the mighty have fallen. Aren't you Olive Peters? Well, I see the apple hasn't dropped far from the tree. The newly moneyed can never break from the past. It takes more than one generation.'

'You would know, Mrs Whitney. My father tells me your father was a wheelwright,' Olive retaliated.

'Olive,' Mrs Jessop reprimanded, turning towards Olive and in the process burning Mrs Whitney's cheek with the curling tongs.

'Good heavens, I'm paying you good money, Mrs Jessop! I don't come here to be disfigured!' Mrs Whitney examined the tiny red mark in the hollow of her cheek.

Olive took one look at the tears welling in her employer's eyes and removed the cape from around Mrs Whitney's shoulders. 'It's not a decapitation, silly.'

Mrs Whitney glowered at her, and Olive returned the favour. She had a whole family from which to draw forth condescending looks. Clearly Mrs Whitney either had few relations or they were unconscionably happy.

'I'm so sorry, Mrs Whitney,' Mrs Jessop apologised. 'Susan, a cold compress for Mrs Whitney, please.'

Susan, who was busy cutting a brown bob, frowned but did as she was told.

Mrs Whitney clasped the compress to her cheek and scattered some shillings on the narrow ledge before the long mirror. 'Well I never, Olive Peters. And to think that your mother goes about putting on airs. You can tell the true nature of people by their offspring, and if you, my dear, are the true indication of your mother's breeding then I pray for the rest of us who have to put up with you and yours.'

The crash of brick and timber sounded and Susan looked skyward, crossing herself in the process. 'Another home lost.'

The noise quite took the edge off Mrs Whitney's comment. She held a handkerchief to her nose, her back straight.

Susan opened the door for Mrs Whitney to leave. 'Maybe your house will be next,' Susan said tartly.

'Here's hoping,' Olive said under her breath. She wasn't brave enough to say the words too loudly. She already feared she had lost Mrs Jessop's most fashionable client.

'It won't stop, you know,' Mrs Jessop announced when Susan's client also excused herself, her hair not quite set. 'There'll be more houses gone, you mark my words.'

Olive had heard similar rumours. 'They're going to have to close streets.'

'Well, they'll have to, won't they?' Susan swept around her chair, gathering the short locks of brown hair into a dustpan. 'The place is going to be like a war zone.'

Mrs Jessop pressed a sodden hanky to her nose. 'There's talk of them moving the Milsons Point wharf and terminal.' She hiccupped. 'There are new train lines to put in, underground. Why, Mr Adler told me that they'd be blasting under the North Shore Grammar School with no thought to those poor boys inside; they're just as likely to fall through to China.'

Olive patted her arm. 'Come on, I'll make you a nice cup of tea.'

'It won't get any better you know, Olive. You and Susan will have to finish up. I'm sorry, I've been meaning to tell you.'

'Finish up? But I've only just started.' Susan and Olive both stared at their employer.

Mrs Jessop blew her nose noisily. 'It's the boarding house. It wasn't Freddy's. I leased it.'

Susan crossed her arms and a bulge of fat strained at the material of her dress. 'I've got mouths to feed.'

'I just agreed on another three-year lease with the real estate agent but I didn't sign anything, and when it was resumed the tenants left.' Mrs Jessop looked at them meaningfully. 'They all left, owing me rent. The boys and I, poor dears, have to move into the shop tonight. I can barely afford the lease on this business now and I certainly can't afford to pay you, Olive. I'm sorry.'

Olive sat numbly in one of the chairs near the shop entrance.

'What about me?' Susan's voice rose. 'You *need* me.'

Mrs Jessop shook her head sadly. 'Not as much as my boys and I need to eat, Susan.'

'Well, I'll take what's owing to me.'

Mrs Jessop unlocked the wall cupboard and counted shillings from a tin. Olive didn't see what Susan received, however by the look on her face it was insufficient. Susan stared for some moments at the coin in her hand and then glared at Olive, her nostrils flaring with each breath.

'You shouldn't be here anyway, Olive Peters. Your family has money. You're robbing an honest person of a day's wage when it's just pocket money to the likes of you.'

Startled, Olive listened as Susan babbled about the state of the economy and the ignorant attitude of those who should know better. By the look on her employer's face, if there had been an intention to pay her it was now lost. Olive collected her hat and gloves and thanked an unresponsive Mrs Jessop. Outside, the street was cold, the air filled with grit and noise. Olive narrowed her vision to the pavement and walked home.

At the entrance to the drawing room, Olive paused. Her mother was giving curt instructions to their maid, complaining about a cracked punch bowl and the benefits of proper packing to prevent such disasters. Although intent on hurrying to her room, Olive turned in a half-circle. The hallway was empty. The Persian runner, which had once graced the polished timber boards, was gone; and a row of hand-tinted paintings, which had hung for many years above a cedar hall table, were also missing, along with the table.

'Well, Olive?' her mother asked brusquely, dismissing the maid. She sat down at her polished walnut desk. Sheaths of creamy paper and a glass oval paperweight competed for space on the desk's surface. An oblong configuration of diamonds as flat as her chest glinted on her hand as she ran a finger down the list. 'Now, if you pack your room by week's end we can all be out by the Saturday. Yes, that should work very well.'

Olive flopped into the armchair of the overstuffed three-piece suite and removed her gloves.

'That suite cost fifty-nine pounds, child. I'll remind you that it is silk tapestry over the horsehair.'

Olive poked a fingernail at the strawberry-pink pattern. 'What are you talking about?'

Mrs Peters twisted on her stool. 'The move, Olive. We did discuss it this morning at breakfast.' She tapped her fingers against the black gabardine of her skirt. 'Then at lunch.'

'I haven't been here.'

'How unusual. Well, your sister and brothers decided to go today – something about rats leaving a sinking ship. Your father has secured a new house for us on the southern side. Do stack the fire a little will you, Olive, it's quite cool in here once one stops moving about and there has been so much to do today. I don't think I've rested even when we lunched. Izzy made a fine beefsteak pie. Very fine.'

'Mother?'

'Yes, right, back to your siblings. They have lodgings in the city until the weekend, when we can all be together again. Of course it suits Henrietta as her young man is on that side of the pond, and Eddy and Hal have always found it a struggle travelling back and forth to the Exchange. Quite frankly, I've been suggesting this move for some time. The North Shore was always so removed from the more cosmopolitan aspects of this great city.'

Olive wanted to pull on her mother's stays until all the bluster puffed out of her. She threw some kindling on the fire instead then kicked the brass fender surrounding the tiled hearth. 'Why didn't you tell me sooner?'

Her mother twisted the beads at her throat. 'Really, Olive, you can't possibly have failed to notice what is occurring not two streets from here. Why, everyone realised that once the resumptions began it would be best to vacate the area.' She raised a thinly plucked eyebrow. 'For an intelligent girl you are really quite stupid at times.'

Olive thought of the wreckage of Blue Street, the inevitable closure of Mrs Jessop's salon and her own unedifying time in the work force. 'Is our home to be resumed?'

Her mother displayed a number of expensive gold fillings. 'No, my dear, your brilliant father has sold it for a hefty price to the Works Department. They are looking for offices close to the bridge construction, and although this street is to be closed your father persuaded the department that it was an excellent position for them.'

'I see.' Now she knew why Henrietta, Eddy and Hal had slunk away so quickly.

'Fortuitous, don't you think, considering the maelstrom that North Sydney will become. I'm moving south before the weekend, so I'll leave the overseeing of the remaining packing and the locking up of the house to you. The removalists are highly reputable and the majority of the furniture will be gone by noon tomorrow. You're old enough – and your father feels you're intelligent enough – to be entrusted with this responsibility, and I have a concert to attend.'

Olive pushed the sole of her shoes into the plush rug on the floor. 'I don't want to leave, Mother. This is our home.'

Mrs Peters directed her attention back to her writing desk.

'Mother, I really don't want to –'

'Five hundred buildings will be resumed, Olive. Then there are the street closures, the shifting of the wharf, the general inconvenience of the demolition process, not to mention the unhealthy air from all this dust and grime.'

'I like North Sydney. My friends are here and –'

'You'll make new ones.' She finished writing and looked at her youngest daughter. 'We're aware of your attachment to the grocer's boy. A change will be for the best, my dear, and with your sister marrying Mr John Eton before the year is out we can't risk a most inappropriate friendship. Although, I've a feeling your childish attachment is an extension of his kindness in saving you from that runaway horse.'

'But –'

'Once you're settled on the south side all your silly notions of work will vanish and then we must find you someone suitable.' She tapped the side of her nose. 'You will be quite in demand once the North Shore is dusted off you.' She smoothed her skirt over her knees. 'And you will adore our new home. We will be close to the water in the eastern suburb of Rose Bay. Very gentrified environs . . .'

Tears pricked Olive's eyes. She wasn't like the others: she didn't want to move south and she certainly didn't want to leave their neighbourhood. Henrietta was four years older and moulded in their mother's likeness, while her brothers were money-market men, impressed with their abilities and well-planned futures.

'It will be wonderful,' her mother said decisively. 'You'll see, my dear.'

Jack knew what was afoot as soon as he saw the two vans outside the Peters's terrace. Beds, wardrobes, lamps, tables and paintings were being wrapped and stacked inside the vehicles. Mrs Peters, dressed in black with a double strand of waist-length pearls and a large hat, motored past in her husband's six cylinder. Jack ran across the busy street. The noise of a jackhammer blasting into rock echoed in the air, and as he side-stepped a youth carrying a crate he envisioned the sandstone heart of North Sydney crumbling.

'Jack!' Olive was at the front door, a handbag tucked under her arm. 'I was just coming to see you.'

'Were you now?' Both of them moved across the tiled porch to make way for the drawing-room chiffonier.

'Come in.'

Jack followed Olive into an empty entrance hall and left as she turned into the drawing room, where boxes and packing were strewn about. A fire glowed pitifully within an elaborately carved fireplace.

'It's good to see you, Jack.'

'Is it?' He backed away towards the window, tugging the velvet curtain open. 'Resumed?'

'Sold to the Works Department as a field office.'

'I see.' He turned his back towards her. 'You were fortunate to make the sale.' The material of his jacket strained across broad shoulders. 'Where are you moving to?'

'Rose Bay. I was coming to see you, Jack. It's just that everything has happened at once. Mrs Jessop couldn't afford to pay me so I lost my job. Then Mother announced we're to leave.' 'I *was* coming to see you.'

'I'm sorry to hear about your job.' He nodded curtly. 'Well, it was good of you to think of me.'

Olive touched his arm. 'Jack,' she said softly, 'of course I think of you. I'll never forget how you rushed across the street that day . . .'

'Anyone would've done it.' He looked about the room. It was as big as his house. Two crystal chandeliers showered light across polished boards and richly coloured scatter rugs. 'My father went over to the city this morning to see someone from the Works Department. I thought I'd drop by on my way to meet him at the ferry.'

'I'm glad you did.' Olive twisted the strap of her handbag.

'He wants an assurance either way as to our future. No one here will talk to him, and frankly I understand.' He gave a half-laugh. 'Things will never be the same again.'

Olive sat the handbag on a tin trunk. 'What will you do?'

Jack thought of his carefully constructed speech, a heartfelt declaration of intent. Words such as starting anew now seemed pitiful. 'Persevere,' he replied flatly, scrutinising the plaster ceiling. In the face of such luxury he was at a loss for words. They walked outside to an overcast sky. The removalists were stacking boxes in the rear of the van. 'When are you going?'

'Everything will be out of the house tomorrow.' Olive stepped beneath the overhead balcony as a light drizzle misted the air.

'Not much time to say goodbye.' He looked at her.

'No, not much.' All night she had wondered whether her sister, Henrietta, was right. Maybe her feelings for Jack were just puppy love. He was, after all, her first beau, and although he'd saved her from the stray horse, a strained ankle was hardly life-threatening. Yet the memory of his kiss lingered. It was her first.

He touched her cheek. 'I've nothing to offer you, Olive. We're like chalk and cheese.'

The head removalist interrupted them.

'We're done, Miss Olive. Be back in the morning for the rest.' He doffed his cap, winked at Jack and walked to the lead van.

Jack took her hand. 'Whatever I do, Olive, I'll never be able to give you this life.'

Was this how love happened? Did you look into a person's eyes and, faced with their leaving, determine you could not live without them? Olive squeezed his hand and willed Jack to utter some declaration of love. Surely things weren't meant to end so hastily, with her left miserable and Jack striding alone towards some manly adventure. Olive thought briefly of her sister. Henrietta would complain that Olive was merely being melodramatic. Was she? She wasn't sure. 'Won't you write me, Jack?' Her lips trembled. Why did she have to follow her family? This was the twenties and people were doing what they wanted everywhere. 'Won't you?'

Jack's lips were on hers. Olive kissed him back, tentatively at first, her heart racing. This kiss – their third – was not tinged with surprise but expectation, and Olive allowed herself to be held within Jack's arms as rain began to fall. Finally they released their embrace to stand opposite each other in wonder. The vans pulled out from the kerb.

Jack lifted a finger to her lips. 'Stick with your plans; follow your parents. I'll come for you.'

From the harbour came the clanging of bells, the ominous siren call of an accident on the water. Jack latched the wrought-iron gate securely between them. The rain dripped from the hydrangea leaves that spilt over the fence, and gurgled along the gutters, washing the day's grit from the road. Olive leant across the dividing fence.

'I'll think of something,' he said. 'Write me your new address.'

He pulled away from her and began to walk briskly down the road, breaking into a run as the clanging from the harbour continued. Olive gazed after him, her clothes sodden. For someone who had spent the last few weeks trying to assert her independence, Olive now felt marooned between the family she was born into and the man she cared for. She brushed droplets of rain from her face recalling Jack's words: *I'll come for you.* Where on earth did he think they were going to go?

Jack ran towards the terminus, his lungs crying out with pain. His father was due in on the three o'clock ferry and the clanging of the siren filled him with dread. He arrived at the ferry landing breathless, and slid the last few feet on the wet wharf into the crowd gathering on the foreshore. Jack elbowed the onlookers aside, ignoring their complaints.

'The Manly ferry's clipped the smaller Milsons Point ferry,' a captain said, pointing towards the water. 'Thirty passengers were thrown in. Luckily a passing punt fished most of them what fell in, out.'

Jack tried to make sense of the sketchy details, however the buzz of the crowd and the pounding rain made questioning the captain near impossible. The punt materialised through the rain. It was a dirty grey afternoon on the harbour with limited visibility, and the open-sided vessel leant heavily to one side in the rough water. With the punt a good ten feet away from the wharf, Jack took a running jump across the gap to land with a thud on the wooden deck. The horses on board were skittish, and their owners tried to calm them as the drays and carts rolled disturbingly to and fro.

'Young idiot!' one of the crew yelled at Jack.

Pushing his way through those passengers eager to disembark, Jack reached the huddle of survivors who were doing their best to get away from the six bodies lying on the boards nearby.

'Father? Have you seen my father, Nicholas Manning?'

'Like we know every person that travels to and from Circular Quay,' a man with a deep gash on his forehead replied. His companions stared blankly.

With a sinking heart Jack turned from the group.

'Over there, lad.' An older man pointed. 'They fished a man from the water; he saved me, he did.'

His father was propped against the wheel of a dray, his face bloodless, his suit coat and shoes missing.

'Father?' Jack squatted by his side and clasped a wet shoulder.

'Jack, lad, I knew you'd come.' His father partially opened his eyes. The punt rocked precariously as passengers began to disembark and another ferry moored alongside them.

'I'm here.' Jack removed his coat, wrapping it about his father. 'We've got to get you home.'

'Never forget the consolation of the Blessed Virgin, my boy. No matter what may happen, stay on the path of righteousness.'

'Don't speak, Father.'

Nicholas Manning grasped his son's shoulder weakly as Jack gathered him up in his arms.

'Make way,' Jack called, pushing through the crowds. 'Make way.' The punt shifted on the water's surface as he carried his father to the safety of the wharf. People milled about them. A queue of walking wounded waited for an ambulance as police constables arrived. People were staring and pointing. Jack strode past waiting horses, noticing a dray plodding slowly uphill. Mustering his strength he yelled to the driver, 'Help me, please, my father's been injured. Please, I only need to go to Miller Street.'

The driver drew hard on the reins and turned in Jack's direction. Jack stood in the rain, his father bundled in his arms. 'Please, help me.'

The driver gave a curt nod. 'Slide him in the back there, lad. We'll see him home.'

## ⋘ Chapter 3 ⋙

## North Sydney, 1923

The morning after his father's accident, Jack woke still dressed. His teeth chattered as his chilled feet landed on timber boards. Pulling on an overcoat, socks and shoes, he looked through droplets of rain speckling the gauze of the sleep-out. Between the gaps in the paling fence he could see a hen scratching in the laneway. A movement caught his eye. Mr Farley was relieving himself over his wife's cabbages in their shared vegetable plot, turning from left to right in a precise effort at complete coverage.

'Right you are, Jack.' He waved, buttoning his fly and glancing to where he'd just urinated. 'Hate cabbage,' he admitted, brushing his hands together as if he'd completed a major task, 'and beans.' He gave Jack what suspiciously looked like a wink. 'I'm a potato man myself. How's your father?'

Jack wiped his face roughly. 'Not good when I left him in the early hours.'

'Hmm. Sorry to hear it,' he said, retreating indoors.

Jack was left alone with the bitter morning wind and light

rainfall. The door was squeaking on the outside toilet, somewhere a baby yelped for attention and the guttering gurgled noisily as rainwater washed from the roof. The morning was the same as any other, yet Jack's life was changing and he was sick to the stomach at the thought of the altered circumstances he found himself in. An image of his father came to him. Jack dreaded returning upstairs. To enter his father's bedroom was to be faced with both his own mortality and the potential loss of a man who represented hearth and home. It was difficult enough last night. For five hours he had sat by his father's side before being relieved by Thomas, then at midnight, having sent Thomas to bed, Jack returned to his father's side. The waxy light from a single candle showed a man hollowed out by his exertions in the freezing waters of the harbour. Yet there was still a slim chance Nicholas Manning would pull through. Hadn't they fished him out of a watery grave alive? And hadn't his father managed a few strained minutes of conversation in the twilight hours?

Jack had fetched another blanket and tucked his father in warmly. Above the bed a wooden crucifix hung silently, while outside the rain battered the window. He hadn't liked the look of the night; it was as if the darkness clamoured for entry. He drew the curtains closed with a sharp tug before picking up his father's Bible and laying the book between his hands.

'Thanks, Jack.' The voice was croaky. A bent thumb rubbed the worn gold cross on the cover. 'This was my father's and his father's before him. It has given three generations solace. When I am gone it will be yours.'

'Father, please don't talk so, all you need is rest.' Jack puffed the pillows behind his father's head.

'Rest is for the old and infirm, Jack. I know I'll not make old bones and I'm content with the Lord's doing. Very soon I'll meet with the Almighty and the petty worries of this world will mean nothing.'

Streaky lightning barrelled across the sky, illuminating the curtains. Jack sat on the edge of the bed and patted his father's hand. 'Don't talk like that, Father. Haven't you always told us not to entice such thoughts?'

Nicholas ignored him. 'You don't want the responsibility an elder son must shoulder. Unfortunately, my boy, duty is a man's lot if he's to prove his place in the world.'

'But –'

Nicholas waved his hand weakly. 'No, my lad, my deathbed is sacrosanct. It's for old men to talk and the young to listen. It's always been such. Sadly, all too soon you'll get your turn and then you'll wonder what all the hurry was about.'

'Rest, Father, please,' Jack pleaded. The doctor had warned of exhaustion.

'You must care for your brother and sister,' Nicholas instructed haltingly. 'For if you fail in your family obligation the saints will look with disfavour upon you. Live a good life, Jack. Be happy, for both your mother's and my sakes. It's important that each generation improves upon the last.' His grip tightened. 'Follow in the path of the Church and you'll always be saved.' Jack's hand was pressed between his father's and the Bible. 'Promise me?'

Jack hurriedly agreed. 'I promise.'

'Then I can find the place God has made for me, knowing my family will be together.'

When Jack left the room the weight of accountability had chased him downstairs.

Now, in the cold light of day, Jack considered the words of commitment begrudgingly given.

A heart-wrenching wail echoed through the house and out into the vegetable garden. He sprinted toward the noise. He could hear footsteps just ahead of him on the staircase and at the bedroom door he collided with Thomas. May was collapsed over their father, her muffled sobbing shaking the bedframe.

'Thomas?' Jack touched his brother's arm. A single glance confirmed the worst. Jack gently pulled May aside, prising her fingers from their father's grip. 'Thomas will take you downstairs, May.' Jack nodded to his brother. 'Come.' He walked May to Thomas. 'Go on, Thomas,' he coaxed. 'I'll be down soon.'

May's sobbing grew worse.

'He should be laid out,' Thomas stated. 'It's what mother would want.'

When the bedroom was empty Jack retrieved the Bible from the floor where it had fallen, placing it on the bedside table. He brushed grey-streaked hair from his father's brow and then gently closed his staring eyes. His throat constricted with emotion and Jack thought for a second how he too would like to collapse over his father's body. Instead he took a steadying breath and fished in his coat pocket for two pennies, which he laid on each of his father's eyes. Jack's chest felt tight and he fought to regain a semblance of composure. He looked up at the wooden cross; Jesus glared down at him. Jack crossed himself, twice for good measure, and backed out of the room.

A week after their father's burial at Gore Hill Cemetery, Mr Farley called Jack into his terrace. They stood in a replica of the Manning hallway, except Mr Farley's lodgings were well maintained, carpeted and sweet smelling. 'Dried lavender,' Mr Farley announced as he led Jack up creaking stairs to a study. Accepting a seat in a swivel chair opposite a leather tooled desk, Jack glanced at the writing paper, books and ceiling-high bookcase that filled a whole wall. A large globe of the world, mounted on a brass stand, sat within arm's reach of Mr Farley.

'My grandfather's,' the old man explained, giving the globe a spin. 'Of course everything pink belongs to the Empire.'

'Of course,' Jack agreed. Although Jack had only had a few years of schooling at a technological college, with an emphasis on preparing the lower classes for a trade, it had still been deemed necessary for all colonials to know the history of Great Britain.

Mr Farley interlaced his fingers. 'Such power – and all of it achieved through tenacity and sheer strength.'

'I suppose.' Jack played with the brim of his cap.

'Never suppose, Jack. Be of strong conviction and stout heart and you can achieve anything.'

Jack straightened his shoulders. He wasn't of a mind to start receiving lectures.

Mr Farley's placid countenance gave way to an uncharacteristic frown. 'I'm well aware that you've no interest in the family business, and with the way things are . . .' He extended his palms upwards. 'I've brought you here to ask you what your plans are, Jack.'

'Get out of the city, I suppose. I just don't see much on offer for the likes of me. Except that now I have Thomas and May to consider.'

'Hmm . . . well, I have an offer to make to you. When I injured my back you didn't hesitate to give me a helping hand, so now you're leaving I'd like to repay the favour.'

'Excuse me?' Jack hadn't actually said he was leaving.

Mr Farley slid an envelope across the expanse of desk. 'Open it.'

Inside was a substantial bundle of pound notes. Jack hesitated as he handled the money.

'You'll find you've been well compensated for your efforts on my behalf.'

'But –'

'Don't say *but,* Jack, say thank you.'

'But, Mr Farley.'

'I always pay my debts. Go out and conquer the world, Jack. And if you're thinking about places to conquer you may consider heading north if you've got the stamina.'

Jack's gaze flicked from the money to Mr Farley. 'North? North to where?'

'Why, north to the bush, of course, the outback. There's nothing to keep you here now.' Mr Farley pushed his reading spectacles higher on the bridge of his nose and selected a book from a dusty shelf. The page he opened showed a map of New South Wales and his long forefinger marked a line from Sydney across the page in a north-westerly direction. 'What do you think?'

Jack leant over the map; looked at the distance covered. 'That's a long way.'

'Eight hundred mile in fact.'

'Eight hundred . . .' Jack found it difficult to comprehend the distance. 'What's there?'

Mr Farley formed a pyramid with his fingers. 'Land, Jack. Land as far as the eye can see. Great swathes of dirt.'

'Dirt?' Jack studied the atlas. He may as well have been looking at a map of the moon.

'Dirt for growing things: sheep for wool, cattle for beef. Wheat for flour too. Maybe even decent vegetables.' He gave a chuckle. 'Interested?'

Jack looked at the map again, at the series of squiggly lines and barely marked tracks; at the mountains and rivers that lay between this life and a brand new one.

'I have these, you see.' Mr Farley slid two pieces of paper across the desk. 'They're title deeds to land in north-western New South Wales. Initially I'd decided on selling them, until I saw this.' He retrieved a shilling coin from his pocket and rolled it across the desk.

Jack stopped the coin's progress with a slap of his palm.

'It's freshly minted. See the ram's head?'

Jack flipped the coin over.

'That –' Mr Farley tapped the desk '– is Waverly No. 4. The finest stud ram in Australia, probably the world.' He formed a pyramid with his fingers again. 'Imagine an animal held in such esteem that he ends up stamped on a coin. Anyway, it got me to thinking about the opportunities there are in this country, Jack. What a man could do if he were young again, eh? Well, I don't expect you to understand – you have youth on your side. But I have land and you have youth, so why not?'

'Why not what?' Jack repeated, studying the coin.

'I'd like to send you out there; see if you can make a go of it. You've money enough there to provision yourself, and I'll transfer more funds to the local stock and station agency when you're ready to buy livestock. I believe sheep are best suited to that country. Fortuitous, don't you think?'

Jack looked at the date on the deeds.

'Soldier settler blocks, Jack. Land resumed from the hoarding squattocracy of last century. It's our turn now. How'd you like to be one of the landed gentry?'

'But it's yours.'

'Look at me. I'm too old for such adventures, but you, my lad, have the opportunity to make a fortune for both of us. If you're willing enough you'll succeed. You'll be my caretaker and manager. I'll expect two payments a year amounting to twenty-five percent of the turnover. Your brother and sister can go with you if you like.'

Jack wondered if the Mannings had ever really known their neighbour. 'And if I make nothing?'

'I don't invest for nothing.' Mr Farley leant forward, the cuffs of his white shirt grubby about the edges. 'However, I don't want anything *the first year*. We'll call that the establishment period. I'll expect detailed accounts to be kept of your daily activities. If you default on one payment, well then –' Mr Farley drew a line in the air '– our contract ends. There's no point in it if there's no money.' Satisfied with his explanation he removed his spectacles. 'What do you say?'

Jack hesitated. 'I know nothing about the country.'

'Neither did that Kidman fellow or the Wangallon Gordons. If a Scotsman can build an empire, you can, my boy. Anyone can learn. Here.' Mr Farley selected a number of texts from the bookcase. 'These are all on animal husbandry – sheep to be exact. That's what you'll be growing, lad, and you'll be growing them for me.'

Jack stared at the map, wondering at the possibilities of such a scheme. *Imagine,* he thought, *Jack Manning: landed gentry.* It meant more than a steady job. It meant a life, with Olive. 'I'd need money for a dray.'

Mr Farley smiled. 'Sign here.'

The typed letter had the address of a Pitt Street law office printed in one corner and there were two pages' worth of numbered points. 'I've never signed anything like this before. What does it say?'

'It simply formalises our agreement, Jack. You pay me twenty-five percent in two payments per annum. I'll give you a copy to take with you when you leave.'

Jack thought briefly of Thomas and May, of his father's words and the family Bible that seemed to seal his fate. If he did this one thing, Jack decided, he would obey the Church's teachings forever after. He glanced briefly about Mr Farley's study and, seeing no evidence of religious persuasion, he wrote his name neatly on the line indicated. Mr Farley shook his hand.

'Welcome to your new life, Jack. Welcome to Absolution Creek.'

Jack was fit to bursting on leaving Mr Farley's house. With his stash of pound notes safely inside his shoe and a letter of employment with a copy of the deeds tucked inside his breast pocket, he entered the kitchen intent on gorging himself on sausages, eggs and bacon. Today they could afford it.

Thomas was sitting opposite the wood stove, his feet perched on the warm cast-iron door. He was morose as usual. In spite of

May's sorrow at their father's passing it was Thomas who now visibly suffered, although May still cried herself to sleep every night. At the sight of their expectant faces, Jack felt awkward. Then annoyance set in. Finally, a door was opening towards a new life and he was saddled with two young siblings and restrained by promises of obligation.

May poured tea and took her place at the end of the table like a dutiful housewife. Jack considered the two and recalled Mr Farley saying they were free to accompany him. Rolling a cigarette, he picked stray bits of tobacco from his tongue. Outside, the rumbling of jackhammers echoed through their once peaceful suburb.

'Mr Farley's offered me employment north of here.' Jack thought of what his mother would say; what his father expected. It was stuffy in the kitchen.

Thomas dragged his chair from the fire to the table. May paled. 'Are you going?'

This was his chance. He flicked ash from the cigarette into a dish of sand. 'There's nothing to stay for here.'

Timber boards creaked in complaint as May stopped her bustling.

'Is . . . Is there a place for us?' Her voice quavered.

Thomas reached for her hand.

'It's a long way from here. Near eight hundred mile, a sheep property.' Jack looked at his younger brother, a softer version of their beloved father. 'I wouldn't expect you to pack up on a whim, especially when it's a trial basis.'

May wrung the end of the tea towel. 'You don't know anything about sheep,' she challenged. 'Besides, Jack, with Father's passing we should stay together.'

Thomas rolled a cigarette of his own. 'What about the store? Our home?'

'Things change, Thomas. I've never been interested in it, you know that. You've got a job, May, and you'll find something,

Thomas, if you decide not to stay in groceries. I need to do my own thing, just me and Olive.' There, it was said. Jack looked at the stove top. He was hungry.

'I see.' May wiped at the kitchen table, scrubbing until her knuckles whitened. 'Ain't no room for us, Thomas, as Jack's taken up with Miss La-De-Da.'

A quiet descended, broken only by the crackle of the combustion stove and Thomas pouring tea into his cup. Jack opened the window and leant against the wooden sill. 'You might want to air this room out a little more often, May. Put a bit of bacon on for me, will you?'

May dumped her tea cup in the sink.

'Cook it yourself,' she answered sharply. 'If your own family aren't good enough, then I'd hardly be good enough to cook for you.'

Wasn't it just like his sister to ruin a moment? Jack turned to his brother. 'You could try and sell this place or lease it, Thomas.'

Thomas's cup clattered on its saucer. 'Me? Sell it?'

'We should all stay together,' May argued, stoking the stove with wood. 'Father would have expected it. Besides, you can't take a girl like that Olive Peters out to the bush.'

'Why not?'

May gave a shriek of amusement. 'Take a good look at her!'

If Jack needed a reason not to take his siblings with him, there it was.

'If it really is just a trial maybe we should stay, May, until Jack comes home.'

May's eyes filled with tears. 'Sure, don't mind us, Jack. We'll keep the family business going while you go off sky-larking. But if we do sell the store, don't expect any share.' Untying the apron at her waist she threw it on the table and walked out.

'And you, Thomas, will you manage?' Jack asked.

Thomas was slow to form a smile. 'Sure, Jack. If you think you should go. Could I come and visit?'

'Of course,' Jack replied quickly, his thoughts already on a dark-haired girl with green-blue eyes. Wait until he shared his news. He, Jack Manning, was to be of the landed-gentry class.

Jack stuck sweaty fingers between his collar and neck and swallowed noisily. At least it was a sunny day. Ripples of white trailed after the craft on the harbour. Although the terminus was busy the majority of the city-bound office workers were already ensconced on the southside. Jack dawdled in the arcade, the glass window of the soda shop reflecting a young man whose spit-and-polished appearance was improved by a barber clean cut and shave. Jack was still beaming from the hot towel and complimentary shoeshine as he jangled shiny coins, contemplating another banana split. He could easily afford one now he was a business man, yet he knew this was no time to be frivolous with money.

At the wharf, construction noise followed his progress. The demolition of the foreshore was ongoing, and a steady pounding of jackhammers, general banging, crashing and despair filled the waking hours. Commuters claimed that mid-harbour you could hear noise from both the foreshores where the bridge approaches were planned. Jack could quite believe it. He thought briefly of Mills McCoy. The man might be a thug but he knew enough to get out of the Rocks.

There were three ferries all loading passengers, a fourth steaming directly across from Circular Quay. Some distance away men were fishing from the end of a jetty while two young children explored close to the blue-green of the water. Hesitating, Jack returned to the entrance of the terminus. The breeze carried the tang of the sea, of batter, fresh bread and the sticky sweetness of fairy floss. The ten-thirty train was already steaming in from Lavender Bay. Olive was late. He rubbed at closely shaven skin. Maybe she wasn't coming.

'Jack.'

Olive stood before him in a low-waisted emerald dress and coat, and a white silk clouche hat. Her black hair shone as she gave a brief twirl for his benefit, her grin infectious.

'Olive.' He didn't know if he could sweat more profusely.

'I'm sorry about your father.' She took a step towards him as the passengers from the train began to bustle past out of the terminus in their rush to reach the wharf and the next ferry.

Jack quickly removed his cap. 'Thanks, we miss him.'

'I heard he saved some other passengers.'

'Yes, two men.'

'You must be proud.'

'I already was, before that . . .' His words trailed away.

'Of course you were.' Olive glanced up the hill to where plumes of dust haloed the surviving buildings. 'I forgot how noisy it was, how dirty.'

'Not how you remember it, eh?'

'I only remember the good things, Jack.' She touched his coat sleeve. A tram was heading downhill towards them. Arm in arm they walked away from the milling train and ferry passengers, side-stepping piles of horse manure to find an empty bench in the adjoining park. 'We may not like the way the bridge is changing our lives, Jack, but if it had already been built your father would still be alive.'

'I guess.' A flock of seagulls circled overhead, then fluttered to the ground at their feet. 'Olive?' He took a deep breath. 'I wanted to tell you that I'm not a grocer's son any more. Well, I am, but I'm not a grocer. I've got land, north-west of here. I've got a living.'

Her slender hands reached for his. 'Jack, that's wonderful. Where? Parramatta? Hornsby?'

'Not quite.'

Olive slid closer along the bench. 'Where?'

'Just let me explain. The thing is –'

'Near the water?'

'Well, no.'

He cleared his throat, lifted his chin. 'The thing is, I know we're different – that our families and such are different – but things have changed for me. I've got prospects. Mr Farley's offered me the chance to manage some land for him. Eight thousand acres and –'

'Is that a lot?'

'Botheration, you have to let me have my say, woman!' Jack knew he wanted Olive by his side, and although May and Thomas's doubts niggled there was little choice if he and Olive were to be together. Besides, he was the eldest. Jack figured he knew what was best for both of them. And hadn't his own mother always deferred to their father? It was best to get the asking over with and *then* tell Olive where they were going.

'Will you marry me, Olive? It'll be remote and hard at first, but . . .' Seagulls fluttered noisily at their feet. 'Olive?'

The girl looked dazed.

'Marry?'

'It's a distance – eight hundred mile,' Jack rushed on. 'I'll have to go ahead and make a place for us. Thomas has agreed to accompany you when the time comes.' It had not taken much persuading to get his brother's agreement.

'Eight hundred mile,' Olive repeated.

'It's a great opportunity.' Jack hugged her slight body. 'This land of Mr Farley's was resumed from one of the big pastoral holdings. This is our chance, Olive. This is my chance to become part of the landed gentry. Look.' Fishing in his pocket for a shilling coin he showed her the famous Waverly No. 4. 'Sheep and land, that's where the money is.' He dismissed the city with a wave of his hand. 'The days of aspiring to be a toffy-nosed office worker are over. Men want to make their name, make a fortune, and sheep will do it.'

Olive plucked at the smooth line of her dress and stared out at the sun-streaked harbour. 'Why not stay here?'

'Because there's nothing here for me.' Jack followed her gaze to the trees frilling the distant foreshore; a small boat was battling the wake of a ferry.

'So you'd go anyway, without me?'

'Olive, I'm doing this for us. If we're to be together it's the only way.' Jack's fingers tightened about her slim wrist. 'Anyway, you can't possibly want to remain in the city, not with the chance we've been offered . . . I'll write regularly. It'll be a couple of months, I expect, before I send for you.'

Olive gave a wan smile. 'I was looking forward to us spending some time together. I thought we could visit each other. You know, take ferry trips, eat ice cream. I never expected all this. It's so sudden.'

'And if I'd had the chance I would have courted you properly. Even if this opportunity had not have presented itself I would have eventually found a way for us to be together.' Jack wrapped his arm about her shoulder. 'This is our adventure, Olive. Our opportunity and our secret. Once you join me we'll marry and then we can tell your family. There'll be little complaint from them when they know I have means.' He gave her a squeeze. 'I know you want to live your life without your parents continually telling you what to do.' Jack spread his arms wide. 'Here's our chance.'

Olive gave a stoic smile. In his rush of words Jack hadn't actually given her the opportunity to say yes or no to his proposal of marriage. 'I, I better go. Mother will be wondering where I am.'

'Already?' Jack queried. 'I thought you had the day free?' With reluctance he escorted her towards the wharf.

'I'm sorry, Jack. All this is a bit of a shock. I need some time to absorb everything.' Olive dabbed at the moisture on her top lip, her thoughts reeling. 'So, this enterprise of Mr Farley's is . . . '

'Is sound,' Jack confirmed, avoiding a dray load of timber. 'I've seen the deeds and of course everyone knows the money that can be made in the bush. You only have to mention the names Kidman or Gordon and men sit up and take notice.' Jack couldn't recall the atmosphere being so humid at this time of the year. Scrabbling to undo the top button beneath his necktie he took Olive's arm more firmly. 'It'll be our great adventure.'

Olive purchased a ticket at the kiosk and, skirting the crowds, they made their way towards the wharf. 'I've a lot to organise so I may see you only briefly before I leave,' he admitted. 'However, once I'm settled Thomas will be in contact. He'll pass on all the details.' They waited as passengers disembarked from the Circular Quay ferry, the foamy water churning only feet away from where they stood. When Jack squeezed Olive's hand the pressure was reciprocated.

'I feel silly rushing off now. Can I see you tomorrow?'

Jack beamed. 'Of course. In the years to come, Olive, our offspring will look back and marvel at our courage. Why, in the years to come I may well be in parliament and you a great lady.'

'Do you think so, Jack?' Pushed along by embarking passengers Olive lost her grip on Jack's hand. 'Do you really think so?' She ran up the gangway and with a little shoving manoeuvred to the stern of the ferry.

'Anything's possible!' The toes of Jack's boots jutted over the end of the wharf.

'Yes, Jack Manning,' Olive cried out. 'Yes, I'll marry you!'

The water lengthened between them as the ferry motored away, a belch of smoke and a churn of grey-speckled foam signalling the beginning of the harbour crossing. Jack watched Olive grow tiny with distance, her hand aloft in an excited wave.

# ❄ Chapter 4 ❄

## The Granite Belt, Southern Qld, 1965

Dropping his hand over the side of the bed Scrubber scrabbled on the floor for his dentures. Dog padded across the floorboards, picked the teeth up in his mouth and dropped them in his master's outstretched hand. It was a hard business this rising, Scrubber thought as he jabbed the unwieldy teeth into place. It took time for his spine to gather the strength needed to participate with the rest of his body.

Once clothed, Scrubber lit the gas stove for the last time, his fingers delving in the mess drawer. He scattered screwdrivers, spanners and redundant salad servers onto the sink. Outside the wind howled mercilessly, rattling broken weatherboard and aged glass.

'Go your hardest,' Scrubber mumbled, stabbing a hole in his belt with a metal kitchen skewer and tightening the leather another notch. By the time the kettle boiled and the tea leaves had steeped good and long, his saddle bags were packed. Supplies, camp oven and billy were about the extent of his needs. What the heck: he threw in a change of clothes. On the sink was a length of rubber tubing, the sawn-off ends smoothed by sandpaper. Scrubber swished it under the tap, dried it on the front of his shirt and rotated it into the hole in his neck. Though he doubted at his age the hole would close over, habit and the slightest improvement in his speech ensured the morning ritual continued. Now he was starting to feel a semblance of his old self.

The black tea made Scrubber's gums ache and his bowels excitable, a familiar bodily state signifying the survival of another night. In celebration of the event he mushed up two slices of toast smeared with a near inch of Vegemite. Dog tilted his head, gobbled up his own share of toast, and washed it down with a bowl of water. If his Veronica were alive, Scrubber knew she'd be telling him to sit down and eat, to steady up a bit. Well, having spent his life either upright or horizontal he wasn't changing now, not even for the whisper of a long-dead woman who'd argued that being pleasantly plump never killed anyone. It did Veronica. She was plain fat.

Now the leaving day was upon him, Scrubber opened the wardrobe. A mangle of clothes that were too big for him and a couple of Veronica's floral dresses sat in a heap on the floor. He kicked the long-unused items to one side, pausing to give one of her scarfs a sniff. It was a mottled yellow affair and it still smelt of strawberries. Veronica's signature scent was, in Scrubber's mind, lolly water. Made from hard candy, he reckoned. However, he stuffed the scarf in his pocket before hesitating at the tin box, which was now revealed in the bottom of the wardrobe. He eyeballed the box for long minutes, his hands reaching out once, twice, before finally making a lunge for it and sitting the box on the end of his rumpled bed.

'What ya reckon?'

Dog cocked his head sideways.

'Hmm, figured as much.' Scrubber eyed the box off a bit, scratched his stubbly chin; eyed it off some more. It was a business this repaying of an old debt. Dog, two front paws on the sagging bed frame, lowered his whiskered muzzle to the sheets and whined. With a glance heavenwards Scrubber raised the latch, the hinge flicking open easily. He took it as a sign and lifted the yellowing newspaper to reveal a leather draw-string pouch. He always was one for good serviceable items, the kind people didn't make any more. Delicately he lifted the pouch clear of its nest and weighed the bag in one hand, then the other. The leather cord was intact and appeared strong. He tested the strength of the roughly modified tobacco pouch, ensuring it looped securely through the hand-stitched hide.

His task completed, Scrubber nodded at Dog, who gave himself up to such determined scratching with his hind leg that he fell over backwards, four legs flailing in the air like an upturned tortoise.

'Dog, this ain't no time for histrionics.' Scrubber tied the pouch to his belt, knotting it once, twice. He grappled with a small brown paper parcel in the tin box and shoved it deep in his trousers. Then he picked up his swag and rifle, flicked off the single bare bulb, slammed the front door and wound the brass key in the lock, tossing it into the dark. There was nothing sentimental left in him, not for material things, anyway. Besides, it wasn't like he could pack it all up in his coffin. Though, come to think of it, he didn't plan on having one of those.

He stood on the hill, the wind blasting his face as it rolled up from the valley below. The eight hundred acres he still owned was a paltry reminder of what lies at the end of a bottle, although to be fair the drink probably didn't come first. This was hard country, where granite thwarted livelihoods and winter could kill man and beast alike. The property deserved a last look at least. The best parts might be long gone, but Scrubber liked to think a cannier, younger person would put his toiling to good use. So he envisaged the wind-cropped paddocks, the rangy cattle, and he meandered along the creek with its rush of water and age-smoothed stones, his body never leaving the worn tread of the front door.

'You ready then?' Scrubber scraped his boots on the edge of the cement step.

Dog yawned into the misting air. Above, the frill of an eagle hawk's wings was silhouetted against the sky.

Satisfied by his reflections, Scrubber skirted the fallen-down garage as he clumped to the stables. Three horses waited in anticipation, their nostrils flaring. They were a knowing triumvirate, and Scrubber, pleased to be fulfilling their fantasies, spoke to them low and gruff, his fingers covering the hole in his neck so the words could escape. He saddled the one he'd named Veronica, loaded Samsara and Petal with his goods, and shut the stable door behind them as he left.

A line of grey cloud hung low on the horizon. Scrubber didn't go much for creeping dawns. The ones that came fast and shiny in summer appealed the most. Funny how these ones appeared more ominous as the years passed, as if they could catch him unawares. Scrubber waggled a finger at the sky. He had an agenda and his own timeframe. Neither God nor that thing in the east were getting him until it was good and done.

He left his turret of a house on the treeless peak as light fingered its way over the tuft of hills in the east. The horses were frisky for old girls and he steadied them with a tug of the halters and a slap across Veronica's boney skull. A man had enough to put up with without suffering an extended show of enthusiasm.

Figuring nine miles a day, Scrubber reckoned on reaching his destination a bit past the winter solstice. It was a manageable ride of some 700 miles and, if done with purpose, achievable. The thing he liked the best about the venture, apart from finally honouring the oath, was the thought of looking over his shoulder as he headed west. The further he rode the longer the minutes would stretch. Scrubber could almost taste the extra days of life this undertaking would afford him.

Dog gave an excuse for a bark and settled into the morning, tongue hanging from one side of his mouth, tail swaying happily.

'Anyone would think this was an adventure,' Scrubber said as he stretched the cotton scarf protectively across his windpipe, patted the pouch at his waist and thought of the men in years past who'd tried to do their best by the girl Cora. None of them really succeeded. One would lose Cora to save her, another would end up dying for her. And him? Well, he killed for her.

## ❧ Chapter 5 ❧

## Absolution Creek Homestead, Northern NSW, 1965

There was a scatter of leaves overhead, the creak of iron. The great branches of the leopardwood swayed above the homestead, the tree's canopy stretching protectively over the building. The highest branches were twisted and dark as if a great fight had occurred to find both air and space as it grew upwards from within the homestead. The remaining branches, dense in both number and leaves, spread from the thick trunk, which leant precariously towards the outside of the building. It was as if some force had leant against the interior of the building and pushed it outwards, so that boards bulged from top to bottom. A single leaf fluttered to the base of the great tree to rest on the uneven floorboards where its roots laid claim to its surrounds. The sun dropped a little lower, the angle of light disturbing a tiny brown lizard on the speckled bark. The creature absorbed the last of the day's warmth before scurrying upwards towards the ceiling.

With open palms, Cora touched the bark of the leopardwood and felt the surge of energy from its living centre. Pressing her forehead against the knobbly tree she felt the great heart of the woody plant wrap her in love.

'So that's it then?' a voice queried, slightly bemused.

She turned towards the rumpled bed and the dark-haired man; one leg entangled in the white sheet, his arm flung carelessly across a pillow. Cora wished she had woken earlier, left before his waking. The cotton billowed out and upwards as he flung the sheet from his body, his lean frame bare. She watched him dress, slowly, methodically: navy work shirt, heavy cable jumper, pale jeans frayed at the hems. When he sat to pull on grey woollen socks, his hair falling over his forehead, she almost relented.

'It would never have worked.' Her words were as crisp as the air. The wind scattered the leaves from the great tree in her bedroom, piling them in a dusty corner of the veranda.

'That's what you said last time.'

'Well, I'm doubly sure now.' The fact that James was smiling only made things worse. It was as if he could see beyond her words to the truth of things.

He pulled on his boots with decisive movements. 'Every time we get close, really close, you pull away from me.' He touched her cheek. 'Nothing else matters you know, Cora, except us.'

Cora visualised her fingers on his, held her breath as the pressure from his touch met the warmth beneath. There was a momentary pause before the inevitable. It was like passing beneath a bridge from shadow to sunlight yet her decision held her fast.

James tucked a strand of hair behind her ear and gave her a wink. He made her feel such a girl again, with his cheeky grin and his habit of standing so close that there was little choice but to look up to him. Nearing his mid-forties, James was in his prime. Any woman would have been proud to have a younger man such as he in her bed. And, ten years his senior, Cora was well aware of what she was giving up.

'We can't live in a vacuum, James, you know that. Life doesn't allow it.'

'Well, you seem to be doing a good job of it.'

Cora directed her attention to the leopardwood tree in the corner of her bedroom. Men were impossible, she mused. Relationships were impossible.

'Ah yes, the silent treatment,' James said lightly. 'What a tragedy you are, Cora Hamilton.'

After he left, Cora sat stiffly on the bed. She glanced at her reflection in the dresser mirror. A straight almost patrician nose was complemented by rounded cheeks and generous lips undiminished by age. Fine lines etched oval eyes. Her neck was not yet scraggly, her hair still black and lustrous. Despite the thin line of a scar that ran close to one eye, some would say she was in her prime. Why then was she so cursed by the past that she was afraid of sharing her future?

The scent of him lingered and warmed her like a caress. Despite the presence of the great tree, the room felt bereft. That's what she hated most, what she'd always hated: the great gulf of emptiness that followed their leaving. And they all left, eventually, in one way or another. She couldn't go through that again: the heart-wrenching hurt. Cora cradled her head, wishing she were different, yet remembering, always remembering.

On the quietest of nights, when the sky was a glassy pond, the memories of the past years hovered about her. They came like drifts of windblown leaves through the blue haze of the scrub and carried the scents of the old days. And like the spirits of the people who roamed the land before white man knew what he trod upon, Cora conjured up her own dreaming, for she couldn't escape from the past.

Cora walked her brown gelding slowly through the grass. The ground was parched. Although January brought rain it was some three months since the heavens graced Absolution Creek with even the slightest spit. With winter coming and the chance of new growth dwindling with each passing day, Cora could smell the approaching dry spell. It hung in the cloudless sky and clung in the shadows when the evenings grew long. Kangaroos, wallabies and emus were increasing in numbers. They were coming in from further afield, from the western division of the state where grazing country was diminished. Cora knew all the signs, and she hated what they foretold. She thought of calling James and chatting about the weather, however a fortnight lay between their last encounter and today.

For April the nights were already cool, the pre-dawn breathing dew across the countryside, a tantalising taste of moisture soon to be stolen by the sun. This day was no different. Droplets of dew were already settling on her thighs and the shoulders of her thick coat. She had been out riding since the witching hour and followed her usual pattern: first stalking the impossibly square garden of the homestead, and then slipping through the fence to the house dam to startle the kangaroos lolling by the leopardwood trees near the edge of the water. They were used to her nightly invasion, and the only responses she elicited were raised heads and a pricking of ears. Cora was a part of their surroundings, night or day. She cut a lone figure in beige moleskin trousers and oilskin jacket, a pistol holstered at her waist, a rawhide stockwhip curled about her shoulder, bridle dangling in her gloved hands. Her horse, as usual, had been girth-deep in water. The animal had stared with unblinking eyes at the still surface of the dam until Cora's whistle enticed him out of his wallowing habit. Three hours on they were still traversing the landscape.

'Come on, Horse.' Cora tugged lightly on the reins, directing them away from the open paddock towards the creek. A waning moon clung mid-sky. A scatter of sheep, the wool on their frames glowing in the half-light, moved methodically across the land. They walked in a staggered V formation, feeding into the northerly wind. Cora twitched the wide brim of her hat and glanced about the paddock, the tang of manure rich in the night air. A line of darkness marked the woody scrub bordering the waterway, and far off to the west a distant treeline defined the edge of Absolution Creek. With three miles of boundary fence already checked, Cora was wary of tarrying in case she missed the object of her ride.

The land was quiet. False dawn appeared with a soft halo of light enticing the bush to movement. A kookaburra flew overhead, a small rodent in its beak. Horse plodded past an ant hill, disturbing a handful of camped sheep as he walked along the edge of the creek. He meandered between clumps of gum trees towards the waterway. A gentle pull on the reins and they were descending the bank. Cora's hand moved automatically to the .38 revolver at her hip.

Horse whinnied quietly. 'Shush,' Cora reprimanded as she ducked to miss a low-hanging branch, the crunch of twigs and branches inordinately loud. They weaved along the water's edge, ensuring a healthy distance remained between them and the creek's murky depths. Cora hated the water, and Horse, sensing her dislike, rarely strayed off their designated path.

'Good boy.'

The tracks appeared almost immediately. The cloven hoofs were imprinted distinctly into the sand and led directly along the creek's edge. Cora counted the impressions under her breath. 'Small ones mainly,' she commented dissatisfied. She nudged Horse and they rode on for some minutes until the green of shrubby lignum choked their path. The dense growth grew in a jagged Z shape, crossing the creek to ensnare a fence and effectively clutter the waterway. Cora and her station manager, Harold, had tried to burn the lignum out last year, however the brimming creek made a strong fire impossible and their attempts simply singed the edges. Only a dry creek would give them the conditions needed to burn the lignum – an unwinnable situation. The creek wound through three of their grazing paddocks and fed two strategically placed dams, providing major watering points for their sheep.

Cora brushed aside a low-hanging branch. 'Where are they?'

Horse pricked his ears. A small flock of green finches flew from the lignum to sweep only inches above the water's surface. They settled as one across the creek, a flurry of tiny flapping wings strung out in a line on the top fence wire. In an instant a big black sow and a litter of screeching suckers tore out of the lignum.

Cora jammed her heels into Horse's flanks and wheeled after the squat dark bodies. Water, lignum and trees flashed past in a blur. Within seconds they were level with the wild pigs. Reins tight in one hand, Cora drew her revolver clear, levelling it at the sow. A surge of adrenalin coursed through her slight frame as she breathed out slowly, simultaneously squeezing the trigger. The wild pig was the size of two border collies. Fat and sleek, the animal hurtled left then right. As expected the litter scattered as the old sow did a direct U-turn to head back towards the sanctity of the lignum. Gripping Horse's flanks with her knees, Cora took aim and fired. The bullet hit the animal behind the ear, killing it instantly. Horse stopped dead in his tracks and Cora's arms flailed in the air as the sudden jolt threw her forward and then back again.

'Damn you, Horse,' Cora complained, pocketing the remaining five bullets from the revolver. 'How many times do I have to tell you not to do that?'

Horse lifted each of his legs in turn, shifting his weight slowly. His large eyes blinked. The rest of the litter dispersed in a crackle of hoofs and drying vegetation. The sow's back legs struck out in the soft sand then stilled.

Cora holstered the revolver, the smell of cordite thick in the air, the barrel hot. 'One less,' she muttered, turning Horse away from the corpse. In a few months the squealing suckers would be another eight grown feral pigs rooting up her precious oat crop or eating newborn lambs in the spring. She wiped at the sweat on her forehead, tucked stray bits of hair behind her ears. Her leg was already aching. The pull of it stretched from her lower spine to her knee. With a grimace she readjusted herself in the saddle, standing tall in the stirrup irons to rub at the knotted muscle in her lower back.

Horse headed along the creek, his hoofs flicking up sand and twigs as they retraced their tracks. Soon Cora was shielding her eyes from the glare of dawn, her weak eye smarting as they cut through the paddock. They crossed the creek at its narrowest point at a cement pipe mounded with dirt, and continued on through the drying grasses. At the box tree, which marked the midpoint between the creek and the homestead, Cora reined in Horse. Balancing the canvas water bag on her thigh she took two Bex powders from her shirt pocket. The powder was gritty in her mouth and it took a good swig of water to wash the medicine down. Swiping her hand across her mouth, she looked out across country she had pictured in every stage of its life cycle for over forty years. The grasses were already drying out with the morning sun. Soon the dewy dark of their stems would grow pale as the cool, dry breath of autumn settled upon the landscape. She tutted Horse into a trot and they padded down the dirt track.

Four miles on, the corrugated-iron roof of the homestead with its guardian tree shimmered with welcome. Curly and Tripod rushed through the open house paddock gate, barking in unison. Despite Tripod's missing hind leg – the result of an altercation with a rabbit trap – the collie was only a tad behind his half-brother, Curly, in speed. He made up for his injury with a screeching howl when it suited him and a less than patient attitude towards sheep.

The dogs did three quick circles around horse and rider, and rushed off towards the stables. En route they stopped at the chook house to bark mercilessly at the strutting rooster. The old rogue never had been much at regular rooster behaviour and could be relied upon to crow night or day, but most particularly when anyone arrived or departed from the homestead. Cora was about ready to put the male renegade out to pasture. You could lay bets that when you wanted chickens he wouldn't perform, and when you didn't he was like a warrior going after his own Helen of Troy. She gave a calming whistle, which quieted the dogs but set the rooster off and set the chooks squabbling.

Horse trotted past the work shed. The bay for the horse float was still empty. Cora just knew it was going to be one of those days and, considering it was only Monday, things didn't bode well for the working week. At the stables she threw her leg over the saddle with a grimace and waited as her lower spine stretched itself out. Horse bore his unsaddling with customary stillness. Cora carried the saddle, blanket and bridle into the tack room, reappearing with a currycomb.

'That'll be it then, mate.' Cora finished brushing Horse down and rested her brow briefly on the bony plate of his head. Digging her hands into her pockets she began the quarter mile walk to the homestead, the dogs nipping at her heels.

The road leading to the homestead was rutted and narrow. Bordered by a western windbreak of towering native gums planted some seventy years ago by the previous owners, the road eventually split into two. One road led out of Absolution Creek: twenty miles of unbroken straightness until a T-intersection appeared as a sudden reminder of life beyond the property. The second circumnavigated the house and garden like a partial ring road, ending abruptly in a maze of wind-twisted pine trees spilling from a ridge. At the wooden gate the dogs ducked between Cora's legs and scooted up the cement path to arrive panting at the back door.

In the kitchen the scent of just-baked scones signalled her house-keeper, Ellen's, efficiency. Freshly gathered eggs sat on the sink, a leg of mutton was cooling under the domed meat keeper, and the scones were huddled within a tea towel. Cora made a pot of black tea, selected three of Ellen's doughy concoctions and some cheddar from the fridge, and sat at the kitchen table, placing the revolver at her elbow. She devoured the food, the tea scalding her throat as she drank thirstily. Some habits were hard to break and eating quickly remained one from childhood. It was always a pleasure to return home after her morning ride. Ellen had a knack for domesticity that more than compensated for her spiky temperament. She had always been very opinionated, whether it be about housekeeping or the best way to eradicate Cora's tree, and over time the two women realised it was best to keep out of each other's way to avoid arguments.

Ellen's husband, Harold, was in town ordering feed corn. Cora hoped they wouldn't need to feed for long. However, with the ewes due to lamb in late August and shearing behind them, she felt more confident with a few preventative measures in place, even though she expected Absolution to have enough feed until mid-winter. She would have to time the feeding carefully, introducing it gradually and in small quantities, for any abrupt change in diet could lead to a distinct break in the wool's staple and a conse-quent downgrading of price. That, however, was the least of Cora's problems this morning.

Twenty-two-year-old Jarrod Michaels was MIA again. This time he'd brokered for half of Friday off, sweetening his request by working part of last Sunday. Cora should have known better. Never-theless she'd found herself agreeing, hoping that a little leniency on her part would be rewarded. At the last minute, in spite of his affa-bility, he'd skipped all of Friday, leaving with Absolution's horse float in a flurry of dust en route to a campdraft over the border.

The kitchen clock on the cream wall was nearing eleven. Cora placed her plate and cup on the sink and gazed through the window at the paddock beyond. Jarrod's future prospects on Absolution were looking decidedly limited, which wouldn't endear Cora to the boy's mother. Mrs Michaels was a widow and a whiner and not averse to making a myriad telephone calls to check on her precious boy.

The blue utility tore around the corner of the house to park in a squeal of dirt, dust and barking dogs.

'Now what?' Cora muttered.

Harold kicked open the back gate and staggered up the path half-dragging Absolution's absent jackaroo. The boy's shirt was ripped and bloody.

'What on earth happened?' Cora grabbed Jarrod's other arm.

'Found him at the second stock grid.' Harold puffed, pulling him into the kitchen. 'Reckon he hit it straight on.'

Cora wrung out a clean tea towel with hot water and began wiping at the boy's face.

'The ute and float are buggered; his horse will have to be put down; and he's drunk as a skunk.'

Cora patted gently around a jagged cut. 'Most of the blood's from this head wound.'

'I'm fine, fine,' Jarrod slurred, pushing Cora's arm away.

'Sure you are, son.' Harold squatted in front of the lad. 'Anything busted?'

'My arm.' The stench of beer and cigarette smoke was atrocious.

Harold and Cora looked at each other. 'Maybe a cold shower would be in order,' Cora suggested.

'Good idea.'

They walked Jarrod back outside to the laundry block where an adjoining shower and toilet were situated. They put a garden chair in the shower cubicle and plonked Jarrod down before turning the cold tap on. The water had the desired effect. Soon Jarrod was abusing both of them as watery blood drained down the plug hole. Curly and Tripod were a delighted audience, snuffling around Cora's ankles.

Five minutes later a dazed Jarrod snatched at the offered towel Cora held. His right arm hung limply by his side. 'What's the matter with you two?' Jarrod complained. 'Jeez.'

'You've been in an accident, Jarrod,' Harold explained patiently. 'Your ute and the float are pretty busted up, which means the police will need to be called in.' He took a step closer to the boy. 'Don't think you want to be explaining yourself smelling like a brewery, do you?'

'No harm in a few drinks.' Jarrod dried his face, wincing at the sight of his blood. 'Is it bad?'

'No it's not.' Cora pointed at his arm. 'What about your arm?'

'No thanks to you, it's busted. You reefed it over your shoulder.'

'Selective memory, eh, Jarrod?' Harold undid a few of Jarrod's shirt buttons. The boy's collarbone was near poking through his skin. He glanced at Cora. 'Reckon I'll take him straight to the hospital. It's a bit much for our doctoring skills.'

'Fair enough.' Cora could set straight arm and leg breaks, but anything else was beyond her. 'I'll call and tell them you're coming.'

Once Jarrod was settled in the front of the utility with blankets and pillows, Harold turned his key in the ignition. 'You'll have to look after the horse.'

'Don't you touch my horse!' Jarrod slumped back in the bench seat.

'You better go.' Cora waved them off, side-stepping the dogs. In the kitchen she made the necessary calls to the police and hospital, the party-line telephone system ensuring the majority of the district would know of the accident within the hour. It only took one interested matron to pick up the telephone and listen in when the manual exchange was rung for the news to travel like the proverbial. Once the authorities were informed Cora holstered her revolver, slipped into her work coat and set her wide-brimmed hat firmly on her head. The business of putting an injured horse down lay ahead, a hateful task.

## ⋘ Chapter 6 ⋙

## The New England Tablelands, 1965

The final rise was a beauty. The high spot gave Scrubber a grand view of the countryside. Spread out like a fancy banquet, squares of jade, brown, gold and murky green were intersected by lines of trees, roads and homesteads. The view folded over slopes until haze met the foothills to disappear into a land not visited by Scrubber for nigh on thirty years. He couldn't smell it yet – the tang of dry dirt and real acreage, of sheep in their thousands, of a land that tempted like a bag of candy. He could remember it, though; could see his arrival at the Purcells' property. Twenty-two years of age, swag at his feet, white gold dangling before his eyes. His missus once said he should have stayed in the flat country. Maybe he should have. He never could forget the scent of lanoline; of a fleece thrown six foot in the air, sunlight catching the burry edges of it before it landed on the wool table to be skirted and inverted into a lump of snowy whiteness. His boots tapped Veronica's flanks as they plodded up the road. The old girl had a tendency to doze off when he tarried. Come to think of it, so did he.

Behind them, cars were starting to protest. Were he a betting man, Scrubber reckoned the young fella behind would overtake, regardless of road rules. They were travelling downhill, the bitumen hard on the three horses' hoofs, the road twisting like a desert side-winder. It was his right to travel the highway like any other person, even if there were now eight cars caught behind him desperately wishing for a slow lane. He patted Veronica on the rump, glanced at Dog padding rhythmically alongside him, and adjusted the scarf about his neck. The car was low and slate-grey; the kind of vehicle that would be invisible in bull dust and eventually get run over by a road train. The double white lines stretched ahead around the next blind corner.

His mount kept her head down and stayed centred on the road. If he'd been a believing man Scrubber almost considered it possible that his Veronica, the woman variety, had come back as the nag he now rode. He clicked his tongue and the mare dropped her head a touch lower. Yep, he mumbled, just like his V. She'd always been stubborn, like the time the doctor warned about dia*beat*es. No one was gonna *beat* her, V bit back. Of course the illness eventually got her a good five years ago at about the same time his own body began to fail him, which was why he was finally heading west to see Cora. With no one left to care for and his own illness worsening, he had no excuses left. Besides which, he had his conscience to clear.

The mare brightened and lifted her head as if attuned to his thoughts. Samsara and Petal weren't so obliging: they pulled on their lead ropes and kicked out at the pushy prestige car behind them. Eventually Scrubber got bored with the noise of it all and gave an off-hand wave to his stalker, narrowing his eyes against flying grit as the car sped past.

◁◆▷

At the end of the first week it was a relief to reach the start of the stock route. The horses knew instinctively when the real part of the journey began. They snuffled at the winter-whipped grass and whinnied when the bitumen grew invisible.

Scrubber stopped early that day. The warm sun was unseasonal and a camp spot hung enticingly in his mind like a good slug of rum. Once his girls were unpacked, their saddles resting at the foot of a gum tree, Scrubber stripped off, sitting the leather pouch on his folded oilskin jacket near a fast-flowing creek. Running into the water he splashed and yelped with delight. This, he decided, was living.

He could have sat by the water for hours, but with his stomach cantankerous he set about getting a feed. A lump of old mutton tied to a bit of string enticed two snappy craybobs to dinner. Scrubber grabbed at their thick slimy bodies, apologising for their unfortunate demise so late in the season. By the time he'd fished, fired up, and roughed together a bit of water and flour, the sun's rays were streaming fitfully through the trees.

Scrubber boiled water in a faithful camp oven and plonked the fractious old man craybobs into the bubbling pot. They cooked in minutes and he tore off their pincers, gnawing at the white fluffy innards with teeth past chewing. Dog, not one for fish, ate damper from a tin plate and drank his share of hot billy tea, belching in contentment as he lay down near the fire.

'Good, eh?' In the past Scrubber had struggled with dinner conversation. Dog turned on his side and rubbed his head in the grass.

The camp fire struggled throughout the night. The wood, leached by numerous floodings, alternated between outpourings of smoke and rare flashes of unenthusiastic flame. When the timber did burn it turned to ash quickly. Scrubber watched the dismal offering with amusement, a piece of grass clamped between dry lips. He'd grasped long ago that some form of genetic flaw had pursued him out of the birth canal and into life, rendering him incapable of following a straight track. Knowing that – accepting that some things from the past were beyond his control – well, it made certain incidents easier to live with. Scrubber glanced at the pouch. He itched for conversation, however the stars were a little too close for comfort, a little too interested in what he planned to say.

## ≪ Chapter 7 ≫

## Absolution Creek, 1965

The sight of the twisted float didn't endear Jarrod to Cora. The boy's utility was buckled head on against one side of the stock grid. The float had jack-knifed, rolled over and come free of the rear of the utility. Cora walked the couple of hundred yards through ankle-high grass to where the float lay on its side. The steel of the horse trailer was ripped jaggedly at the front, and she could hear from within the horse's laboured breathing and the float wall being kicked intermittently.

She scrambled up onto the side of the float. Inside, the chestnut mare glared back at her with wide, frightened eyes. There was a deep gash along her rump and another on her chest where she had hit the front of the trailer on impact. These wounds probably would have healed nicely under the care of the local vet were it not for the extent of the mare's leg injuries. Both front legs were broken, and a hoof partially torn away. A crow flew overhead and gave a single vulturous cry. Slipping a bullet into the chamber of the revolver, Cora took aim and fired. The animal stilled.

In the silence that followed, Cora examined the scene. The mare was still saddled and, judging by the extent of the caked dust and sweat along her girth and legs, hadn't even warranted a rub down at the end of yesterday's draft. Aware that young men were inclined to be foolish and that the float was insured, Cora might well have only reprimanded Jarrod and deducted his wages for being thoughtless; what Cora couldn't abide, however, was injury to animals.

'You could have called me.'

James Campbell walked towards her, vet bag in his hand. 'I didn't hear you.' Cora clambered down from the float. 'Who called you?'

'No one. I was on my way to check on some calving heifers next door. The pistol shot was the giveaway. I'd recognise it anywhere. How's the kid? I assume it was Jarrod?'

Cora nodded. 'Drunk as, with a busted collarbone and more attitude than a cut snake. Harold's taken him to the hospital.'

'Looks like he was lucky.' James peered into the float. 'Well, it was a nice clean shot, Cora, not that I would have expected anything else.' He looked at the wreckage. 'All this will have to stay as is until the police arrive.'

They walked back through the grass to where their vehicles were parked. 'So, how's business? I didn't think you had the time for it any more.'

James patted his bag. 'Just keeping my eye in: all those years of study and then half the family clears off to the big smoke and the rest are pushing daisies.'

'You're lucky. At least you've got something to fall back on if things go pear-shaped. So, how are things going over in squatter-dom?' James's property was six miles away as the crow flies and a good thirty by road.

'Not bad. The clip will be patchy though. The season hasn't been too kind to date. And you?'

Cora pinched the bridge of her nose. A headache loomed. 'Staff problems. There are always staff problems.'

'I'm hearing you.' James dropped his bag through the passenger door of his utility.

'This accident will just about pull Jarrod up at Absolution. I've been thinking of getting rid of him – he's just too unreliable.'

James glanced over his shoulder at the wrecked float. 'Well, I can't blame you. Anyway, miss me?' He was leaning against his ute, arms and legs crossed, hat tipped back on his forehead.

'Nope,' Cora replied quickly as an image of a billowing white sheet came to mind. 'I mean –'

James lifted his hand. 'Don't worry, I know how you like your space. You forget we've got a history, Cora, and neither of us are selling out any time soon.' He gave her a lopsided grin and opened his car door. 'I'll be seeing you, kiddo.'

Cora waited for him to look back, for their eyes to meet, and was surprised when disappointment swelled inside her as road dust smothered his departure.

'You can't fire the kid while he's still in hospital.'

They were sitting outside beneath the kitchen window. Some years ago Harold had helped her dig out a few feet of dirt in a sizable square, and now the second-hand pavers they'd laid supported a peeling wooden table and three chairs. Cora sipped her tea, a diary and paddock book beneath her elbow. 'I guess you're right.' One night's observation had turned into a week. Jarrod's arm was broken in three places, his collarbone too. 'At least he'll be dried out by the end of it.'

Harold added another teaspoon of sugar to his tea. 'I feel sorry for him.'

'What's to feel sorry for?' Cora asked. Tripod followed Curly in a limping gait through the flower bed adjoining the chicken wire fence.

'Well, he's only got his mother and they reckon she's a tough master. Anyway, he's out for the count now by the sounds of it.'

'Would you keep him?' She set her cup down on the table.

Selecting a pre-rolled cigarette from his leather hat-band, Harold lit it and coughed thickly. 'He's a good worker.'

'Too unreliable. I just don't know why we have to put up with people like that. Either they want work or they don't.' Cora called the dogs over, affectionately pulling each of their ears. 'Don't get me wrong, Jarrod's great, when it suits him.'

Harold drained his cup and flicked ash onto the patchy lawn. 'Well, I can't make staff out of a broom and a bucket.'

'Some of the ones we've employed on Absolution have been about as handy as that.' Cora sighed. 'No, I think Jarrod's days here are over.'

'How about I tell him?' Harold suggested. 'He's still pretty fired up about you putting his horse down.'

'Like his hide.' Cora stacked the cups and empty cake plate noisily.

After Harold left, Cora stayed out in the weak autumn sun. Jarrod's accident disrupted everything. Now they were down one jackeroo, jobs were postponed – including the corn delivery date – to be rearranged accordingly between visits from the police, the dealings with the insurance company and an irate mother. Close to informing Mrs Michaels of what she really thought about her beloved boy, Cora managed to listen for all of five minutes before putting the receiver down.

Cora scribbled some stock movements in the diary and wondered about her staff conundrum. Absolution Creek was a middle-sized holding of 8000 acres. Not massive by any means, but large enough for a single woman to need the assistance of Harold and a jackeroo to oversee. As Absolution's seventh jackeroo in seventeen years, Jarrod followed a line of bush-bred greenhides who needed to be broken in. Stupidity was fast becoming an employee characteristic she could do without. It seemed best to employ a qualified station hand; not only would that alleviate the hair-tearing rigmarole of the past seventeen years, it would relieve some of the strain.

Cora knew eventually her injuries would make full-time work on Absolution difficult. The fall that occurred forty years earlier damaged her eye, leg and hip. If such an accident happened today she would have been treated for breaks, fractures and muscle tears, and perhaps something could have been done for her wounded eye. She did what she could, of course. Long walks, hot-water bottles and hanging from the door to stretch out her spine. Old wounds, however, were hard to heal and increasingly she relied on Harold for the more labour-intensive jobs. Over the last three years she'd stopped drenching the sheep, fencing, carting hessian sacks of chaff, lifting small bales of hay; separately they were small tasks, but combined they took away a great part of her work day, relegating her to the office or her daily rides about the property. These rides were Cora's salvation, for at night the land spoke to her, reminding her of another time and place. Like her injuries, there were some things a person could not be free of.

Having acknowledged she could never forgive those who had made much of her life difficult, Cora nonetheless tried to keep past hurts firmly in the past. It took some time for her to discover that she was incapable of setting memories aside or compartmental-ising her anger. Everything from her earlier life continued to directly affect her present and future, including her failed love affair with James Campbell.

It was time, Cora decided, to repay her sister Jane Hamilton. There was the very real possibility that her future at Absolution Creek could be cut short by management agreements put in place decades ago, and it was important to Cora that she still be on the property when the injuries done to her and her family so long ago were finally brought to light. She wanted to be on the land she loved.

Her plan involved employing someone under the guise of a paid female companion. 'A malleable female companion.' Cora looked at the tea leaves in the now cold cup. Why bring a perfect stranger into her home when one could nab a relative? Jane's daughter, Meg. The great pity of life was that one couldn't choose their own relations. Still, she satisfied herself with the belief that surely Meg couldn't be as troublesome as her mother. Meg's birth had been announced somewhat triumphantly in the 'hatches' section of the *Sydney Morning Herald* in the early forties, and although the silence between Cora and Meg's mother extended over forty-two years, a quick search courtesy of the Sydney telephone exchange had located her sister.

I'll just have to try and see, Cora thought. She attempted to list the benefits of the arrangement from the girl's viewpoint. She could dangle the prospect of some form of inheritance. It didn't matter really. Her aim was to take from Jane her only child and show the woman that Cora had not forgiven her or forgotten. Cora put pen to paper.

*My dear Meg,*

*At some stage in your life your mother may have mentioned me. Although she and I are not close, I am your aunt and I live quite a distance from you on a property in north-west New South Wales. I am younger than your mother but I find myself in need of a companion, and of course immediately thought of you. I am by no means an invalid, however I do require some assistance indoors, and how wonderful it would be if you decided to leave dreary Sydney and join me. In return I offer you a place in my spacious homestead and, of course, a most generous allowance.*

*Absolution Creek is a large well-known holding which produces beef and wool. It is a beautiful, productive property with the added benefit of fresh air and unending space. I have no children of my own, which is why I have decided to make contact with you. Your mother will see little benefit in such an arrangement, however do believe my heart-felt invitation.*

*With best wishes,*

*Cora Hamilton*

Cora briefly thought of Jane Hamilton and when she finished writing the letter – addressing the envelope to Meg – a grim smile of satisfaction settled on her face.

Later in the afternoon Cora walked around the corner of the enclosed veranda to the room where she intended Meg to sleep. The bedroom was musty. Crossing the dusty floorboards she opened the faded curtains and casement window. The breeze encircled her, lifting dust from a leather chair, narrow wardrobe, hardwood dresser and four-poster bed. Cora ran her fingers across the polished brass bedknobs, her eyes drawn to the bunched mosquito netting hanging from the ceiling. The netting was shadowy with dust; fragile with memories.

The bedroom needed to be painted before her niece's arrival. She could probably even find a picture or two to tart up the walls. A scattering of leaves on the corrugated-iron roof startled her. For a moment Cora imagined it to be the heavy step of a man and she closed her eyes, constructing his image. He was with her still, breathing life into every new day. The man who saved her and deserted her.

Jack Manning.

Sneezing, she sat at the writing desk and ran a finger across the cracked surface. It was purchased from Anthony Horden's mail-order catalogue in the summer of 1924, and remained unused. Inside one of the drawers sat a tub of unopened furniture wax, a stubby pencil and . . . the coin was cool beneath the pad of her fingers. Fishing it out, Cora rubbed the metal on her moleskins. There he was, Waverly No. 4, Mr Purcell's prize merino stud ram rendered for posterity in metal in a swirl of horn and woolly growth.

Flicking the shilling coin high in the air, Cora caught it with a determined swipe. In spite of everything, there were some good parts in the weather-beaten chronicle that was her life. Some.

# ⪻ *Chapter 8* ⪼

# *The Queen's Club, Sydney,*
# *1923*

Olive and her mother were already seated in the dining room of the Queen's Club when Henrietta appeared in a waistless crepe chiffon gown of palest blue. The waiter escorted her with the minimum of fuss to their corner table overlooking Hyde Park.

'Gracious, Henrietta,' their mother exclaimed, 'late again.' Nevertheless she nodded approval at Henrietta's pearl necklace, the longest strand of which reached to her waist.

'Well, you do persist in dragging us to your Club, Mother, when there are any number of fashionable eating houses.' Henrietta glanced around the damask- and crystal-burdened room, nodding to a number of older matrons who had their own daughters and daughters-in-law in tow.

'Even if they had not closed the tea room at the Queen Victoria Building we would still be ensconced here,' Mrs Peters argued as a waiter draped heavily starched napkins across their laps. 'This is fast becoming *the* most fashionable place in Sydney. Besides, membership is very restricted.' She flicked open the menu.

'The modern set spends the midday hour in mixed company.' Henrietta retrieved an ivory fan from her purse and began wafting it about. 'This club has only been opened for a few years and already I can feel myself becoming crusty,' she whispered behind her fan to Olive.

A waiter hovered close by and poured water into stemmed glasses.

Mrs Peters addressed the waiter smoothly. 'Steamed snapper with parsley sauce, cabbage and mashed swede and –' the menu was subjected to a final withering gaze '– walnut trifle for dessert.'

'For everyone, madam?' the waiter enquired.

'Everyone,' Mrs Peters confirmed, closing the menu with a decisive snap.

Olive stifled a giggle: Henrietta detested parsley sauce and cabbage.

'Marjorie Madgewick was telling me last night that the new Parisian designer, Coco Chanel, caused quite a sensation recently. It would appear tans are now de rigeur.' Henrietta enjoyed being at the forefront of knowledge.

'No, really?' Olive was intrigued. Madame Chanel had the European set wearing jersey men's-style jackets and bell-bottom trousers.

'It's true,' Henrietta enthused. 'Apparently she was horribly burnt while on holidays and, voila, suddenly brown skin is in fashion.'

'How appalling,' Mrs Peters lamented. 'I myself will never understand the interest you girls have in the European set. Why, it was only a handful of years ago that they were blowing everyone up over there – including our own countrymen.'

As their fish arrived the business of eating took over. Olive looked at the sunken-eyed fish laid out like a sacrificial offering and wished for veal cutlets and spaghetti. This dish, like so many things redolent of their life in North Sydney, had been condemned to history, as had the unfortunate inhabitants dwelling in the path of the great bridge construction. She had long since learnt not to argue. Patience and agreeability were now Olive's greatest virtues, especially as nearly four months had passed since Jack's departure. His absence left a gap in Olive's daily life too large to fill.

Mrs Peters chewed. 'Tasty, is it not?'

Olive's cabbage was well boiled and the parsley sauce was concocted of such finely chopped amounts of the plant she could hardly complain. She gave the expected smile, receiving a nod of approval from her mother. She missed Jack's company. He wasn't as reserved as the young men Olive now mixed with and his conversation was never limited to the polite chitchat that centred on boring financial or legal institutions.

Henrietta poked uninterestedly at her food. 'So, you've been behaving yourself, little sister?'

'She's been out with the Gees twice this month. Their son Archy is –'

'Boring,' Henrietta interrupted. 'Haven't you seen Martin Woodward? He's dreamy.'

Olive brightened. 'Well, I met him –'

'He's sailing to Great Britain in the New Year,' Mrs Peters interrupted. 'Apparently he hopes to continue on to Cairo to see Lord Carnarvon's discovery.'

'They opened the burial chamber belonging to the boy king Tutankhamun, Henrietta,' Olive began excitedly. 'Buried treasure in this day. Isn't it amazing? How I would love to do something as thrilling as travel and adventuring.'

'Anyway, you can forget the Woodwards, young lady. The wealth isn't there. Your sister has set high standards.'

Henrietta Eton was very much the wealthy wedded woman. In the short month since her marriage she had become something of a benefactor to a number of less fortunate women with some musical ability.

'I did ask, Mother, if Mrs Eton senior could source someone

suitable for your household. I suggested even a housekeeper would suffice, but things haven't improved, staffing wise. There has been a massive decline in the number of those in service since the war.'

'Tell me something new, Henrietta.' Mrs Peters sniffed. It was a matter of contention between mother and daughter that Henrietta should have three servants by December and Mrs Peters still made do with one. 'How people in the classes can get uppity and choose not to follow a profession required by many of us is beyond me.'

The arrival of the trifle, wobbling unceremoniously on gold-ringed plates, was a pleasant distraction. A great spoonful of cream was arranged indulgently on her plate. Her mother excused herself and went to the powder room.

'Are you happy?' Olive asked her sister. 'Aren't you bored?'

Henrietta laughed. 'Lack of work is something our class aspires to, Olive. It leaves those of us fortunate enough to be born into a life of privilege free to pursue other interests. You're still not thinking of employment? You know neither Father nor Mother would allow it, and the Etons' tolerance for such inclinations is non-existent.'

'So, you'd see me bundled off to the wealthiest man I could nab, with the prospect of idleness as a future?'

Henrietta played with the cream around the trifle, her round diamond and sapphire ring glinting beneath the electric light of the chandelier. 'What a ridiculous attitude you have towards life, Olive.'

'It is my life, Henrietta,' she reminded her sister. 'I should be able to choose how I live it. The world is changing yet you seem stuck in the past.'

Henrietta set her spoon down. 'Maybe I like the past; the security, the comfort of it. You're quick to judge, but how do you think you would fare if you were left to your own devices to clothe, feed and shelter yourself?'

'And what would you say if I told you I'd formed a liaison with a land owner?' Olive took a sip of water, the time allowing her to gauge her sister's reaction. Henrietta's demeanour improved considerably. 'This land was built on the sheep's back, by men such as Kidman and Gordon. Everyone knows that's where the true money in this country lies.'

'Good heavens.' Henrietta's perfectly coiffured bob shook with excitement. 'Haven't you been busy! And who is this wealthy squatter? Certainly there are few in my circle.'

'You wouldn't know him, Henrietta, but when we marry it will be for love, and I hope to be involved in the running of his business. It will be the absolute most.'

'I thought you'd forgotten about your silly notions of romantic love, Olive,' Henrietta replied in a clipped tone. 'You'll come to realise that these aspirations you and your young friends harbour may seem quite modern, however the realities of life outweigh the emotional. Still, if the gentleman in question has money our parents can hardly disagree to the union, especially if the wool clip is large. Your friend will be requiring financial advances and our brothers are well positioned in the money market to afford such a service. The Etons have superlative contacts so he'll be welcomed into the fold. That's how dynasties are forged through marriage. You must purchase a house nearby for the coming season. Oh, you and I will be quite the pair. Well done, Olive. I believe your coming nuptials will eclipse even mine!'

Olive gave a choked reply. How one sentence could be so construed quite flabbergasted her.

'I thought Jack Manning would soon fade from view,' Henrietta continued. 'Of course it's terribly difficult for young women of means these days. The magazines and papers daily describe the 1920s as a period of change and everyone talks about the modern woman and her ideals – that romance and romantic appeal are far more important than class distinction. It's all rubbish. But, my dear sister, if you achieve both love and wealth while satisfying your penchant for remaining active, well, you will be quite the example of female possibility.'

It was exactly the reinforcement Olive required as her time apart from Jack grew longer. He was the type of man the modern girl clamoured for: a handsome adventurer who lived his life according to his own terms. Maybe Henrietta was correct. Perhaps her Jack would become all her worldly sister imagined.

'Shopping time,' Mrs Peters announced, rubbing her gloved hands together. 'On the account, thank you, Mathews.' She tipped the head waiter a shilling.

Olive whispered fiercely in her sister's ear, 'Not a word.'

The afternoon passed in a blur of chiffon, voile, silk and printed rayons. If there was one thing Olive's mother was born to do it was shop, and she could argue with the best of them when it came to quality and price. While the general populace worried about increasing food prices, for Mrs Reginald Peters money was no object. Her grosgrain ribbon-tied boxes screamed new money.

It was dusk by the time they returned to Rose Bay, the heady scent of jasmine following them up the pavement and into the single-storey building. The house with its cream stucco finish, wrought-iron window grilles and arched porch was in a relatively new style known as Spanish-American, and her mother's latest concern was the sudden interest in such buildings. God forbid everyone should end up having a house similar to theirs.

Once in her bedroom Olive dumped her shopping on the bed and sat lengthways on the wide windowsill, breathing in the fresh sea air. Her world was so different on this side of the harbour. Every part of her life was changed and in some respects it was for the better. Everyone was happier, more settled. With her brothers barely home, Olive assumed a more central role in daily life. It was as if her parents finally took note of her existence. Apart from lectures on the importance of marrying within one's class, and the necessity of shared values – and, by extension, affluence – it was actually now quite fun to be in her mother's company. She had become surprisingly tolerant of her *modern* values. And when her father wasn't at his Club he regaled them with tidbits of social scandal and business acumen that set them all to laughing for hours on end. How much more difficult this made Olive's current scenario. None of them were aware of her imminent desertion – a looming event, and one that she pinched herself about on occasion.

The breeze stirred the lace voile curtains. Taking a last sniff of jasmine- and salt-scented air, Olive selected a floral perfume from her dresser and spritzed the nape of her neck. Jack's last letter explained that Thomas and May had closed up the shop and that Thomas would contact her in a fortnight to advise her of their anticipated travel date, and the boarding house on the North Shore from which he would collect her. Not a word was to be said to anyone. Olive was to slip out the front door and leave her family behind without a goodbye. It was best that way, Jack wrote, it was the *only* way. Olive thought of Jack's constant letters, a swell of guilt hounding her thoughts. She did write back, yet her life seemed so inconsequential in comparison to his that she rarely went beyond a page. While she'd wavered over leaving her family, Jack continued to write of his experiences, of the countryside, of his unfailing desire for Olive to join him as soon as possible. He made everything sound so tremendously exciting and romantic.

The noise of her father's six cylinder sounded in the driveway and then the front door slammed. Olive could smell kidney being sautéed as she walked swiftly down the hall and greeted her father. She took up her usual pre-dinner position in a chair directly opposite the fireplace. Her father stood at the mantelpiece and her mother handed him a brandy. She could do this, Olive told herself sternly. She would do it. Women were capable of living extraordinary lives, romantic lives; even if she were a little afraid.

'Oh, Reginald, our first of the season.' Mrs Peters picked up a green and silver card from the mantelpiece and waved it in the air. 'I love Christmas. It's just so festive.'

Her father sat down in his armchair, shook open a newspaper and frowned. 'Hmm, it's a good month away.'

Christmas remained one of Olive's most favourite times of the year. For a moment she wished she hadn't agreed to leave Sydney before the holiday season.

'Another squatter has filed for bankruptcy. Smaller holdings, following the resumptions late last century, and increased taxes have not helped the landed, and the Country Party still hasn't quite enough weight to assist.'

'What party is that, Father?' Olive enquired, although her thoughts turned to presents.

'It was formed to improve the status of graziers and small farmers, and to secure subsidies, however wool isn't the growing centre of economic activity that it once was.'

'Oh, but there's money to be made from sheep, everyone knows that,' Olive insisted.

Her father peered over the top of the paper.

'If you are the owner or investor, Olive,' he corrected. 'For the rest it's slab huts, flies and toil.'

'The outback always looks so much better in oil,' Mrs Peters offered. 'Tom Roberts really has an artist's eye for the romantic.'

Olive squirmed in the horsehair armchair. Staying on for Christmas seemed a remarkably good idea. 'What's a slab hut?'

Her father folded the newspaper, resting it across his knee. 'My dear girl, you really don't want to know.'

## ≪ *Chapter 9* ≫

# *Absolution Creek,*
# *1965*

Cora was on the left wing of the sheep. Horse ambled through a stand of box trees, the winter-dried canopy of leaves rustling like paper. Her breath came out in white puffs as she squeezed her chilled fingers clad in leather gloves. Meg's response, received in the mail a fortnight ago, was totally unexpected.

*Dear Aunt Cora,* the letter had begun and was followed by the usual pleasantries. Cora could still see the words *excited* and *delighted* on the lined paper, even though the letter itself was now ash in her fireplace. It was the next paragraph that almost made Cora withdraw her offer.

*We would absolutely love to move to the country. I say 'we' because I am actually married with twin girls. My husband, Sam, is a mechanic, and I'm sure on such a large property there would be any number of vehicles that would require his attention. As for our children, they will be ready for primary school next year and would hardly be a bother in your large homestead. I know my married state is probably unexpected news, however . . .*

A male in her house and two young children – hardly the arrangement she was hoping for. The dialogue went on for another paragraph before Meg's closing statement.

*You were right about Mother. She is against the idea. As a mother myself I can understand her concern at my moving so far away to start a new life . . .*

The knowledge that Meg's mother was against her daughter's move was enough for Cora to send a positive reply. Sometimes even the best plans went slightly askew, although she had to admit she was annoyed with Meg. The girl could only be in her early twenties. What was she doing with her life? With a sigh Cora looked across to the adjoining paddock.

Through the fence the rams grazed into the easterly wind, heads down in an arrow formation. Having fulfilled their yearly duties they were pleased to be free of their demanding harem. Not one looked up from the grass as the ewes passed, except for Montgomery 201. Absolution's prize stud ram stood apart from the rest of the mob on a slight rise, head high, his nostrils sniffing the wind. Cantering to the fence on Horse, Cora looked across at the great animal. A descendant of Waverly No. 4, he was pure perfection. Big framed with soft rolling skin – an almost perfect staple in terms of length, colour and strength – he also had a propensity towards siring twins. His genetics were already evident having improved Absolution's flock and wool clip in the three years since his purchase.

'How are you going, Montgomery?' she said as Horse gave an unfriendly snort.

The ram reciprocated with a haughty stare, lifted his front hoof and gave a single strike to the ground before walking away.

'Good to see your temperament hasn't changed.' Horse gave a whinny in agreement. 'Worth the money, don't you think?' Cora doubted her ride would agree. Horse and Montgomery had a strained relationship that extended back to Montgomery's first day on the property. Horse had lifted the wooden latch at the yards to sneak a mouthful of Montgomery's lucerne hay and had quickly found himself on the end of a charging ram. By the time Cora reached the yards to investigate the ruckus, the lucerne was trampled into the dirt, Montgomery was standing sentry next to it and Horse was high-tailing it through the scrub. 'Come on, Horse, let's go.'

Horse managed a quick two-step over a rotting log and made a beeline for Tripod. Clearly he was in one of his moods today, more interested in irritating the dogs than keeping up his pace. When the three-legged musterer slowed, Horse nosed him in his bottom, which led to Tripod barking and snapping.

'Horse!' Cora reprimanded. Twice Horse's abrupt manoeuvre jolted her forwards. Cora pushed her knees tight against his flanks and gave the reins a tug. There was already an ache in her leg, although for the moment it was more chill than pain.

'Must be the cool morning,' Harold commented, walking his roan mare towards her. His Kelpie, Sue, was bringing up the rear as usual with an *I may or may not work today* attitude.

Cora sniffed. She'd never been one for sundowners – dogs that only came to life at dusk.

Harold drew abreast, cleared his throat and spat over his shoulder. 'My nephew's coming out again in a few weeks.'

'Didn't take to his apprenticeship then?' Cora asked, surprised the boy's father had even suggested a cadetship at a newspaper. What teenager wanted to interview stallholders at a Sunday afternoon market?

Harold hesitated. 'Hated it.'

Ahead the mob of sheep threw up a curtain of dust. 'You're not surprised?' The firm set of Harold's jaw suggested something was amiss.

'I suppose not.' Selecting a pre-rolled cigarette from his hatband, Harold lit up with a silver lighter. It had been a gift from

Ellen on their wedding day – a perfect present for a bush man who rolled thirty cigarettes before breakfast, slipping them through his hat-band for easy access.

Cora tapped Horse lightly on his flanks and closed the distance between the mob. Overhead, swallows were flying directly towards the wool shed, readying to clog the eaves with their nests and splatter everything with their droppings. Harold was still riding beside her, which meant the conversation had some way to go. She mumbled under her breath about not having children and *still* being subjected to everyone else's problems with their offspring, and waited for the next instalment. Kendal White was the youngest of three children belonging to Harold's sister and had spent half his school holidays, and a bit of time in between, at Absolution. When the teachers decided that a period of suspension would be beneficial to both parties, he was packed off to his uncle.

'Another scrape?' It seemed to Cora that Kendal never initiated any problems at his fancy school in Brisbane yet was always in the thick of things at the end. 'He should be sent out to the Territory for a year or so. A bit of time jackerooing on one of those big stations wouldn't hurt him,' Cora suggested. It wasn't the first time.

'His mother won't have it.' Harold ruffled his horse's hair between the ears.

'What about a fitter or turner? Or a boilermaker?' She pulled on Horse's reins, steadying him so that Tripod could gain some space between them. *Candlestick maker, she mused.* Why the silly dog just didn't move out of Horse's way was beyond her.

'He wants to come here,' Harold announced as if the decision were already made.

Cora whistled at Curly. He'd bailed an old ewe up under a Wilga tree with a handful of other stragglers. One by one her companions left to rejoin the mob until she was alone, stamping her foot and bowing her head in anticipation of a charge. The tail of the mob slowed to watch the show.

'Here?' Cora asked Harold, whistling again. Having managed to rid themselves of Jarrod Michaels, she was still coming to terms with her decision to trial Meg's husband as a station hand. It appeared Absolution was becoming a home for waifs and strays. 'I don't think so.' Once before, Harold had approached Cora with the suggestion of taking Kendal on as a jackeroo – he'd even coerced his wife, Ellen, into putting in a good word for the boy.

'I don't expect you to understand, Cora, but I'd appreciate it if he could come for a bit.'

'I don't know, Harold.'

'The thing is, what with Jarrod's leaving I thought we could do with the help.'

Cora's intuition told her that employing relatives of staff could come to no good. They invariably expected special treatment and one could be assured that their bush ability never matched their perceived levels of importance. 'I certainly can't afford to pay him.'

'I told him that.' Harold rose up in the stirrups and whistled again. The ewe turned and walked back to the mob, but not before the right flank took the opportunity to charge across the paddock in the wrong direction.

Cora spun Horse around and galloped after the bolting sheep. There was a water hole ahead and if the ewes reached it, it would take some cajoling to move the old girls from its tree-shaded banks. Horse galloped towards the lead. Tripod was quickly left behind and, although his three legs worked overtime to keep up, he was engulfed in Horse's billowing dust.

Twenty minutes later the ewes were in the next paddock. It always amazed Cora how they knew instinctively which clump of trees to head to on arrival. They could remember where the tastiest grass was and the location of each specific watering point with a brief sniff of the air. Harold closed the gate behind them and lifted an exhausted Tripod up to her. Cora patted him as the dog settled on her lap.

'About Kendal, I just don't think I should be saying no to him. This is the only place he ever comes back to,' Harold stated.

'Out of necessity,' Cora replied.

Harold's voice was hopeful. 'And I'll watch over him.'

'While you're working?' Cora placed a steadying hand on Tripod's back. Give it a couple of days and the kid would be out helping to muster and then what? Then everyone would be expecting him to be paid, including the lad himself. 'I already have Meg's husband coming. I expect I'll have to pay him something if he proves to be handy.'

Harold gave a disapproving snort.

The trouble with having a manager who had been with you for more than ten years was that they felt they had a claim to any decision made. 'If Kendal comes he's your responsibility and he won't be paid. Secondly, if he comes this close —' she held her thumb and finger together '— to causing a ruckus, he's gone. No excuses.'

'Thanks, Cora.' Harold's tone was flat. 'He'll understand. We've decided he doesn't need any more schooling.'

As they neared the house paddock Sue detoured towards Harold's house, while Tripod jumped to the ground and headed straight for the chook yard. Curly, who had followed the returning riders at a distance, stopped a few yards short of the yard. The rooster was already on guard, his chest puffed out in pride. The chooks fluffed their wings and a babble of noise filled the air.

At the stables Cora and Harold unsaddled the horses.

'Do you think this arrangement will work then with this city lot?' Harold asked.

'We'll see.' Cora brushed Horse down, amused at the way the animal closed his brown eyes and hung his head, his breath softening into a sound like a cat's purr.

'Always hard bringing city folk in.'

The noise from the chook yard was becoming cacophonous. Cora yelled at Tripod and Curly to quieten down. Horse twitched his ears in irritation and walked away.

'Might have a bit of smoko and then see about repairing the mincer. Thought I'd kill that wether for a bit of mutton later.'

'Sounds good, Harold.' Overnight the station's fortnightly kill ration had gone from feeding three to eight. 'By the way I've decided to get that old dam delved in the 1500-acre paddock.'

'It hasn't been used for years. It'll cost.'

'I figure once it's cleaned out and enlarged I'll run a channel across to the bore drain. That way we can fill the dam from the bore when it's dry. You can never have too much water.'

Harold pushed his brimmed hat back on his forehead revealing deep sun-etched lines. 'Well, it's not a priority. I'd like to be clearing the lignum, doing some work on the woolshed, tacking a wall on the end of the hayshed.'

Cora ignored him. 'We'll be needing to take down the old fence from around the dam. That'll be a good job for Meg's husband to start on.' She brushed her hands together. 'And Kendal. When is he due?'

'I'll give him a bell tonight,' Harold replied, his mouth fixed.

Cora figured the boy would be sitting by the phone. They both knew she'd been stitched up good and tight.

## ❈ Chapter 10 ❈

# Middle Harbour, Sydney, 1965

Meg ran her fingers across the springy grass and pulled her knees tight beneath her chin. The scent of salt drifted up on the wind from Willoughby Bay as the many homes skirting the shoreline came to life. Primrose Park remained her favourite place since childhood. As a young girl she would scramble from her home down the hill after school, ignoring her mother's instructions to keep away from the park with its sewerage works history. Yet what child wouldn't want to run across spongy grass down to the shore, where the comfort of land met the unknown expanse of the sea. This was a place of butterflies and seagulls, barking dogs and fruit bats, driftwood and a cliff face of dark, dream-harbouring trees. Meg recalled collecting shells in the winter, when the cold sea breath had stung her neck and ears. There was a mossy log near the base of the tree-covered cliff. Beneath, in a shadowy depression, lay her most favourite shells; the skeleton of a baby bird thrown from a tree; and a piece of china stained blue like a baby's eyes.

Meg walked slowly back to the flat she shared with her mother, husband and children. Her aunt's letter sat tucked in a top drawer of her dresser. There were only a handful of days before they left. It was funny. Having been so excited at her aunt's offer and then thinking it would be dashed by her married state, now she felt nervous as their departure neared. At the stone wall marking their block of flats, Meg paused. She had a mind to find her special log and dig up the shells, the dead bird and shard of hard-baked china. The cliff beckoned as Meg lifted the latch and walked through the gate. Everyone needed a special place, even if it could only be reached by way of memory.

'You sure you want to do this?' Sam asked Meg. He was sitting up in bed smoking, waiting for her to finish brushing her long hair. 'It sure came out of the blue. Who would have thought the old sheila would have picked us.'

*Me*, Meg corrected silently. She tied her hair back with a scarf, checked on the sleeping twins and climbed into bed beside Sam, wrinkling her nose up at the smoke.

'You know we've got a roof over our heads and food.' Sam puffed out a perfect circle of smoke, grinning at his creation.

'Thanks to my mother taking us in, Sam. And it's my job that's feeding us.' Meg adjusted the bed covers irritably.

'Want a smoke?' he asked quietly. 'Always settles me for the night.'

'No thanks.' Meg could never be certain where her husband's good moods would lead, especially when the whiff of rum escaping from his skin was stronger than the tobacco smoke hugging him like a cloud. As she wriggled down beneath the covers a tail of smoke wafted into the air above her. Her aunt's letter was so unexpected that she'd hugged it to her chest in wonderment before giving thought to its ramifications. Her carefully written reply, which revealed her married state, was sent immediately. For two weeks her correspondence remained unanswered. For two weeks Meg bit her tongue, scared that if the offer was so much as uttered aloud a letter would come immediately, withdrawing the chance of a new life.

'Don't you think it's too good an opportunity to refuse?' she asked. Sam's eyes were glassy. 'Sam?'

He shrugged his shoulders. 'I ain't been much good to us so I reckon we should have a go.' He sat the ashtray on his chest. 'Besides, it's a bit late to be talking yourself into it now she's said yes to our moving up there.' He gave a chuckle. 'From what I hear the bush is full of toffs. They all made their fortune from sheep in the fifties when the boom was on. You've heard the stories. The papers were full of it. My pa still tells tales about the squatter who walked into the Hilton Hotel and offered to buy drinks for the bar. All them suits, can you imagine it? Course, next thing the squatters are all buying Rolls Royces. Country people ain't like us any more, Meggie. We're poor and now they're the toffs.'

'So you're saying my aunt could treat us like poor relations?'

Sam yawned. 'Who knows?'

Meg turned to her husband. 'Well, I think she sounds really nice in her letters. It'll be such a big change, but I think of the girls and the space and the chance to have a place of our own eventually, and a job for you . . .' She said this quietly, the words trailing off into the room.

'She hasn't actually said she'd leave the place to us, Meg,' Sam reminded her. 'Glorified housekeeper and companion is the role you're setting yourself up for. Looks like I'm along for the ride.' He gave a rum-enriched belch.

'She said that the property was beautiful and that she had no other relatives.'

'Well, she can't turf us out when there's a couple of ankle-biters in tow – her own blood – and we've given up our lives in the city for her.'

Meg figured her aunt knew they weren't giving up that much. 'Mum never talks about her, you know. Never did, not even after Dad died and it was just the two of us.'

Sam dragged on the butt and then stubbed it out, wincing as heat met his fingers. 'My grandfather had a farm, out Windsor way.'

Meg sat upright in bed. 'You never told me that. So, you've had a bit of experience then? You know what we're in for?'

'Sure. Sure thing, love. I might be an unemployed mechanic but I've seen a bit, you know. I'm a good five years older than you.'

Meg lifted her hand to cuff him playfully on the shoulder, before thinking better of it. 'Well, aren't you the cagey one.'

Within minutes his breathing changed and the snoring began. One of her girls gave a whimper in her sleep.

The next night four of them sat in silence around the yellow laminated table. Meg's mother continually glanced towards Sam's vacant seat as if she expected the occupant to materialise at any moment. The two adults and two children chewed their way through sausages, potato and cabbage. The sound of their swallowing and gulping seemed inordinately loud within the confines of the small kitchen. Jane Hamilton's flat only boasted two bedrooms and a sitting room, kitchen and bathroom; Sam's first comment on arrival was that the place wasn't big enough to swing a cat. *Or a punch*, Meg's mother retaliated. Although her son-in-law rarely raised a voice indoors, he was not averse to fighting and one such incident had ended Sam's job as a mechanic, eventually rendering her daughter and grandchildren homeless.

'Pass the salt, Meg,' her mother said archly. She doused her sausages liberally and then watched the twins poking at their food. 'Jill, Penny. Stop that.'

The five-year-olds jolted to attention, all sausage-grease smiles and swaying legs, their focus directed at Meg.

'Time for bed,' Meg ordered, ushering the girls from the kitchen.

'You've made your mind up then?' Jane asked, her eyes never leaving the food on her plate.

'Yes.' Meg collected her plate, tossing the uneaten food onto a sheet of newspaper on the sink. 'Sam will be back later. We're leaving early in the morning.'

'I've asked you not to leave and you're just ignoring me.'

'It's for the best, Mum. We both know that. And Sam –'

'He's a handy one, isn't he? Just follows you about waiting for everyone else to do the providing.' Her mother squished sausage meat and potato onto her fork. 'You can bet he'll be out drinking now.' She chewed thoughtfully. 'I wouldn't bother waiting up for him. If you're off tomorrow he'll be on a right bender tonight.'

'Knock it off, Mum.'

'Don't speak to me like that just because you managed to get yourself caught up with the likes of him. My heavens, marrying the first boy you had a liking for and then getting with child, all when you'd barely turned of age. It's not right.'

'Neither is sending a girl to work instead of letting her finish her schooling. And you wonder why I was married at nineteen.' Meg watched her mother scrape her plate clean with a scrap of bread.

'Well, as it happens you didn't need much of an education. Once you leave here you'll be in the back of beyond.'

Meg turned the hot water tap on, and the water spurted out, hitting the plates in the sink and splashing back to burn her hand. 'Damn.' She faced her mother. 'There's no point you being angry about this. You could have helped us. You had your chance but you rented the upstairs flat instead of giving it to Sam and me and the kids.'

'And what am I?' her mother asked loudly. 'A goddamn charity? I've looked after you, haven't I? I've raised you, haven't I? Just because you go and marry a no-hoper doesn't mean I have to pick up the mess.' She waved her fork in the air. 'And what about payment? Do you think that husband of yours would've kept the rent up? No. How could he? You'd be stacking the grocer's shelves and scraping to feed your young'uns, and the rest of it he'd be spending down the pub.' She fumbled a cigarette from the packet on the table and lit it. 'No point all of us being homeless, just because you were too scared to go it alone for a while. Wait for the right man.'

'And was your man the right one, Mum? There's not a single photograph of him, not one letter, not even his dog tags.'

'You leave your father out of this. He's dead, and the dead deserve respect.'

Some days Meg wondered if she'd ever had a father in the truest sense of the word or if she was simply the product of passion during the terrible war years. Her father was just a telegram on yellowing paper. Another soldier missing presumed dead, a man unknown to her, his whole family unknown to her. Meg snatched a cigarette from the packet, lighting it with her mother's discarded box of matches. She wasn't having this argument again. She wasn't going to ask for the hundredth time why there was no contact with her paternal grandparents or aunts and uncles. It never got her anywhere. 'Well, maybe if you'd been a bit kinder I wouldn't have felt the need to marry early.' She regretted speaking the moment the words spilled from her mouth.

'It's a weak person that blames another for their choices.'

Meg took two good drags and stubbed her fag out in the sink. 'I just don't understand why you're so upset about our leaving.' Jane was in her late fifties, yet life had left its mark on her in the listless way in which she moved, and the half-tilt of her head as she stared vacantly into space.

'I told you a dozen times, she's no good, that woman. Tricking you to go north to some property. What property? I say. Cora Hamilton doesn't want you, girly. She's only sent for you because she's decided it's time for a little payback.'

'Payback for what?'

'When you do get up there she'll set about telling you a lot of things that simply aren't true. She'll make me out to look nasty, when it was her that always had the bad blood.' Jane slammed the table with the flat of her palm. 'How her father ever bred a girl like that I'll never know.' She pushed her plate aside. 'You shouldn't be going.'

This was the nearest they had come to an amicable conversation in a fortnight. As mother and daughter they'd never been close. 'You have to explain why you dislike her so much, Mum, and why you've suddenly decided that you don't want us to leave. I know you haven't liked us living here for the last eighteen months, and the kids can be difficult.'

Her mother stubbed out her cigarette and reached for another. 'I'm past young'uns. Leave that husband of yours and I'll evict one of the tenants early.' She clamped the cigarette between her lips, lit it and took a drag. 'Give the place to you and the kids.' The cigarette dangled from her mouth.

'I can't leave Sam.'

'You don't love him,' Jane said bluntly. 'You *depend* on him. There's a difference.'

Meg opened her mouth to argue.

'Anyway, no good will come of moving to be with that woman.' Jane scratched her neck. 'I should've known she'd come back into my life. Those sort of people can never be trusted.'

'Why can't she be trusted?'

'The years pass and you think you've done enough to be rid of them.'

'Mum!' Meg said, horrified. 'How can you talk about Aunt Cora that way? She's your own sister.'

Her mother stubbed her cigarette out absently in the leftover cabbage on her plate. Lifting her head she looked Meg directly in the eyes. 'I should know then.'

'It's not a bad place,' Sam stated, waking Meg. They were out of Sydney and crossing a long low bridge over the Hawkesbury River in their station wagon. The water was a dull blue, the banks smeared green by the thick trees that covered the surrounding hills. The sun was hot for mid-winter, the twins overtired and cranky. Meg wound the window down a little further and pulled her sweater off.

'A mate of mine's been through that neck of the woods. Reckons it's pretty good country. A bit isolated though,' Sam said, one hand on the wheel.

'Isolated? No pub you mean.' Meg folded the sweater. Sam's meal of sausages and cabbage had eventually been fed to the next-door tabby.

'She'll have staff. They all have staff apparently: managers, overseers, cooks, governesses. All the big stations run that way.' He grinned. 'Always fancied myself part of the landed gentry. Anyway, I don't know nothing about farming, but how hard can it be?'

Meg stared at him open-mouthed. 'But your grandfather, the farm. I thought . . .'

'Good old fella, my grandfather. Had a few acres out near Windsor. Long since gone now. Lost it during the depression.' He gave Meg a quick side-long glance. 'I can ride, although I haven't done it for a while.'

Meg felt the bile rise in her throat. 'You said –'

'*You said*,' he mimicked, his fingers tightening on the steering wheel. 'You didn't know what you wanted, Meg, and you still don't, so I helped make the decision. Anyway, I had to get out of Sydney.

I got myself into an altercation with a bloke – laid him up pretty bad.'

Meg's shoulders drooped. 'Oh, Sam. You know what the magistrate said after your last bar fight.'

Sam shrugged. 'Well, that's the worst of having a one-time professional boxer on your hands. As soon as there's a fight, I'm to blame.'

'It could mean gaol, Sam.'

'She'll be right. I don't think old Jeffo'll die. Anyway, what does it matter now? We're off to a new life. The old girl wants a companion and you wanted to accept. The worst thing that can happen is you'll get bored and we come back to Sydney once Jeffo's well. And the best thing.' He grinned and leant across to squeeze her arm. 'Fell on our feet this time I reckon, Meggy. This one could set us up for life.' Sam concentrated on passing a Bedford truck. 'All we have to do is hang around for a while, see if she intends to leave the place to us.'

'You do know how old my aunt is, don't you, Sam? She's a bit younger than Mum. This isn't going to be an overnight thing. I don't think she intends to drop off the perch anytime soon.'

'Well, I figure that if she was all fine and dandy she wouldn't have made the offer. And it seems to me that as you're her only kin then it would be worth our while for you to make yourself indispensable to the old girl.'

Meg reluctantly agreed. 'It's a great opportunity for us. A chance for a fresh start.'

'That's the way, Meggy. Think of the money that was made in the bush in the last decade when wool was a pound a pound. Think of the advantages that Penny and Jill will have away from the city.'

Meg glanced at the twins who were currently comparing the shape of their knees.

Sam patted her arm. 'And good farming land will fetch a pretty price. A mate of mine has a mate in rural sales who has a mate who reckons we'll be made.'

Meg gasped. 'If anything does happen to my aunt I'm not rushing out and selling the place.' She could only imagine how long the money might last if Sam got hold of it.

'Well, we'd hardly be interested in keeping it,' he argued.

'Why not?'

'Why not? Are you mad? We don't know anything about farms.' Sam shook a cigarette from its packet and gripped it between his teeth. He pushed the lighter button on the dash. 'It's one thing to take advantage of something that falls in your lap,' he said as the lighter popped out and he lit his cigarette. He drew heavily on the tobacco. 'Quite another to bugger things up.'

'This is about financial security,' Meg replied quietly. 'Besides, I think we're getting a bit carried away. We've got lots to learn and, who knows, you might like working on the farm.'

Sam stared blankly at the road ahead. 'Not likely.'

Meg opened her mouth to retaliate then pursed her lips instead. Experience taught her that arguments once started could last for hours, particularly in a closed environment from which there was no escape. She looked at the highway, thought of the wonderful city she was leaving behind: the harbour and bridge, the picture-postcard park of her childhood. It was harder to let go of than she had imagined.

# ⤐ *Chapter 11* ⤏

## *Absolution Creek,*
## *1923*

Placing a boot firmly in the stirrup iron, Jack wrapped his hand around the pommel of the saddle and hoisted himself up onto the roan mare. He tightened the reins, gripped her flanks with his thighs and dropped his heels in close. The mare steadied, snorted into a hot breeze and gave a single stroke of hoof to dirt. Theirs was a tentative relationship forged through two days of testy riding lessons from the blacksmith in Stringybark Point and the occasional pointer from the postal and supply rider, an Irishman by the name of Adams.

With a touch of spur to horse hair, they were off spinning through trees sappy with new growth, and careering over grasses and soil, leaving behind a doughy imprint of their passage. Jack firmly pushed down his wide-brimmed hat, making it a little more secure. A few days back he'd spent an hour or more retracing his steps when it had blown free at the gallop, and he wasn't of a mind to go through that rigmarole again. The mare slowed to a walk and Jack rode on, oblivious to the sun piercing the countryside. He was conscious only of the horse moving beneath him, of muscle and sinew stretching and lengthening with each stride.

A light wind teased them onwards over lightly timbered plains, and through shrubs and saplings. They passed scrub-reared animals appearing like jack-in-the-boxes from behind trees and clumps of grass. Kangaroos and wallabies, startled at his approach, bounded across the paddock in mobs of thirty or more, their long tails stabilising every move. Ahead, twenty or more emus were strung out across the grassland, all long legs and bobbing heads. Jack twitched the reins and ducked low-hanging branches. Every single day since his arrival at Absolution Creek he found himself reminded of what it meant to be a city lad. There was much to learn.

At the creek he dismounted, leading the mare down to the water's edge. The horse drank thirstily, her nostrils flaring just above the water as she swallowed and breathed simultaneously. Once finished, Jack tethered the mare at the base of a gum tree, tying the reins good and tight.

'You stay put,' he cautioned. The mare, whom he'd christened Pat after Olive's mother, was a wanderer. Jack already knew the pain of a five-mile walk home when the sun threw no shadow. As he turned, the mare bit him on the shoulder. 'Mary, Jesus and Joseph!' he exclaimed. Pat blinked large brown eyes as Jack rubbed the paining flesh. It took a scant two days following the mare's purchase for him to discover that the blacksmith who'd sold him the horse was not the obliging man he appeared. The man had even thrown in a pair of hobbles. 'Just in case,' he'd said smiling.

'Just in case, my foot.' Jack scowled as he left Pat to the soft herbage edging the creek.

Stretching his fingers to the sky and humming quietly, Jack knelt to splash water on his wind-burnt skin. The creek water was cool and he ran handfuls through his shaggy hair, which was in want of a cut. On the opposite bank five grey and pink birds, long-legged and sure-footed, spread their wings wide as they danced slowly in a circle. Their feet tossed up puffs of sand as they moved, their heads swaying from one side to the next. Jack sat at the water's edge, watching them.

It intrigued him that he'd not once missed Sydney since his leaving. He thought of the North Shore on occasion – often dreamt of the white spray of the ocean and the screeching calls of the seagulls, of car horns and the salty kiss of a dawn shore walk – however, the memory was eroded by the continual pounding of the jack hammers, the sound of which even now reverberated in his brain.

He lay flat on his back with his hands behind his head, the sand cushioning him as mid-morning light brightened the narrow strip of treeless space above the creek. He'd had a mind to build a hut right here on the water's edge, but one night's camping with mosquitoes that nearly carried him away quelled any such idea. The hut on the eastern side of the creek was his current home and, having just pegged out a proper homestead block not two miles further on, it was on this space he currently daydreamed about.

Jack dreamt of the completed structure nightly, saw it rise from the misty swirls of sleep like a magnificent castle. At its centre was a snug bedroom with a soft thick mattress and sheer-netted mosquito veil. Olive lay on the bed dressed only in a sparse white slip that clung to her thighs and stomach, and rested lightly on her gently sloping breasts. When Jack drew close to her, close enough to see a vein pulsating through the warm skin of her neck, Olive spoke to him softly, beckoning. It was always at this moment that Jack awoke, agitated and restless, eager for the rest of his life to begin.

The mare whickered quietly, bringing Jack to wakefulness. It was just as well, he decided, for he wasn't sure of what came next, when the bedroom door was closed and the candle blown out. He thought of his father's Bible sitting snug in the saddlebag and wondered if he should take up from where he'd left off last night. He'd been a stickler for his Bible readings, finding it eased the night-time hours and provided a semblance of normal life. And his conscience reminded Jack daily of the promise he'd made in Sydney. Having disregarded his dying father's wishes, and aware further transgressions were not advisable should he need to call on the Saints' assistance, his devotion to the Church's teachings were now absolute.

Scraping sand into his palm, Jack felt the weight of it before flinging it in an arc across the water's surface. The grains fell in a spray on the sunlight-speckled water. He expected Olive to arrive before Christmas, and as the days disappeared in a blur of gratifying toil he could scarcely keep the grin from his face. There was so much to show her. Apart from the boundaries of the property, the different sizes of the paddocks and the two thousand head of sheep that now grazed happily under his care, there was the land. Each new day brought with it a glimpse of heaven: the musty pinks of dawn and the flaming reds when the sun sank, the warbling of birds in the early morning and the rustling of wind through the trees. It was getting hot – hotter by the day – but that change carried with it a new beauty. By mid-afternoon the earth shimmered in spun silver. Land and sky merged together as waves of heat buckled the natural symmetry of the air. It was then that the bush grew melancholy. Stilled by the sun's heavy hand, the countryside slept for those few heat-held hours.

'Come on then, Pat.' Jack untied the mare's reins and she nibbled at his back as he remounted. 'You can do that all you like, but we both know neither of us is going anywhere so you may as well behave.' His foot found the stirrup and Jack settled in the saddle. With the arrival of two thousand ewes on Absolution Creek less than a month ago, there were now fences to check and more yard building to continue with. He'd given up on trying to build the house prior to Olive's arrival. There were simply not enough hours in the day to do everything. Besides, Thomas would be here soon and with his brother by his side the whole exercise would be far easier.

A Sunday morning ride had become habit, although in truth most days blurred into the next. No longer stymied by shop opening hours, regulated mealtimes or the obligatory Sunday mass, Jack discovered the benefit of bush living. He sensed city folk probably needed such methods to keep them in order, like a well-oiled machine. Out here it didn't matter so much. A man could live according to his own inclination, his life structured only by the hours of daylight available to him and the work required. Freedom was now his and it came with a swathe of land only a magician could conjure. Jack held aspirations of eventually owning Absolution Creek, for the Farleys were without children and he'd done the man a good service for many years in Sydney. Certainly good enough to warrant such a gift. Nevertheless, Jack knew a person couldn't be forward about such a transaction. He would bide his time, keep his part of the bargain and eventually sound Mr Farley out as to his future intentions. Only last month he'd received word from Mr Farley requesting Jack sign an updated leasing agreement. It appeared that a maiden aunt was entitled – by a recent will – to financial assistance. Jack had proudly signed a ten-year lease agreement and, in doing so, protected Mr Farley's current asset and cemented Jack's future. Absolution Creek, Jack decided, would be his land one day. It would be his place in the world – somewhere safe to rear a family, somewhere where a man could love his wife and provide for her.

Jack manoeuvred his horse through a clump of tight spiky-leafed trees. The postal rider Adams called them belahs, and they dotted this part of Absolution like hairs on his arm. The whippy branches yanked at his shirt and hat. Sticky cobwebs were an added obstacle. It was with relief that Jack reined Pat out towards open country again.

When Pat reared, Jack was ill-prepared. He slipped to the ground with a hard crunch, landing solidly on his back. Some feet away the mare reared again and struck out fiercely with her front hoofs. Jack stood shakily. He collected his hat from the dirt, watching as Pat kept striking at the ground. Whatever it was, the mare was clearly frightened. He glanced at the rifle holstered by the saddle. 'Hey, girl, are you right?'

The mare's ears twitched as Jack took hold of the reins. On the ground was a large brown snake, its hoof-shredded body already attracting ants. Taking hold of its tail, Jack stretched the creature out. It was nearly seven feet long.

'You got a bit of a scare, that was all.' Jack inspected the mare's fetlocks, pausing at the coronet where the front leg merged into the hoof. He couldn't see any bite marks and from what he'd read there would be a distinct puncture mark. *What he'd read*, Jack thought with disgust. Everything he knew about the bush came from a book. Sometimes he wondered if it was enough. Mounting up he turned the mare homeward. It was a ride to the hut – at least four miles. The horse grew slower, finally dropping to the ground halfway home, her back legs kicking out, her breathing ragged. Jack patted the mare's neck and then set about undoing the saddle and removing the bridle. There wasn't anything to do except wait until she breathed her last, so Jack sat in the dirt as she shuddered and whinnied, her hind legs striking haltingly at the hollowed-out dirt. An hour later she was dead.

The landscape looked washed out and vacant in the growing heat. Jack slung his rifle and waterbag over his shoulder and slid his father's Bible down his shirt front. Perspiration blurred his vision and he wiped a hand across aching eyes. At dusk he would return with the pack horse to collect the hog-skin saddle and bridle. For now he concentrated on the road home, as crows cried out soullessly above. So much for his dreams of rising to be a respected squatter. At the moment Jack just hoped to survive.

## ⫷ *Chapter 12* ⫸

## *Absolution Creek, 1965*

'You're looking well.'

Ellen sported a red cardigan, woollen skirt, and a rarely seen slash of lipstick on her thinning mouth. 'I'm having lunch in town today,' she announced to Cora, scraping dirt from her heels at the back gate.

'Well, good for you.' Cora was expecting James at any moment. Horse had gone off his feed and she wanted him checked out.

'I finished the house; it's in tiptop shape.' Ellen gave a satisfied smile. 'Now that I'm close to being officially off the payroll I wanted to say to you that I have never once considered you to be quirky in nature –'

'However?' Cora wondered if Ellen would seize the opportunity for one final rebuke. She was the type of woman adept at point-scoring and if queried on any matter inevitably responded as if she were being poked in the chest. While Cora remained confident Ellen's personality was formed well before her arrival at Absolution Creek, she was equally convinced Harold's wife found employment here quite beneath her.

'However, the tree has always been one thing that I've considered to be unusual.'

'Apart from my nocturnal jaunts?' Cora loved to antagonise Ellen.

Ellen fiddled with the fine chain around her neck.

'Many would no doubt agree with you,' Cora continued, as Curly and Tripod snuffled past to lie in the shade of the meathouse eaves.

'Anyway, if you need me, I'm only a phone call away and I promise to give Meg some pointers over the next couple of weeks until she gets the run of things. After that you'll find me at the Town and Country Club, arranging flowers and playing bridge.'

Cora wished she could be a fly on the wall at the Club. Ellen Morrisey was not quite one of the establishment in the committee's eyes and it appeared she'd only passed muster due to a maiden aunt's daughter marrying a prominent pastoralist some thirty years earlier. Nevertheless she was in the door, whereas Cora would never be Club material. Ellen's cheeks coloured as Cora thanked her for her help over the years. Theirs had been a less than cordial relationship at times.

Cora took her boots off at the back door as Ellen drove off. This was the beginning of the transition from lone household inhabitant to instant family. The arrival of the Bell family was certainly changing the landscape and Cora was beginning to realise that it probably wasn't a popular decision. Although Ellen was pleased to be retiring, her husband had apparently complained to his wife at the loss of income. Ellen was, in fact, casualty number one in the Bell saga and despite their differences Cora would be sorry to see her go. There was little to be done about the situation, however, for she didn't need two housekeepers and nor could she afford to pay for such. Casualty two, in Harold's eyes, was Kendal, and she couldn't help wondering if the Bells' imminent arrival had somehow stymied Harold's future aspirations in regards to his family's involvement on Absolution. Cora was still considering the altered arrangements on Absolution when James's vehicle drew up at the back gate.

'So then, we're expecting visitors?' he queried, cracking a toothy smile as he walked up the path.

He always did look good, Cora mused, noting her own saddle-greasy moleskins.

James looked at his watch. 'Yep, you're dead on. I'm ready for a cuppa and a scone myself.'

Cora rolled her eyes. 'You better come in. How's Horse?'

James took a seat at the kitchen table as Cora stoked up the Aga with a log from the pile on the floor.

'He's got a small abscess on a tooth. I syringed it, but it will probably be a bit tender for a few days.'

'Thanks, James. I appreciate you looking at him.' The kettle hummed on the stove top as Cora set cups and saucers on the table. The scones were cooling, the radio was playing softly and a stew was warming on the slow-cooking plate.

'So then, how have you been? Ellen tells me you have rels coming to stay.'

Cora made the tea, strong and black, and plonked the scones that were now cooling in the tea-towel-lined colander in the centre of the table. 'Well, we've had a few changes recently. Ellen's retiring and Kendal's coming back for a few months.' Cora added cheese to the table's contents.

James stretched his legs out as if playing lord of the manor, and gave a groan. 'Not that little twerp?'

'The one and only.'

'How'd you manage –?'

'Don't ask,' Cora interrupted. She knew that if she explained that Harold had insisted, James would wonder about the control Absolution's manager held, and Cora wasn't ready to talk about her reluctance to put Harold offside. It was difficult enough to find staff and nigh impossible to retain someone of Harold's ability when Cora Hamilton was in charge.

James took the hint. 'What's the go with the relatives?'

'They're on their way from Sydney now.'

'I know how you love your space, Cora, so I have to wonder about you having them to stay.'

'Why do I have to justify my actions to you?' Cora placed a heaped teaspoon of sugar in her cup. 'I seem to recall that we're no longer an item.'

James leant back in the wooden chair. 'We slept together more than a dozen times before we were officially an item in the district's eyes. By my count we've been outing for four years, although, considering I can count on one hand the number of times we've been together in public, maybe *outing* isn't the right word.'

Cora opened her mouth to speak.

'And, Miss Hamilton, during those four years you broke off our relationship three times, argued with me more than necessary and generally became a right pain in the arse.'

'But –'

'And now we're having another *break,* which seems pretty ridiculous when we both love each other.'

Cora threw her head back in exasperation. 'What is it with you? Can you never take no for an answer?'

James looked as if he were seriously considering her question. He took a sip of tea and then bit into a dry scone. 'Butter and jam would be good on these.'

'Anything to stop an argument.' Cora fetched the butter and jam, then plates, knives and a jam spoon. She dug around in a rarely opened drawer before finally locating butterfly-patterned paper serviettes.

'Now we're talking. Did anyone ever tell you you're a right little scone burner?'

Without hesitating, Cora lifted a scone and pelted it at James's head. The doughy ball hit him clean on the nose.

James brushed crumbs off his thick grey jumper and picked the scone up off the floor. 'Well, that's lovely, that is.' Dolloping strawberry jam on the former missile he stuffed the entire half in his mouth. A smidgen of jam clung to his lip and he slowly licked the sticky blob.

'You're incorrigible,' Cora said.

'Come back to me,' he said softly. 'I miss you.'

Cora clipped the saucer with her teacup. Flustered, she dabbed at the spilt liquid with a serviette.

'Cora, you know you mean the world to me.'

She closed her eyes. 'Please don't do this.'

'Why not? I know you still care.'

'Relationships – I'm just no good at them.'

James gave an easy smile. 'What are you afraid of?'

'Nothing.' Cora took a small bite of her scone, her appetite non-existent.

Resting his elbows on the table James stared at her. 'One day you'll tell me.'

For a moment Cora considered doing just that, but the words floated unintelligibly and she ended her brief attempt with a shrug of hopelessness. James wouldn't understand. How could she expect him to?

'Anyway, I started this relationship. I don't see why I have to agree to ending it just to appease you.'

'What? You have to agree to it because I don't want to be in it any more,' Cora argued.

'That's a poor excuse.'

Cora laughed as she poured more tea. 'James, please listen to me.'

'I have, on more than one occasion, and you're wrong.'

'I'm wrong?'

109

'Yes, it does happen. You can't be right all the time. Now I can hear *your* brain ticking over.' James made a show of dabbing at the corners of his mouth with a serviette, before realising his finger was sticking through the paper. 'Okay, let me appeal to your business mind. Don't think about us as a relationship, think about us as a business.'

Cora had to hand it to him, he was nothing if not persistent.

'Apart from the fact that we're good together, which is a given –' he paused for emphasis '– if we put your eight thousand acres with my twenty we'd have a fairly handy property. Add that to the fact that you do care for me even if you won't admit it, you have to agree the scenario's pretty attractive.' He screwed up the serviette and with a cricketer's flourish overarmed the paper into the sink.

'It is. I particularly like the part where I'm running this empire, including the share owned by your city-based siblings, while you return full-time to your vet stuff and spend your days sticking your arm up the backsides of neighbours' cows.'

'I'm not going back to the veterinary practice. You know that. Sure, I help the odd neighbour out occasionally, but really, Cora, I'm being serious. With my mother's death and none of my siblings interested in coming back to work Campbell Station, there's only me left on the property. If Dad hadn't died so long ago things may have been different.' He gazed momentarily out the kitchen window. 'Anyway, it's nearly three years since Mum passed on.'

'I know you miss her.' Cora rattled cups and saucers together and began stacking the crockery on the sink. 'I'm sorry I never got the chance to meet her, although I realise she didn't share my feelings.'

'Anyway,' James persisted. 'Forget love. Every time the word hovers around your general vicinity you go cold, so let's go the business route. Hey, if you were interested, with your land we'd have enough collateral to buy out my sisters.'

Cora puffed air into her cheeks. 'They've chosen a different life.

I really don't see why they deserve an entitlement in return for zero contribution. Anyway, why don't you just sell a block and pay them off?'

James sighed. 'Because I'm like you, Cora: I love Campbell Station. I don't want to see the property broken up in any shape or form.' He looked at her. 'Think about it. You and me living and working together.'

'And arguing,' Cora added. James's image of their potential life was so picture-perfect at times even she believed it were possible. How then did she go about explaining to him that what he wanted and what she longed for – a joining of hearts and businesses – was impossible? All relationships were impossible. There had been other men in her life: the occasional drover passing through, a stock inspector, even an encyclopaedia salesman. The 'book man', as she fondly remembered him, had lasted three years. A length of time made enjoyable by the fact that he travelled through Stringybark Point every six months and on arrival at Absolution Creek stayed for an average of ten days. Yet despite these romantic interludes no one had touched her deeply. As soon as Cora felt the stirrings of something more than mutual companionship, she backed off, haunted by a past that scared her away from any form of commitment, and by memories of a man whom no one, to date, could compare with. 'For a smart man you really know how to capture a woman's heart; a marriage and a business transaction all in one.'

James made a show of noisily scraping his chair back across the linoleum floor. Cora waited for the final retort. They'd always been like this: the bantering, the playfulness, and then the moment would turn and Cora would come face to face with her feelings and find escape through a single throw-away line. She followed James outside and watched as he pulled on his boots, his old collie, Tag, lolling patiently in the dirt with Tripod and Curly.

'Gidday, Tag,' she called. The dog sat up, looked from her to his owner and moved to James's side. 'It's a conspiracy,' she commented.

111

Her attempt at levity didn't work. James walked down the back path and soon after she could hear his utility start up. Was it her imagination or had she really murmured the words *Don't go?*

Cora scuffed her feet against the worn burgundy runner as she walked along the enclosed walkway dividing the living areas from the bedrooms. She turned onto the veranda ringing the outward facing bedrooms. Only Cora's bedroom was big enough for a fireplace. A wall had been knocked down in the forties and a fireplace put in at her instruction. The twins' bedroom faced the east, their single casement windows offering a view of the edge of the ridge with its pine trees. Cora hoped they would be cosy enough. She banked on the warmth of her fire to keep this part of the homestead liveable. The girls' bedroom, dusted and polished by Ellen, was so clean not even the most canny daddy-long-legs spider could hide from view. It was true that the creamy paintwork had seen better days, and the single beds creaked when you sat upon them, but the dusty pink bed covers and curtains looked rather pretty next to the timber wardrobe Ellen had managed to freshen up with white paint. There was even a navy rug on the floor, retrieved from a camphor box, the thick pile now quite passable thanks to warm water and soap.

Cora wondered about the family due to descend on Absolution Creek. She could only imagine the discussions that would have gone on between Meg and her husband. Uprooting their family was no small matter, especially when the transition involved heading northwards from a city life into a new environment. The Australian bush. She wondered which of them had made the final decision or whether the knowledge of Cora's childless state and the asset involved had been enough to warrant their speedy agreement. In Cora's view it was a win-win situation. Her niece had been enticed by the offer of a paying job in the country and would by now have visions of inheriting the land one day. And Cora wanted to inflict some form of pain on Jane Hamilton. She wanted Jane to feel as lonely, angry and betrayed as she had once felt.

Cora hoped Jane would miss the girl so deeply it hurt. She hoped Jane would lament the loss of her grandchildren, and wake every morning feeling helpless and alone. She hoped Jane would be furious at Cora and that the fury would make her pick up the telephone, or travel northwards to have it out with her. It was a confrontation long overdue, and Cora was already basking in Jane's annoyance and frustration. Meg didn't know anything about Cora and Jane's past, and Cora was sure Jane had every intention of keeping it that way. Either way, Meg and Sam Bell's arrival would bring changes for everyone. Especially Cora. She would have family around her again for the first time in more than forty years. She tried to imagine what it would be like – how she would react, how they would. And children: Cora never expected to have children living at Absolution Creek. She was suddenly wary and excited.

Before her father married Jane's mother, Abigail, following the death of Cora's mother, her family had been a wonderfully close-knit unit. Then Abigail arrived with her *holier than* attitude and a spiteful daughter. Jane hated Cora and Ben from the very beginning. She sneered at them and complained to Abigail, who in turn whined to their father. However, if Jane was embarrassed by her stepbrother and stepsister, she was also jealous of the love they received from their birth father. Looking back it seemed to Cora that Jane was intent on getting rid of them in order to have her stepfather's undivided attention. How a kid could have so much hatred within her at such an early age baffled Cora. Maybe Jane suffered from some type of mental deficiency that served to emphasise the worst parts of her personality. Either way, in the end Jane won, although Abigail had played a significant role in Jane's eventual short-lived victory. What a pair for her father to become tangled up with: a thief for a wife and a conniving stepdaughter.

Now Jane's daughter, Meg, was coming to live at Absolution Creek. Closing the casement window, Cora looked out at the wind-blown day. The grass was brittle and yellowing from successive frosts, and a draft crept in from beneath the sill. She recalled that chilly whisper of air sneaking into her own room long ago. Of course back then she'd been prepared to freeze at night. As a young girl she spent hours watching the tips of a branch of the leopardwood sway out the window, as if cautiously testing the landscape beyond. The pale leaves billowed in blustery winds.

On a timber dresser on the veranda stood the last of the boxes previously lining the bedroom. During the fifties Cora had given thought to packing the lot up and railing it south to Sydney. They were not her keepsakes after all; they were Jack's. And with sentimentality not high on the list of her preferred characteristics, Cora speculated that an antique shop would no doubt have a customer interested in such collectibles. Yet somehow the items remained in the house, until now. Cora lifted the folded cardboard and was immediately assailed by the pungent aroma of a bull mouse. 'Jesus, Mary and Joseph!' she exclaimed, taking a step back. This *was* fire material.

Over the previous weeks Cora had burnt whole piles of New York's *Saturday Evening Post,* water-stained and stuck together, ten years of the *Australian Agricultural Gazette* with its outmoded agricultural implements and a carton of sale brochures.

Cora leant delicately over the box and lifted a wad of old *Sydney Morning Heralds* from their smelly resting place. Most were dated around the early twenties, with one from 1931 commemorating the opening of the Sydney Harbour Bridge. She blew at the dusty type, careful the mouse droppings remained in the box and didn't escape onto Ellen's polished floor. Despite having never been to Sydney, the arch amazed her. Its whole construction seemed a modern miracle even if Jack always lampooned it. She remembered this particular copy of the paper, for she'd saved it herself. It was a window into Jack's world. She gave a brief thought to salvaging the best of the papers and then changed her mind. The past was the past, and had she not spent half her life trying to forget it? With a heave she lifted the box and carried it outside.

There was an old 44-gallon drum sitting on bricks behind the meat house. Tripod and Curly kept a respectful distance as she removed a stack of the newspapers and dropped them into the drum. There were small holes in the base and sides of the drum to draw air. When Cora threw a match in, the aged papers caught light quickly. Smoke streamed from the top and as the flames rose she added more papers by hand before upending the box's contents into the drum. A shower of sparks rose up to assault her nostrils as papers, magazines and a book curled beneath the heat.

'A book?' Cora said loudly. She peered through the gathering smoke as the flames took hold. The blaze leaped across a skinny volume. It was pale green, with a faded red binding. Cora lifted her bad leg and kicked at the drum. A tongue of flame reared up angrily. She kicked at the drum again and it toppled, falling on its side with a great whoosh of ash. Cora too fell with the force of her movement, and by the time she scrambled to her knees the book was already smouldering.

At that moment Harold arrived, struggling with a dead wether over his shoulder. He dropped his load when he spied Cora and rushed to help her up.

'I'm okay, really,' she said shakily. 'I was burning off and, well, I slipped.'

Harold righted the drum and did his best to tidy the mess blowing about the garden. He gave a nod at the blackened remains she clutched. 'You're all right?' His hands were bloody and the air about him carried a curious mix of fresh meat, lanolin-rich wool and manure. Cora hated the stench of a fresh kill.

'Yes, sorry to startle you.' She clutched at the book. There were streaks of black ash on her moleskins, shirt and hands. 'An old book,' she explained. 'Hadn't seen this one. Guess my curiosity got the better of me.'

The growling of dogs had Harold running to the freshly slaughtered wether. Curly and Tripod were pulling on a leg apiece. 'Get out of it, yah mongrels,' Harold yelled, doing his best to kick at Curly and missing by a foot. Curly growled in response, but the dogs reluctantly backed off as Harold heaved the carcass over his shoulder. 'You okay, then?'

'Sure.'

Harold carried the carcass into the meat house to hang by its shanks, and the door slammed shut. Cora tried to open the book, pulling at the hardcover until it ripped away to reveal a mass of blackened pages. For a second, just a second, Cora could have laughed. What she thought had been destroyed long ago had remained intact beneath her roof for nearly forty years. She'd found Jack Manning's diary and lost it; once again destroyed by her own hands.

## ⋘ *Chapter 13* ⋙

## *Absolution Creek,*
## *1965*

They arrived near dusk at a boundary gate just as the twins began to cry in unison. Unwrapping the last Vegemite sandwich, Meg passed a slice each to her girls, before clambering from the vehicle. Stretching the small of her back she opened the wooden gate to let the car through. There was a jam tin nailed to an iron post and a peeling painted sign that said *Absolution Creek*. This was it. They had arrived.

The wind made Meg's skin prickle with cold, yet it was unlike the chill of built-up Sydney. This air was bracing, fresh, new, and despite the long journey and the hours of mulling over Sam's idea of selling Absolution Creek, Meg felt renewed. The trip had ended up taking two days. Penny had become car sick and then the radiator overheated. Still, they were here now. A sense of pride swept through her as her gaze encompassed the dirt beneath her feet and the grass swaying across the paddock. A flock of white birds flew overhead. Low on the horizon the sky turned from a dusty pink to a wavering line of red. They had crossed mountains and hills, watched as the countryside flattened and stretched itself into unknown horizons, all the while Meg smiling inwardly as they grew closer to this great adventure: their new life, their new home.

The beep of the car horn swept away her thoughts.

Meg got back in the car and they drove along a further five miles of road before reaching a second gate. A single row of wavering gums lined the western road ahead while a dense hedge hid what Meg assumed was a stately homestead – for the only thing visible beyond the hedge was the crown of a large tree. Sam stopped the station wagon outside a single wooden garage. Darkness was descending on the land. The southerly had increased in strength. Sam hurriedly wound the window up, turning to the back seat to cluck Penny and Jill under their chins. He received buttery Vegemite grins in return.

'Yuck,' he complained, screwing his nose up at them. Penny and Jill giggled.

A distant line of outbuildings and a windmill smudged the skyline.

Sam opened the car door. 'Well then, here we are,' he commented with a distinct lack of enthusiasm. 'Hope the old girl's got a couple of beers.' He rubbed his hands together. 'Or rum.'

Meg frowned and the twins scrambled out of the car. 'I'll take them inside, find my aunt and we'll go from there.'

'Righto.' Sam began unloading their belongings, placing them in a neat pile as Meg, holding her children's hands, walked through the open back gate and up the path. There was a laundry block on the left and a gauze-walled building on her right, which she guessed was a meat house. Two steps led to the door of the homestead. Meg quickly took in the louvered glass shutters, peeling paint and uninteresting squareness of the home, and swallowed.

'Is this it, Mummy?' Jill asked.

'Pooh!' Penny said loudly.

The scent of meat hung in the air. It was a ripe, chewy smell, more overpowering than any butcher's shop.

'Look!' Penny pointed a finger towards the skinned carcass hanging in the meat house. All three of them walked closer and, looking through the gauze, stared into a cast-iron bucket filled with offal.

Meg put a hand over her mouth. 'Let's stretch our legs before we go inside,' she said, fighting the queasy sensation in her stomach. She dragged the girls away into cleaner, crisper air.

A narrow cement path bordered the house, which was set within a garden consisting of partially dead grass, a scraggly green hedge and tall trees. Everything was perfectly square. Even the chairs and tables scattered on the verandas had a uniform look about them. As they walked further, Meg noticed that the house appeared to be split into two, with a vine-covered walkway joining the two rectangular buildings.

'Look, Mummy, a tree.' Jill pointed ahead. Together the three of them stared at the great hulk of tree poking out from the low roof. For the briefest of moments Meg thought it was an optical illusion, however the wall inside the veranda was clearly misshapen by the growth within.

'Heavens,' Meg mumbled.

'Will it fall, Mummy?'

Meg wasn't sure. 'Of course not, Penny. I think the branches have grown that way to find the light.' Her girls were still staring. 'I think we'd better go inside. It's getting dark.'

'What's that?'

Despite her inclination to seek the safety of the house, Meg allowed Penny to drag her towards a small shed that stood some yards from the homestead. The sky was turning from blue to black, blurring the space between ground and air as Penny led them along a worn path to what they soon discovered was a toilet.

'Why's there a toilet outside, Mummy?' Penny pushed at the creaking wooden door.

Meg looked at the outdoor toilet and at the tree cradling the house below. A scatter of stars dotted the sky.

'Mummy?'

'I don't know, Penny,' Meg answered, firmly clasping a small hand in each of hers. She quickened their pace, glancing up at the towering tree as they walked the length of the homestead. The wind nipped at their cheeks. Ahead two dogs barred their path. Meg skirted around the animals, a child pressed close on either side. The dogs growled softly. So then, this was Absolution Creek.

Meg knocked on the back door while the twins fidgeted at her side.

'Come on in,' a female voice invited.

Meg opened the door and hurried her children into the glass-enclosed back porch.

'Just walk straight down the hallway,' the voice continued.

Meg followed the direction of the voice along a narrow hallway, the uneven floorboards slowing her progress. They found themselves in a large kitchen lit by an overhead light and heated by a wood-burning stove on a far wall. The black cook top and flue, with its plate racks on either side, was clearly warped, for a thin stream of smoke wafted upwards in the draft. A radio crackled the six o'clock news. At the end of a long wooden table, which could easily have seated twelve, sat a woman totally unlike Meg's mother. Where her mother's face was creased with dissatisfaction, this woman was almost wrinkle-free, apart from the crow's feet around her eyes. She was full featured with a wide forehead, generous lips and glossy dark hair.

Leaning nonchalantly against the kitchen bench was a man in his sixties. Short and stocky with a basin-shaped haircut, he gave Meg a nod.

'Well?' Cora barked. She was wearing pale trousers and a lemon-coloured shirt.

Meg jumped. 'Hello, Aunt.' She was shocked to discover the youthful woman opposite and quickly stepped forward to grasp her hand.

'Meg, this is Harold. Meg's fortunate to be the only child of my sister, Harold, and so through sheer genetics is my first choice as companion, although I daresay each of us believes the other's on trial. Harold's my manager.'

Harold nodded again and shook Meg's hand. She found his grip reassuring, his glance less so. Meg had been subjected to the sweeping head-to-foot gaze of other men, but she doubted she'd ever rated so poorly.

'Pleased to meet you.'

His mouth twitched. Meg wondered if he were responsible for the slaughtering of the animal outside.

Her aunt took a cigarette from a packet on the table, inserted it into a slender holder and lit it. Fingernails shone in the harsh overhead light. She drew in the nicotine steadily, exhaling through her nose. 'Harold's been here for many years. He's what you call a station manager.' She puffed again. Penny and Jill tightened their grip on Meg's hands.

'Do you know you have a tree sticking out of your house?' Jill said, standing with one ankle crossed over the other and her fingers in her mouth.

Penny nodded in agreement. 'A big one. You're very brown.'

'These would be your children, then?'

Meg pushed the twins forward, their reluctant feet fighting against the linoleum flooring. 'Penny and Jill,' Meg introduced them, giving them another shove. The floor covering was quite worn in places and Meg snuck a glance at where the linoleum was upturned and pulling away from the cracked skirting board.

Her aunt laughed. 'Sounds like a nursery rhyme. Never mind, we all have our crosses to bear. And your husband?'

'Sam's unpacking the car.' Immediately the scrape of boxes sounded from the porch.

'Well, I wasn't expecting you to have a ready-made family at your age, but there's not much we can do about it.' Cora stared at the twins. 'I've put you in the bedroom on the right. The children can have the one next to you. They look to me like they're ready for schooling.'

'Next year, Aunt. They turned five a few months back.'

The back door opened and the noise of Sam sliding boxes and suitcases onto the porch halted their conversation. 'I see you haven't taught him how to knock.'

Sam entered the kitchen with a smile and hearty hello. His greeting stilled when he took in Cora sitting serenely at the end of the kitchen table. Hesitating, he shook Harold's hand. 'Nice to meet you all . . .'

'Cora Hamilton.' Cora reached out a slender arm and shook his hand. 'And what's your trade then?' She turned his hand over, briefly studying the smooth palm. 'Pen pusher?' She stared at his twice-broken nose. 'Street fighter?'

'Mechanic.' He took a step back to place an arm around Meg's shoulders. 'Long day. We're pleased to be here.' Sam ruffled Jill's hair while his other tightened on Meg's shoulder. 'Gee, I didn't realise there were good sorts up this way.' There was an edge to his tone. Meg knew what he was thinking. Neither of them had been expecting the likes of Cora Hamilton. She was certainly not a doddery aunt.

Cora flipped the lid on an ashtray and stubbed her cigarette out. The lid closed with a snap. 'We rise early here, Samuel. I'm up well before dawn, however if you breakfast at six-thirty, you'll have time enough to meet with Harold at seven-fifteen.'

'I'll give you a tour in the morning, Sam,' Harold advised. 'There's a bit on. There's an old fence to be pulled down and some yard repairs.'

To Sam's credit the expression on his face didn't change. 'Sounds good to me, Harold. How many staff do you have here?'

Cora gave an engaging smile. 'We have a team, Sam, and including you that would be two at the moment. The thing is, what Absolution needs is someone with experience, but now you're here we can put you to good use. After all, you have to earn your keep somehow.' Cora lit another cigarette.

'Thanks, Miss Hamilton.' Harold dipped his head in deference and left the kitchen, side-stepping the luggage. The back door clicked shut quietly.

'Dinner's at seven, Meg. You might like to wash and change. I'm putting you in charge of meals from now on. Harold's wife, Ellen, will still come in the mornings to explain how things run, at least for the next couple of weeks until you get used to things.'

'Okay.' Meg hadn't exactly envisioned herself as a housekeeper. 'The girls are fed.'

Sam gave her a *told you so* look and lifted a yawning child in both arms. 'Bedroom?'

'Go straight through, Samuel.' Cora pointed towards a door at the opposite end of the kitchen. 'Along the walkway, turn right onto the veranda. The girls' room is first on the left.'

Sam glanced at Meg.

'Off you go, Sam,' Cora directed. 'I'm sure it doesn't hurt for a father to put his girls to bed occasionally.' She waited for the sound of the kitchen door closing. 'How's your mother?'

'Good,' Meg answered warily. There was a large crack in the wall above where Cora sat. It extended from the floor in an arc to the corner of the room.

'That woman was never good – she was either sour, argumentative or spiteful.'

A small *oh* escaped Meg's lips. Of course it was to be expected. If her mother hated her sister then it only made sense for the feeling to be reciprocated. She suddenly realised she had unwittingly placed herself in the most unenviable of situations: in a war between siblings.

'Plates in the cupboard,' Cora called over her shoulder as she walked to the fridge, returning with a tray of ice. Meg tried not to stare at her aunt's slight limp. She foraged through the cupboards, locating condiments and cutlery as ice clattered into a glass. 'Drink?' Cora asked.

'No thanks.'

'Bet you've never had one.'

'Beer,' Meg admitted.

Cora was sipping on a tall glass of rum. 'I'm a gin martini girl myself, however I find rum more warming in the winter and it's a better painkiller.'

Meg glanced at her aunt's leg. 'Are you in a lot of pain?'

'Some. Arthritis during winter. That's when it's worse. I had an accident a long time ago.'

'What happened?' Meg asked.

'It involved a horse and a dray. You should ask your mother.' Cora's eyes were bright. 'She was there.'

At the tight look on her aunt's face, Meg decided against further questioning. At least for the moment.

Cora crunched ice. 'I'd imagine that husband of yours likes a few. '

'I'm sorry?'

'Drinks, Meg. He's a drinker, isn't he?' Cora twirled the ice in her glass. 'Unhappy people with a fondness for the bottle take to it pretty quickly out here. It's the isolation.' Cora took a sip. 'I'm thinking he thought he'd be here to see the old girl out – that old girl being me – then sale-o!'

Meg experienced more than a twinge of guilt. '*I* didn't think that,' she blurted out.

Cora laughed. 'So much for matrimonial loyalty. Don't look so concerned, Meg. I'll take honesty any day. Did she remarry?'

'Who? Mum? After Dad?' Meg queried. 'No.'

Cora drained her glass, looked as if she might say something, and then changed her mind. 'Go wash and change,' she commanded Meg. 'I'll set the table tonight.'

Sam was still in the bathroom when Meg finished rummaging through her suitcase. She brushed her hair, dabbed on some lipstick and felt somewhat better once dressed in her best grey sweater, black skirt, stockings and lace-up shoes. She glanced around the white-walled bedroom, which smelt strongly of fresh paint, and decided against waiting for Sam. She walked back to the kitchen. Finding it empty, she investigated the rooms leading from the hallway. The room to her left was like an Aladdin's cave. Art deco side tables and coloured glass lanterns competed with an eclectic selection of trendy plastic furniture, including large Acapulco chairs with their iconic saucer-shaped backs, and smoky glass-topped coffee tables. Different varieties of lush green ferns trailed down the sides of tall mahogany planters and a myriad tiny dried leaves lay scattered across the black-and-white floor tiles. This, she supposed, was used mainly in the summer, for the room was quite cold.

The dining room opposite was totally different. Here the walls were a pale yellow and the curtains framing the six long casement windows a faded red silk. Meg's eyes were drawn to the fireplace. Framed by shiny red timber with a single column on either side was a mantelpiece with an oblong bevelled mirror. The interior of the fireplace was decorated with an etched canopy, with a fire grate of quite gothic design. It would have been magazine perfect were it not for the cracks that spread across the plaster walls like varicose veins. Meg was sure light could be seen through the crack in the wall closest to the hallway and there was a definite gap running the length of one wall where the floor had dropped a number of inches. In spite of the evident state of disrepair, strategically placed lamps gave the room a warm glow.

Her aunt was already seated at the dining table. Steaming plate-fuls of an aromatic stew wafted into the air.

'Have a seat, Meg.'

Meg did as she was told and they began eating without Sam. She was frightened of dropping food on the polished table and conscious of her manners. Her aunt certainly didn't stab the air with her knife, like her mother did, or position her knife and fork in the quarter to three position on her plate. Nor, she noticed, was there the obligatory cabbage her own mother so loved. Meg did her best to emulate her aunt, eating slowly and carefully, and straight-ening her back so that she too sat upright. She crossed her fork over her knife in a delicate V between mouthfuls. She was sure her aunt gave a slight smile.

'Where have you been?' Meg said as Sam entered the room.

Sam, who had showered and changed, ignored his wife. He looked around expectantly at the sideboard, but then noticed its empty decanters and the water jug on the table. He frowned before slumping into his chair. 'Sorry.' He didn't sound at all apologetic. 'I didn't realise there was a train to catch.'

Cora tapped her nails on the table. 'You'll appreciate an early dinner after a few days with Harold.'

'Sure.' Sam shovelled stew into his mouth. 'No need to go to all this trouble for us though, Cora.' He waved his fork at their surroundings. 'We're kitchen people.' His eyes fell on each painting, each lamp, the height of the pressed metal ceiling. One of the ornate cornices dangled a good foot from where it should have been secured.

'I always eat dinner in here, Samuel.' Cora shook a cigarette out of its packet and lit it with a sigh of satisfaction. 'People dress for dinner in the bush. We always have.'

Sam swallowed noisily. 'Thought I might go to town tomorrow, pick up some supplies.' He pushed his chair out and leant back on two legs. 'Nice table.'

'Mahogany.'

'Hmm, matching chairs?'

'Burr walnut,' Cora answered.

'Pricey, eh?'

'Yes.'

Sam brought the chair back down so that it rested on all four legs.

'We don't need anything in town, Sam. Besides, this is a six-day-a-week job.'

'Well, I've a mind to go exploring.' He pushed his plate away sulkily.

'Town is a once-a-fortnight event for supplies.'

Sam glared at her. 'Meg and I didn't come here to be bossed around, you know. I never actually said I'd be working for you.'

'And what did you actually think you'd be doing? Living here under my roof gratis?' Cora exhaled cigarette smoke, which drifted up towards the embossed metal ceiling. 'If you intend to find work elsewhere – which, I might add, I'd be happy to see you do – I'd charge you board accordingly. That's fair.'

'Fair? There's fair and then there's downright bossy.' The crockery rattled as he stood.

'Is that right? Well, in the meantime have a think about what you'd like to do. Work here or elsewhere, remembering that you'll be on trial anywhere you go. There are no free rides out here.'

'Who do you think you are?'

'The person who owns the fuel bowser. Did you fill up when you came through the village?'

Meg knew Sam was far better off working here and keeping a low profile, at least until his latest fighting debacle was forgotten. Although she doubted the police would chase him this far north, it would be a different matter if the man called Jeffo had ended up with serious injuries or worse.

'I don't know where you get off –'

'I'm the owner, Sam,' Cora pointed out, 'and your prospective employer.' She leant towards him. 'My offer was for your wife. You're lucky to be here.'

Meg's heart felt as if it was slowly detaching itself from the inside of her chest.

Cora took a sip of water. 'And I'll remind you both that there's no corner shop here. It's a 200-mile return trip to Stringybark Point, so keep a list handy if your memory fails you for when we do go to town for supplies.'

Sam glared at her. 'Well, ain't that some sort of welcome. We come here in good faith –'

'This is my home, Samuel Bell.' She leant forward in her chair. 'There's little point you trying to throw your weight around here. I'll remind you once only: Meg is family, and while you are both to a certain extent on trial, *you* have to earn the right to be here.'

Meg widened her eyes in response to Sam's furious stare. He'd not once raised his hand at her or the girls, but there was always a first time. 'Sam.' She knew how her voice must sound – plaintive, pleading.

Cora took a long, languorous draw on her cigarette and blew the smoke directly at him.

'Sam, please.'

Sam walked briskly from the dining room. Meg unclenched her fists. There were deep red welts across her palms.

'He's a difficult one, isn't he? No need for explanations. He'll get used to things,' she said amiably. 'It'll be difficult for him, though. Men hate reporting to women.'

Clearly her aunt's anger didn't extend to Meg. 'Harold obviously doesn't,' she said.

'Oh, I'm sure it irks him some days, but the truth of it is that Harold's a perfectionist. That's how he lost his own place in the early fifties. He was so busy trying to make everything perfect that he spent himself out of his only asset, his land. I don't intend to see that happen here and Harold knows it. If an increase in expenditure doesn't increase production, and by extension income, we don't do it.' Cora finished her cigarette and stubbed it out in a porcelain ashtray. 'He didn't want to come here, did he?'

Meg gave a small shrug. At this moment she didn't want to be here either.

## *Chapter 14*

# *Mrs Bennet's Boarding House, Chatswood, 1923*

Olive peered out the top-floor window of the boarding house. She lifted the casement window and a cool billow of wind ruffled her carefully groomed hair. She sported the latest hairstyle, known as a shingle, which finished just above the shoulders. The permanent wave suited her dark hair and she patted a stray lock back into place, noticing the small clouds on the horizon. It would storm later in the day; a Sydneysider knew such things. She craned her neck in the hope of glimpsing the street below, but a patch of lawn and a wooden paling fence were the limits of her view.

Olive flipped the brown curtain and sat on the bed, smoothing her tubular crepe tunic across her knees. Her suitcases were packed and ready. She scanned the room that had been her virtual prison since arrival. The walls were bare and peeling, and despite being early December a chill settled about her. She thought of her buttercup-yellow bedroom with its view over the waters of Rose Bay, and glanced at her sister's early Christmas gift, which she felt sure was more a token of approval following her revelation at the

Queen's Club. Strands of seed pearls were interspersed with beads of lapis lazuli, the bracelet quite at odds with the room she now inhabited. Her fingers plucked at the worn brown coverlet beneath her. Her fancy wristwatch with its mother-of-pearl face told her only half an hour had passed. Thomas was coming tomorrow.

'One more day. One more night,' she repeated softly.

Olive thought of Jack; tried to recall his face. She brushed away gathering tears and recollected the slab hut pictured in a book at the State Library. There had been another image as well: of a woman behind a one-way plough. Of course there were also photographs of picket-fenced dwellings, black-skinned maids and grimacing children, but it was the toiling woman who occupied Olive's thoughts. It wasn't her fault. She had no photograph of Jack and, having been apart for months, her resolve was weakening. She believed she loved him, yet a growing awareness of what she was giving up ate at her. Worse, now she was at the final, irreversible stage of Jack's plan, she was holed up in a boarding house, hiding out like a common criminal from family and friends. What would happen if Jack couldn't make a go of things? Would they end up paupers – she with her skirts tucked up as she dragged her feet through yards of dirt, and Jack dulled by disappointment? What would *she* do out there? Have babies, Olive supposed. Help Jack, perhaps. Help him do what? She was about to run away to join the man she loved, yet her resolve was failing her and she realised she was giving up far too much to risk it on a dream. Why couldn't Jack have stayed in Sydney? Why did they have to build the bridge? That great blasted bridge, Olive thought sadly. Despite the massive structure and the eventual uniting of the city, it had created a chasm that she now knew was impossible to breach.

She wrote the letter quickly, using the thin paper supplied on the dresser, only pausing to re-read it when her tears had dried.

*My dearest Jack,*
*Don't think my affections have diminished. I write this knowing*
*you have gone ahead to make a place for us and I admire your*
*courage for setting off into the vastness of this country to follow*
*your dream and carve a place in the world beyond. Sadly, I*
*have come to realise such a place is not for me. In the months*
*we have been apart I have found myself appreciating security,*
*love and the familiarity of hearth and home. Both our worlds*
*have changed, Jack, perhaps for the better. Forgive me, however*
*I lack the courage to venture into the unknown, to live an*
*isolated existence far away from family and friends.*
*Olive*

Olive hastily folded the letter as Mrs Bennet's footsteps sounded
on the stairwell. The woman jumped visibly when Olive opened
the door, her fist mid-air.

'I was just letting you know that you're late for breakfast. Again.'

Olive handed the older woman the letter and enough coins for
postage. 'Mrs Bennet, I will be leaving today. Can you arrange
transport to the city?'

The widow looked at her suspiciously. 'Transport to the city?
I thought you were . . .' She paused to examine the letter before
slipping it into her apron. 'Never mind. You'll be telling me it's none
of my business.'

'I believe I owe you monies for my stay.' Olive counted out the
coins required. Each movement she made, every thought, seemed
to be that of another person. In her mind she was walking towards
the Milsons Point terminus, her arm linked through Jack's. Then
they were sitting eating a banana split . . .

Mrs Bennet cleared her throat. 'My gardener's off on an errand
this afternoon. If you like he could take you to the train station then.'

'That would be fine. Thank you.' The train, ferry and cab ride
home would give her time to contemplate her arrival at Rose Bay.

After two nights' absence, Olive's excuse for her disappearance – a pre-Christmas house party with the Gees – would soon be revealed as a sham. Mrs Gee and her mother spoke weekly and Olive knew she must return home and face punishment. Her parents would be horrified by the truth, yet what else could she do? As Olive closed the bedroom door she rallied, straightening her shoulders and firming a smile. What had she been thinking? A woman such as herself, a settler's wife! Why, she had not the first idea about the country.

Olive changed into a pink silk dress and grey overcoat with matching silk lining. It was a little overdone for travelling, but she was determined to return to Rose Bay with her head high. Adjusting her grey clouche hat so that it sat low over her forehead, she assessed herself in the mirror. She dusted powder across her nose and applied a coral pink lipstick. When the knock came on the bedroom door she was quite ready to leave.

'The weather's turned,' Mrs Bennet warned, letting Olive struggle with the two suitcases down the stairs. 'I've no spare umbrella for you. It'll take some twenty minutes to get to the station.' Mrs Bennet's sturdy lace-ups echoed down the stairs and along the hallway. 'I'd be suggesting you wait till morning.' The hall table bulged with picture frames and knick-knacks, all highlighted by a weak light emanating from the tasselled lampshade.

Olive lifted her chin a touch higher and walked down the gravel path to where a dray waited. She looked left and right, expecting an automobile, but instead Mrs Bennet's gardener, a rough-looking individual with old man eyes approached her. He took hold of her suitcases and threw them into the back of the dray.

'Visiting, was you?' He manhandled her aboard. She sat squeezed tightly against him on the wooden seat.

'Are you going home now, lass?'

Olive detected a slight Irish accent in the guttural voice. 'Yes.' A sprinkle of rain moistened her palm. 'For Christmas.' Olive lifted a perfumed handkerchief to her nose, the reek of onion and sweat unavoidably strong as the horse trotted off down the road. Above her, the sky was thickening with heavy cloud. They turned from Mrs Bennet's street and the dray rolled past a number of timber houses.

'Christmas, eh?'

'Yes, it's only three weeks away.'

'To be sure it is. Live on the city side, eh? I used to live there too, till the bridge, of course.'

Olive nodded, loath to move her handkerchief from her nose and mouth. 'The bridge development has changed many people's lives.'

'Not yours, eh?' His eyes strayed to Olive's pearl bracelet.

She tucked it under her coat sleeve. 'Is it far to the station?'

The gardener pulled his cap down, flicked the reins and turned to the right. They were on a rutted track with fewer houses and many more trees.

'Used to be a lot of orchards around here, and Chinese. Modernisation, eh?' He spat over his shoulder.

Olive opened her mouth to check directions, a fierce thunder clap drowning her out. The gardener flicked the reins and drove some way in the streaming rain before seeking cover beneath a large tree.

'Nice watch.' He thumbed at her wrist.

The canopy above provided only the minimum of cover and Olive huddled into her coat, feeling the water seep through the fine cloth until the back, shoulders and skirt of her dress were soaked through.

'Nice ear bobs. Pearls, is they?'

Eventually the rain began to lessen.

'I'll be having that fancy bracelet of yours, lass.'

Olive started at the gardener's voice. 'Excuse me?'

'Give it here.' He reached for her arm.

134

Olive struck out with both hands, slapping at the man wildly. She twisted in the wooden seat and aimed at him with her feet.

'You're a bloody holy terror.' He slapped her once across the face and succeeded in wrenching the pearl bracelet free. Dazed, Olive drew back and fell from the dray onto the muddy ground. She landed heavily.

'All I wanted was the bracelet.' The gardener sounded quite annoyed. He propped her against a tree, taking a step back to look at her closely. 'Watch and ear bobs.'

Olive threw the jewellery on the muddy ground and, with shaking hands, tugged at her dress, which had ridden up to reveal the tops of her stockings. The man was searching her handbag, whistling when he found her clutch of pound notes.

'How we gonna get you to the station now, eh lass? You look a right fright to me. Pretty silly just for the sake of a bracelet.' He tilted her chin.

The sound of a horse clip-clopping down the muddy road carried on the slight breeze. A dirty hand quickly silenced her. They remained in that position for some minutes until the splatters of raindrops showered them from above. Olive struggled beneath the man's weight. His breathing was laboured and the heat of him through the wet material of her dress seemed to scorch her. When she cried out again she was rewarded with a stinging slap. The gardener glanced over his shoulder.

'The thing is, if you'd given me the bracelet, lovey, you could have been on your way. But looking the way you do now, with your hair all mussed, your clothing muddy and ripped, well, if you do put me in – which you will – the coppers will assume the worst when you've only got yourself to blame.'

Olive turned her head from him. 'Just go, please. Let me be.'

'So it's a bit of a wasted exercise, if you know what I mean, leaving you looking like you do, with no violation even been attempted.' He grinned happily. 'Besides, toffs like you, well, you've had no experience, and me father always said a little training never went astray.' He put his hand over her mouth and, dragging Olive sideways, fell upon her. 'If it's any consolation, you'll be my first under these circumstances.'

## ⋙ Chapter 15 ⋘

# The New England Tablelands, 1965

Lifting the homemade swag, Scrubber scooped out a shallow hole in the dirt, sat the leather pouch inside and lay on top of it. There were still some hours to endure before sunrise, and if sleep did come to him he figured it was best to be prepared – a failure due to lack of attention couldn't be risked. He didn't want anyone to feel tempted. After all, a fella might think anything was in that pouch. Scrubber burrowed his bony spine further into the dirt and said a few words he thought passable prayer-wise.

Through the dark of the bush night Scrubber listened as the horses ambled across fallen leaves. Their hoofs crushed branches, and soft whickering floated through the air. Scrubber turned towards the smoking fire, flinging his arm across Dog. With a full belly and a drowsy mind it was real easy to wallow in memories of times past. And tonight in particular his mind kept meandering, as he recalled the man who once saved him, who in turn couldn't see that he needed saving from himself . . .

Matt Hamilton was tall and built like a red brick out-house. He had a face women loved and the poorest ability when it came to judging a person's character. Of course from Scrubber's viewpoint that was the most positive attribute Matt could have had. If his pa were around he would have told Scrubber that meeting Matt Hamilton that day was akin to finding a four-leaf clover. Unfortunately the reverse couldn't be said of Matt's association with Scrubber.

It was late December 1923, and Scrubber just twenty-two years old, when he arrived on the slopes. Worn out and hungry he was about ready to turn himself in. The day before, a group of Aborigines had accosted him on a dirt track. It was some altercation. Having discovered there was nothing worth stealing, they spat on him, following a good rubbing down in the dirt. That was near it for Scrubber. With busted ribs and his water bag stolen, he figured he was done for. Then providence led him to gaze across the paddock to where two men on horseback came into view. They were a good mile away, riding into a dipping sun, and in spite of exhaustion Scrubber slipped through the fence in a bid to follow them. The rocky ground tested his knees and feet. By the time Scrubber reached the camp it was dark, his mind numb with tiredness. He could barely move for the pain of his ribs. Grasping the trunk of a silver-barked tree, he slid to the ground, his calf muscles quivering. Scrubber couldn't remember his last meal. He peered out from behind the tree.

Only feet away the men talked of women and of kids, and of a man called Purcell, as saddle bags were unpacked and meat began to sizzle. Scrubber's stomach gurgled and he nearly teared up from the inglorious act of his hiding.

'You gonna stay out here all night?'

While the sudden voice was friendly enough, the barrel of a rifle was wedged between Scrubber's ribs.

'I don't mean no harm,' Scrubber replied, his strength nearly gone. This was it then – a bullet in the back just as his father foretold.

The barrel poked him.

'Geez, mate, you don't look so good.'

When the rifle's owner realised he was injured, Scrubber was half-dragged forward to the blazing fire. There was a haunch of sizzling meat on it, and in spite of his wounds Scrubber's mouth watered.

'What happened?' the two men asked in unison, silently measuring his desperation: a fortnight's growth on his face, a patchwork of dried blood across torn and filthy clothing.

'Blacks,' Scrubber answered coughing up blood.

The one called Matt Hamilton was open-eyed, with an easy smile and skin tanned a wrinkled brown. He handed Scrubber a water bag, helped him drink and then wiped his face clean with a damp rag.

'He's just a kid,' Matt advised.

With shaking hands Scrubber gulped the cool liquid and ate bits of warm salted meat that were offered to him. 'It's me ribs. They laid into me, them blacks did.'

Matt shook his head. 'Well, mate, lucky we found you. It's ten mile to the nearest water. You'd never have made it in your condition.'

The men were off a big sheep run owned by a squatter named Purcell, Matt explained, and were a week into searching for a wing of seventy ewes missing from the count. The one called Evans reckoned the sheep were over the border by now. Scrubber didn't go much on Evans. The man glared at him across the camp fire as if he'd attacked his kin.

'You're not exactly the type of straggler we expected.' Evans plugged a wooden pipe with tobacco. 'How'd you get lost?'

'How'd the sheep get lost?' Scrubber replied as Matt poked at his ribs and then wrapped strips of torn shirt around his torso. His skin was speckled blue-black from bruising.

'Walked away from their mob,' Matt informed him, surveying his handiwork.

'Well –' Scrubber took a slurp of water '– so did I.'

When Matt laughed, Scrubber knew he'd be all right. This was the bush after all. No one knew him or of him, he was safe. 'I could do with a job,' he wheezed.

'A job?' Evans laughed.

'Aye.'

'You can't even walk, mate, and we can't sit around waiting for you to come good.'

'Sure we can,' Matt disagreed. 'You can't leave him here.'

Evans spat into the dirt. 'You always were a do-gooder, Hamilton. Leave him with a waterbag and a bit of meat and in a week's time he can walk on. He ain't our problem.'

'In those boots?' Matt commented, pointing at Scrubber's shoes, which were part leather and part twine. 'A day's rest and he'll be up to riding.' Matt turned to Scrubber. 'It'll be painful with those ribs of yours and all that bruising.'

Scrubber gave a grateful nod.

'Can you ride? Shoot?' asked Evans. 'Know much about sheep?' Food bulged in his cheek.

Scrubber studied his filthy hands. There wasn't much he could do at all at the moment.

'Leave him alone, Evans. The lad can barely stand.' Matt gave a nod and offered him a pannikin of sugary tea. 'Bet you can fight.'

'Aye.' Scrubber gulped at the scalding black tea, savouring the taste of it. 'That I can do.'

'You're Irish then?' Matt asked.

He kept the pannikin close to his lips. 'We all gotta come from somewhere.'

Evans puffed out a string of smoke. 'Where do you come from then?'

'Not here.' Scrubber took a careful breath. His ribs hurt something fierce. 'South,' he decided to reveal. A man couldn't appear too cagey.

Matt gave him a friendly smile. 'Reckon Purcell would take you on if you're willing to work. What's your name?'

'Scrubber.'

Evans took a puff of his pipe. 'How'd you get that?'

'A fella called me Scrubber when I appeared out of the bush one day at his homestead and asked for directions.'

'Scrubber it is. You want to smear a bit of mutton grease on those feet of yours,' Matt suggested. 'Here.' He tossed him a saddle blanket. 'A wash and a shave will set you right.'

Evans grunted. 'This one's on you, Hamilton. I wouldn't go near the likes of him. I reckon he'll be trouble.'

Scrubber settled down in the dirt, his body paining something fierce, and looked through the ring of trees to the sky above. His belly groaned and he imagined the meat swirling in his starving guts as his body tried to suck the food into itself. Although he'd been on the road for more days than he cared to remember, this was the first night he'd actually looked carefully at the stars, really seen them. Scrubber, eh? A new name for a new life.

Scrubber stretched out on his back, his spine finally locating a less painful position. He wondered if the same stars were above him now as those at that first meeting with Matt some forty years ago. Back then he'd wondered at the contrast of so many stars sprinkled close to the dark of heaven. Time made a man appreciate the night sky. Life didn't have so many bright spots in it as you hoped for. He wormed across the puckered ground, manoeuvring the tobacco pouch beneath him. It was a fine thing this remembering, if it wasn't tinged with regret. He wondered if Cora Hamilton ever gazed at the stars, if she thought about the old days. Well, he'd know soon enough.

Scrubber guessed everybody wanted the same things. All those years ago as he lay by the spitting fire with Matt's saddle blanket under his head, anything had seemed possible: food, the chance of a job and the world spinning above. The offer of the saddle blanket had sealed his relationship with Matt Hamilton. An act of good will that stuck in Scrubber's mind. If things were different they'd all be here now: him, Matt Hamilton and Jack Manning.

But, of course, that was never going to happen – not with a thief among friends.

## ⋘ *Chapter 16* ⋙

# *The North West Slopes, 1965*

The billow of bulldust hung low and heavy, inescapable. Scrubber would have ridden past the drovers were it not for the young fella hanging at the rear like a willie wagtail trying to claim his territory, all puffed chest and attitude.

'Three hundred head walking in a tight circuit of two hundred mile,' he told Scrubber, a cigarette stuck to his lip. 'The owner's giving his paddocks a spell after recent rain. Figured on a month's destocking. No one told the old man that with the cold weather not much would be growing in the mob's absence.'

'That so,' Scrubber croaked, keeping his throat covered. The boy was dressed for the part: jeans, boots, pocketknife, flapping oilskin, newish hat. Bit stiff in the saddle though – left hand dangling as if he didn't know quite what to do with it. Injury, he reckoned. A splatter of blood stained the lad's thigh; something had recently had its throat cut.

The youth spat his smoke into dry grass. 'Where you going?'

'West.' Scrubber watched the cigarette butt flare in the leaf litter. He clucked his girls on.

The lad was quick to stay abreast, spurring a flighty gelding with a wily eye. 'You ever been droving? You need a station hand?'

'Never been that desperate and no.' Scrubber clicked his fingers at Dog to keep up.

'There's the camp.' The boy pointed.

Scrubber didn't think two trees and a cattle truck dressed roughly with a tarp was a mirage.

'And we've got fresh meat if you're partial.'

Scrubber scratched his stubbly cheek. Was the Pope Catholic? 'Have you now?'

He watered his horses while the three drovers yarded the mob. They pegged a square out with posts and wire, packing the cattle in good and tight. Scrubber contributed by gathering a bit of wood to keep the fire going, dragging a log up to lean against, and sitting his belongings close to where he intended to sleep, right by the fire. It was a rough camp: two scribbly gums with a rope stretched between them to tether the horses, a patch of dirt, a truck, and a half dozen dogs scrabbling over something dead through an adjoining fence. Still, a man could put up with plenty when it came to a free meal cooked by another.

The drovers returned and introductions were done intermittently as the men took turns to splash water on their faces from a bucket. They threw handfuls of the stuff sparingly about their necks. They were lean, roughish types with the names of Tyrell, Cummins and Jarrod. Scrubber could still smell them after their wash, which was saying something. He used one of Veronica's old tea towels dampened with water to clean himself up a bit, running his fingers through his best feature: his snow-white hair.

Cummins appeared from the rear of the truck, walking gingerly down the ramp, a leg of mutton dripping blood over his dusty shirt.

'Fresh kill,' he announced, sitting the leg on a tin plate and cutting the flesh into steak-like wedges. With the incisions made, he stabbed the knife in the dirt and then drove a small tommyhawk into each cut mark, splintering bone and buckling the plate. He threw the hunks of meat into a skillet, and chucked the ruined plate over his shoulder.

Tyrell roughly peeled potatoes, whistling while he worked. Two loaves of bread and half-clean plates were handed around. Not a bad camp, Scrubber decided. It could be real tasty.

The meat spat and hissed, the potatoes burned slowly, and tea was made bitter strong. The drovers were friendly enough, Scrubber thought, not that Dog agreed. He growled low and often, occasionally standing to bark at the pack of dogs through the fence. Scrubber pushed him down with his hand. 'They're not your type, mate.'

'Good dog?' Tyrell asked, as he speared a piece of barely cooked meat with a fork and sat it in between two pieces of dry bread. 'Always was partial to long-haired collies.'

'Biter,' Scrubber supplied. 'Not me – anyone else.'

Dog growled.

'He's hungry.' Scrubber nodded at the skillet.

Reluctantly Tyrell handed Dog a bit of bread and mutton. The mutt snaffled it up. Scrubber made a show of taking his scarf off, stretched his neck sideways, and tapped at the bit of rubber piping wedged in the hollow. Three pairs of riding boots scratched in the dirt. Jarrod passed him a slice of the meat and two bits of bread, but wasn't so talkative any more. Eventually, when the silence had got past the comfortable stage, they all asked a question: where he came from, where he was going, about the hole in his throat.

'Forceps delivery,' Scrubber explained, his thumb covering the hole as he spoke. 'Buggered up my vocal chords.' As expected no one queried him. Cummins offered him a splash of rum, but cautiously, like he didn't want to get too close.

'You know anyone in need of a station hand in a month or so?' asked Jarrod, the young lad he'd met first. 'I'm only here on account of an accident.' Pulling roughly at his shirt he revealed a knobbly collarbone. 'The boss put my horse down without asking – fired me because I couldn't work.'

With the lad's shoulder exposed, Scrubber caught sight of a rugged red line and jutting bone. 'There's always a cocky that enjoys belittling another.'

'Any advice?'

'Aye, lad. Sue 'em,' Scrubber counselled, saving his speech to concentrate on fresh mutton and potatoes. In his experience every effective team needed a thief and a whinger. Scrubber figured Jarrod fitted the mould. 'You get the tucker?' Scrubber asked, forcing a particularly tough piece of flesh down his gullet.

Jarrod chose not to answer and ran greasy fingers through his hair.

'Slaughter it yourself?' Scrubber persisted. He prided himself on judging a person. 'Takes a bit to blood a sheep properly, especially if you eat it fresh.'

'I know how to stick something if I have to.'

Scrubber felt the boy's eyes drift to the pouch at his waist. 'I'm sure you do.'

None of the drovers slept by the fire. They packed themselves into the back of the truck, tossing out gear to make space: a suitcase, a trunk, jerry cans of fuel, rope, rifle and spare supplies. Scrubber weighed up if he needed any of it, but he was used to travelling light and better for it. His bones were aching tonight and a bit of extra heat never went astray, so he hollowed the dirt out a little closer to the fire, resting his rifle nearby, and burrowed his cheek into the soil, his nose inches from Dog's warm breath. His horses stayed close by, sensing his distrust, eating the meagre rations by the road. Tomorrow he'd make it up to them: put their stomachs before his own. A man couldn't go very far without them, after all.

When the hand reached for the pouch by his waist Dog growled in warning. Scrubber straddled the youth in a dusty flurry of kicks. A blade glinted in the dwindling firelight.

'I reckoned you'd come for me,' Scrubber growled in a rush of indistinct words. A dribble of moisture seeped from the hole in his neck. 'You feeling particularly tempted to meet your maker tonight, Jarrod? Cause it don't mean nothing to me, killing a man.' He gave an unintended wheeze. 'Watching 'em die . . .' A drip of neck fluid splattered the boy's cheek. 'Seeing his blood.'

Jarrod tried to move, but was pinned by bony knees and a razor-sharp elbow. Dog's nosed pressed tight and hot into his cheek. 'You're mad,' he gasped.

Scrubber sheathed the knife. 'Maybe I am. I've got crimes attended to that no confession could ever cleanse, and no sense of respect towards another man's life. What you got apart from youth and attitude?'

Jarrod shook his head. 'Get off me.'

Scrubber lifted a gnarled fist. 'Never show the enemy your weak spot,' he said and cracked it into the boy's collarbone. The lad howled like a girl.

'Well, what do you think of that?' Scrubber said to the pouch, patting it as he resettled himself. 'Haven't lost my touch.'

Jarrod scrambled backwards and looked from Scrubber to the pouch. 'You're mad.'

Scrubber pushed his neck scarf about his throat. 'Amen.'

The altercation put Scrubber out of sorts for a couple of days. By the time he made camp next to a set of ruined sheep yards he'd already been on Purcell land for a day. He'd know it anywhere: the engulfing flatness of it, the parched ground, and the sense of accomplishment that still wavered across the now tree-covered paddocks. The government had bought all of Waverly Station for a poor price – a mandatory resumption of criminal proportions couched in a great environmental quest to save some lizard that no one ever saw. Now the land was ruined, wasted, a sorry mix of feral pigs, kangaroos and wild horses. Natural pasture no longer existed. Highly paid stupidity, and the men in suits wondered why folks did their best to cheat paying taxes.

Still, it was good to be back. That first day he'd ridden in with Matt and Evans all those years ago, with a week of half-decent food down his gullet and one of Matt's shirts on his back, he'd felt like a king. They had walked their horses down a dray-wide road past outbuildings that resembled a small town. Shearing shed, men's quarters, overseer's house, Matt's house, stables, yards: Scrubber remembered them all. He recalled kids running across a paddock, windmills turning, dogs barking, the smell of food in the air and the tang of sheep droppings. Then the sheep appeared on the horizon like a great moving blanket. Scrubber had watched bug-eyed as the mob grew closer, until they were all he could see: a great shining carpet of blinding whiteness.

Matt had pulled a shilling coin from his pocket. On one side was the head of a great ram, his horns almost running over the rim of the coin. 'You keep it, Scrubber,' Matt had said. 'That there ram, he's from here. Welcome to Waverly Station.'

Of course it was another man's empire, another man's legacy, but Scrubber couldn't help but feel a sense of pride that day.

And now here he was back on Waverly, forty-plus years on and pleased as punch. Scrubber patted the pouch at his waist. This then was where it all began for the Hamiltons. The place Matt's wife made infamous by default. She'd been a woman in the wrong place all those years ago, and although Matt must have loved her, as it turned out love didn't equate to trust.

# ≪ Chapter 17 ≫

## Absolution Creek, 1965

'Are they asleep?'

Sam was huddled in a weathered cane chair outside their bedroom, a bottle of rum in one hand, cigarette in the other. It was easily one of the coldest spots to sit. A sharp wind had arrived with the night and it rushed the length of the veranda, carrying earthy unknown scents.

Meg closed the door to the twins' room. 'They're exhausted. It's cold out here.'

'Half their luck. Three hours I've been awake. You?' He took a swig from the rum bottle and flicked ash on the floor.

Even if Meg hadn't been kept awake listening to Sam's brain turning over, she knew sleep was impossible. 'Where did you find that rum?'

'Can you believe this place? There's a great tree growing out of her bedroom, straight through the roof, if you please.' He took another swig and wiped his lips with the back of his hand. 'An outside dunny – now that's modernity for you.' He tapped his foot on the floorboards. 'The foundations are buggered, some of the walls have great gaping cracks in them, and here we are sitting down to dinner like she's lady muck. And wait for it –' he waved his arm around as if presenting a prize '– no staff. *We're* the staff.' The end of his cigarette glowed brightly. 'Top that off with an attitude that would tell her own grandmother to go suck eggs and, geez, well that aunt of yours wrapped you up good and tight. We've landed ourselves in a right dump, we have. Well done.'

Meg snatched the rum bottle from his hand. 'Stop it, just stop it. Sometimes I don't know why I married you.'

'Sure you do, Meg,' he slurred, 'you did it to spite your mother.' He whipped the bottle from her hand and dropped his cigarette butt on the veranda, grinding it in with his heel. Then he walked away.

Picking up the butt, Meg peered out at the dense blackness and returned, shivering, to their bedroom. She tossed the remains of Sam's cigarette into an overflowing ashtray and crawled into bed. The yellow shade on the bedside lamp reflected a halo of light on the freshly painted walls, the only bright part of the one-window room, which was otherwise cramped with dark wooden furniture. When she turned on her side the brass bed squeaked and swayed; when she pulled at the covers the springs poked and pinged. No wonder sleep was impossible. Meg squirmed her way to the middle of the bed and lay very still. She could see part of the cornice had split and was protruding slightly from the wall. Dirt, dust and leaves were partially visible beneath it. The house really was in disrepair. What had she done bringing her family here?

From the ceiling came a scurrying noise. There was a whoosh of wind through trees, the lone mournful howl of a dog and then the sound of something sliding down the corrugated-iron roof. Meg thought of the great tree above her, its outstretched arms protecting her family, and finally slept.

She woke to a blast of freezing air and Sam's finger poking at her shoulder. 'There's someone walking around outside.' The lamp was still burning, and from behind him the open door revealed the night. Her brain fought the urgent awakening.

'I was in the kitchen and I could have sworn someone walked straight past me. I heard the back door slam. It's after midnight.'

Meg tried to stir some saliva in her mouth. 'I suppose you finished the bottle?'

Sam sat on the edge of the bed. 'I'm serious, Meg.'

'Well, it could be Cora or your imagination.'

'Aren't you worried?'

'Believe me, I've got plenty of things to be worried about, and spooks are not one of them.'

'Fine.' Sam lay down fully clothed beside her and within minutes began to snore.

Meg turned the light off and tucked her head under the pillow, then threw it across the room as Sam let out a snore that was accompanied by a series of loud belches. She crept from the bedroom silently and padded along the veranda. She was of a mind to go to the toilet, however the night's shadows and coldness put her off what would be a sprint in the dark to the long-drop. Instead she hung on the veranda, staring at a crescent moon, her feet aching with cold.

There was movement: a flicker of something beyond the shadowy outline of trees. The moon profiled the elongated A-frame of the windmill as it turned, a continuous low whine marking each rotation. Into Meg's field of vision walked a horse from the direction of the dam. A scattering of kangaroos moved in tandem as the horse lifted his head and whinnied. A second figure appeared, a person with hands outstretched as if in supplication to the moon. Meg, unsure of what she was witnessing, backed into her bedroom and closed the door.

Penny and Jill took the egg basket from their mother and smiled sweetly in unison.

'So, all you have to do is walk straight into the chook yard,' Meg reminded them. 'No dawdling.'

'We know, Mum,' Jill answered. 'The rooster won't hurt us and the hens won't peck us.'

'Zactly,' Penny confirmed with a single nod of her head. 'And we'll get all the googy-eggs.'

'Are you sure you don't want me to come?' Meg wondered how she would ever catch up on her chores this morning. It had taken half an hour to get the wood stove roaring again after she had inadvertently let it go out. She couldn't help it. Having spent forty minutes under Ellen's watchful tutelage – learning how to skin membranes from kidneys and liver, and remove the veins from this favourite of bush breakfasts – she was beyond thinking. In fact, dry-retching was about the only thing on her mind; that and having to cook the awful stuff. It was 9.30 am; Cora usually returned by eleven at the latest.

'We can do it, Mum.' Jill backed away down the path.

'Mummy always shuts the gate. You will remember to shut the gate?' Meg cautioned.

Both girls nodded their heads. 'Yes, Mum.'

'Hmm.' Meg looked at her two daughters, their hands clasped around the wooden handle of the basket. In the doe-eyed silent pleading that followed, the twin tub washing machine started to make an ominous clunking noise, and the telephone rang.

'Okay, go.' Was that their ring? Meg wondered as three longish *bring bring brings* echoed through the house. Still unused to the party-line system of communication, Meg decided against answering it. Cora explained that if in doubt when it came to deciphering the morse-code rings she should simply pick the receiver up and listen. It was an open line between the five households and it appeared no conversation was sacred, for if your neighbour wasn't listening in to your call the telephonist at the local post office probably would be. The phone rang out.

Jill and Penny slipped through the back gate and ran towards the chook yard.

'Doggies,' Jill called, dropping to her stockinged knees in the dirt. Penny followed suit. Soon Tripod and Curly were licking their faces, and knocking both girls onto their bottoms in excitement. Tripod nosed the empty basket and Curly gave it a quick chew. Eventually Jill tired of the game. 'Go away,' she said with her best frown. Pulling her sister to her feet they walked to the chook yard. On their approach the rooster appeared from the rear of the yard to take up his normal sentry position near the gate. Jill looked over her shoulder. 'I don't think the dogs are meant to be here.'

The dogs were sitting to attention, eyeballing the rooster. Curly took a step forward. The rooster bobbed his head and crowed indignantly. Tripod hopped forward.

'Why, will they eat the eggs?' Penny asked.

'No, but the chickens don't like the dogs. Remember? Aunt Cora told us that.'

Tripod and Curly began to growl softly.

The rooster walked towards the gate.

'You can get the eggs,' Penny said, shoving the basket at her sister.

Jill looked at the rooster. Some of the hens had stopped their dirt pecking and were waiting expectantly, their heads darting from side to side.

'Look, the doggies are coming,' Penny squealed.

Jill took the basket and checked the steady progress of the dogs, who were about ten feet away. She was sure Curly had a smile on his face.

'Are you a scaredy-cat?' Penny asked, her small hand reaching for the gate's latch.

The rooster was stamping his clawed feet. Puffs of dust were rising in the air. Jill slipped through the gate, followed the chicken wire wall around to the laying boxes and quickly gathered the eggs.

'Hurry up, Jill!' Penny called as the chook yard disintegrated into a deafening noise of squawking hens. The rooster flapped his burnished red wings and raced to the gate, where Curly had sneaked up behind Penny.

'Open the gate,' Jill hollered as she tried to shadow the chicken wire and escape the screeching hens.

Penny lifted the latch, took a step backwards and promptly fell over Curly. The rooster was out the gate in an instant, running head down like a one-hundred-yard track star. Jill slammed the gate closed and together the girls took off in pursuit of the rooster, who had the lead on both Curly and Tripod.

'Trouble,' Penny squealed excitedly as they stumbled across the rough dirt road in the direction of the homestead.

'Big trouble,' Jill agreed, as the rooster disappeared into the garden.

Cora arrived back from her morning ride quite refreshed considering the length of time she'd been in the saddle. Having decided to leave Harold and his two protégés – Sam and Kendal – to their mustering job, her own ride out to the north-west boundary had been uneventful. Her annoyance at Kendal's presence was soon eradicated by a band of gradually lighter blues, which signified the dawning of a perfect day. It had been two weeks since her niece's arrival and the household had settled into a wary armistice that may not have come about were it not for the presence of Meg's girls. Penny and Jill were dear little children who played, argued and cried as if each day were their last. Despite Cora's limited experience with anyone under twenty years of age, she had already grown fond of them, especially as she saw them only a few hours each day.

The house was full of life, and after years of rambling about within its secure walls with just herself for company, it almost made Cora cheery. And Meg was more than she hoped for. She had taken to her new duties with careful efficiency under the watchful eye of Ellen. Now it remained to be seen how she would manage the homestead. It appeared the girl's life had revolved around child-rearing and stacking shelves in a grocer's shop. Not exactly the type of training conducive to being an independent woman. As for Sam, Cora's initial disappointment had settled into a more amenable *wait and see* attitude. Harold's work ethic and Sam's resultant exhaustion had ensured early nights with none of the attitude he'd had the affront to address her with on his arrival. Just as well, for Cora Hamilton never carried anyone and she wasn't about to now.

The sight of Curly with a ribbon around his neck and Tripod trussed up in something that looked like a nappy, certainly wasn't the welcoming committee Cora expected at the back gate. Both dogs looked decidedly unhappy. Tripod in particular appeared most put out. He fell on his back at her approach, growling and biting at the offending red-and-white checked material. Curly on the other hand began a stint of head-shaking that she felt sure would disable him. Quickly disrobing both animals, Cora picked up a dog-chewed child's skivvy from the dirt, noticing a trail of egg shells on the cement path. Kicking her boots off at the top step she soon realised that inside things were little better.

Jill and Penny were cooking.

A mountainous formation of flour sat on the sink and a line of yellow yolk seeped from the edifice and ran down the front of the white cupboard. Cora lifted a sock-covered foot from a mess of gluey flour on the floor and discovered a trail of tiny footmarks leading to the pantry.

'Jesus, Mary and Joseph!' Cora exclaimed when she opened the door. The girls were rummaging in the pantry, their discarded findings lying in a heap on the vinyl floor where they sat.

'What are you doing?' Cora demanded.

'Nothing,' Penny answered, shoving sultanas into her mouth.

'Cooking,' Jill replied proudly, wiggling a white finger into something brown and liquid on the floor.

'Oh, Jill, please. Not the treacle,' Cora admonished.

Jill held up a stained finger.

'Where's your mother?'

'Catching the blasted rooster,' Jill said solemnly, sticking her treacle-covered finger up her sister's nose. Penny squealed and retaliated with a sharp pull of her sister's hair.

'And where's your father?'

'Mustering the bloody back paddock,' both children replied.

It didn't take long to find the girl's mother. Meg, hair askew and scratches up the length of one arm, appeared at the back door. Outside the kitchen window, a rooster crowed. Considering there was only one on Absolution, Cora could only guess at what happened.

'Harold will catch the rooster.'

'You're sure?' Meg tucked stray bits of hair behind her ear. She looked as if she'd been climbing a tree. 'The girls left the gate open and –'

'Probably best if you're with them until they get used to things,' Cora suggested.

Meg glanced apologetically at Cora and sat the kettle on the stove.

'The twins are in the pantry when you're ready to deal with them.'

Meg moved towards the door.

'If you don't mind, Meg, you might save it for after I'm finished.' Cora gratefully accepted the tea her niece made and swallowed two Bex powders with the scalding beverage.

'Bread and jam?' Meg offered.

'Yes, I suppose.'

Meg placed strawberry jam, butter and two slices of bread on a plate and sat it in front of her aunt. 'Look, Cora, I'm sorry, but kids are kids.'

Cora removed her revolver, placing it on the table. 'I've been up since midnight, Meg. I'm not inclined to come back and find my home a disaster zone.' She bit into the bread, silently cursing the loss of her morning staple – scones and cheese. 'It's been two weeks since your arrival. Have you got the run of things now?'

'Yes. I just got waylaid.' Meg glanced at the wall clock. From the pantry they could hear the twins singing. She was starting to wish she were back in Sydney. At least there it was easier to keep an eye on the girls, and she had enjoyed a semblance of a life. So far, all she'd done at Absolution was listen to Sam complain and try to remember everything her aunt told her to do. She wasn't sleeping very well, and as yet hadn't managed to muster the courage to ask Cora about the strained relationship that existed with her mother. Then there was Cora's sleeping habits. Meg was pretty sure she stalked the house in the dead of night before heading outdoors. 'Can't you put that revolver somewhere else instead of sitting it on the table beside you every morning?'

Cora glanced at Meg in surprise before looking aimlessly about the kitchen, finally holstering the gun at her waist. 'Your girls aren't bush kids, Meg. There are any number of places they could hurt themselves: the dam, the dipping trench, playing with old wire and tin. The dogs could even bite them – they aren't used to being played with.' Meg didn't respond. The fiftieth rendition of 'Row, row, row your boat' sounded loudly from the pantry.

'Do you go out at night, Aunt Cora?'

Cora cupped her hands around her teacup. 'What do you mean by go out?'

'In the evening after dinner. It's just that Sam isn't a good sleeper and on a few occasions he's thought someone was outside.'

Cora hid her smile and took a sip of tea. 'There are plenty of things outside to disturb a person not used to the sights and sounds of the bush.'

'You're never here for breakfast, you come back mid-morning, sleep during the afternoon.'

'I have a routine I keep to.'

'I once thought I saw you near the dam with your horse.'

Penny and Jill appeared, food filthy.

'I'd appreciate it if you two behaved yourselves,' Cora admonished. 'No more playing in the pantry or cooking or playing dress-ups with my working dogs. Is that clear?'

Penny and Jill stared wide-eyed at Cora. Then, as if on cue, both girls burst into tears and ran to their mother.

Maybe she had been too harsh, Cora thought.

As Meg consoled her children, Jill turned her treacle-covered mouth towards Cora and poked out her tongue.

The knock on the bedroom door came just as Cora was about to put head to pillow. It was 3 pm and she expected it to be Meg. She raised herself up on her elbow. 'Yes.'

'Gidday, Cora. See you're ready for me.'

'James.' Cora swung out of bed, pleased her change of clothing before her afternoon rest consisted of a baggy cream jumper and matching long johns, and not her favourite flannelette nightie and bed socks. 'What are you doing here?' Although the afternoon was chilly the sun streamed in through the louvered windows, silhouetting him.

Removing his hat, James closed the door. 'I've dropped by a couple of times but the place is awash with kids and staff. Figured as I know your habits I'd have to catch you and everyone else unawares.' He nodded at the bed. 'Maybe take the opportunity to create a bit of gossip.'

Cora caught her smile before it appeared. 'Behave yourself.'

'Yeah, right. Anyway, for someone who likes their space you seem to have a full household.'

'My niece, Meg. The rest of them – husband included – came with the deal.'

James looked about the room, at the great tree filling the opposite corner, before sitting at the desk. 'So I've heard. You didn't actually mention the other morning it was a permanent arrangement.'

'You didn't ask.' There were only a few feet between them and Cora could already feel her heart trying to take control of her mind. James smelt of wet dogs and antiseptic, reminding her of warm days.

'The husband's in a spot of trouble with the Sydney police. I reckon that's why he slunk up here. Clobbered some fella in a bar fight.'

Cora tidied unruly hair. 'So, you've been checking up on me.'

James fingered the brim of his hat. 'You know I always figured we couldn't get it together on account of you being the independent sort. Guess I was wrong on one count.'

'There are some things in my family that needed sorting, James, and I owed my sister.'

He fiddled with a polished black stone holding down some accounts. 'I wondered when you'd make your move.'

'What's that meant to mean?'

'Well, getting the girl here to spite your sister, for one. Payback time, eh?' He adopted a soothing tone. 'It was a long time ago. Why not let it go?'

'Because I don't want to.' Cora tied her hair back with a length of ribbon. 'You forget, James, things happened, people are dead.'

She bit her lip. 'Anyway, I don't see why the girl shouldn't know the truth of things.'

'How'd you entice them here?' James asked. 'It had to be something attractive enough to get Meg away from her mother.' He rubbed the stone paperweight. 'Something feasible.'

Cora hated the direction James was taking their conversation. Why was he making her out to be the dastardly relative?

'Oh, I get it.' James dropped the paperweight on the desk. 'You've dangled Absolution Creek in her lap, made vague promises to gift it to Meg despite your own intentions of not leaving until you're carted out on a door.' He scratched his cheek. 'Wow, that makes me look like a bit of a fool. Here I've been talking joining forces and living happily ever after, and you're too busy plotting revenge to bother with me.'

'James, look I'm –'

'So what are you going to do, then? Tie your niece up and force-feed her your side of the story?' He held his hand up. 'No, I've got it. You're going to hold Meg here against her will, deprive her mother of her only child as she deprived you of your loved ones. That's it, isn't it? It's as simple and as sad as that.'

'You're being unfair,' Cora retaliated.

James shook his head. 'Actually, I'm just plain annoyed at both of us. I didn't realise I was barking up the wrong tree. I guess it's one thing to have a bit of a fling and quite another to commit; especially when you're obsessed with righting the past.'

'James –'

'Well, I wouldn't hold your breath. After all, she's city bred and her husband's a no-hoper.'

'Meg's smart, everything's going like clockwork and she deserves the opportunity to –'

He laughed and shoved his hat firmly on his head. 'You're not doing it for Meg. You're doing it for yourself and probably *him*, his memory.' He pointed a finger at her. 'Sometimes I wonder if he's not the reason you can't commit to me.'

He always was one for riling her, reason enough to keep him at arm's length. 'That's ridiculous.'

'Is it?'

'Why shouldn't she know the truth?'

'Because you're not doing it for your niece, Cora. The only thing you're doing is wrecking your own life and buggering up hers.'

'You mean I'm wrecking your life, James Campbell.'

James opened the door leading out onto the veranda. Outside a rooster raced past, wings flapping, squawking in terror. Harold was only a few feet behind, rifle in hand. 'Good to see things are running like clockwork.' Hot in pursuit came the twins, squealing with excitement, and finally Meg, dark hair flying as she called after her daughters.

'So that's Meg,' James commented. 'Well, she's a bit of a looker.'

As the rifle shot sounded and the twins cried out in unison, James slammed the door. Cora clenched her fists and expelled a hot burst of breath. She stalked the bedroom, glancing at the great tree as if it could provide answers, then she began to rummage through her dresser drawer. Eventually she found the wooden-handled mirror stuffed in her sock drawer. The glass steamed up under her breath. Satisfied, Cora tucked the mirror safely away. Outside the twins were crying. Meg's words of comfort floated in the garden, softening the angst both outside and within the homestead.

Cora lifted the stone paperweight. It was reassuring to know James was nearby, even if no one could help her. If only she wasn't so mindful of her past, so protective of her person. All her life she'd felt as if her heart were a captured bird within a wooden cage. So many times the cage door had been left tantalisingly open only to be slammed shut when least expected. James was right. It *was* her past that stopped their relationship from being all that it could be, and she couldn't escape it.

## ⇜ *Chapter 18* ⇝

# *The North West Slopes, 1965*

The place was laid out in his mind like a map. The dray-wide track Scrubber remembered was overgrown, the collection of buildings on the slight hill resembling a skeleton. On approach the bones became wind-blown bits of walls and roof. Timber and corrugated iron stretched across the area, caught in fences and trees, lying on the ground between thick stands of saplings. Scrubber knew by location whose house each pile of rubble once was, and he mumbled the name of each owner, visualising the inhabitants.

Matt Hamilton's old cottage was roofless, the narrow veranda rippled. Scrubber gave the horses their freedom and stepped into a world lost some forty years ago. Now he was here, part-way through the journey, Scrubber wondered how a mere slip of a girl could have enticed him to take this one last ride. The boards crumbled under his step: soft wood consumed by white ants, bleached by the wind and sun, ruined by time.

He tripped and fell, his hands managing to shield his face. Dog was there immediately, licking him, cajoling him, willing him to life. His old dog knew he was tired, knew that his every move was gradually becoming eroded by pain. Scrubber heaved himself from the hole in the floor and retreated to the rear of the house to sit in the sun. The view was limited to a stand of old trees, a flattened dunny and a sapling-invaded paddock. Scrubber untied the pouch at his waist and sat it on a weathered log. He faced the cracked leather square-on, and rubbed at a scabby lip.

He had been on the road some weeks now. It was time to have a bit of a yarn to his old mate. Although he wasn't one for believing in spooks it seemed a mite silly to be picking a fight in an isolated spot, even if the six-foot-tall bloke he conversed with was packed in an old tobacco pouch. He'd start real slow, he decided.

'Well, it's not the same, mate.' He gave a noise that was once a laugh. 'It's all fallen down, dilapidated, buggered.' He glanced up at the sky. 'If you were here you'd be shocked by the waste of it, by the barrenness, by . . .' He looked at the pouch. 'How you travelling then? Me, I'm not so good.'

He prised a tick from Dog's ear, squeezing the blood out of it between his fingers, then turned his attention once again to the pouch. 'I've took my time and all, I realise that. The thing is, you dying left me in a spot.' Scrubber found a lump of chewing tobacco in his pocket and crammed it into his mouth. 'I never was the smartest one in the mob.' It was difficult, this chewing and talking when a man had a hole in his neck.

The horses roamed past the flattened dunny and whinnied into the rising wind. 'I couldn't look after the girl after you and Jack Manning were gone. I had to do a runner. Anyways, in the end the kid looked after herself. So, I just wanted to say that if you were alive now I'd hope we'd still be mates. Even after everything I did to you and yours, I hope we'd still be cobbers, cause you were real good to me. And I'm real sorry that you ended up . . . well, like you are.' He spat tobacco juice into the dirt. 'But I'll be a goner myself soon, if it's any consolation, and I'd like to think that my bringing you back to your daughter like she wanted all those years ago, helps to make amends.'

Dog gave a bark. A clatter of something on iron mingled with a shifting wind that roamed the old buildings. Scrubber almost believed he could see sheep, hear voices, smell the old days. The doc said it would happen; that the pain would eventually cause him to hallucinate. Digging his fingers into a trouser pocket, he placed the shilling in the palm of his hand. With a bit of a clean the image of the ram on the 1923 coin would come up good as new. Just as well he still had it, Scrubber decided, clutching the metal in his fingers. A man needed something tangible to remind him that the old days existed.

Scrubber replaced the coin in his pocket and patted Dog on the head. 'I'm going to have myself a bit of shut-eye, Dog. Just twenty winks and then we'll be off.' Dog sat by his side, watchful, patient. Scrubber stretched his back against the wall of the cottage, as his innards complained. He too was being white-anted.

Waverly Station's great ram had appeared from behind a box tree the first week of Scrubber's arrival on the property, the week before Christmas, 1923. With the experienced stockmen away for a few days mustering in a mob of ewes, Scrubber was left in Dobbs's control. The old cook and bottle-washer gave him the guided tour of the outbuildings and sheds. Halfway between the woolshed and the ram shed, Dobbs started talking about the Gordon family of Wangallon Station. It seemed that Luke Gordon wanted some of Purcell's merino bloodline, and Purcell refused to sell him any rams.

'Why?' Scrubber asked.

'On account of the Gordons having everything else, including the biggest spread in these here parts. What they don't have though, lad, is a ram on a shiny coin.'

When Scrubber laid eyes on Waverly No. 4 he understood why Luke Gordon wanted one of Purcell's rams. He was a huge animal – broad of back with a proud, disdainful gaze, a roll of wool falling to the ground from his throat and scrolling horns. He was running with thirty of Purcell's top females in a specially fenced paddock and he clearly disliked having his territory invaded.

'This is him. Beautiful, ain't he?' Dobbs sounded love struck. 'Evans looks after him, although I don't think Waverly likes him – always snorting and striking the ground with his hoof. He doesn't mind Matt's kid though, Squib. Anyway, better Evans than me. If the ram dies on Evans's watch, well, it'll be . . .' He ran his thumb in a cutting motion across his neck.

Scrubber was dumbfounded. 'For a sheep?'

'This sheep's the national champion, lad. He's legendary and he's made Mr Purcell very high and mighty in the sheep industry, and very rich.' He tapped Scrubber on the shoulder. 'This will be about as close as you and I will ever get to something famous. Now, let's get you on that gelding and see how your riding's progressing.'

It wasn't. Firstly, it was an effort to mount and dismount thanks to his damaged ribs. Secondly, the gelding clearly didn't take to young try-hards trotting around a yard. Scrubber landed in the dirt, clutching his wrist and yelping at his jarred ribs before squeezing through the timber railings, intent on escaping from Dobbs's offer of medical ministrations. He wasn't sure how a pocketknife could help a busted bone.

He escaped to a stringybark tree, guessing he'd be run off the place within days. A one-handed man was no good to anyone. Sympathy wasn't strong in his family. Having been raised on a lifted hand and the expectation that a child could earn coin at the age of six, it was a shock to discover that now, in his early twenties, he felt a bit sorry for himself. At the rate he was going he would end up a homeless cripple.

'Are you awake?'

Scrubber blinked and opened a drowsy eye. Flies plastered the kid's face. A girl was sitting beside him, sharing the shade of the same tree. 'What do you want?' he asked, instantly awake. He looked around. There'd be a parent nearby – someone to snatch her up and holler at him to stay away. The girl poked at his busted hand. 'Get away with you.'

'Dobbs said you gone hurt yourself. That you fell off Mr Purcell's gelding.'

The calico bag by the kid's side was upended; strips of cloth, two stout splints and a flask of brandy spilled onto the dirt. He eyed the spirit hungrily. Purcell ran a dry camp.

The girl pointed at his hand. 'I can fix it.'

He grabbed at the flask and took a satisfying swig. 'Get away with yer. Yer not big enough to fix anything.'

She snatched back the brandy. 'Can so.' She replaced the stopper. 'Youse want it fixed or not?'

He guessed he did. 'You're Matt's kid, ain't you?' Gingerly he held out his hand to her and she returned the flask.

She nodded. 'My name's Squib. And you're called Scrubber on account of the fact you appeared out of the scrub. Near death, my father says.'

'Saved me life, he did. And he put in a good word for me so I'd get a job here.'

'Yeah, he's real good, my father. Now, wrap your good arm around the tree and hang on.' She pointed at the flask. 'Normally I wouldn't be saying this but you better drink that down.'

'Doctor's orders, eh?' He gulped the spirit down, his empty stomach lapping up the fiery drink. As he swallowed the last of it the girl pulled on his hand. Two definite clicks sounded. The pain was shocking. 'God's holy trousers, girl. You're frightening.'

She laughed then as if it was the most normal thing for a kid to do. Squib splinted his wrist up good and tight, binding it with strips of material. Her knots were firm and clean, the material torn with the aide of her teeth, her dark hair brushing his forearm. He hadn't been that close to a woman who didn't want something, ever.

'How'd you learn doctoring then?'

Squib gathered her things together. 'My stepmother, Abigail. Her father was an animal doctor, excepting he was self-taught, and when he killed a nob's racehorse, well, that was when he went to Come-By-Chance to be a publican. Anyway, he had real doctoring books with pictures and everything.'

'Of animals?'

'No silly, people. That's how come I can do some doctoring, like my father. We got it out of Abigail's father's books. My father can stitch. Once he put thirty stitches in a man when an axe head flew off and hit him in the leg.'

'What would your father say about this, then?' Scrubber extended his neatly bandaged wrist.

The girl put her slight hand on his shoulder, gave a crooked smile, eyes as clear as rain water. 'He'll say I've done good.'

'I owe you.'

The noise of men talking and the clip-clop of hoofs stopped their conversation.

'The men are back,' Squib announced. 'You better go.'

Scrubber watched the flurry of dust the kid left behind as she skirted the trees and ran back in the direction of her cottage.

Reluctantly he walked the half-mile to the stables. He was only a week into his new job and with a buggered wrist Scrubber worried he'd be kicked off Waverly Station. The only thing in his favour was that Matt Hamilton had recently been promoted to overseer. Dobbs reckoned Evans would have it in for Matt. The two men were pretty even when it came to ability, however Matt was the fairer of them and he had the type of personality that made a man keen to please him. A fact Evans hated. The previous overseer, a gruff southerner named Martin, had hanged himself in the woolshed after downing a quart of kerosene. Dobbs, always full of knowledge, reckoned Martin had a few kangaroos loose in the top paddock. It wasn't until the older man tapped his head that Scrubber realised what he meant. Of course the end result of the woolshed hanging was that now Matt Hamilton was the boss man.

Scrubber found his new place right at the bottom of the feed chain, although with the benefit of the dead man's boots. Even Dobbs, when dishing up his food last night, somewhat affectionately called him the scum feeder in reference to the slimy yard troughs it was now his job to clean.

At the stable entrance Scrubber met Dobbs.

'Hand's fixed, I see.' He gave a nod of approval. He turned to the five stockmen unsaddling their horses in the cavernous stables. 'Got ourselves a right quick learner we have.'

Evans undid the girth strap on his mare. 'What's a city kid doing out here, anyway?' he asked, walking past him with a saddle.

'Trying to work like the rest of youse,' Scrubber countered.

Dobbs gave a rattling cough. 'Lay off him, Evans. He's young, but keen. You were that way once.'

Evans sniffed.

'Have I told you about tonight's feed? I've enough damper to bind up a fancy city fruit-eater, and kerosene-strength billy tea.' Dobbs removed his hat and brushed his wiry hair flat with the currycomb. 'Salted mutton, fresh eggs –'

'Potatoes and damper,' Evans interrupted, making a show of inspecting his mare's shoes.

Dobbs gave his own horse a swipe with the currycomb, and with a firm pat on the rump sent the animal trotting into the paddock.

'Afternoon, Mr Purcell, sir.'

The stables went quiet.

Having not laid eyes on the man before, Scrubber stood stock still. Tall and stringy looking, with a pencil moustache and army-shine boots, Mr Purcell's three-piece suit clung to him as if it had been specially made. Purcell spoke briefly to Evans before running a well-trained eye across the gathered men. Scrubber knew immediately what it meant to be a ram poised on the brink of being culled. The squatter's eyes fell on him, a riding crop pointed in his direction. Scrubber sensed the other stockmen backing away into the shadowy recesses of the stables.

'Hamilton recommended him,' Evans volunteered.

Scrubber waited anxiously as the squatter gleaned his life story from his appearance.

'I don't take to fighting, womanising or the bottle out here. The men tell you that?'

Everyone nodded, including Scrubber.

'Good.' Purcell's gaze fell on a basket of eggs sitting atop a chaff bin. 'Bring those eggs to the main homestead, boy.'

There was a chuckle from the recesses of the stable. Purcell narrowed his eyes and then turned and walked away.

Scrubber trudged the two miles to the main homestead, his sight fixed on the shimmering corrugated-iron roof and the blindingly white walls. Purcell's homestead was set within a paling fence. Large trees bordered the raked dirt path, which led directly to a bull-nosed veranda of polished timber and curving corrugated iron overhead. There were long casement windows, curtained on the inside, a solid front door with a blackened horseshoe-shaped knocker, and chairs scattered the length of the veranda. Books were perched on one of the tables, along with a jug of something that was obviously real drinkable, for flies buzzed around a cloth protecting the contents.

'You shouldn't be here.' A young woman appeared from around the corner of the house, a basket over her arm. She plucked at it with her fingers, swayed slowly from side to side; her bare feet were tanned gold by the sun.

'I've got these.' Scrubber held out the basket of eggs.

The girl inspected them, pursing her lips. She had a pair of dusty lace-up shoes strung over one shoulder.

'I mean Purcell – Mr Purcell – said I should bring them.'

She was a plain girl, Scrubber thought, and largish, but her teeth were good.

Extending her free hand she took the basket from him. 'You're new.'

Scrubber nodded. 'Started a month or so back.'

'What do you think about the place then?' She swung the egg basket to and fro.

What Scrubber wanted to say probably wouldn't have any credit with her: that it was a disappointment to discover that even out here, in the back of beyond, he remained a have-not. Worse, he was at the bottom of twenty have-nots all vying for food and coin and a trip to town. 'Good.'

'You're a bad liar.'

Scrubber thought her canny. He liked that. 'I used to be pretty good.'

'Veronica, is there a need for you to be conversing with that stockman at the front of the homestead?'

'Mrs Purcell,' Veronica hissed before calling out, 'He dropped off some eggs, Missus.'

Dressed in ankle-length grey, Purcell's wife appeared. She was a raw-boned, wide-hipped woman with white hair and a thick string of pearls. Scrubber figured she'd blend into the landscape without them; certainly they were the only thing worth remembering about her person – they gleamed white like gull's eggs. His fingers itched at the sight of them.

'Well, move on, the both of you. We don't need loiterers here.'

They parted under the dragon's stare, although Scrubber made a point of turning to watch the girl walk around the corner of the homestead, scuffing the dirt with her bare feet, her skirt swaying slightly as she moved.

# ⚹ *Chapter 19* ⚹

# *Waverly Station, North West Slopes, 1923*

A collar of sweat itched her neck. Outside the cottage the call of an owl broke the night's silence. Squib rubbed her eyelids. Great shafts of moonlight poured through the roughly fitted timber walls, tracing a path over clothes hung on pegs; a table piled with children's Learners and devotionals; and her brother's much coveted single bed. The moon highlighted Jesus writhing on a wooden cross, a faded picture of Mary and the toes of her stepsister, a scant inch from her nose. Crawling over her sleeping sisters, Squib's foot became entangled in bedclothes and she landed with a thud on the tampered dirt floor. Despite the daily watering of the floor and a solid sweeping, the dirt clung to her sweaty legs as she shoved her hands through the armholes of her dress. Once outside on the sloping veranda, Squib brushed the sticky grains with determination. The floorboards were thick with dirt. They usually slept outside in the summer, but a howling dust storm had struck at dusk, forcing them indoors to a night of heat-wrecked sleep and midnight squabbles.

Her father was sitting on the edge of the timbered flooring, a curl of pipe smoke rising toward heaven. 'That you, Squib?' His gaze was fixed on the illuminated trees edging their world.

She sat beside him and wove her fingers between his. Matt Hamilton squeezed her thumb, once, twice. She hated her nickname, yet somehow it sounded better when her father used it.

'Your mother always liked these nights when the moon was fat with light. Me, I can never sleep.'

'Me neither. Too hot.' Her mother used to call her father 'her Matty'. Squib liked it, liked the soft sound of it. It was much better than Mr Hamilton or plain old Matt.

'Be hotter when daylight comes.' He took a swig of water from his canvas bag.

Squib could already taste the grit on her lips, could imagine the sun prickling her skin to redness. Accepting the water she took great mouthfuls of the bark-tinged liquid. It ran down her chin to wet her dress and splatter the timber flooring. She gulped, then hiccupped. Her father's heavy hand ruffled her hair.

'Everything all right with you young'uns?'

She shrugged. 'I guess.' It had been a subject of consternation between them when her widowed father took another wife. It came soon after her mother's death from a snakebite when Squib was just eight years of age. She recalled the day clearly on account of the fact that her mother had stolen money from a village store, and then admitted the theft to 'her Matty'. Instead of returning the coin they had run. That night while camped in the bush, Squib's mother was bitten.

It wasn't that Squib didn't like her new mother, it was just that she preferred her old one, the one that birthed her, loved her. The new one came with a lemon-sour daughter older than Squib, and managed to birth a new one named Beth with her father. *We're stuck with her now*, her brother Ben commented upon noticing his stepmother's bulging belly for the first time. Ben was the one who explained that things would never be the same. That their step-mother wouldn't take to them on account of their dead mother.

Inside the hut, Beth began to whimper. Her father glanced at the fat moon dropping towards the horizon as Beth let out a dog's howl of complaint. 'Come on, Squib.'

They walked the half-mile guided by moonlight, reaching Mr Purcell's stable as a breeze rustled the leaves in the surrounding trees. With her father's horse smartly saddled, they mounted up and were soon trotting off into the scrub, Squib wedged between him and the bobbing horse's neck. They rode for some time in silence. Pre-dawn teased them with a moment of coolness as a breeze picked up before gradually dropping away to the hills in the distance. Hair stuck to Squib's forehead as she accepted the reins from her father and eased the horse into a walk. The scent of dust was thick, tinged with smoke from a bush fire far to the north.

Being the Sabbath, her father was free from work. As Church was a day's ride away they were left to endure scripture readings from Abigail instead of the free time once given with a motherly kiss. It had become something of a rigmarole this Christian thing, Squib decided. Saturday night was now bath time, and the tub was dragged into the kitchen and filled with murky dam water, the surface greasy with homemade soap and water that bathed four children. This procedure was followed by de-lousing with a sharp comb, oil and lice powder and a dose of Epsom salts. At the thought of it Squib grimaced. Abigail was convinced she and Ben were the bearers of the lice infecting the household on a regular basis, and they had both been subjected to a severe hair cutting. Squib didn't bother arguing that sharing towels and beds probably didn't help. The only good thing about it being Sunday tomorrow was that Tuesday was Christmas. Their father always made them something each. Last year Ben and she had both got catapults.

They were heading back towards their cottage, which in compari-son to the Purcells' low-slung homestead looked like a shack. Squib was glad her father was now the overseer – it meant a new house. They were just waiting for the dead overseer's wife and kids to leave. Her father thought they'd have to be thrown off the place.

'Abigail doesn't really like Ben and me, you know, Father.' The horse slowed its rhythmic gait and stretched its hind legs out lazily. Her father took control of the reins.

'Sure she does.' He twitched the leather and clicked his tongue in encouragement. 'It's just a bit different for her. She's used to better things.'

'What things?' Squib looked over her shoulder at her father's creased face as the glow of dawn shadowed their progress. Things could have been worse: it might have been her father who'd died from snakebite; his body laid out on an old door while the coffin was hammered together.

'Anyway, with Mrs Purcell taking her on two afternoons a week, things will change.'

'Why can't Mrs Purcell read? Why does Abigail have to read to her?'

'It's a squatter thing, I guess. They've got more money than they know what to do with and Mrs Purcell wants the company.'

Being a squatter was something Ben aspired to. Rich people had sheep and land and paid others to work it for them. Squib waved away an insect and curled her fingers through the horse's mane. All that reading to Mrs Purcell meant she now had twice as many chores to do. Her stepsister could never be found when it came time to take the washing off the line or being nursemaid to Beth or carting in wood for the fire or drinking water. Even supper had fallen to her to prepare on the two afternoons Abigail was away. Squib didn't mind that much, except she would have liked to have known what her stepmother was doing with the money she earned.

He rubbed her shoulder, his touch light. 'Don't you get yourself all mussed up before the Bible reading. You know how she likes you all to keep clean.'

'No, Father.' Light was beginning to stream through the hills to the east of them when they arrived back at the stables. Squib gave the horse a good brush with the currycomb while her father greased his saddle, and then begged him for a piggyback.

'You're thirteen, Squib.'

She grinned all the way as she bobbed across the paddock. The cottage stood on a low rise and was flanked by a row of crooked trees on the western side and an expanse of nothingness on the east and north.

'Your older sister will be leaving at the end of the week, Squib. I've not told her but she's at the age for work. Mrs Purcell has applied to the Gordon family of Wangallon Station on her behalf and they're expecting her.'

Squib's eyes widened. 'Jane won't like that.'

Her father nodded. 'Neither will her mother. You'd best clear out when I tell them.'

Squib reckoned she would. Jane had done her best to keep an eye on both Squib and her brother, Ben, since her father remarried. If she couldn't accuse them of some minor crime on a daily basis, she'd make something up.

Half a mile away they could hear the four-year-old Beth screaming, the sound carrying towards them like a wounded animal. At the cottage her father faltered, dropped her, straightened his back with an exaggerated sigh and walked inside.

'Psst.' It was Ben, crouched at the corner of the house, a wedge of damper in his hand. 'She's blaming you for waking Beth,' he whispered as Squib trailed him out past the vegetable patch. 'Here.' He handed her a bare mouthful of bread before stuffing his with the greater portion. Squib chewed the dough hungrily, pinching her nostrils as they passed the dunny.

'Rank,' Ben commented. 'Come on.'

They quietly circumnavigated the cottage and raced each other towards the stable where Mr Purcell's young colts were already yarded for a mustering job the next day.

'Beth's been crying since you left.'

'I couldn't sleep.' Squib scrambled through the wooden railings.

Ben gave a snort. 'You never sleep.'

In the yard, Ben separated one horse from the others, direct-ing the animal into a large yard with a single thickset hitching post in the centre. 'Best of three,' he called, climbing on top of the post. Squib chased the colt directly past the post. Ben leapt for the animal's back and landed heavily in the dirt.

'Clean miss,' Squib yelled, clambering onto the post. She stood silently, balancing carefully as her brother brushed himself off and ran behind the colt, chasing the horse towards her. As the horse trotted past, Squib gave a yelp and sprang from the post. She too landed in a spray of dust on the hard ground. 'Touched him,' she called proudly. 'Your turn.'

'You're bleeding.' Ben pointed at her knees as he readied for the colt to pass. He sprang forward quickly on his second attempt and landed on the horse's back only to slip to the ground. 'Ouch.'

Squib balanced on the post and counted softly to four as the colt raced past in a flurry of dust. She leant forward, pushed off with her toes and launched herself into the air. This time her aim was straight. The horse was beneath her. Quickly flinging her leg over and grasping the colt's mane, she yelled with delight. 'I did it!'

Ben's mouth turned. 'Dumb luck.'

'Well, dumb luck's better than no luck.' She wiped at the sheen of perspiration with dirt-smeared hands and slid from the colt's back.

They mucked about in the yards until it neared Bible time. Ben looked at her from head to toe. 'She'll give you a roasting,' he warned. 'You're filthy.'

Squib figured she probably wasn't at her best. Her knees were bruised and bleeding, her dress torn, and dust seemed to be sticking with equal determination to skin, hair and clothing. Worst of all she was starving and she wasn't of a mind to be withheld a meal just because she'd wanted a bit of fun. The trough next to the iron water tank was full and it was into this she sat fully clothed. Ben's mouth gaped.

'It'll be almost dry by the time we get back.' She rubbed at the dirt on her dress, scrubbed herself and then dunked her head under the algae-slimed liquid as Ben busied himself, splashing water on his face. The sides of the trough were slippery and sludge plastered the bottom. Squib managed to get out without falling and promptly shook herself like a dog. 'Ready.' She patted her hair into order, ignoring the stinging grazes on her knees. Ben gave her a shake of his head.

The dog appeared on Monday. He was all bony rib cage and large droopy eyes, and Squib knew immediately she wanted him. She named him Dog, tied him up under one of the crooked trees on the western side of the house, gave him water and fed him scraps of bread snuck from the kitchen. At nearly fifteen years of age, Ben was taking lessons from Mr Purcell's farrier. His hands ached from belting in horse shoes. Quite often he returned to the stables at dark to be with the horses. With the heat making the air almost too dense to breathe, any stock work was completed by midday, which left the afternoon for the men to attend to yard building and fence repairs. For once Squib liked the hazy heat-filled day. There was no one around.

That first day the yellow dog wouldn't let her pat him, but by dusk he was nuzzling her arm and by midnight, when the cottage was bathed in darkness, he was lying stretched out by her side with his head on her arm, both of them gazing into each other's wide brown eyes. Squib spent the night outdoors, cool and uncramped, her timber confines exchanged for a web of stars. Tomorrow was Christmas and she dreamt of a horse she could call her very own.

From the cottage came the sound of Beth whimpering, and her father and stepmother arguing. Their voices rose and fell intermittently.

'They've got no proof, Matt,' Abigail was saying. 'Tell them to search the cottage. Ask Mr Purcell if I can speak to his wife. She'll believe me.'

'It's gone too far for that, Abigail. The necklace went missing after your last visit to the main homestead.'

'But I didn't take it. You believe me, don't you?'

'People get an itch for wanting more, Abigail. I can't blame you for wanting to better yourself. Why, my first wife –'

'Your first wife knew no better. I do.'

'It's a loose loyalty that exists out here in the bush. One man's problem is another's boon. Evans has pointed the finger and the men are beginning to take sides. There's talk that Martin didn't hang himself, that maybe I wanted the overseer's job too much.'

'Evans? That jumped-up –'

'He'll be the next overseer, Abigail.'

'But I didn't take the necklace.'

'I can't risk the authorities getting involved. I've got two kids to think about.'

'You have four, Matt.'

'Two kids that will be taken away from me if I'm not careful. You know that.'

'How a man like you ever married a woman like that –'

'She was a good woman and she didn't breed a conniving daughter. I want you to start packing. If things turn real sour, we'll have to leave and soon.'

Squib lay bug-eyed awake. The lamp went out in the cottage and a door slammed. She couldn't believe what she'd just overheard. Abigail must have stolen Mrs Purcell's pearl necklace and because of that her father would lose his job as overseer. What was worse was that now they would have to leave just in case

Mr Purcell called in the coppers. Her father always said that she and Ben would be safe on Waverly Station, that Mr Purcell would turn a blind eye to their presence just as long as the work was done on time and there wasn't any trouble. Well, now there was trouble. Big trouble.

Eventually she slept, only to awake in the dead of night. The moon hung like a teardrop above her. Dog whimpered. It was nice to have a dog, Squib thought, nice to have a –. Something made Squib sit upright. She scanned the shadows cast by the moon's glow: cottage, vegetable garden, outdoor dunny. Nothing moved. The space lived in by her family was still. Then Dog stirred and gave a low growl and she spread herself flat against the trunk of their tree.

'What is it?' Squib whispered, taking hold of his back. Again the same long, low growl.

Squib saw them then: a line of black fellas walking single file across the face of the paddock beyond. Their long, lean legs shone in the moonlight as they swished through the grass, faces turned towards a scrubby rise in the east. They carried shields and long hunting spears and walked westwards into darkness. Squib wanted to run after them, to ask where they were going, yet something held her to the earth. She finally gained the courage to take a step in their direction only to find a lone man waiting in the shadows near the creaking toilet door. He was dressed in white man's clothes. He squatted in the dirt, his knees creaking.

The hairs jumped to attention on Squib's arms and she bit her lip, tasting blood on her tongue.

'One day the land will call to you, little one, and you must listen.'

Squib was sure her own eyes were as wide and as white as the man's opposite. She twisted her arms behind her back. 'Why?'

He placed a hand on her shoulder. 'Because she needs to know we can still speak her language. When the people of the night sky come together in battle you will understand, for this will be the sign. This will herald the ending to the beginning of it all.'

⌐◇⌐

'New friend?'

Squib picked at the sleep crusting her eyes. It was daylight. The men on walkabout were gone. Crawling into a sitting position she brushed dirt from her face and hair. It was then she noticed the heavily bandaged wrist. 'His name's Dog.'

'Good choice. If I have a dog I'll be sure to call him that. Anyway, I just wanted to say thanks for what you done with my wrist.' He held it towards her, flexing the fingers. 'It's fixed and I'm off scrub cutting.'

Squib took his hand, prodded at the bones. The dog nuzzled her arm. 'It ain't, you know.'

He lowered his voice. 'Well, if I stay, Evans will throw me off the place on account of not being able to work. Your father knows that. It was him that got me the work scrub-cutting.' He gave her a wan smile. 'Look out for the Boss Cocky. He probably won't like your dog,' he said.

'Even if he's my friend?' Squib wondered how a man got such a stretched out nose.

'Don't make no difference.'

Squib swatted at a black fly. 'Suppose not if you're a dog on a sheep place, but my father says if you're a friend then you're a friend for life.'

'Maybe, I wouldn't know. I ain't never had one.'

'Hey,' Squib called after him, 'you've got a friend now.' He gave her a look like someone had just offered him two bob for nothing. Squib figured it for a smile. 'Merry Christmas,' she called after him. He answered with a wave.

⌐◇⌐

It was a whole day before Ben knew of her pet. Christmas Day passed barely noticed, with their father away all day and Abigail and Jane hunkered in the kitchen whispering. Squib kept to herself, afraid for the dog, waiting for the worst to happen. Afraid to mention her father and stepmother's argument to her brother for fear the talking of it would make things worse.

'You can't keep him,' her father said on catching sight of the stray at dusk. 'Mr Purcell doesn't allow feral dogs on the place. You know that, Squib.'

Ben kicked at the dirt. 'He doesn't have to know.'

Their father plied the soft plaited leather of his hat-band. 'He'd find out.'

'We won't tell him,' Squib argued. 'We promise.' Ben nodded in agreement.

'He'll know.' Their father's mouth thinned.

'Only if *she* tells him.' Ben gestured towards the cottage.

'Don't talk about your mother that way. She's doing her best.'

Ben sat down by the dog and scratched him between the ears. 'She's not my mother.'

Squib readied herself for an argument, for her father's belt to be loosened from his trousers. Ben was fast for a kid, but their father could run like the wind, especially when it came to giving them a hiding. Ben firmed his jaw. A pale blue blood vessel pulsed in his throat. 'I think we should be able to have a pet.'

Ben's calm words settled their father. He scratched at his crotch, gave a trademark sigh. 'Mr Purcell reckons any stray dog ends up being a sheep killer. Don't forget what ram lives here on Waverly Station.'

How could they forget? Mr Purcell handed out a shiny new shilling coin to every man and child on the property when Waverly No. 4 became famous. On that day Squib determined that she too would have such a grand animal and a dog.

Their father left them sitting under the tree, the dog flanked by his protectors. Squib knew she wouldn't have him for long.

'I hate the blasted Purcells. I wish we could leave,' Ben said, stroking the dog's back.

'And go where?' Squib asked hesitantly. Clearly her brother knew nothing of the argument.

'Anywhere, Squib, almost anywhere. If we could leave *her* behind it would be even better.' Ben's gaze was on the house again. They could hear arguing. 'I don't like her. Never have.'

'Me neither.' Squib drew a pattern in the dirt with a stick. The dog licked her arm.

She was lying in the dirt, the sun bearing down on her legs like a fire. As she drew her body beneath the tree's shade a lone shot rang out. The dog was gone. Ben appeared from around the cottage, his eyes red-rimmed.

'Father came with his rifle. I let Dog off so he could get away but he went straight over to Purcell's.' He gave his customary kick of the dirt. 'Sorry.'

In a few more years Ben's eyes would be hard like their father's. Squib blinked, jabbed a stick into the dirt. At least her father knew how to shoot. He was real careful with his rifle, holding his breath and letting it out gradually as he slowly pulled the trigger. It was an art he'd explained when he'd showed her how to shoot, like those clever people who could paint. When the second shot echoed across the slopes of the property, Squib knew her father hadn't done the killing.

'Anyway, there's some good news. We have to leave, tonight.'

'Leave?' Squib scrambled to her feet. 'Tonight?'

'We're not to say a word, just pack up real quietly.'

From inside the cottage they heard their father and Abigail arguing. Her voice was brittle, defensive, their father's wounded.

'Abigail stole Mrs Purcell's pearl necklace.'

Ben's mouth sagged. 'I know. There ain't no proof, but Dobbs told me the talk is real bad and Evans wants Father's job.'

'He's leaving because of us, Ben. If the coppers come out here and see us –'

'I know. They'll take us away. Put us in an orphanage.'

Squib studied the crooked trees and the cracked ground, and thought of the yellow dog. He'd been the only thing worth packing, although she would have liked to have seen the man with the busted wrist one more time. Scrubber was her first real friend.

## ◁ *Chapter 20* ▷

## *Mrs Bennet's Boarding House, Chatswood, 1923*

Olive felt as if she were floating above the earth. Her limbs were weightless and although she was aware of space and freedom, her mind was a blank. It was only when the incessant light kept beating against her face, when she was conscious of someone tugging at her, that she experienced a drawing back to a world she didn't want to enter.

'Olive, can you hear me? Is this right, Doctor? Surely a person can't sleep for days.'

'Considering the circumstances I would have let her rest a little more, however the police will have their statement and, although the identity of her assailant is undoubtedly Mrs Bennet's missing gardener, a report is required.'

'When can she travel?'

'Travel? My dear lad, your friend has suffered quite debilitating injuries. No, I see no chance of travel in the foreseeable future.'

Olive opened her eyes to a world gone blurry. Pillows were stuffed behind her and water offered. She drank gratefully, feeling the liquid spill over her lips to settle in the soft hollow at the base of her throat.

'Olive, how are you?' Thomas shook his head. He turned to the doctor. 'What will I tell –?'

The doctor removed the stethoscope from around his neck. 'Her family?' He pursed bulbous lips. 'Things were done.' He glanced at his patient.

'But she will recover?'

Olive heard the concern in Thomas's voice.

'Nearly fourteen hours before she was found. It's a time for a young lass to be lying in the cold.'

'But apart from the broken arm she has no bad wounds, mainly grazes. You said so yourself.'

The doctor snapped his bag shut. 'It's the wounds we can't see that are unlikely to heal, my boy.'

It was nearly three weeks since the attack. Olive was staring out the casement window at the wind-blown treetops when Mrs Bennett appeared. Without a word the older woman bustled across to the window and opened it, the gusting breeze sending a shiver across Olive's skin. She sank deeper into the sagging mattress.

'Just a minute or so of fresh air, Miss Peters. We can't have you suffering from a want of nature's own healing powers.' The woman dusted the dresser and washstand and topped up the ceramic water jug with a bucket. 'Miss Peters, I want you to know that I won't be charging you for the use of the room these past few weeks since the incident.' She wrung chapped hands. 'And please know I never knew that lad was such a criminal. You know I never would have left you in his care otherwise.'

'Mrs Bennett, please –'

'Having said that, well it's just not proper; a young woman

travelling alone. I used to say to my late husband that modern girls eventually got themselves into trouble, and you have, my dear.'

Olive closed her eyes. There was a fierce clarity about the morning.

'Well, it's done now and I daresay you've learnt your lesson. However, things can be done, to fix things if need be.'

'What do you mean fix things?' Olive blurted.

The widow gave a knowing nod. 'Well, my dear, you're my responsibility while you're under this roof and the doctor felt it only proper I understand your *situation*.'

Olive blanched. 'My situation?'

'Yes, your womanly monthlies have not come when expected.'

'That is none of your business.'

'I don't believe in it myself, however I've sent word to a Mrs Harper. Now, now, don't look so perturbed. She's quite reputable in her circles. No knitting needles or such and anyway you're too early for that with it being only weeks since the . . . the occurrence. Anyway, she'll be paying you a visit when your arm's mended. The doctor says another five or six weeks, so we'll work on that.' Mrs Bennett smoothed her long black skirt. 'Of course, it could be the shock and all that's disrupted your, well, you know what I mean. Anyway, if the worst eventuates we'll be ready, and once you're rid of the child you can be on your way and no one will be the wiser as to your folly.'

Olive sat upright. 'I don't want to see Mrs Harper.'

Mrs Bennett's face reddened. 'Don't be ridiculous, Miss Peters. You're not thinking straight. No woman in her right mind would want to birth a criminal's bastard. Besides which –' the widow lowered her voice '– such doings are quite against the letter of the law. I'm putting myself out for you, on account of feeling some measure of responsibility for your predicament. If I were you I'd be grateful. What's a bit of warm water and disinfectant after all? I daresay Mrs Harper's procedure will be a lot less uncomfortable than what you've already endured.'

Olive was dozing in the wooden rocker when Thomas arrived mid-afternoon.

'I didn't expect to see you up.' It was clear he was pleasantly surprised, for Thomas's usual non-descript expression was replaced with a smile of perfectly straight teeth.

Olive used finger and thumb to rub at the corners of her eyes. 'Thomas, it's good of you to keep coming.'

He took her hand briefly. 'I'm so sorry, Olive, about all of this.'

'Thomas, please stop apologising. You've been saying the same thing nearly every time you visit.' She forced herself to smile and gestured for him to sit on the poorly made bed. 'How is May?'

Thomas coloured. 'Quite well, thank you. She wanted to come and visit . . .'

Olive picked at the fringe on her shawl. 'Tell May I understand. My predicament is not something a young woman should be exposed to.'

'Not at all, Olive.' Thomas leant forward. 'She will come eventually, when you're up and about and have put this terrible thing behind you.'

'I'm quite a sight really, Thomas. The independent, upwardly mobile twenties girl who ran away only to be attacked and . . . and ruined.' Despite her best intentions Olive broke down.

Thomas concentrated on the wooden floorboards. 'May thought perhaps Jack should be told.' He faltered. 'I could write a letter telling him of your . . .' Again the search for an appropriate word. 'Misfortune.'

Olive thought of Jack's sister. May was giving her older brother the opportunity of breaking their engagement, something Olive could not allow to happen, not now. She tried to recall the days before the accident. It was all so hazy. She vaguely remembered that she had been going to write to Jack to tell him it was over, but she couldn't for the life of her recall if she had written the letter in the end.

Thomas interrupted her thoughts. 'I've already written to say that you were ill and that our journey north has been postponed.'

'No. No letter. Please thank May for her concern.' Olive thought of Mrs Harper. She would hardly stoop to such lower-class tactics, regardless of her dreadful predicament. 'Do tell May that I would appreciate her understanding as to my privacy. Meanwhile we will continue as planned. We will leave when my arm is quite mended.'

'The doctor said –'

'The doctor knows very little other than what he reads out of a book, Thomas.'

'Mrs Bennett said you were going to the train station the day of the attack. Why were you going there?'

'I was coming to find you.' Olive found herself lying smoothly. 'There is a Mr Worth staying here and he became suspicious.' How the circumstances of the past weeks had altered her. Now she was blatantly lying.

Thomas furrowed his brow.

'Spying,' Olive emphasised.

'I should have found lodgings more appropriate for you. When Jack finds out –'

Olive dragged herself up from the rocker to clutch at Thomas's arm. 'He must not find out. Neither you nor I will tell him.'

'But surely you can't keep such a thing from him.' Thomas ran a hand through glossy hair. 'I promised Jack on my life to watch over you, and instead –' he could barely meet her eyes '– you've been attacked and . . . and violated. And by all people it had to be Mills McCoy. Mrs Bennett tells me they still haven't tracked him down.'

'Mills McCoy? I didn't know his name. But it is of no matter.' Olive squeezed Thomas's arm. 'If I can bear it, you can bear it, Thomas. Swear to me that you will not say a word.'

'Olive, I'm –'

'Swear it!'

He gave a single, miserable nod. 'Come for me when my arm is mended and we'll make plans.' She pushed aside his attempt at an embrace, inwardly shuddering at the thought of a man touching her. 'Leave now, Thomas. I'm tired.' She closed her eyes, keeping them shut until Thomas's footfall sounded on the staircase.

All Olive wanted to do was return to her family, however if Mrs Bennett was right, if she was with child, she could not bear to bring such embarrassment upon them. Heavens, how she would miss them. She thought of her father standing by the fireplace, of her mother attentive and adoring as she poured him an evening drink. Even worse was the worry that would beset them as the days drew on, and there remained no sign of their youngest child. Were they searching for her? Had Henrietta revealed their discussion at the Queens Club that day they lunched? Did her parents believe she'd run off with her lover, or worse, Jack Manning? If so they would be so distressed by the potential scandal it was likely they'd chosen to wait and see what eventuated. Olive closed her eyes tightly to ward off the ready tears waiting for release. She had to be strong. She had to carry on. She was, after all, a victim of her own stupidity. Besides which, there was no alternative. A second violation, as insinuated by Mrs Bennett, was equally distasteful and quite simply beneath her. The brown coverlet on the bed muffled Olive's sobs. No eligible man would want her now. Her best hope lay in joining Jack and, if she really were pregnant, passing the child off as his. This then was her life's path, and Olive knew there was little alternative than to make the best of it.

## ≪ *Chapter 21* ≫

# *En Route from Waverly Station,*
# *1923*

The horse-drawn dray careered violently to one side of the dirt road, throwing Squib, Jane and Beth onto their sides. Tin plates fell from a stack and a kettle hit Beth, before rolling towards the open end of the dray. Beth began bawling immediately. Jane clutched at the precious kettle, which she had caught just in time, and proceeded to kick the spluttering four-year-old in the leg.

'Plain Jane, plain Jane,' Squib antagonised, trying to divert the girl's attention from Beth. Her stepmother turned and barked at them to all shush and hang on. Beth cowered as Jane grabbed the stacked tin plates to stop their rattling and then, manoeuvring her skinny body against their piled belongings, kicked out her feet. Her aim as usual was perfect and Squib cringed as her thigh became numb. 'Stop it,' she yelled, grasping at the splintery sides of the dray as the wooden wheels travelled back over the rough corrugations of the road to the opposite side. 'Just because youse wanted to have babies with Jimmy Winter doesn't mean you have to be nasty to us.'

The three girls looked sullenly at each other as they bounced up and down on the wooden boards. Jane scowled and folded her arms. Beth stopped crying. 'Are you having a b-baby?' she asked between hiccups.

Jane's neck twisted towards the front of the dray. Sweat stained the puddle-brown of her mother's dress, the material taut across the breadth of her back as Abigail hung on grimly to the reins. Ben turned from his seat beside his stepmother and grinned knowingly.

'No one's having a baby, silly,' Jane said to Beth who was now sucking at a length of her short dress. 'We have enough of those in this family already.'

Ben poked his tongue out in response.

Squib moved to the rear of the dray and dangled her legs over the end. Beneath her bare feet the road moved quickly. A lone magpie swooped low across the dirt track, the trees sucked away by distance until they became a blur of brown-green mingling with blue sky. She swiped at the beads of perspiration on her face and thought of the crooked trees fringing their house. She would miss riding with her father at dawn when the others were still waking. She would miss the paddocks and sheep yards and Waverly No. 4, and she would miss the overseer's house that was meant to be theirs. For a moment Squib believed that the past two days were only a dream. How else could she explain the events that had forced them to leave Waverly Station? Yet those days now lay behind them and her memories of Mr Purcell's sheep station were already unravelling in her mind like a ball of twine. The narrow track carried them onwards, tufts of dry grass and coils of dust springing up from the road's surface. The grit sprayed her bare feet like handfuls of thrown sand as Squib tilted her head towards a sky wispy with white cloud, and tried not to think of the tiredness that made her ache. She was already sick of travelling and sad that they were running away.

The whinnying of a horse quickly drew everyone's attention. Squib swivelled in the direction of the noise, pulling uncomfortably at her dress, which had caught on the wooden splinters beneath her. It was their father. Tall in the saddle he cantered towards them, straight down the middle of the road, a plume of dust tailing his approach like a guardian angel. The dappled mare slowed with the barest of pressure on the reins and he pulled level with the dray, his hat low, his face streaked with dirt.

'If we follow the creek I reckon we'll find ourselves a place to cross eventually. I'd like to be doing it before dark.' He pointed at violet clouds gathering in the east as he walked his horse beside them.

'Righto,' Abigail replied with a sniff. She'd been crying for most of their journey.

Squib scrambled across the bumpy dray to be near her father, ignoring Jane's kick. 'Where are we going, Father?' The wooden boards dug at her knees.

He slowed his horse and came level with her. 'Hopefully somewhere I can get a bit of work.' He ruffled her closely cropped hair.

*'Where are we going, Father?'* Jane mimicked softly.

'Don't annoy your father.' Abigail tucked a tendril of hair behind her ear and pushed at the straw hat shading her face. 'Can we stop for a break, please, Matt?'

Squib caught the quick look of annoyance that crossed her father's face. He gestured to a large box tree and the dray creaked to a jolting stop in the shade. Squib slid from the dray and was off and running with Jane and Ben in the direction of the creek. Soon they were splashing and kicking cool water at each other.

'Where do you think we'll end up?' Jane asked Ben when exhaustion left them standing ankle-deep in silty mud.

Ben jutted out his chin in imitation of his father and pursed his lips. 'I heard Father say last night that we'd keep going until he found work. Maybe a boundary rider, maybe a stockman. He might even go droving.'

'Droving?' Squib repeated. 'What about us?' They all stared at each other.

'Squib and Beth should stay with Mother. They're the youngest.' Jane gave Ben a rare smile. 'As the oldest we'd be more help to him.'

'You're meant to be a maid at Wangallon Station,' Squib argued. 'Father says it's time you went to work.'

'Who told you that? It's not true! My father –'

'He's not your father,' Squib yelled. 'You lost yours. He ran away when you were little and never came back.'

Jane clenched her fists and in two strides crossed the sandy dirt. Squib landed with a thud on the ground. 'He *is* my father now. You say otherwise and I'll make you sorry.'

'Me sorry? It's your mother that got us into this mess.'

'It'd be better if we all stayed together,' Ben said, trying to placate. 'At least for the moment.'

Jane, hands on her hips, looked sullenly at the water's surface. Squib brushed dirt from her dress and rose to her feet. One day she'd show Jane.

'Anyway, Father wouldn't leave us unless he had to,' Ben added. They each nodded in agreement as he kicked at the water. 'If he does leave, though, maybe we should take off. If your mother –' he looked directly at Jane '– if Abigail gets caught . . .' He swallowed, studying the older girl. 'If the worst happens, you can bet they won't let us kids stay together, alone.'

'My mother did nothing wrong,' Jane complained. 'We ran on account of you two being –'

'We wouldn't of run if it wasn't for your thieving mother.' Squib clenched her fists.

Ben flicked a stone into the sluggish water. 'We could go somewhere else and wait for Father. Set up our own place.'

'What about Beth?' Squib asked.

'We can't take a baby with us. Besides,' he reasoned, 'she's not like a real sister.'

'Thanks. What does that make me?' Jane turned briefly in the direction of the road as if checking for eavesdroppers. 'She's the only mother we've got,' she snapped.

'She's *your* mother, Jane, and Beth's. Not ours.' Ben looked to Squib for confirmation. Squib pressed her lips together. Sometimes *no speakies* was the best answer.

'Well I'm not going anywhere.' Jane crossed her thin arms across her chest. 'And you won't either, Ben Hamilton.'

Ben threw another stone into the water.

'Squib's right. If we'd stayed at Waverly you'd be keeping house as a maid by now,' Ben reminded Jane. 'Once we're settled, Father will send you away to earn your own keep. He says you're past the age for it already.'

A tangle of limbs rolled across the ground. Squib wasn't sure who would win this fight.

'Kids? C'mon.'

Squib kicked at the two bodies. 'It's Father,' she yelled, booting Jane's bare legs. Ben and Jane scrambled apart. Their father's voice had them running across fallen logs, prickly grass and side-stepping a large mounded ant hill. They arrived breathless to stand by the dray, the sun's rays quickly erasing the memory of the cool creek.

Their father sized them up briefly, ruffling Squib's lice-controlling shaggy haircut for the second time that day. 'I want you to all have a bit of bread and a swig of water and then we'll keep going.' He looked down to where Beth lay asleep in Abigail's lap. 'I don't want to be stuck on the wrong side of the creek in case that storm arrives early. There's nothing for us on this side.' He paused and checked the road in the direction they had so recently travelled. 'The sooner we're on the other side the better.'

'What's on the other side?' Ben asked.

Their father scratched his head. 'Dunno.'

'Dunno?' Ben repeated. 'We want to know, Father. It's bad enough we had to leave because of what *she* did.'

'Don't talk about your mother that way.'

Ben jammed his hands in the pockets of his shorts.

Matt Hamilton's hand struck Ben's cheek with a loud slap. Father and son judged each other, Ben holding his cheek silently as tears welled. 'Get in the dray, Ben.'

Ben ignored the command and sat heavily in the dirt.

Squib looked at the woman who had replaced her mother. Their reason for leaving Mr Purcell's had festered like a blister waiting to break and now Abigail Hamilton's actions were beginning to poison the family she'd married into. Squib wished her stepmother and Jane would walk into the bush and disappear. The stout woman was staring out towards the gathering storm clouds, her eyes red-rimmed and vacant. Jane lifted Beth from her mother's arms.

'Don't wake her,' Abigail cautioned, clambering to her feet and dusting off the dirt from her ankle-length dress. 'And I won't be talked to that way, Ben.'

Despite the edge to her voice Squib knew that Abigail Hamilton no longer wielded authority.

Ben spat in the dirt. 'A fly,' he responded in defence at his father's glare.

'I don't think you should go droving, Father,' Squib blurted. 'I think you should stay with us.'

Her father lifted Squib, sitting her gently on the rear of the dray. 'Things will work out. You'll see.' He touched her nose briefly.

'Move over,' Ben complained, spreading his legs until Squib was left with only a few feet of space. Beth curled up behind Jane and Ben, who after a series of angry kicks took ownership of separate sides of the dray. Squib found herself sitting upright at the rear, Ben's feet only an inch from her behind. Their father tied the dappled mare to the rear of the wagon, before seating himself by Abigail and taking charge of the reins. The dray trundled onto the road and Squib let her body relax into the rolling, bumpy progress of the cart. She looked to where her father and Abigail sat, their backs straight, voices silent. They hadn't always been like that; now a whole day could pass with the sun glistening between them like a third person.

As the sun began to sink in the west, Squib thought of the crooked trees, the stockman with the busted wrist, the yellow dog, and Mrs Purcell in her high-necked blouse and fancy pearl necklace. She didn't like to think about Abigail stealing the necklace as it reminded Squib of her own mother's thieving. For the second time in her short life they were on the run. Tiredness seeped through her. She wondered if she could squeeze up between Jane and Ben. Surely there was room enough for her as well. The shadows lengthened. With a sneeze and an itch of her sunburnt neck, Squib's head began to droop.

It was dark when Squib woke. She felt herself slipping and her slight fingers grappled for something firm to cling to. A beam of moonlight breaking through overhead cloud revealed the outline of a person. Slowly her stepsister's features came into view. Squib opened her mouth to call out as a jolt bumped her partially off the end of the dray. She could feel her feet dragging on the dirt. Her father's horse struck her leg, once, twice, and she frantically reached for Jane's legs, her fingers touching the older girl's toes. Jane withdrew them abruptly and, in the instant that her pleading eyes met her stepsister's, she slipped off the end of the dray into the night.

## ≼ Chapter 22 ≽

# The North West Plains, 1965

Scrubber picked the bindi-eye burr free of Dog's paw and flicked it into the grass. He had awakened in pain at daybreak and managed to down half a pannikin of lukewarm tea before setting off. Four hours on, a stretch of the legs was more of an ordeal than a man supposed. He straightened stiffly as Dog tested out his burr-pricked paw.

'Get on with you, Dog,' Scrubber hollered, scrambling atop his ride. 'No time to stop now.' Dog gave a lazy yawn and trotted on ahead. Scrubber checked the pouch at his waist. It made for some good conversation having a mate tied to your belt. You could speak when you liked about what you liked, although Scrubber refrained from antagonising the dead.

A few weeks after Scrubber's arrival at Waverly Station the Hamilton family were gone; the troublesome elder daughter, the boy, Ben, and the one called Squib, all packed up in the dead of night with an ankle-biter in tow. The demise of the Purcells began soon after, not that Scrubber cared, not after he heard the story.

They were on the boundary where the slopes spread out into the plains; ten men with axes and enough trees to keep them busy over summer. It was the last area to be tamed by Purcell, and Scrubber enjoyed seeing the land made useful, wanted to see the white gold of the north. Day after day he swung at the thick woody plants, his shoulders aching, palms splitting open and rehardening. His bandaged wrist suffered. It was a rewarding job, though. A man could see where he'd been and Purcell left wind breaks and shade lines, wise enough to the mechanisms of nature to know what both earth and animal needed to survive.

As fading light streaked the countryside, they sat around the open fire. 'Welcomed Hamilton's missus into the big house like an equal, Mrs Purcell did,' the camp-boss, Archie, informed them. He was new to their team, having arrived only that afternoon from Waverly Station. They chewed on roasted rabbit and doughy damper. 'Next thing, old Dobbs reckons a fancy necklace is missing, and a few days later the whole Hamilton family have run off,' the man continued.

Scrubber paled. 'Are you telling me –?'

'Guilty as.' Archie nodded. 'The new overseer, Evans, said Hamilton's missus stole the necklace, and –' He leant towards the fire, drawing the nine men together in confidence '– there's talk that the old overseer, Martin, who was found hanging in the woolshed, *didn't* kill himself.'

The listening men craned forward.

'Evans says Hamilton really wanted that overseeing job.' Archie brushed dirt from his patched trousers, his words hanging in the air.

'That's a lie,' Scrubber said loudly.

'How would you know?' one man asked, narrowing his eyes.

Scrubber chewed over his words. The air tensed. The men looked at him.

'If you know something, kid,' Archie warned, 'it would be best to come out with it now.'

Scrubber was beginning to feel sick. He'd only taken the scrub-cutting job because it gave him a reason to leave Waverly Station. The timing had been perfect. In a week or so he'd intended to high-tail it out of the flat country. 'It's just that Matt Hamilton practically saved my life and he got me the job with Purcell. Then his kid, Squib, fixed my wrist.' He held his hand aloft for inspection. 'I could've been a cripple. Ain't no one ever helped me the way the Hamiltons did. Not even my own family.'

The men relaxed. 'Well, kid, you never can tell with some people,' Archie replied. 'Anyway –' he sucked on a bone '– they set black trackers onto them. They finally caught up with Matt Hamilton and his missus and clapped her in gaol.'

'Was there any proof?'

'Mr Purcell's word is good enough and his missus swore it must have been Abigail Hamilton that done the thieving.' Archie rubbed his greasy hands on his shirt front. 'As for Matt Hamilton, well, they let him go. Whether that's right or wrong –' He shrugged '– who's to know? They reckon he was a right mess. One of his kids had fallen off the back of a dray while they were on the run. They never found her.'

'Her?' Scrubber swallowed. 'Was . . . was it Squib?'

'Yeah, yeah, I seem to recall Dobbs said the name was something like that.'

Scrubber found it painful to breathe. He'd barely known Squib, yet when he closed his eyes the only people he gave a thought for was the girl and the man who'd showed him kindness.

He looked at his left wrist and formed a ball with his fist. In the end freedom didn't taste so good.

# ∝ *Chapter 23* ∝

# *The North West Plains,*
# *1924*

Squib awoke to the earthy smell of rain. Splats of moisture struck her face and back, growing steadily heavier until her dress was sodden and her skin cold. Struggling into a sitting position, she touched the side of her pounding head, pressing tentatively at puffy skin. One of her eyes was shut tight. Drops of rain mixed with streaks of blood when she drew her hand away. Where was her father? Squib wondered. Why had he not got them to cover before the rain came? Gingerly she stood, then screamed, her right leg buckling in pain. A curtain of heavy rain blocked her view in every direction.

'Father? Ben?' Squib cupped her hands as she'd been taught, waves of pain shuddering through her head and leg. 'Ben? Coo-ee?' She dragged herself from the road, her toes sinking into an ooze of mud and grass. Slipping through a stand of skinny saplings she huddled beneath a thick-girthed tree. Teeth chattering, she inspected her leg, poking at it carefully. She had seen a broken leg before. A tree had fallen on a man at Waverly and he had ended up with bone poking out through his skin. The men pulled the leg straight and then set it with splints, much like she'd done for Scrubber's wrist. Squib figured that even if her leg wasn't broken all the way through it still needed attending to, however she had nothing to tie splints with even if she could find two straight branches. She prodded at her closed and swollen eye. With a sob she squeezed her good eye shut. It was then she heard the roar.

When the surge of water came Squib was lifted up in a torrent of froth and sticks. Grappling uselessly for something to hang onto, her slight body hit floating timber and tree trunks. Murky water engulfed her nose and mouth, and she was barely able to keep her chin above the water. The water kept sucking and swirling, flinging Squib continually from one obstacle to another. Eventually her good leg gave way and the air she so desperately gasped at didn't seem to want to come to her any more. She thought of her father and closed her eyes.

The tree Squib struck held her firm in its dense arms, and had she not opened her eyes and seen a glossy brown snake curled only feet away on another branch, she happily would have remained in its clutches. Instead she searched frantically for an escape, launching her body at a large piece of wood as it sailed past. She clung fiercely to the board and twirled through waterlogged trees. Then the board was knocked from underneath her and the world became dark.

'Mary, Mother of God. What have we here?'

Squib looked up into a man's face. There was a bright light behind him, a glow that haloed his face. Lifting a weak arm she wondered if she were in heaven. If so, was this man God? She thought of her father. She expected she would float away with the angels, perhaps see her dead mother.

'That's better,' God said lifting her and moving her to dry ground.

God squatted beside her. There was a dead pig on the bank. It lay on its back with two of its legs pointed skywards.

'You've got yourself a nasty bump over your eye, and your leg looks –'

Squib yelped in pain.

'Sorry.' God pushed his hat onto the back of his head. 'What's your name, then? Where did you come from?'

Squib opened her mouth to speak, but her tongue was dry and the words wouldn't come. Nothing seemed to be working. Not her legs so she could stand, nor her arms so she could wipe her eyes, which had filled with tears. Through her one good eye she saw kangaroos hop past and a short distance away an echidna ambled to the creek's edge. There were spiky-looking trees and wavering grasses and God smelt of pipe smoke and a sort of thick pungent scent that Squib knew well. 'Sheep,' she said loudly.

God sat back on his haunches and rubbed his chin. Actually, he looked a little young to be God, Squib decided. Maybe this wasn't heaven. Maybe she'd been saved.

The man gulped water from a canvas bag like her father's and swiped the back of his mouth. He was writing something down. Every few minutes he'd pause and stare off into space before returning to the book, his thumb and forefinger twirling a lock of brown hair. A pile of books sat to the left of his elbow, a slush lamp to the right. The stink of the lamp reminded Squib of home. A dirty wide-brimmed hat rested on an outstretched knee and a cracked leather boot moved occasionally across the dirt floor of the hut, piling sand from left to right. He looked at the scraped-clean plate beside her on the camp bed and pointed at it.

'You finished?' he asked quietly, putting his pencil down and wiping a hand on his trousers.

Squib nodded. The food had been good. She prodded the sturdy splint on her injured leg. It ran from the top of her thigh to her foot and was tied on with lengths of material.

'I'm no doctor, but I figured that was the best thing to do.'

Squib nodded.

'I don't know if it's actually broken or not.' He frowned. 'There wasn't any cracking sound when I pulled your leg straight. It could be a bad fracture.'

Squib nodded again.

'Do you want some more water?'

'Yes.' She watched as the water bag was lifted from a peg on the wall. Streaks of morning sun inched through the split timber walls. The slabs of wood were piled one on top of the other and were held in place with wooden stakes. It was an old hut. Squib hadn't seen anything built that way before.

He passed her the water. 'What's your name?'

She wondered how much she should tell this stranger. 'Squib.' She gulped as the liquid dribbled down her chin.

'Squib? What sort of name is that?' A fly buzzed through the open door.

'Where's my father?'

The man closed the book he'd been writing in. 'I'm Jack, Jack Manning. I left a branch there for you to lean on if you want to get up.'

Squib glanced from the solid piece of timber back to the man who'd saved her. He was thickset across the chest and tall, with brown-blond hair, smooth skin and a smile that made Squib want to smile back. She figured him to be a bit younger than Scrubber. Taking her plate he went outside to the open fire where he dished up food from a black pot. Squib watched him through the slats of the timber walls. A horse was hobbled beyond in the clearing. Grass fanned outwards in a soft pale wave to end in a tangle of man-high trees. He returned to sit at the rickety table and started shovelling food into his mouth. Squib stood carefully, her head woozy. Balancing on the makeshift crutch she limped across the dirt floor to stand a few feet from Jack, who barely looked up.

'Reckon you had a good fall, kid.' He picked at his teeth, examined a morsel of food retrieved from a rear molar, and popped it back in his mouth. 'You've been asleep for a bit.'

Tinned foodstuffs and bags of flour, sugar and tea lined the far wall along with a handful of books. Squib made out the name Ivanhoe and Sir Walter Scott on one red cloth volume; it was one of her father's favourites. In another corner were two tin chests. There was no window, just the bed and rough blankets, the table and chair and a rifle and saddle near the door. A candle crate held a quart pot and potatoes. A writhing Jesus was nailed to the split timber walls. Squib turned her nose up at this show of religion, wondering if the same bathing rules applied here. The dirt floor was patterned with boot marks, and there wasn't a single sheepskin rug to make the place a bit homey; not even a length of material to mark the space between the bed and the table. A dark leather-bound book sat squarely on the edge of the table. Squib read the gold lettering on the spine and immediately thought of her step-mother, Abigail. *Holy Bible*.

'Where's my father?' Squib pulled at her dress. The material felt stiff. 'Where's Jane and Beth and Ben and Abigail?'

Jack creased his forehead. 'I don't know. I found you by the creek when I went down to check my traps; figured you'd been washed up by the flood.' He looked at her carefully. 'There was no one else.' He fell to eating the remains of the food, keeping his head low to the plate until the tin was clean. He licked the spoon a couple of times and then took up a wooden pipe.

A flicker of pictures ran through her head. 'I fell off the dray. We were leaving the Purcells on account of –' Squib stopped, wary of sharing the truth.

Jack halted in the stuffing of the wooden pipe. 'On account of what?'

'Nothing. You know the Purcells?' she asked hopefully.

Jack shook his head. 'They're not from around here, that I know of. Which town are they close to?'

Squib shrugged. In all her time at Waverly Station she'd never been to town. The match flared against the tobacco as Jack drew on the wooden end. There was a billow of smoke and the pipe went out.

'Where were you heading with your family?' Jack lit another match and gave a series of puffs, which set him to coughing and spluttering. The tiny flecks of embers died again.

'You don't smoke much, do you?'

Jack concentrated on the pipe and gave a scowl Squib figured was just for show. The man's eyes were soft and pale in wrinkle-free skin, although his face was very brown.

'Anyway, Father said we had to cross the *crick* before the rains came.'

Jack re-lit his pipe and gave three strong puffs, his satisfaction at the glowing tobacco evident. 'I reckon he missed his opportunity.' He looked her up and down. 'If you want to wash up there's a barrel of water outside. Reckon you'll have to stay with me for a while, though, until your leg mends a bit and Adams comes. He can take you back to Stringybark Point after he finishes up his mail run.'

'Can we find my father?'

Jack looked out the door. 'Best thing to do is get you back to town with Adams.'

'Will he find my father?'

'In town they can telegraph the right people about you being . . . lost.' He pointed to a tin on the table. 'You might want to put some salve on those grazes once you've had a wash.' He glanced around the hut as if seeing their surrounds for the first time. 'You be right here.'

Squib wasn't sure if it was a question or a matter of fact, so she gave a brief nod.

'I'll be out all day.' He waved his arm vaguely. 'You might keep the fire going if you've a mind.'

After Jack left, Squib limped outside with the tin. Her injured eye still wouldn't open fully, but she could make out that miles of flat country peppered with trees surrounded the hut. She drank thirstily from a barrel and then, filling a cast-iron bucket with the red-tinged water, stripped off to wash both her clothes and herself. Once clean she quickly re-dressed and applied the sticky salve from the tin to her grazed legs and arms. There wasn't much to see at Jack's hut. It sat within a ring of tall trees and scrub, as if a giant had dropped it into the clearing. The roof was bark with saplings rested crossways to hold it down, tied on with woven grass and twine. On the coolest side of the hut was a meat safe, empty. Three distinct tracks led out from the rough building. Squib limped about very slowly. The first track only went a short distance and finished at the base of a tall tree. There were piles of mounded dirt as if someone had been digging at its base and a bit of prodding with a stick soon led Squib to discover that this was where Jack did his morning business. The second track, the one Jack took that very morning, meandered across the grassy paddock forever, so she turned homeward. The third track wove eastwards through wavering grasses, eventually narrowing until it reached the creek.

Squib came to an abrupt halt at the sight of the swiftly flowing current. On the opposite side three kangaroos were nibbling grass. Disturbed, they raised their heads, pricking their ears at her intrusion. Sunlight streamed down through the gum and box trees framing the waterway as the kangaroos hopped to a grassy hollow. Squib glanced again at the hated water, wondering how many days her father was from finding her. It didn't matter, Squib decided, she simply had to wait.

A partially skinned rabbit lay in the dirt. In the late afternoon light the carcass looked a blue-grey colour. It still had its head on and its eyes were glazed. Jack washed himself in the bucket, before wringing his shirt out and hanging it from a hook near the hut's door. He returned to squat by the fire, building it up with branches before decapitating the rabbit and roughly cutting it up. He threw it in the pot on the fire.

Squib couldn't help but stare at Jack's bare body. Muscle rippled across his stomach as he moved and a thin line of hair disappeared into the top of his trousers. Reluctantly Squib drew her gaze back to the fire. 'Where's your family?' she asked quietly. She'd slept the afternoon away, her injured leg spread out in the dirt like a wounded animal. 'Are you lost too?' She didn't like that word. It reminded her of the yellow dog, of her own misadventure.

Jack looked at the contents of the pot and frowned. 'What happened to the rest of it?'

'I ate it.'

'What do you mean?'

'I was hungry.' She was still hungry.

'What are you wanting a meal in the middle of the day for? And what am I supposed to use for beginnings for the stew?'

'Everyone eats three times a day,' Squib answered. 'Anyway, all we need is dripping and flour.'

'Well, there's no dripping. So we'll have to make do with a bit of water and salt.'

'Cabbage?'

'No. Does it look like I have a vegetable garden?'

'Well, you've got flour so we can make damper. And I saw potatoes.'

Jack glared at her. 'True enough. Guess I'll go get some then.' He walked to the hut, returning with the potatoes.

They sat in silence until the smell of cooking rabbit and dough filled the dry air. Jack dished up a plateful for each of them. The rabbit wasn't so good this time. When they'd finished, he pulled a night log across the fire, sat the pot to one side and walked wordlessly to the hut. Squib limped slowly after him to sit on the narrow camp bed, watching as he lit the slush lamp and began reading a letter. Within seconds the hut was invaded by whirring insects. They came through the open door and the ill-fitting slats, biting and buzzing until Jack appeared to sit within a blur of cream-coloured wings. With a sigh he carefully folded the letter and placed it securely inside the book.

'Is that from your family?'

'They've been delayed.' His voice was low. 'Shouldn't you go to bed?'

'When does Adam come?'

'Adams? A few days, a week, can't always be sure.'

'Why not?'

'Cause I can't.'

'But why?'

'Cause things don't run like a clock out here, Squib. That can't be your real name. What's your surname?'

Squib lifted her splinted leg onto the bed. She figured she could tell him her name. He had been good to her. 'Hamilton. Where's your family?'

'Coming.'

'From where?'

'You sure do ask some questions for a kid.' Jack blew the lamp out and walked to the door of the hut. 'Time for some shut-eye.' He closed the rickety door behind him.

Squib peered through the slats at Jack's silhouette as he stalked about the campfire in the gathering darkness. She wondered what he thought about, where his family was. He was a big man – bigger than her father – with a kindly face, except that Jack's nose was a bit crooked and his teeth were slanty at the top, like someone had pushed them all to the left. Squib nosed closer to the timber walls, her face pressed hard against gappy boards. Her breath caught in her throat. The light fell softly to highlight his muscular shoulders and broad back. Jack Manning certainly wasn't like her father or brother, or Scrubber for that matter.

At some time during the night Squib awoke with a start. A wind had blown up and it ruffled her hair through the gaps in the hut's walls. The small space was criss-crossed with light from the moon, and through a gap in the bark roof a sprinkling of stars brightened the dark sky. Night was the time to stay awake, Squib decided, for everything bad that happened in her short life had occurred when darkness covered the earth. Her mother died during the night. They had left Waverly Station during the night. And the water came for her in the night. There was something else that had occurred, something so awful and sad it clutched at her chest like a hand twisting at her heart. And then she remembered. It was Jane. Jane had watched her fall.

## ≪ Chapter 24 ≫

## Absolution Creek,
## 1965

Harold took one glance at Sam's seat on the dappled mare as he tore past him, and knew he was looking at a rooky. Although in truth his yelps for help were also a bit of a giveaway. Oh, he'd put on a good show, there was no doubt about that. It was so good that Harold didn't pay much attention to his skill level the first day. Sam had been late and so Harold had saddled the mare for him. He'd talked about a strained shoulder muscle and backache from the previous day's work in the machinery shed, and sure enough he looked a bit stiff in the saddle. He followed rather than rode abreast and seemed a bit unsure. Preoccupied with scheming to ensure his nephew ended up with a paying job, Harold had ignored him. Who'd watch a learner when you could ride with a natural – and Kendal White was a born horseman. Where he got it from, with city slickers for parents and professionals for siblings, was anyone's guess. The kid had a good seat, kept his heels in and the reins firm, and rode with the nonchalance of an old hand despite his intermittent stints in the saddle.

A week ago they'd mustered a 1500-acre paddock, moving a mob of wethers westward into country the boss had been fallowing for six months. With the flighty wethers taking off in every direction Harold hadn't been able to keep much of an eye on Sam. Meg's husband drifted in and out of the scrub, gathering a few head as he went and, whether through default or ability, was with them at the end. That was as much as Harold could expect of a city-born recruit in a big paddock. Today, however, they had mustered and yarded the rams in old set of sheep yards over the creek. The area had been well rung in the early twenties and the lack of timber meant Harold was quick to notice Sam's reluctance to be up front and centre; most of which stemmed from his inability to control his horse.

Cora hardly ever used these yards. Today's exception to the rule came in the form of Montgomery 201, a stud merino sire purchased in 1962 at the Premier Merino Show & Sale down south. Joined to the pick of Absolution's finest females he'd produced a drop worthy of a major stud, and when he started roaming a year back, preferring the eastern side of the creek, Cora let him be, as long as he did his duties and took care of his harem first. The old patriarch had been running with the flock rams for the last couple of months and Cora rarely brought him to the main yards unless necessary.

Although smoko was high on Harold's list of priorities as they headed home, Kendal was on for a gallop. He took off into the bush yelling something about getting 'the gloss off' his bay gelding, and soon the three of them were tearing through the scrub chasing a mob of pigs – at least Harold thought there were three of them.

Harold pulled on the reins and his horse breathed heavily. There was a splash of water and Kendal appeared through the trees to trot his horse alongside his uncle's, his dog, Bouncer, keeping abreast.

'Did you see Sam?'

Kendal laughed. 'Sure did. He went this way and I went that way.' He twisted his hands in opposite directions. 'I said to Knuckle here –' he patted the gelding's neck '– "Where'd he go?" Then I heard a scream.'

Harold's impatience rose. 'Kendal, where is he?'

'Beats me, Uncle Harold. He took off like a kid on red cordial. Suppose you're going to tell me it's work time.' He turned the collar up on his coat to ward off the cold southerly.

'As long as the boy comes back in one piece.'

Kendal stretched his fingers where they clenched the reins. 'He was hanging on for dear life when I saw him. Anyway, his horse will bring him home.'

'I guess.' Harold gestured over his shoulder. 'He won't last, you know. He's a green hide through and through. Heard tell up at the pub that he's a mechanic by trade. Reckon Miss Hamilton will palm him in a month or so. You gotta give it to him, though. Said he could ride a bit – a bit being the operative word. I didn't realise until today that he was so ordinary in the saddle.'

Kendal snorted back mucus and spat in the dirt. 'We'd be better off with a broom and a bucket for all the use he'll be.'

'Well, if he didn't have a liking for the bottle he might have a chance,' Harold said thoughtfully. 'At that age – well, it's a waste of a life. It's pathetic really.'

Kendal was goggle-eyed. 'You're telling me he's a drinker as well? Oh, this is too good.'

Harold laid a steadying hand on his nephew's shoulder. 'Don't count your chickens yet. There's plenty an alcoholic who can manage a job. In the meantime we'll have to give him the benefit of the doubt.'

'I give him nothing. He took my job.'

'He doesn't know that,' Harold warned.

They walked their horses towards the hayshed, bush quails rising into the air as their horses disturbed the tufted grass. Sue and Bouncer rushed after the low-flying birds, ducking and weaving with little success.

'We'll have some smoko first then we'll let the boss know we're right to go through the rams. The next job after that is to drive out to the dam in the ridge block. There's an old fence we've got to pull down; she wants the dam delved.'

'What's the point of that?' Kendal asked. 'There's a bore drain running through that corner. It should just be re-fenced.'

'You're right but we aren't giving the orders.'

'More's the pity.' Kendal grinned. 'So what about the jackeroo?' Behind them the bush was quiet. 'Why'd she do it?'

'Age, I guess.' Harold could only surmise that loneliness finally got the better of the stout-hearted spinster. He only knew of one 'serious' relationship in Cora's life since his arrival in 1952 and that was James Campbell, one-time local vet and owner of Campbell Station. It seemed to Harold that their relationship existed solely on Absolution Creek, for they ventured out as a couple only a handful of times in the four years they were together. Then just recently the relationship ended. Of course, such a liaison could never have worked, at least not while the vet's indomitable mother was alive. Eloise Campbell was not a woman who bore such dalliances. One's position in society was everything. So it was surprising that now the Campbell matriarch was gone, Cora and James couldn't get it together. Not that Harold was complaining. It was one less hurdle to jump. That was, until Meg and her brood turned up.

'When I think of the work I've done here over the years – yes Miss Hamilton, no Miss Hamilton, three bags full Miss Hamilton. Well, geez, she's just ungrateful,' Kendal said.

Harold repositioned his bum in the saddle and gave his customary click of the tongue. 'Steady on a bit, Kendal. You can lead a horse to water . . .'

'Yeah, I know, I know. I just thought this jackeroo job was a sure thing, and it's not like I can't do the work.'

'It's the money.'

Kendal took a swig from his canvas water bottle, wiping his chin clean. 'See, that's what I don't get. You told me she made a pretty good sum during the wool boom, that the place still does. So what happens to it?'

'Who knows? But she certainly doesn't spend it on the house or flash trips to Sydney. There's no David Jones department store paddock here that funds a high life. She doesn't have one.'

'So what's your next move?' Kendal flicked his reins, whistled for his dog to keep up.

Harold snorted. 'Next move? I'm buggered. While there was no family around I figured there was a chance Absolution would eventually be left to me to manage. She can't do the work that she used to on account of that leg of hers, so I figured that eventually she'd be looking for someone to leave it to. After all, what else would a single woman do with it? In time I expected you to take over the running of it.' He gave Kendal an apologetic shrug. 'Nice little spread like this . . . well, you could have had the pick of the local girls when it came to marriage and eventually I'd have a fine view of those box trees outside the cottage in my retirement. I had no idea there was any family left. Hell, I thought the Hamiltons and the Mannings were done and buried. The best I can hope for is that this current job I have continues and then I'll slowly drift into retirement. But you, my lad, well you're buggered.' Harold swatted at an unseasonal fly buzzing around his face.

'This is ridiculous. There must be something we can do,' Kendal replied.

'If it all goes to the dogs I'll become another busted-arse unemployed bushman. Ellen will love that. She's spent twelve years trying to become a member of the local Town & Country Club. She'll just love it if we have to move.'

'I don't get how Cora Hamilton can even own this land. It's just wrong.'

Harold reined his mount in. There had been speculation aplenty over the years as to whether Cora actually did own Absolution Creek. There had been talk of leasing agreements and management fees, but no one he'd ever spoken to could confirm or deny that particular piece of information. Everything else, however, had damn well happened in the main street of Stringybark Point. Harold knew those bits – the worst bits – were true. 'Don't be thinking you can change things here on Absolution Creek, Kendal,' he warned. 'Everyone for miles around knows who Cora Hamilton is and where she came from and she's been left alone.' He spurred his horse onwards.

Kendal drew abreast with his uncle. 'So are the rumours true?'

'Yes –' Harold flicked the reins and trotted onwards '– they're true.'

The hay shed was only a short ride ahead. The twenty-six-foot-high wooden roof was an obvious landmark. Over the years Harold continually pestered Cora into boarding up the northern end, the direction most of their weather came from, but she'd refused. Harold didn't agree with her argument that the oaten hay at that end was always fed out first, negating the need for the expense of protection. This year he wanted it done.

Kendal glanced over his shoulder. 'No sign of him.'

'You go ahead. Once he reaches the fence line he can only go left or right. I'll see him from here.'

A half hour later, Harold was on the verge of considering a search party when Sam appeared. Sure enough he'd followed the fence around and was now cutting across the paddock towards the homestead. Harold raised an eyebrow. The man had a bit of a sense of direction at least. They met up at the gateway leading into the homestead block.

'Everything okay?' Harold leant down, unhooked the chain from the gate post and rode through.

'Fine,' Sam replied through gritted teeth.

'Shut it, will you?'

214

'No problems.'

It was ten minutes before the lad caught up. Harold waited under the shade of an old brigalow tree; his left leg strung out across his mount's long-suffering neck. He slapped at sticky flies, cleaned saddle grease from his thumbnail and pulled at a sun scab on the back of his hand with his teeth. He had to admit, it irked him his own nephew had to take second place to an ignorant try-hard.

A hazy mirage of horse and rider finally appeared on the dirt track. Harold held few expectations regarding Sam's mustering ability, however the lad did have enough nous to follow his lead. And he'd stuck to him like the proverbial, shadowing him as they walked the rams to the yards, only moving to a wing when directed. He got points for that at least. Unfortunately, Sam Bell was a poor rider with no livestock experience, and now here it was late morning with a good day's work ahead of them. Harold was too old for this stuff.

'How're the legs?' Harold reckoned the furrow between Sam's eyes had more to do with pain than glare. The boy rode with a stick up his arse, and those washy green eyes made you feel he was accusing you of something.

Sam tried to give a nonchalant flick of the reins, but struck his mare in the eye and a second later found himself sitting in the middle of the tack-hard track.

'I should have said bum,' Harold stated solemnly, dismounting his own horse and extending a hand to pull Sam up from the ground.

Sam brushed himself down. 'Not sure what happened.'

'Save it for the women,' Harold advised remounting.

'That obvious?' Sam winced.

'I didn't pay much attention at the beginning.'

'Too busy watching the young fella, eh? He's a bit of a tear-arse.'

Harold burst out laughing, holding the mare still as Sam did one, two, three, eventually five standing leg hops to mount up.

Harold flinched, expecting Sam to go straight over and land on the impressive ants' nest on the other side. The mare whinnied in disgust.

'What's so funny?' Sam queried, pleased at last to be moving again.

'Tear-arse, you say? Didn't think he was the one yelping?'

'What's wrong with Cora's leg?' Sam asked, choosing to ignore the manager's remarks. The old man was forgetting something: he was family, not staff.

'Accident. Long time ago,' Harold replied. 'We'll be out again day after tomorrow. You better get yourself a pair of pantyhose.'

'Pantyhose? What the hell for?'

'It'll help with the chafing.' Harold nodded at Sam's look of scepticism. 'You'll see what I mean in a few hours. Everyone uses a pair in the beginning.'

'Yeah right. Anyway, what accident?'

'One that you'd know about if she wanted you to.'

'Secret, is it?' Sam gave a snort.

Harold walked his horse on ahead. 'You ask her yourself,' he called over his shoulder, 'you're family. In the meantime you better tell Cora that the rams are yarded. We'll have a quick cuppa and be ready to go in twenty.'

There were five sets of sheep yards scattered around Absolution Creek, as well as the central main yards at the woolshed. The yards they approached carried memories so raw that Cora barely used them, electing instead to walk any sheep on this eastern side of the creek across to the main yards, much to Harold's continued frustration. 'Time is money,' he would comment. Cora knew that better than anyone. Nonetheless, when she did choose to sleep she wanted her time on the pillow to be free of dreams of the past.

This year her paddock rotation had all the flock rams running on this part of the property, along with Montgomery 201 and a two-year-old drop of his son's selected as weaners. Montgomery, in the habit of wandering in an easterly direction, usually pulled up stumps from his flock of ewes once he'd considered his business concluded. Meandering across the creek a good three miles, his preferred spot was a patch of soft green grass that was bordered by gum trees. Cora couldn't blame him. It was a nice spot, with water views of the creek when there was a run down it.

Today Montgomery was standing in the middle of the large receiving yard when they drove up. Dust swirled around him as the rest of the rams ran away to bunch up in a far corner. Cora could tell Montgomery was peeved. A single strike of his hoof in the caked dirt confirmed her suspicions. Curly and Tripod, the only dogs allowed near the rams in an onlooker capacity, trailed Cora as she walked through a gate into the sheep yards. They sat obediently near the gateway, their eyes fixed on Montgomery.

'Have you got that dog of yours chained up, Kendal?' Cora checked.

'Sure thing. Bouncer's in the back of the work truck inside the sheep crate.' Kendal nudged Sam in the ribs as he walked past and said under his breath, 'Might be safer if you get up in the back too.'

'Very funny.' Sam, hands on hips, admired Montgomery as the ram turned sideways to display his full glory. He was a large-framed animal with a soft white muzzle, an apron of wool that clung to his front like ermine on a king, and large horns that scrolled impressively. 'Nice sheep.'

'You should see him when he's in full wool,' Harold replied, keeping close to the fence as he skirted Montgomery to open a gate.

'We shear the rams twice a year on account of the flies,' Cora explained as Kendal followed his uncle. 'Old Montgomery here will never quite look the way he did when he first arrived on-farm.'

217

Harold and Kendal walked around the main mob of rams, pushing them into the next yards. They avoided Montgomery, who stalked their every move.

'He's not very friendly.' Sam nodded to where Montgomery was following Kendal. The animal rushed forwards and bit the jackeroo on the back of his leg. Kendal turned and raised a leg to kick out at his attacker. Montgomery quickly backed up, dropped his head and was striking the ground again with his hoof, readying for another go.

'Don't even think about it, Kendal,' Cora warned. 'He's always been a pretty good judge of character. Well, Sam, you better go learn something.'

'What about him?' Sam pointed to Montgomery. 'Shouldn't he be with the other sheep?'

'Sure thing.' Cora nodded. 'So, do you want to be the one to get him up the drafting race?'

Sam looked at Montgomery's horns and hurdled the fence.

Kneeling in the dirt, Cora scrimmaged in her pocket and held out a piece of apple on the flat of her palm. Montgomery trotted over and nibbled delicately at the offering.

'Good boy. How are things going then?' Montgomery blinked large brown eyes and, finishing his apple, stood stock still. Cora ran her hands lightly over his frame, double-checking for any injuries or the slightest sign of fly strike. 'You're good to go. Not sure how your offspring will do, though. Not all of them will be up to the task of following in your footsteps.' Montgomery snuffled for more apple, nudging Cora in the thigh before tailing her to the gate. Curly and Tripod padded quietly aside as the ram lumbered out into the paddock.

'Look after yourself, Montgomery.' The old bugger cost Cora a fortune in '62, but there was no doubting the benefit he'd given the flock. This year's wethers carried Montgomery's larger frame genetics and as proof had cut nearly five per cent more wool compared to last year.

'Are you ready, Cora?' Harold called from the drafting race.

Kendal and Sam were on either side of the timber railings as Cora took up position under the bark-covered shelter, which ran the length of the narrow race. With instructions to her two youngest crew members to watch for any rams who attempted to leap over the railings, Cora went through the young rams carefully. Montgomery's drop were boxed with the rest of Absolution's flock rams and she made certain they were all packed two abreast within the narrow race for ease of inspection and to prevent injury. In the past plenty an aggravated ram had jumped over or upwards to knock down an unsuspecting stockman.

Cora had selected twenty young rams originally, giving them time to grow out to assess their potential as future sires. Running her hand down each of their backs, she parted their wool carefully on the shoulder, back and side, mindful not to pull at the wool and therefore the sensitive skin beneath. After an inspection of staple length and colour she then ran her palm over the opening, ensuring the wool closed up properly. A check of their body confirmation and teeth came next. Harold stuck beside her like glue, a blue raddle stick in hand that he used to dab on the muzzle of any ram that didn't make the cut.

'He's a bit small,' Harold commented.

'There's nothing wrong with him.' In spite of the cold breeze Cora wiped perspiration from her brow. 'We'll leave him in with the pick.'

Harold let out a barely disguised sigh.

They were just nearing the end of the race when a four-year-old reared upwards. Cora backed off quickly.

Harold had the raddle out. 'He got me last year.'

'Laid him out flat in the dirt he did.' Kendal gave a low whistle. 'Like a dropped bag of flour.'

'Thanks for that, Kendal. I don't think we need details,' Cora reprimanded.

'Bet you ain't seen nothing like this before, Sam.' Kendal lit a cigarette. 'That one looks blown.' He pointed to a ram stained along the flanks. 'Have a look.'

Sam walked forward, deftly jumping over Kendal's outstretched boot. 'Nice try.'

'Nothing's blown here.' Cora straightened her back. 'And you forget, Kendal, you're from the city too.'

By the time they finished going through the mob there were only six young rams that Cora was happy with. 'Well, let's draft the pick into this yard and then we'll double-check their confirmation.'

'Whatever you say.' Harold opened the drafting gate at the opposite end, switching the two-way gate from left to right as he speared the culls into one yard and the remainder into another. Out of nowhere, Kendal's dog Bouncer flew over and into the race. The kelpie went berserk, biting and barking as if his very life were under threat.

'Get out of it!' Cora yelled, trying to grab the barking dog.

Kendal rushed forward yelling obscenities, as Harold secured the gate. Curly and Tripod arrived to stand by their mistress's side, barking in solidarity. The rams buckled backwards and three jumped the railings and immediately boxed themselves with the culled mob. Another struck Cora in the shoulder as he leapt skywards, collecting Harold as well. Both of them ended up on their backs in the dirt.

'Cora, can you hear me . . .?'

*Sunlight filtered down through the bark roof caressing the papery wood worn soft by the elements. Jack was balanced on the railings, hammering a lifted piece of bark back into place. He turned towards her, his hand reaching for hers. Cora lifted her fingertips towards him, strained with all her might to close the distance between them.*

*A gust of wind blew up, turning the yards hazy with twirling dust. The draft blew Jack's hat up into the heavens, then it was tumbling over and over, across the earth's crust . . . 'What would I do without you?' he called after her as Cora chased the spinning hat. 'What would I do?'*

'Cora?'

She woke to Harold kneeling by her side.

'I'm fine.' Accepting his hand, she got to her feet, her head reeling.

'You okay?'

Cora felt her shoulder. 'Jarred, that's all. But you're bleeding.'

Harold touched his forehead. 'Flesh wound, I'll survive.'

They brushed their clothes free of dirt and then turned towards Kendal, who was chasing his dog across the paddock in the opposite direction to Montgomery. Sam meanwhile was walking the boxed rams back around to the penning-up yard so they could be re-drafted.

'That's what I'm meant to be doing, yes?' Sam checked, a worried expression on his face.

'Yeah, you're right, mate,' Harold answered.

'One of them's bleeding,' Sam yelled from three yards away. 'Back leg.'

'We'll cart the culls home and they can run in the house paddock,' Cora told Harold, walking back towards Sam, her mind fighting an image so real she could have reached out and touched Jack again. Joining Sam in the yard she scanned the mob as Harold rushed in and, grabbing the injured ram, flipped the animal over onto his back.

'Well go on, Sam,' Cora ordered, 'give him a hand.' She inspected the wound as the two men held the animal steady. The ram was ripped near its backside. 'He'll have to be taken home and dressed.' She didn't like the sheep's chances. Rams were proud animals with a bad tendency to end up dead under a tree even with blanket and bottle care. Curly and Tripod slunk under the railings to sit at Cora's feet. 'You might want to have a word with Kendal,' she suggested to Harold as they set the ram free. 'There's no place for a dog like that on a sheep run.'

'He's never done it before.'

'Makes no difference. The dog has to go.' Cora rubbed at her shoulder, her thoughts going back to another dog, a yellow one, on Waverly Station. 'Will you be right?'

'Yeah, no worries. We'll finish up.'

Cora felt both the men watching as she walked back to the ute. While her shoulder was sore, her back and hip were also suffering the repercussions of being slammed into hard ground.

'Is she okay?' Sam asked.

'Tough as nails, Cora Hamilton,' Harold replied gruffly.

Cora gave a grimace and opened the utility door. Curly and Tripod were inside in a flash, fighting over the prime position next to the passenger window. Ignoring their antics she delved through the mess on the dashboard. Notebooks, a busted wool bale stencil and spent cartridge rounds cluttered the surface. Eventually she located the emergency box of Bex powders. 'Thank heavens.' She downed the powders with a swig of rainwater from a bottle and leant back against the cracked upholstery. In the swirl of yard dust mushrooming skywards, Cora envisioned Jack Manning, saw him standing in the yards, perspiration mixing with dirt on his tanned face, his grin lighting up the longest day. Sometimes it was pretty hardgoing being tough as nails.

## ❈ Chapter 25 ❂

## Absolution Creek, 1924

Every day at dawn Jack rode out to check on his sheep. By late morning he would be back, cutting scrub in a circle leading out from the rear of the hut, piling and burning it as he went. He hoped to have a substantial area cleared and ready for the spring rains. Sweet green grass was a high priority for his fledgling flock. Squib followed Jack about slowly, helping to stack branches and swish any sneaky tongues of flame escaping into the grass. The heat and smoke from the fire stung her eyes, especially her injured right eye. It was now open but was fuzzy to look through, and weeped as if it belonged to a sick person. Jack had told her that she'd had a cut near her eye the day he'd found her and Squib could feel a slight indent beneath the skin. Her injured leg complained continually. She had two sturdy sticks to lean on now, however she was always tired. Her body compensated for the injured side and she walked leaning one way to take the weight off her still-splinted leg. Jack and she rarely spoke, although he showed her how best to light piles.

'Walk around until you feel the wind on your face, then make a hollow at the base of it. Add some dry leaves and twigs. See?' He hollowed an area and made a nest of grass and twigs and then, with a burning branch from one pile, lit the new one. 'Can you do that?'

'Of course.' She gritted her teeth as she circled the next pile and then, finding the wind's direction, carefully made a nest. The lighting of it proved more difficult. The splint on her leg prevented her from bending over so she slid to the ground.

'Blow on it. A fire needs a bit of fanning. Didn't your father teach you anything?'

The question hung between them. Squib wondered how many days a woman had to put up with a man's mood. 'He told me there's no need to be grumpy.' The fire caught quickly, crackling loudly as it wove through branches and leaves. When her father was in a bad mood he was like Jack: not wanting to talk to anyone, and only remembering half of what you told him. Her real mother once said that when a man grew sullen and cranky a woman had to let him alone; let the problem work out of his skin. Squib reckoned she'd have to do the same with Jack Manning.

Flecks of charcoal dirtied the creases around Jack's eyes. 'What's the place you're from like?'

Squib crawled backwards from the fire and drew a rough map in the dirt. 'There are hills to the east of us, a big river and lots of paddocks fanning out like this.' She drew a myriad of box shapes. 'Mr Purcell grew sheep. Ain't lots of trees like here. Father says they were rung years ago, although he still sends men out scrub-cutting near the slopes.'

'You can't possibly remember all those paddocks.'

'Why not?' Squib looked at the map; it was pretty good. 'Maybe the ridge paddock is more square.' Squib straightened the line with her finger and sat back to study her handiwork.

Jack glanced from the map to the girl and back again. 'You know anything about sheep?'

Squib knew from experience it was best not to be too capable else you'd soon be working like a dog. She crossed her fingers behind her back. 'Nope.'

Jack's almost hopeful expression sunk to disinterest. Soon he was back swinging an axe and piling up scrub. Squib would have liked to have told Jack about Mr Purcell's sheep and about Waverly No. 4 and the shilling coin, but she figured there would be time enough for that. Besides, he had to be in a better mood first, otherwise it would be just like her mother said: he wouldn't remember anything.

Around mid-afternoon every afternoon, when the flies were settling on backs and faces, Jack read for a few hours before heading to the creek. The book he read was the Bible and Squib sure wasn't showing interest in that, not after Abigail's attempts at *churchifying* them. Instead she too took refuge from the day's heat inside the hut, resting her leg and eye by sleeping during the long afternoons. By the time the sun was weaving its way through the trees, boredom usually set in and Squib took to trailing Jack to the creek. He reminded Squib of Ben: half-daydreaming and doing boys' stuff; including her only when he needed help.

Squib hid behind a tree while Jack set his traps and threw in a line. She watched as he settled beneath a low-hanging branch. He perched himself on his fishing log, a line in one hand, a book in the other.

'You don't have to hide up there.'

Squib pressed her lips together. She'd been as quiet as a mouse. 'I don't like the water.' She moved to sit five feet further down the bank, spitting on her ankle where a stick had grazed it and then throwing a branch into the water. A ripple formed across the surface.

'Squib. Don't.'

Squib thought of the times she'd fought to be heard amidst the clamour of her own family and wondered if Jack's family were like him. Maybe they didn't speak much either, except in short bursts.

'Hot doggedy.' Jack gave a toothy smile as he landed a fat yellow belly.

'It's a good one,' Squib agreed as Jack grasped the thrashing fish, cut its head off and split him clean down the middle. 'Yuk!' she exclaimed as the guts spilled out onto the sand.

'You say that now,' Jack commented, running a knife blade against the silvery skin, 'but wait till you've tasted it.' Scales glistened on the hairs of Jack's hand as he washed the fish clean in the creek. 'Wrap it in that piece of wet calico.' He passed the fish to Squib, who fumbled with her crutches and dropped it in the dirt.

'Squib!'

'No need to get crotchety.' Squib wrapped the fish securely in the wet cloth, smiling at Jack. He'd already turned his back, concentrating on his fishing.

'Jack?'

'Hmm?'

'I can't remember what my father looks like anymore.'

Jack's hand twitched. He was playing tug-o-war with another fish. 'Me neither.'

The box tree dappled the water with sunlight, as Squib rested her hand lightly on Jack's shoulder for balance. There were so many questions sitting unasked in her head, like a dusty shelf spilling over with piled-up objects. Where was Jack's father, for instance, and how come Jack hadn't mentioned him before? And why was he out here all alone? She kept staring up into the leaves, her hand on his shoulder, comforted by the knowledge that Jack Manning wasn't grumpy at her. Like Squib he was just sad.

When Jack caught the next fish it flapped and splashed its way from the creek, spraying them in an arc of water before landing with a thud in the sand. They both squatted back on their feet, and looked at the large fish glistening on the bank. Their eyes met across their dinner.

'You hungry?' Jack gutted the fish quickly, stowing it in the damp calico. Before Squib could answer, her stomach rumbled. Jack burst out laughing.

Squib was prodding at one of the smouldering heaps the morning Adams arrived. The smoke spiralled up around her as she flicked at a lady beetle, coercing it to safety. The gruff coo-ee echoed above the crackle of the fire, and at the sound of the unknown voice Squib ducked behind the heap. Jack gave an answering yell and was quick to leave his cutting and walk to where the man tethered his horses to a hollow tree stump. The stranger was shorter than Jack, with a black beard reaching to his chest and a thick-legged stride. As the men disappeared into the hut Squib limped as quickly as she could past two pack horses, their saddle bags bulging, to the rear of the hut where she slid down against the timber walls in the hope of eavesdropping.

'Appeared like some wraith in the mud of the creek after the flood,' Jack explained. 'Nearly scared the ghost out of me she did. Most of her hair had been shorn off and I thought it was a boy until I saw the dress; she even called me God. I thought she was done for.'

'Well, that's the strangest story I've heard tell.' The man's voice was scratchy and slow.

'I'd say her folks reckon she would have drowned.' Jack cleared his throat. 'The kid thinks her father will be looking for her. But he would have given up by now.'

Squib clenched her hand over her mouth.

'Depends,' the gruff man answered.

'She says she fell off the back of a wagon.'

'Hmm, she probably did. Either that or she was pushed.'

Squib squished her nose against the timber. Adams had a perfectly round face and a pink tongue that darted out of the furry blackness, like a small animal.

'She's got a problem with one eye. The way she looks at me sometimes I don't think she can see out of it clearly.' Jack got a bottle and poured a splash of something into two glasses Squib had not seen before. She figured they were Jack's special things from the piled-up goods and trunk against the wall. 'It looks to me like she was either kicked by a horse when she fell from the dray or it ran over her.' Jack took a sip of his drink. 'I put a splint on her leg. I'm no doctor but by the way the kid yelped when I first examined it I reckon it's either fractured or broken, or both.'

'Well, you've done your best. Who knows how far she travelled downstream, Jack. Did you ask her what the country looked like where she comes from? If it was flat or hilly?' Adams took a good slug of the dark liquid.

'Hilly. She mentioned people by the name of Purcell.' Jack sipped his own drink.

Squib thought his voice sounded hopeful. She pressed her ear against the timber.

'Purcell, Purcell. Seems familiar.' The sound of coarse scratching was loud in the hut. Adams's fingers disappeared into his beard. 'Course there are the Waverly Station Purcells. You know, the ones that own that ram on the shilling coin. But I can't imagine she'd be from there. Anyway, those Purcells run a tidy show from what I hear and they wouldn't be bothered with the likes of some waif after her family had done left.'

Unfortunately Squib knew Adams was right. The Purcells weren't any good to her now.

'It's not like she's gentry,' Jack added.

Adams slurped from the glass. 'I reckon you're right, Jack.

The parents would think she'd drowned or some such.' He gave a throaty cough. 'She'd be an orphan then. What age is she?'

Jack hesitated. 'Maybe twelve, thirteen.'

'Nearly fourteen,' Squib mouthed, tears stinging her sore eye.

'I was hoping you'd take her back to Stringybark Point and telegraph the right people. Maybe one of the town women would take her in while the authorities tried to find her kin; one of the publicans?'

'Maybe.' Adams didn't sound convinced. 'Don't go much on them women in them pubs. Oh, they're good for a banging and a bit of information when a man needs to know the happenings about him, otherwise . . . I suppose I could ask Lorraine. I'm a bit on and off with her.'

'Well, she can't stay here with me.'

'I reckon they'll pack her off to some orphanage in Sydney. That's the place for a kid like that. Eventually they'll put her out to work and then she'll have to fend for herself. When's your woman and brother arriving?'

The breath left Squib's throat in a tight squeeze.

Jack gazed about the sparse cottage. 'My brother wrote to say Olive had fallen ill, but she's recovering well. As it turns out I've only managed the foundations on the house so I'll be pleased when I have some help. I can't manage it what with looking after the sheep and clearing country as well.'

'They've been slow to arrive,' Adams pried. 'I'm guessing it takes a bit to coerce a woman out here. Anyway, I can't understand why you don't move into the homestead over the creek.'

Jack swatted at a fly. 'I thought Olive would like a brand new house, not some old wreck. She's used to better.'

Adams looked about the dingy interior of the hut. 'The girl could be helpful, you know, especially out here, and you with a city-bred woman.'

'A man gets used to being alone, and with a girl and all, well it's not right. She's of an age where –'

Adams winked. 'Got an inkling for her, eh, Jack? Nothing wrong with that. I meself have taken to a bit of young skirt on occasion. Me own brother married a fourteen-year-old. They're good breeders – young and strong – and before a man knows it he's got a ready-made work force. Worth considering.'

Squib's good eye widened.

Jack put the cork in the bottle. Adams wet his lips and drained his glass. 'I just don't think Olive would take to her. It'll be hard enough for her to get used to being away from Sydney. She wasn't born to the likes of this, and then to be lumped with a lost girl . . . Well, I just don't want to make things more difficult for her.'

Adams placed his glass on the table. 'Tell you what. Once I've finished my run I'll swing by and pick her up in a month or so. You never know, if a kid can make themselves a bit useful it's a different story.'

'No sooner?'

Squib thought about the afternoon at the creek. Weren't they friends?

'I've got myself a returned soldier who took up with a full blood a few years back. They tell me the fella's got a few loose in the top paddock, but a man can't be worrying about a fella's mentality when there's a job to be done.'

Jack took a swig of water and offered the canvas bag to Adams. 'What's the job?'

'Two half-caste children.' Adams sloshed water down his throat, beard and shirt. The liquid sparkled in the dark fuzz of his face. 'We can't have this sort of cohabiting going on, Jack. Them half-castes will be sent somewhere to be looked after, maybe even a good white person's home so they can be reared proper.'

Adams left after a drink of tea and a bit of damper. He had a half-day's ride to the next property, and told Jack that if he timed things right a bed and a feed were provided. Squib was pleased to see him leave. She didn't like the way he looked about the outside of Jack's hut as if he were visiting Mr Purcell's chook pen.

'A man gets a hankering for something different now and then that he hasn't had to kill with his own hand.' Jack poured tea from a spluttering billy into a tin pannikin. The camp fire glowed hot and bright. They sat apart from it, chewing on stringy salted mutton delivered by Adams, along with fried potatoes and johnnycakes made by Squib.

'How'd you know how to do that?' Jack blew on the little damper cakes, which were sweet and soft.

'I know how to do a lot of things.' Finishing her mouthful, Squib took a sip of the tea. As usual it was overbrewed and too strong. 'I don't want to go to an orphanage. I want to stay here.'

Jack wrapped the joint of mutton up in a swathe of calico. 'You been sticky-beaking?'

'If I go my father won't find me.' The tears were running down her cheeks, regardless of inclination.

'Well, you've already been here for a few weeks, Squib. He hasn't found you yet.' Slurping his tea, Jack kicked the ends of a log into the crackling flames.

'And I d-don't want to l-live with whores.'

'Well you can't stay here,' Jack said softly. 'And there's no point getting upset.'

'Why not? Why can't I stay?'

'Because it's not proper. You should be at school or something.' Jack scraped his plate and tossed the contents of the pannikin on the fire, the liquid sizzling.

Squib poked at her food. 'I've been schooled. I had my learners. I know how to write and read. Anyway, maybe your wife would want me.' She began undoing the splints on her leg.

231

Jack looked up from his book. 'You don't want to stay here, Squib. I can't look after you. Hell, I can barely care for myself. Hey, don't undo that!'

'My leg's itchy. Anyway, if you build a house with a fireplace I can cook on that. I can cook corn meat, mutton, pig and rabbit.'

'You should be in a town with other kids your own age.'

'If you got a copper I could do your washing.'

'Maybe if you were in a town your father would have a better chance of finding you.'

'Do you believe that, Jack?' Frowning, Squib untied the last strip of material from her injured leg. It looked paler and smaller compared to her other one, as if shrunk from lack of use.

Jack began stuffing his pipe. 'Of course.'

She looked at him doubtfully, whipped the pipe from his hands and began packing it as her father had taught her. 'I was washed down the *crick*. If I was washed down the *crick* then my father will ride along the *crick* until he finds me.'

'How do you know that?'

Squib fiddled with the hem of her dress. There were two new holes in the skirt and a worn patch in the back of it, which she could see when she dunked it in the wash barrel and held it up to the light. 'I can cook and clean and look after babies. I looked after Beth when she was just a wee thing.'

'How's your leg?' Jack took his pipe and lit it with a glowing twig from the embers. The tobacco flared nicely.

'Fine!' Squib wiggled her toes. Her leg felt stiff. She stood shakily, only using one crutch for support. Gingerly she placed her weight evenly across both her legs. The pain was gone to be replaced with a dull ache.

'I left a bit of material out with a needle and thread. They're sitting on the tin trunk. I thought maybe you could patch your dress.'

Squib gritted her teeth and began walking slowly towards the hut to fetch the sewing things. 'I'll sleep out here.'

There was no moon – only the whirr of insects and the tang of smoke from the smouldering scrub to keep her company. Cocooned beside the fire, Squib stitched material across the holes in her dress as she imagined playing blind man's bluff with Ben or skylarking down at the stables. Even his face was fading. It was as if being swept down the creek had gradually washed away all memory of her family. Squib tried not to think of them. She tried not to cry. She knew Jack wouldn't like her to cry. He'd think she was a baby, and he and Adams already thought she was just a kid. A kid nobody wanted. A kid who was lost. A kid who would never be found by her father. As Squib's eyes filled with tears the myriad stars blurred together until a sea of whiteness danced before her. She dreamt of running away, but the dream ended in a strange land where her days were spent tearing at green shoots of grass with her teeth, of fighting with the kangaroos for a soft hollow at night, of ending up a pile of sun-shrunk bones.

The next morning Squib washed her face in the water barrel. Her eye was better now but it still didn't like daylight much, and only stopped weeping when the sun sank to the other side of the world. There was no chopping noise coming from the scrub; no smoky scent winding itself towards her on the wind; no Jack. A pile of horse manure, still warm when Squib held her hand over it, marked the track eastwards and she set off into the path of the rising sun. She could move a lot faster with two crutches, and with her leg freed of the splint she managed a half-hop, half-step which was almost a slow run. Soon she was travelling through a paddock scattered with timber and knee-high grass, the butts of the plants tinged the palest green. Her leg quickly began to ache from the exertion, yet the rush of adrenalin spurred her onwards. Bush quail scampered across her path. Off towards the south-east an ambling horse and rider disappeared into the scrubby horizon. Squib, eager to catch up, placed a little more weight on her injured leg.

Weaving through a clump of trees she slowed, listening as Jack's horse whinnied a few hundred yards away. Her leg ached, sweat dripped from her face and her feet were sore. When she looked again in Jack's direction he was nowhere to be seen. Disconcerted and a little bewildered as to where she actually was, Squib sat heavily on the ground. There was a soft rustle of grass, the squeak of leather. Jack appeared, leading his horse by the reins.

'I was wondering how far you'd get. Pretty impressive, kid. C'mon. Hop up. Old mate will give you a lift. We're only about half a mile from the yards.'

Squib flew up onto the saddle, dragging her leg over the horse's back, and waited for Jack to hand up her dropped crutches. He was still staring when she held out her hands for the reins.

'I didn't know you could ride.' He kept the reins tight in his hand.

'You never asked. Besides, everyone can ride.'

Jack lifted a bemused eyebrow. 'I see you didn't waste any time on repairing your clothes.'

'Well, I'm handy to have around. This horse is pretty old.' Squib patted the animal's neck. 'You can give me the reins.' Jack wrapped the leather about his hand more securely.

From a distance the sheep yards appeared small yet well shaded. Two large box trees towered over the largest yards while a pretty pepper tree provided shade for the business end of the drafting race. They were pretty much the worst set of yards Squib had laid eyes on, and she'd seen plenty at the Purcells'.

'What do you think?' Jack led her on horseback through a series of yards towards the drafting race. It was a narrow affair with one side collapsing inwards, so that any self-respecting horny ram would baulk immediately and either go backwards or over the railings – any direction except straight ahead. Across the race two yards were full of sheep. The animals stood to attention, heads erect, the leaders stamping their hooves in disapproval. Warning puffs of dirt rose a few inches above the ground with each movement. Squib automatically picked out scrabble holes, where a canny ewe could escape, and broken railings. She noticed many of the gates were affixed with twine. Although Jack was obviously proud, Squib reckoned her father would say the yards weren't worth a spit.

'Are those sheep meant to be out there?' She pointed to where sixty or so stragglers were feeding into the wind.

'Jesus, Mary and Joseph,' Jack muttered, bashing his hat on his leg before sticking it firmly back on his head. 'I've got 2000 of these ewes. I purchased them joined at the saleyard, and do you think I can find them all now? How am I gonna keep a handle on the flies?'

'You open the gate, Jack, and I'll ride around the back of them.'

'They'll take off.'

'Not if we're quick.' Squib grabbed the reins from Jack and steered the horse around the yards, circumnavigating the escapees just as Jack reached the yard closest to them. He dragged the gate open, ducking around the opposite side of the escaped mob. It took time, but eventually the mob caught sight of their compatriots inside the yards and with a little cajoling they raced towards them, jumping into the air as they passed through the gate.

'Thanks.' Jack walked on ahead of her. 'I thought you didn't know about sheep.'

Back in the yards, Squib slid from the horse's back. Jack passed her the crutches. 'Where's the shearing shed?' she asked, ignoring his query.

'On the other side of the creek.' He hurdled a timber fence and began carrying fire wood from a pile back to the yard adjoining the race. Squib met him at the fence, shaking her head doubtfully. 'I reckon we're going to be busy come shearing time then if it's just you and me doing the mustering. Is the shed far away? Is it big?'

Jack dumped the wood on the ground. 'Big enough.'

He wasn't going to need much of a shed with 2000 head, Squib decided. But then she figured you had to start somewhere. It might take Jack a while but he had land and sheep; one day he'd also have a thirty-stand shed with lanolin-smooth boards, large wool tables and sprawling yards that practically ate sheep up and spat them out naked the other end.

'I need to make a fire to –'

'To boil up the bluestone?' Squib arranged the wood in a pile. 'You haven't been here long, have you, Jack?'

Jack piled the wood, scrunching bark, twigs and a handful of dry leaves into a protected hollow. His match flared and, with much cupping of hands across the weak flame and puffs of air, gradually a pale yellow flicker snuck across the dry tinder. They watched the growing fire in silence until it was ready for the old copper that lay upturned under the pepper tree. Jack sat it in the fire, adding water to it from a couple of empty ceramic rum flagons he'd filled from the creek over the preceding days.

'Is your family from the bush, Jack?'

He poked at the fire. 'Sydney.'

'Syd-e-ney? Where's Syd-e-ney?'

'It's south of here – a big city with a beautiful harbour that splits it in half. Well, not for long. They're going to build a bridge that will unite the north side with the south.' Unwrapping a block of bluestone he dropped it into the simmering water. 'You know what a harbour is, don't you?'

'Of course, silly.'

Jack proceeded to push the sheep through three yards until they reached the area that fed into the drafting race. Clouds of dust billowed up from the trampling hoofs. The dirt stung Squib's eyes and throat and settled on her sweaty skin. The ewes baulked at the narrower pen, and despite Jack's best efforts he was soon cursing their stubbornness. Squib left the fire and walked slowly in the opposite direction to the ewes, her movement quickly spurring the sheep forwards. Jack glanced at her but said nothing.

They spent a good part of the day checking the ewes for flystrike. They filled the race and inspected each animal before turning them out the opposite end to escape to the grassy paddock beyond. The slightest discolouration of wool or dampness was double-checked by Jack's probing fingers and then swabbed with the bluestone. Ten ewes were badly struck across their backs. Flies had already nested in the thick wool staple leaving a nest of maggots to eat away at soft flesh. Jack cut away at the worst areas with a pair of sharp shears, removing the matted wool so that the bluestone could be applied directly to the wound.

'Shear it all the way back, Jack, until you've a ring of clean, dry wool around the wound.'

Jack looked up from the matted stench of maggoty wool. 'Would you like to do it?'

Squib squashed the wiggling pale maggots with a stick as they fell to the ground. 'My wrists aren't strong enough.'

By the time their shadows were long on the ground the job was finished. Jack kicked the copper over, the blue water extinguishing the fire. Squib swallowed great gulps of water from the canvas bag, her hands tinged blue, her hair dark and matted with dust. When Jack mounted up, he pulled her up behind him. Her leg ached with exhaustion, however Squib wasn't telling Jack.

Close to the hut Jack detoured through the trees. They moved through the lengthening shadows silently, the air growing fresher as the trees grew denser. Eventually they arrived at a small clearing further along the creek. It was here Jack had laid the foundations and framework for his four-roomed home. Two lines in the dirt marked an eventual covered walkway, which he intended to lead to a kitchen. 'In case of fire,' he explained as he led Squib around the perimeter of the building. 'These wooden uprights are four feet in the dirt, packed solid.' Taking hold of one of the tree trunks he gave it a quick shove. 'I'll mix up mud and grass, form them into bricks and make a proper waterproof wall.'

'With no holes.'

Jack ruffled her hair. 'No holes.'

Squib was impressed. Mr Purcell's house was made of mud brick, which meant Jack was secretly rich. 'It's called pise.'

'Well, aren't you the know-all.'

They rode back to the hut in darkness. Squib figured they were due for a full moon. The stars hung low and bright, and beyond the rim of the camp fire the shadowy scrub was quiet. Jack threw another piece of wood on the fire, the embers fizzing into the air. They chewed on salted mutton, exhausted. Squib knew this was one night when she'd sleep like a baby, at least for a bit of it. And if her father didn't come for a while longer she reckoned that would be okay too. 'My real name's Cora.' Squib scratched at the dirt by her side. 'Cora Hamilton. I got called Squib on account of being small for my age and for being . . .'

'Being what?'

'Unimportant – at least that's what Abigail and Jane said.'

Jack stretched his legs out. The sole of one of his boots was flapping. 'Well, I think Cora's a real fine name.'

Squib pointed at his boots. 'You should be wrapping leather about them for protection; they'd last longer. Roo hide's good.'

Jack passed Squib his pipe and tobacco pouch. 'Better go shoot myself one. Guess you wouldn't know how to tan it?'

'Of course, silly. Everyone knows how to do that.'

Jack folded his arms around his knees. 'If you weren't here I'd learn from one of those books.'

'Sure you would,' Squib agreed.

'I've been told there isn't much spring or autumn out here. The weather doesn't seem to be interested in a kindly lead into summer – or winter, for that matter.' Jack lit the freshly packed pipe, took a puff and inclined his head in thanks.

'My father always said it was important to keep a property's stocking rates down. You know, on the conservative side. That way when a tight time comes around the ground isn't already chewed out.'

Jack scraped bits of meat into the fire and gave the plate a lick. 'For a kid you sure know a bit. I'll be sorry to see you go.'

'Go?'

'Well, yes. The thing is, you do have your own family and as none of them have shown it's best you go into town and see what the coppers can do for you.'

Squib was stunned. 'I thought we were friends.'

Jack edged his way from the yellow flare of the fire. 'I just want you to find your kin, Squib. Everyone deserves to have family.'

'But I could stay and cook and clean and wait for my father to show up.'

Squib's words floated in the night air as Jack walked away.

# ≪ Chapter 26 ≫

## Absolution Creek, 1965

Morning light glazed the condensation on the louvred glass shutters, competing with the flickering fire to turn the cypress floor into a variegated pattern of light and dark. It stretched towards the speckled bark of the leopardwood tree as two inquisitive field mice raced from their hidey-hole beneath the hardwood dresser to seek cover at the opposite end of the room. Returning to the paperwork on her desk, Cora checked the monthly outgoings in the station ledger. The only notable gains were in the form of Kendal, who admittedly could work like a Trojan, and he was currently doing so for free. The other bright spot was shearing. This year's clip had been excellent, the prices obtained good. The result ensured the station bank account would be out of the red for at least seven months or so until the next payment was due. They had Montgomery 201 to thank for that. The prize stud ram purchased at great cost was the shining light in Cora's flock improvement plan, and so far her gamble was paying off. In spite of these positive developments, the new bank manager, Mr Harris, had happily informed Cora only last month that they would no longer be willing to provide credit if Absolution Creek exceeded the agreed overdraft limit. It was inevitable that the previous manager would eventually retire, but after a banking relationship spanning thirty years it was still a shock for Cora. His departure came at a time when the banks were questioning their exposure to the fluctuating agricultural markets. The wool boom of the fifties was over, the season was iffy, and credit wasn't something the banks were excited about.

She wrote out two cheques – one to the general store for their monthly account and the second to the rural produce and supply store. With no other major expenses until the delving of the dam, which was booked for late August, and the dipping of the flock six weeks after lambing finished, Cora anticipated they wouldn't go beneath the bank agreed debt amount. That was a relief. There was more at stake now than a fight with the bank for a short-term loan. The previously amenable leasing relationship she'd enjoyed with the Farley Family Trust had ended with a new generation.

The leasing arrangement of Absolution Creek was a convoluted affair. Cora had renegotiated Jack Manning's initial ten-year lease in 1933, an arrangement which, thanks to her not once defaulting on a payment, led to an ageing Mr Farley agreeing to a further fifteen-year lease of the property. With the Second World War falling into that period and then the dustbowl weather of the forties nearly blowing half of the bush out to sea, a further renego-tiation in 1948 was easily accomplished. However, that was when the difficulties began for Cora.

Although thoughts of purchasing Absolution crossed her mind almost daily, Cora was afraid to take the step. Once the district became aware of the lease arrangement and her intention to buy the property, her past would be dug up and those people who had stayed quiet in the area for so long would surely complain. They wouldn't want a woman such as herself owning Absolution, and Cora was convinced someone would draw the government's attention to her existence. The 1948 lease signed by a widowed Mrs Farley continued past her death in 1960. Since then the twice-yearly payments required had been renegotiated and increased. Cora had little choice. The Farley Family Trust made no secret of their wish to end the leasing arrangement. Cora could either agree to the new terms or leave Absolution Creek. Her hand was being forced and there was little she could do. One payment default and she was out.

Cora shook away images of losing Absolution and checked the rest of the paperwork on her desk. There was her list for today's shopping trip to Stringybark Point and an unopened letter addressed in an unknown hand. Unfolding the thick paper Cora scanned the contents.

'Heavens.'

Jarrod Michaels was suing her for injuries sustained while in her employ. The phrases *partial disability* and *loss of income* were quickly followed by the amount of £50,000.

Pushing her chair out, Cora studied the tree as her heart steadied. It sprouted from the corner of the bedroom to rise up through the homestead like an ancient monolith. Grazing the edge of the partially sawn-off cypress ceiling, it extended into a shadowland of exposed roof beams and faint splinters of light before finally escaping through a circular hole in the corrugated-iron roof. Beyond this partial entombment it flung itself gloriously into sky and space to stand sentinel over her land. For how long?

Thanks to the bank and the Farleys, the property now teetered on a knife-edge. Fifty thousand pounds was too much; solicitors cost too much. Cora scrunched the letter into a ball and then flattened it out again. Ignoring the problem wouldn't help the situation. A visit to her solicitor while in Stringybark Point was now required.

'Damn it,' she muttered.

From next door came the sound of running, then giggling. The twins were ready for town. It had become abundantly clear over the last few weeks that companionship was one thing, but it couldn't be turned on and off like a tap. One moment the twins could be as quiet as baby pigeons asleep in a nest, the next as determined as wild cats seeking food. There was no in between, no appreciation of the silences, of the breaths between breaths. Penny and Jill were tiring and fascinating and sadly indicative of the changes from one generation to the next. When only five years older than the twins were now, Cora had assisted at the birth of her half-sister, Beth, carrying boiling water and swaddling clothes. That same day her young hands had swirled bloodied sheets in a boiling copper, and plucked black duck for dinner. She'd ridden bareback alone to find her father. Of course, those days were gone. So much of everything was gone.

'Are you ready?' Meg's knock on the door and the opening of it occurred simultaneously. Her niece was dressed in a grey skirt and cream twinset, with a hint of blush and a rose-coloured lipstick. The local matrons would be impressed.

'Ready.' Cora gathered the mail. 'Have you got your list?'

'Double-checked.'

'Yeah, double-checked,' Penny copied, skating to her mother's side.

'Me too,' Jill agreed.

They were a matching pair dressed in red velour dresses and white tights. 'Well then.' Cora smiled. 'Let's go.'

In spite of the gradual decline in population over the decades, Stringybark Point remained a small yet prosperous centre. The main street juggled the standard assortment of businesses, with the post office, bank and the long-running offices of Grey's Solicitors deemed the town's historic buildings. Cora parked outside the General Store, amused at the level of excitement a trip to town generated. The twins were desperate to get out of the car, desperate to visit the park further along the street and desperate to get inside the store. They scrambled from the vehicle in a flurry of red and white, long plaits flying. Eventually all four of them were standing on the kerb, Meg and Cora discussing their list of jobs.

'I'm a bit underdressed,' Meg commented as two women similar in age walked by, neatly attired in serviceable suits, hats and gloves. 'Did you see how they stared at me?' she remarked as the women walked across the road to the post office.

'Oh, I don't think it's you.' Cora slipped the car keys into her pocket.

Another group of townsfolk walked by. Cora recognised one of the older women as a particular friend of James's mother, Eloise. She smiled a greeting and received a curt nod in reply.

'Happy bunch,' Meg observed as the twins rushed to their reflections in the shop window.

'Women in moleskins and work shirts don't fit into their view of the world,' Cora explained. 'In fact, I don't fit into their view of the world.'

'What dear children,' a shopper said as she stepped out of the General Store, a bulging brown bag on each hip. Pausing, she watched the twins as they twirled in front of the shop's glass window.

'Bloody bastard,' Penny chimed, mimicking her father's voice.

'Good heavens.' The shopper heaved the bags a little higher and left quickly.

'I'm terribly sorry,' Meg called after her. 'I don't think we should have come, Cora.'

'Rubbish!' Cora laughed. 'You go and get the groceries. I'll drop the mail off and meet you back at the car in an hour.'

'Come on, girls,' Meg called to the twins. 'I want you to be on your best behaviour. If you're good I'll buy you a lolly each.'

'Really?' Jill swayed from side to side. Meg nodded. Bribery usually worked. On the other side of the road the same two women with their pert hats and gloves departed the post office, stepping from the kerb and detouring in an obvious effort to avoid Cora. They crossed the road and, spying Meg, headed directly towards her, offering polite hellos.

'I hope you don't mind us asking,' one of the women began, her white handbag strung across her arm like the Queen. 'We noticed you talking to Cora Hamilton and we wondered what she was like.'

'And how you know her?' her ash blonde friend added. 'You must be terribly brave.'

'Excuse me?'

'Well, everybody knows of Cora Hamilton.' The white handbag slid to the crook of the bearer's arm. 'And she looks like such a nice person.'

'Tomboyish but nice,' the handbag's friend corrected. 'What we were really wondering was if it was true.'

Confused, Meg looked from one woman to the other. 'If what were true?'

'If there really is a tree growing in the middle of her house?' the ash blonde asked.

'And if she really does ride with the ghost of her dead lover at midnight,' her friend said excitedly.

'What?' Meg looked down at her daughters; their faces were agog. 'Please, my children.'

'And –'

'Go on, ask her.'

'No, you ask her.' Ash-blond hair was tucked behind an ear.

'Fine.' The handbag was grasped securely beneath a woollen-clad armpit. 'Well, everyone knows that Cora Hamilton was left Absolution Creek by Jack Manning. The talk is that she bewitched him all that time ago; that's how she got the property. So we're wondering, as no self-respecting man in his right mind would go near her, do you think she did the same thing to James Campbell?'

Meg took each of the twins' hands. 'I'm sorry, I don't follow.'

The handbag switched arms. 'Bewitched him? Well, did she?'

'He's so dreamy,' the ash blonde concluded. 'It's such a waste.'

Meg wasn't sure what world she'd stepped into. Giving polite excuses she dragged the twins through the plastic flyscreen strips and into the General Store. A row of tables and chairs lined one side of the shop and a sign read, *Best vanilla milkshakes in the north-west*. The storekeeper behind the counter wiped his hands busily on a white apron and beamed a greeting.

'Well, well. I was wondering when she'd let you into town; you and your little 'uns. There you go, girls.' He extended a large glass jar over the counter. The twins accepted the stick candy eagerly and with bulging cheeks began inspecting the comic rack next to the newspapers and magazines. 'We're so used to boxing up a standard monthly order that sometimes we forget people actually live out at Absolution Creek.' He wiped his hands for the fourth time. 'So then, how are things going out there?'

'Fine, thank you,' Meg answered cautiously. 'Like all properties.' She made a show of examining the wares behind the counter. Assorted cookery items such as egg beaters and saucepans were strung from the ceiling; dry goods were on shelves, while under glass sat fresh sausages, cooked meatloaf sold by the slice and a myriad mutton chops.

The shopkeeper gave a knowing smile. 'Yes, but you're not on any property, my dear. You're on Cora Hamilton's Absolution Creek.'

'So it seems,' Meg replied, passing the shopkeeper her list.

## ⪻ *Chapter 27* ⪼

## *The North West Plains, 1965*

The cold air bit at Scrubber's throat. Not even the collar of his oilskin could keep the wind from that most delicate of crevices in his neck. Spurring Veronica onwards he rode without a break. Groaning helped alleviate the pain. Biting the back of his hand until his skin bled distracted him. Abusing Dog to hurry and keep up also relieved the discomfort.

Dog bailed up at noon. Since then he'd been perched on Scrubber's swag atop Samsara, a rope lacing him down lest he doze off and forget where he was. The cold eventually forced Scrubber to make camp early. Having finished the wallaby leg he'd been chewing on for the better part of a week, Scrubber was of a mind to catch some pigeon. He wasn't a dietician but even he knew it was important to vary his food a bit. He'd even gone so far as to buy a couple of apples from a homestead, although he'd had to mush it up a bit like an old woman. The signs weren't good. Even his throat was starting to close up on him.

Scrubber let the horses wander across the grassy flat while he scattered a bit of damper on the ground and backed off twenty paces to sit at the base of a wilga tree. The birds were twittering through the spiky branches of the surrounding timber and it was some time before a couple of topknot pigeons landed on the ground. If he'd had the materials Scrubber would have done the whole exercise properly, with a crate and a piece of string. Instead he sucked in his breath and waited for the pain in his guts to subside. Then he popped one pigeon in the head and blew the wing off his mate who had come to investigate the ruckus.

'Sorry about that,' Scrubber said as he lifted the mangled bodies and carried them away from the hunting ground.

With a fire going and the partially plucked birds roasting whole, Scrubber draped his swag blanket over some bushes. He'd not been near water for two days, but with all the signs of a dewy morning brewing he could rely on a sodden blanket for a morning cuppa. He stocked up on fallen timber to ensure the fire stayed good and hot, and cut belah branches for extra warmth. If he layered the branches above and below him he could be assured of a warm night. Splitting the pigeons down the middle with a knife, he scooped up the cooked innards and then chewed the carcasses, bones and all. He was a guzzler for a bit of bird meat and hot black tea; Veronica's favourite. Ah, Veronica. Occasionally he did miss the old ball and chain. He remembered the day they got together like it was yesterday.

'You came back then?' Veronica stated with obvious surprise.

Scrubber turned to see the young woman with a basket of eggs over her arm. She was standing in the dirt. Dobbs needled him in the side with his elbow.

Lighting a smoke he leant against the stable door. 'Wouldn't have got my pay otherwise.'

'Go on,' Dobbs whispered over his shoulder. 'You won't get better out here.'

Scrubber walked out into a morning glazed with heat. The distant paddocks were hazy, the usual twittering birds quiet. He never was one for a stillness that made you look over your shoulder.

Veronica rubbed at an ankle with her toes. 'Things sure changed after you went scrub-cutting.'

The girl's blouse and skirt, although clean, were worn in places. Scrubber figured she'd be lucky to be sixteen. 'I reckon.' Matt was on the run, the kid was gone – dead most likely – and there was a new overseer. He took another look at her, a good slow one. Either Veronica appeared better now compared to a few months back or he'd been in the scrub too long. 'Pity 'bout Matt.' That was why he'd come back. To find out if Dobbs had any news.

Veronica gave a series of sniffs, finally dislodging whatever troubled her. 'Yeah, I heard youse were particular friends with him. How will you go with the new overseer then? Evans.'

Scrubber took a drag of his smoke. The girl held out her hand for it and reluctantly he passed it across. 'Don't reckon I will. Reckon I'll hand in my notice and head to the hills for a bit.' He rubbed at his neck and shoulders. 'I'm no full-time scrub-cutter.'

Veronica puffed and coughed, fiddled with the eggs in the basket, and waited as Dobbs left with two horses strung out behind him.

'There's a storm coming,' Dobbs warned. 'Youse better get to some shelter. I'll go double-check on Waverly No. 4.'

Veronica brushed the cook and bottlewasher's words away with a flick of her wrist. 'Dobbs would have told you then 'bout what happened. That uppity Abigail Hamilton stole Mrs Purcell's necklace and then cleared off. Mr Purcell was real disappointed in your friend, Matt. Anyway, Mr Purcell put the black trackers onto them when the coppers had no luck. They caught up with them and now she's in gaol. Imagine stealing from Mrs Purcell. They still hang people, you know.'

Scrubber spat a strand of tobacco into the dirt. 'Only for murders and such like. Anyway, I just don't understand how they could accuse her.' He took a breath. 'I heard there wasn't any proof.'

Veronica took a step closer, real confidential like. 'Why, cause Mrs Purcell employed her on account of the fact she was an edumacated woman.' She gave a matter-of-fact nod. 'She could read, and Mrs Purcell she's real lonely, so Abigail Hamilton would sit up there in the big house and read to her of an afternoon. Perfect opportunity, that's what Mr Evans said. Imagine being paid to read.'

Scrubber snatched the cigarette back, took an angry puff and stamped it out under his boot. The wind gusted over them, swirling dust into the air. Beyond the stables low brown cloud was rushing towards him. The wind picked up and Scrubber screwed his eyes against the flying grit.

'I'll never get back in time,' Veronica cried out, suddenly anxious, as strands of hair flipped about her face.

'Back for what?'

'To get out of that.' She pointed at a dense brown haze that was already upon them, dimming the daylight to a rust colour. 'Dobbs was right. It's a dust storm.'

The wind howled, shaking the corrugated iron on the stables. Dust choked the air. Dirt began to invade the whorls of Scrubber's ears and nose, to get into his eyes. He pulled Veronica into the stables, eggs and basket flying, and together they managed to shut the double doors. They dropped the wooden cross bar to lock it and set about closing the single shutter window before backing away into the middle of the ten-stall structure. Timber and iron groaned above and around them.

'Will it hold?' Veronica looked anxiously at the visibly moving roof.

'Buggered if I know,' Scrubber yelled as the stables filled with dust. He could almost swear something was being thrown against the timber walls. Dirt was mounding up beside the door. Red dirt the colour of which Scrubber had never seen seeped inside. The world turned dark. They ran to the middle stall to crouch amidst tamped dirt and aged manure.

'Is it the reckoning?' Veronica asked, huddled beside him.

Scrubber had to think about that one. He'd done some bad things in his life but . . . 'Nuh, don't reckon. That's meant to be thunderbolts and fire and stuff.' Dirt and dust layered them. Veronica started coughing and couldn't stop. 'What's the matter with you?' He could barely see her.

'Can't, can't breathe,' she wheezed.

*Damn it all*, Scrubber mumbled. 'You going to be right or what?' He reached a hand out towards her. She was lying in the dirt. 'Hey girl, sit up.' That was all he needed. He put his cheek to her mouth, a hand on her heart. That'd be the next thing: she would die and the blame would be his. Scrubber looked through the haze of thick dust – inside or out would make little difference. Best they were apart when they found her.

Carrying Veronica to the door, he lifted the latch and shoved it open against the mass of dirt. She awoke, gasping for air and wheezing, and he dragged her along the side of the stables using the shaking wall for guidance. She clung to his body like a frightened bird and when they finally reached the yards he decided against dumping her. He pushed Veronica through the railings, going on memory as to the direction they should be heading. The wind was beginning to lessen; the girl was livening up. The yards were a swirl of murky brown objects. Reaching the water trough, Scrubber quickly lifted the girl and dumped her in. She spluttered and drank, and coughed and complained, until finally the wheezing eased and she had the strength to slap him across the face.

'Eh, what's that for? I saved your life!'

Veronica scrambled from the trough and slid down by the water tank. Now she was crying. Scrubber didn't have much experience with the crying types. Dunking his own head in the water he stripped off his shirt and wet it good and proper. 'Here.' He sat beside her and flipped the wet shirt over their heads. 'Breathe through this, it'll keep some of the dust out.' It was difficult not to look at the outline of her breasts, at the sodden material moulding her thighs. He wrapped his arm about her waist and pulled her closer. The girl was a misery of dust. 'Where you from then, eh?'

'T-Tamworth.'

'Well then, you and me, we've got something in common,' Scrubber lied, squeezing her about the waist. He turned his face to hers, and rested his hand on her thigh.

'I'm starving h-hungry.'

Scrubber licked his lips clean of dirt and dust. 'So am I.'

251

## ≪ Chapter 28 ≫

## Absolution Creek, 1965

They drove away from the homestead in the old blue Holden utility, with Sam squashed between Kendal and Harold on the bench seat. The road was shadowed by the line of native trees. Extending out from the base of each gnarled trunk was an expanse of frost-free ground. The remainder of the thinly grassed paddock was glassy with cold. Even the chook house was quiet, the inhabitants fluffed and hidden deep within their roost. A frost layered the house paddock gate, strings of ice hanging like shredded paper from the frame. Sam wondered why Harold persisted in starting so darn early when anyone in their right mind would have been snuggled in bed with a cuppa.

The radio was playing a Dean Martin song, 'Pour the Wine'. It had been a while since his last drink – a single rum and milk with Cora and Meg to mark six weeks on the property – and despite the early hour Sam swallowed. Cora had quickly got a whiff of his sneaky drinking and hidden her stash, which left Sam to keeping a bottle in the bedroom. It was an easier alternative, except when you ran out and the fortnightly trip to town was a few days away.

Harold switched the radio off, wound down the window and began whistling. Already the customary silence that marked the start to their days irked Sam. On average Harold needed a good ten minutes before he could construct a complete sentence. This early morning reticence was usually complemented by coughing, whistling and . . . there it was: the worst smell in the world. Sam reckoned Harold could power his own vehicle with the amount of methane he produced. Harold wound his window up. Like clock-work Kendal wound his down.

The utility moved along the pot-holed road at a slow pace. It seemed every few hundred yards they were stopping for something: cows, kangaroos, wallabies, sheep, even birds. As usual nothing seemed to be particularly interested in getting out of their way. It was as if the ute was part of the bushland; a pale blue inhabitant in a winter grey world. Kangaroos in particular were in the nasty habit of jumping directly in front of them, like crazed kamikaze animals. Why Harold just didn't put his hand on the horn Sam couldn't understand. This sort of driving wouldn't cut it in the city. People had places to be. Harold wound his window down again. The blast of cold air from both sides knocked Sam breathless. Ahead the road was physically barred by two Hereford bulls camped in the middle of it.

'They like the warmth of the road,' Harold explained as the utility bumped off the track to avoid the animals.

They turned right to drive along a fence line as the sun struggled over the horizon. In the distance came the sound of a sharp crack, then another. Sam jumped. 'What in the name of Moses was that?'

Harold shifted down a gear. 'That'd be your boss.'

'My boss?'

'Yeah,' Kendal drawled, 'the one and only Cora Hamilton.'

'She goes out shooting of a morning,' Harold revealed.

'Of a morning. Half the night more like it,' Kendal corrected. 'Mad as a cut snake that one.'

'Kendal.'

'Well she does, Uncle. She gets up when the rest of us normal people are still in bed, saddles that poor horse of hers and takes off into the bush. It's just not natural.'

Sam knew Cora was a bit of a night owl. He'd heard her stalking the house on numerous occasions and she was never around at breakfast, which didn't bother him. However, midnight rides were out of his comfort zone. 'Why does she get up so early?'

'Ask some of the locals – they've got some interesting takes on that.' Kendal flicked a dried piece of snot out the window.

Ahead a white mound of earth came into view. Harold drove straight towards it, picking a track through a stand of stringy saplings, and headed straight up the degraded incline. The sides of the dam were deeply cracked. They breached the top of the bank, and Harold slowly drove down the other side. Sitting in the middle seat, Sam was flung from one set of shoulders to another as the utility navigated the deeply eroded bank. The dam had been fenced in. A muddy pool of water filled a tiny section of it, and a number of carcasses – ragged flaps of protruding bone and dark hide – straddled the remains of the water hole.

'Well, bugger it.'

Sam quickly saw the cause of Harold's annoyance. A live emu struggled feebly, caught in the fence. Feet away a calf had not been so lucky.

'Must 'ave ducked in through that broken wire.' As Harold spoke a cow appeared from amid the prickly briar bush on the other side. 'One of the bulls got in with some of the old girls before the joining date. There's a handful of young'uns that have dropped in the last week. Too damn early to be calving, probably froze to death.'

'Hypothermia,' Kendal agreed.

On their approach the cow bolted back into the bush. 'Beats me why they come here when there's a bore drain not half a mile on.' Harold stopped the vehicle near the edge of the dam. 'There's rope in the back. You boys pull that dead calf out and I'll put the old runner out of his misery.' Harold fetched his 22-calibre rifle from behind the bench seat, loaded the magazine and let off a single shot. The emu dropped like a stone.

Sam tossed a coin. 'Heads for staying dry.' The metal landed with a thud in the dirt. Swearing roughly, Kendal took his boots off and walked straight into the dam to loop the rope around the calf's neck. 'Righto.' Together he and Sam pulled on the rope until the ooze of the mud loosened its hold and freed the stiff body. They dragged the calf up the embankment, leaving it to the crows. Kendal poured water on his feet and hands from a bottle, shook himself like a dog and redressed. 'Unreal,' he muttered. 'Here I am, the unpaid worker, and I'm the one covered in mud and shit.'

Sam sniggered.

Kendal picked dried mud from the backs of his hand. 'You're only here cause of your missus.'

'That's enough,' Harold ordered. He cut the wire trapping the emu with pliers, and the bird slumped heavily. 'Get the gear out of the back and get to it.'

Sam began rummaging around in the tool box. Next to it, Harold's foam esky was tied up with an old leather belt, and a large thermos was strapped on top. Sam's own lunchbox was rattling around on the dash, minus the thermos. Distracted by whining children, half-cooked eggs and a wife who'd let the wood stove dwindle to nothingness, he'd left it on the kitchen table. His head was pounding; he really needed a drink.

'Well, come on, then,' Kendal called. 'Have you found the pliers?'

Sam gritted his teeth. 'Here, catch.' The metal pliers spiralled through the air to land with a thud at Kendal's feet.

'Hey, they could have hit me!'

Harold looked up from where he was repairing the wire spinner. Although the fence was well past its prime he grudgingly admitted that some of the wire could be reused, just as Cora suspected. No doubt she'd been out in the dark, spotlight in hand, to make sure. Kendal was busy sniping at the short lengths of wire that held the barb to the tops of the upright iron posts while Sam was testing the strength of the posts with his own weight. Harold lifted the wire spinner as a loud 'coo-ee' echoed through the scrub. A mob of pigs rushed out of the tangle of undergrowth. Close on their heels came a half-dozen trotting cows and a handful of bounding kangaroos. The menagerie converged up the dam bank towards the startled men. Harold waited patiently by the utility, Sam raced for a tree and Kendal was caught between the fence and an irate cow. The pigs and remaining cows soon scattered, leaving Kendal with nowhere to go. The trembling cow put her head down and charged. Kendal dived over the fence and rolled awkwardly into boggy silt.

'Nice one.' Sam let out a bellow of laughter that set Harold chuckling as the cow trotted away.

Kendal dragged himself out of the mud, reaching the dry bank on his hands and knees. When he finally stood he found Cora staring at him, a grin on her face and a freshly shot bush turkey hanging across her thigh.

'Women in the city pay a fortune for that sort of skin treatment.'

Kendal grunted at Cora as he trudged towards the utility, and grunted again at his uncle, who was perched on the bonnet having a cuppa.

Sam was still laughing. He was stretched out against a box tree, oblivious to the nest of ants at his feet, until they started nibbling. 'Ouch, ouch, ouch.'

'Ants,' Cora commented dryly as she flicked Horse's reins. 'We've got three types out here, Sam: the white ones, which will eat your house; the black ones, which will eat your food; and the green ones, which will eat you alive.' She nudged Horse closer to where Sam was flicking frantically at his clothing. 'Those would be the green variety.'

'They sting,' Sam complained.

'Cheer up,' Cora replied, giving Harold a wink, 'there's turkey for dinner.'

'Pull up a stump.' Harold gestured to Sam and Kendal as Cora trotted away whistling. 'Do you want to go home and get changed?' he asked between mouthfuls of a cheese, onion and pickle sandwich.

'No.' Kendal took a slurp of tea. 'Only half of me's wet.'

'Suit yourself. Forget your thermos?' Harold asked, passing Sam the lid off his. 'Happens.'

Sam took the tea appreciatively and bit into Meg's butter and Vegemite saos.

Harold pointed a knobbly finger at him. 'A man will die out here if that's all she's feeding you.'

'Don't usually eat much.'

'You will,' Harold assured him, gulping down his tea. 'Right, back to it then.'

Sam looked at his half-drunk tea and partially eaten biscuit. Kendal dropped his mug in the esky, tied the strap around the lid and moved to follow his uncle.

Sam took another sip of the scalding tea, and decided Harold had to have a mouth lined with asbestos to drink that quickly.

'Well, come on then,' Kendal said gruffly. 'This ain't the city now.'

Considering Harold had managed to put off this fencing job for quite a few weeks, Sam couldn't understand why, to use Cora's phrase, they needed to go at it like a bull at a gate.

He settled back on the log and, looking at Kendal over the rim of the thermos lid, took a long slow sip.

It was near dark when Meg heard the utility idling outside. Wiping her hands on a tea towel she poured two glasses of milk for the twins and watched as they squashed their peas with the backs of their forks. Jill, a fast if messy eater, was already halfway through her roast turkey, while Penny was in the middle of transporting mushy peas from one side of her plate to the other.

'Eat up, Penny.'

The back door slammed. 'You look exhausted,' Meg observed as Sam slumped into a kitchen chair. She turned off the radio. She'd scream if another weather report came on.

'Buggered more like it,' he admitted. 'How're my girls?'

'Good, good, though Cora's bush turkey isn't going down so well. It's a bit tough.'

'I'm not surprised. Who knows how long it hung from her saddle.'

'Yeah well, at least I didn't have to pluck it.'

'Finished!' Jill held her plate up proudly.

'Finished!' Penny drank down the rest of her milk.

'Go, the both of you,' Meg said. 'Clean your teeth and go to the toilet, you little ragamuffins.'

Penny shook her head. 'But we can't go out there by ourselves. The bogeyman will get us.'

The outside toilet was not something the girls had taken to. Actually, neither had Meg. The dash in the dark or on a frosty morning was made worse by the continual checking for spiders under the wooden seat. 'Use your potty then.' Meg waggled her finger. 'But only number ones, not a number two.' The twins scooted out of the kitchen. There was the clanging of doors and screeches as they ran along the cold walkway out to the veranda and their bedroom.

'Well, one thing about it, this place agrees with the girls,' Sam commented.

Meg cleared the twins' plates. 'So, how are you getting on with Harold and Kendal? Any better?'

Sam flipped open the door to the wood fire and warmed his hands. He was red from windburn and his lips were dry and cracked. 'Put it this way, I'm regretting popping old Jeffo one in the nose. Gee, that seems like a lifetime ago now.'

'That bad?'

'Seems to me Kendal still isn't being paid. Can't blame him for being annoyed about that.'

Meg figured Sam had got a drink from somewhere and he'd had just enough to be amenable.

'How are things going with –?' He nodded towards the dining room. Cora would be reading in front of the fire, a relatively new arrangement now the kitchen was no longer her domain.

'Fine, although she tells me I've ruined her news hour, now that the kitchen has been overrun with children at 6 pm.'

Sam yawned. 'I had a couple over at Harold's place. I think he must be working on the "keep your friends close and your enemies closer" mandate. Anyway –' he lit a cigarette, cocked his head sideways '– you don't know where her stash is I suppose?'

'No,' Meg lied. She'd mistakenly thought he was cutting back.

'Just checking.' Sam's work coat concealed half a bottle of whiskey, thanks to Kendal. 'You know she rides in the middle of the night – goes out hunting wild pigs. She's different.'

Meg lowered her voice. 'The people in Stringybark Point certainly take a wide berth when they see her. It's like they're scared of her, and there're some wild stories doing the rounds too.'

'I'm not surprised.' Sam took a long drag, blowing the smoke into the expanse of the kitchen. 'A lone female running a property with all-male staff isn't exactly the norm. I reckon you're here to help repair her reputation.'

Meg stirred the gravy on the stove top. 'Somehow I don't think my aunt's worried about that.' She rested the steel egg flip on the sink.

'You heard from your mother?'

'No. I wrote a letter letting her know we'd arrived safely and I've heard nothing.'

'Well, you might want to try again.' Sam belched. 'We'll want to go back eventually. What about Cora? Do you know what happened between them?'

'No.'

'Have you asked?'

'No.'

Sam dropped his half-finished cigarette into the remnants of Penny's milk glass. 'Aren't you interested?'

Retrieving the glass, Meg rinsed it out. 'Yes . . . no . . . maybe. I'm not sure if I want to know. I don't want to end up in the middle of –'

'A family argument?' Sam finished. 'I think it's a bit late for that.' He heaved himself out of the chair. 'I'll go have a shower and have an early dinner. I don't think I could do the whole dining-room thing tonight. I'll tuck the girls in.'

Meg looked out into the wintry void above the sink. Beyond was a low hedge hemmed by three willowy gum trees, a square of grass, scraggly geraniums and ghost bush. A faded yellow blind cut a third of the view, however having spent the better part of her days at the sink Meg knew the landscape intimately.

'Do you want to know?'

Cora's voice jolted Meg from a daydream of Primrose Park and the harbour. Her aunt was slouching against the pale timber of the door, a pair of reading glasses dangling from her fingers.

'I didn't know you were listening.' Meg turned her attention once again to the gravy. Privacy was a hard-won commodity under this roof.

'Tell me about your father,' Cora said.

'I never met him. He died during the war,' Meg replied sharply.

'Do you know that for sure?'

'I know what Mum told me.'

Cora grimaced. 'No need to be defensive.'

'Fine. They met in Sydney, fell in love and then he was shipped off to the war. He died in Tobruk.'

'Well, that's pretty true. It's the order of things that have been rearranged. Your father left your mother when you were two years of age. She never saw him again. He probably did die in Tobruk. At least he was listed as missing in action, presumed dead.'

The clang of the metal egg flip hitting the floor startled Meg into action. She swiped at the greasy splats of gravy with a dish-cloth. 'How do you know that?'

'I'm sorry, I don't believe in perpetuating lies. I've had experience with them.' Cora sat the book and reading glasses on the kitchen table. 'Actually, I rather thought you knew.'

'But how? Why would Mum lie?'

Cora tucked the book under her arm. 'Your mother never suffered from a shortage of self-preservation, Meg.' She gave a brittle laugh. 'Anyway, I might dislike your mother but that sentiment doesn't extend to you. Ask her next time you speak to her. Write her a letter.'

Meg rinsed the dish cloth. 'She hasn't answered my first one.'

Cora looked as if she were about to say something, but instead she opened a cupboard and retrieved a rum bottle secreted inside an empty flour canister. She poured herself a drink. Ice and rum filled a glass. 'It was your birth notice in the *Sydney Morning Herald* that piqued my curiosity. I came across it by chance. I actually thought there may be a chance for, if not quite a reconciliation, at least a confession of mistakes made in the past.'

'That's very cryptic.'

'Anyway, I wrote to your mother, congratulated her on your arrival. Two years later she wrote back – a little belatedly, don't you think? – to tell me that Geoffrey had left her. She blamed me for his leaving.'

'Was it your fault?'

Cora wagged her finger. 'Oh no, my dear. No apportioning blame on me, thank you very much. I never met your father and so, in truth, I don't think it was my fault. I blame love.'

'Love?'

'Your grandfather's love for his first wife. You see, your mother and I are stepsisters.'

Meg removed the bubbling gravy from the stove top. 'I don't understand. Stepsisters?

Cora skulled her drink, the ice clattering. 'No, I don't expect you do.'

'Mum never said anything about you being stepsisters.'

'Actually, I doubt she said much about me at all. Yes, well I can see by your expression that I'm right on that account.'

'I need to know, Cora. I've never had any grandparents, or any aunts and uncles, until now.'

'Believe me, Meg Hamilton Bell, I know how that feels.'

'Mum never talks about you or Granny. It's like she never had a mother.'

'I expect she feels let down by her. Why my father ever got caught up with the likes of that woman, Abigail . . . Well, let's just say she was an embarrassment to the family. I blame her for some of what happened. For the rest of it I blame your mother.'

'And what happened?' Meg asked desperately. 'Tell me.'

Cora sat tiredly at the kitchen table. At last here was her opportunity to reveal the truth.

# ≪ *Chapter 29* ≫

## *Absolution Creek,*
## *1924*

Squib lit the slush lamp on the table. Jack's diary was in its usual spot, his cramped handwriting noting weather conditions and stock work. Not once was her name mentioned – not even when they'd worked together in the sheep yards. Well, he could do it by himself and see how he managed, Squib thought angrily, noticing the name Olive scrawled in a corner margin. 'Olive.' Squib's lips pinched. Olive was the reason Jack didn't want her to stay.

*I've my own family coming.*

Squib knew that if she were sent to an orphanage, her father would never find her. It was better to leave Jack before he sent her away, and walk upstream from the direction she'd come. With a sob she flung the waterbag over her shoulder, inadvertently knocking the lamp. The flickering flames spread swiftly over the diary, letters and books. Squib gave a gasp, her first instinct to smother the fire with the scratchy blanket from the bed. As she watched the flames, however, a feeling of righteousness spread through her body. Gathering her crutches, she walked out the door.

At the creek she turned right, following the curve of the waterway to limp over fallen logs, the sand cool beneath her feet. She hated the creek. It had taken her away from her father. She only bore being so close to it in the hopes it would lead her back to him.

She kept moving until the sun rose and birdsong drifted down from the trees. Once daylight arrived she rested her injured leg every hour.

At noon she slurped water from the canvas bag at the base of a gum tree as a flock of ibis took flight. At least it was cool near the creek. There was a slight breeze and the closely packed branches overhead shaded her from the sun.

By mid-afternoon Squib could barely walk. Her feet complained and her hands hurt from the makeshift crutches. She knew eventually she would find someone, although an image of Jack riding up, his hat pushed low on his head, a tuft of grass between his lips, haunted each step.

By late afternoon her legs could carry her no further. Turning a bend in the creek, she scattered a mob of sheep at the water's edge. Skirting their soft piles of droppings she ran up the slight bank. Ahead lay an expanse of grassland broken up by patches of trees. Exhausted Squib lay down in the long grass and slept.

Squib awoke to a low-hanging moon. The wind rustled the grass, blowing the tips of it so that it appeared like a grassy sea in the moonlight. Her nostrils twitched as the wind briefly changed direction. The scent of roasting meat floated on the breeze. She was not alone. She could see hobbled horses feeding into the northerly wind. There was the creak of leather, unmistakable in the clear night air, and the low murmur of voices interspersed with the occasional laugh. Squib peered across the grass to where a group huddled around a campfire. She knew too well the sound of marrow being sucked from a bone and the fatty juices that smeared your chin. Soon theft would be added to her list of sins.

When the moon passed its midpoint in the sky, Squib walked stealthily towards the glowing embers. The smell suggested a morsel of their meal remained somewhere among the snoring bodies. She circled the camp carefully, picking her way around a freshly killed sheep that had been left lying in the grass. Congealed blood oozed from its slashed neck, and the partially skinned animal's flesh glowed white under the moon's gaze. One of its legs had been hacked off, and the rest of it – meat that would have fed a family for days – left to rot.

The three travellers were nestled around the dying fire, snoring intermittently. Squib took a single, silent step towards the stacked dirty plates and reached across for the lump of meat.

'What 'ave we got here?'

A strong arm grabbed her ankle. Squib squealed as her make-shift crutches fell and she landed heavily on the ground.

'I'm reckoning this would be the kid I was telling you about – the one staying with Jack. What you doing out here then?'

Squib struggled against the thick arm, tilting her head away from the stench of sweat and mutton fat. It was Adams. 'And I'm reckoning you'd be the lot that killed that sheep,' Squib retaliated, finding herself subject to the scrutiny of a young man and woman. 'Sheep stealing's a crime.'

'Is your leg hurt?' the younger man asked.

Squib gave a brief nod.

'Sheep stealing. That's rich coming from a runaway,' Adams replied.

'She's a bit old to be a runaway.' The woman turned to the young man at her side. 'She's not exactly a child. And you say she was with Jack, Mr Adams?'

Squib stared at the woman opposite her. There were hollows beneath her eyes and her pale skin was emphasised by flecks of red in her short dark hair. How on earth would this woman know Jack? Squib sucked in her cheeks and let out a long breath. She spoke very distinctly and politely and she appeared to be younger in age than her stepmother, Abigail. Was this woman Jack's Olive?

Adams nodded. 'You're never too old to be a runaway, ma'am. And yes, this is the girl. I told Jack she'd be best sent to an orphanage.'

'I'm not going to any orphanage,' Squib said defiantly as Adams tied a rope about her waist, holding the end firmly. Her fingers picked uselessly at the knot.

'We'll see about that, girly.' Adams tightened the rope.

'Must you do that, Mr Adams?' The woman's smooth forehead had the slightest indentation of a frown.

'Ma'am, she'll wander off into the night and end up being taken in by the blacks if we don't keep an eye on her.' He looked at Squib. 'It's to Jack's tomorrow.'

The woman passed Squib a plate with a bit of damper and meat, and peered at her over the camp fire. 'Are you a runaway?'

'No. Jack found me when I got lost. I fell off a wagon and got washed down the *crick*.'

'Likely story.' Adams huffed.

'It's true.' Squib took a mouthful and chewed quickly. 'My father's looking for me.' She tugged on the thick length of rope. Only animals were tied up.

'How do you know?' the woman asked, leaning forward.

'I just know.' Squib bit into the meat. It was tough, tasteless. No wonder – meat had to be hung for a good few days in the winter or salted immediately in the summer before it was edible. She dragged the bread around the ring of her plate and drank the water offered from a pannikin.

'How long have you been with Jack for?'

Squib looked at the woman. 'Long enough.'

The woman's cheeks turned red.

'You're Olive, aren't you?'

There was a gasp and then the man sitting beside the woman finally spoke. 'How did you know that?'

Squib ate some more food under the glare of the travellers. 'Because he's been waiting for you.' She pointed an accusatory finger at Olive. 'People need their family, you know. You shouldn't have left him out here alone for so long.'

For a moment Squib thought the woman looked guilty. Although it was a hot night the woman wrapped a blanket about herself, shifted in the soft dirt like a burrowing animal, and whispered to the young man by her side.

'Get some sleep,' the young man suggested, rolling onto his side.

Squib licked her plate clean. Jack's Olive pulled the blanket over her head. Adams belched and stretched out in the dirt. For a long while Squib sat beneath the glow of the moon as sleep overcame her companions. Try as she might she could not undo the knotted rope.

'How'd you get out here then, my pretty?' It was Adams, his voice low, his fingers creeping to her thigh.

Squib grabbed one of the crutches, aiming for his crotch. He swiped her aside with a well-aimed slap and she fell backwards, her head hitting hard dirt. 'I'll tell Jack.'

The young man stirred and turned on his side.

'I don't reckon you'll be telling Jack anything.' Adams breathed over her. 'I reckon I know who you are, I do,' he said quietly. 'There's this interesting tale doing the rounds 'bout a girl who fell off the back of a wagon whilst her kin were running from the law. Your mother's the Purcell thief, ain't she? The one who took that fancy bit of jewellery?' Adams's eyes dared her to deny it. 'Well, she's in gaol in Sydney now – the State Reformatory for Women – so it's real unlikely a single man's gonna put himself out for a kid, especially when he's got a whole lot of coin in his pocket. I reckon you ain't told Jack that snippet. After all, he's a good Christian man; he wouldn't hold with the likes of thievery and you not coming clean about it.' He leant towards her. 'So my advice to you, girly, is to be real nice to me. In return I'll keep my mouth shut.' He glanced across at the two sleeping bodies before running a calloused palm across her leg. 'It'll be up to you to convince old Jack to keep you. Course in return I'll be expecting some gratitude when I swing by on my usual monthly run.' His grip tightened on her leg. 'You understand what I mean, don't you?'

Squib edged away from Adams as he shoved his saddle backwards and forwards in the dirt, finally using it as a pillow. Overhead a tangle of stars spread out across the night. Squib hugged a saddle blanket about her thin shoulders and stared at the vast sky. 'Find me, Father,' she whispered softly into the wind. 'Please find me.'

Adams led the way on a spindly wheeled cart, his bay horse trotting behind him. The dark cloth of his suit was just visible between a jumble of chairs, mattresses and a cupboard. Tethered to the bay was an ageing packhorse. Squib was at the rear of the crowded dray, wedged between two leather-strapped suitcases and tin trunks. No longer bound by rope thanks to Olive, her waist remained sore. It was a slow, uncomfortable ride. She felt every bump through the boards, although she figured she was more accustomed to this type of travel than the woman up front. Jack's Olive seemed awfully out of place in her grey dress and matching coat. Even the hat she wore was strange. Pulled down over her short hair it resembled a bed pot.

'Where you from then originally?' the young man called Thomas asked. They had been travelling since dawn with little conversation.

'A sheep station,' Squib replied politely. She liked this man with his soft cow eyes and wide smooth face. His forehead was quite big, which Ben reckoned meant a person carried a lot of brains.

'Why don't you send them word about your father?' Thomas suggested.

'He's left there,' Squib answered quickly.

'Thomas,' Olive interrupted, wiggling to try to get comfortable on the folded blanket that was supposed to cushion her ride, 'she's just a child.'

Thomas elbowed her. 'She only looks to be a few years younger than me.'

'I'll be fourteen soon.'

When the sun reached its highest point and Squib's skin reached roasted meat stage, they passed through a stand of tall gum trees. For a few blissful minutes they were sheltered by the brown-green canopy above. Rays of light criss-crossed limbs and possessions, and Squib held out her forearm as the play of light danced across her skin. She had been thinking about Jack, about Adams's threat about the orphanage, and this woman, Olive. She wondered what would happen next. If her leg hadn't been paining so much after her long walk yesterday, she would have jumped off the dray and run.

The scent of smoke drifted through the trees. 'Here we are.' Adams turned in his saddle. Ahead, framed by the boughs from low-hanging trees, open country beckoned.

Squib ducked as they passed beneath the low branches, her hands clutching the back of Thomas's seat. For a moment she didn't recognise their destination. A wide circle of burnt-out earth greeted them, a thin stream of smoke lifting into the air from a pile of rubble. Across the desolate space sat a rickety table she found familiar, which held a selection of foodstuffs. A trunk was nearby, burnished dark by the fire.

The dray jolted to a stop. 'Must have been some fire,' Thomas exclaimed, jumping to the ground.

The smoky air made Squib cough. Many of the larger trees Jack retained for shelter were scorched, and spirals of blackened earth were being lifted into the air by the wind. The clearing, which once housed a myriad of birds, was totally devoid of life.

Thomas placed firm hands around Olive's waist as she climbed carefully down from the dray. 'Thomas, surely this isn't the place.'

'Adams says it is.' He stretched his arms upwards. 'If I ever sit in a dray again it will be too soon.'

'Coo-ee,' Adams called through cupped hands.

'That's the bush call,' Squib explained to Olive as a figure appeared from the ridge of trees beyond. 'In case you get lost.' Squib's voice faltered. There on the edge of the ridge was her Jack.

'Jack, Jack, I'm sorry! I didn't mean to cause the fire.' The dirt was warm underfoot as Squib limped across the charcoal ground. She grasped his shirtsleeve. 'I'm sorry. It was an accident. Don't send me to an orphanage, please!' She winced as Jack touched the bruise left by Adams's hand.

'You've gone injured yourself.' Even as Jack spoke he was staring in the direction of the dray. Impatiently he loosened Squib's arms, then broke into a run. When Jack reached Olive he drew her against his body, holding her for long minutes before throwing his hat in the air and hugging Thomas. Squib's shoulders drooped.

Adams shook hands with Jack and gestured towards the devastation of the fire as the group surveyed the damage. They walked towards her, their boots crackling twigs and leaves. Olive, in her heeled shoes, kept going over on her ankle with every second step.

'How on earth did the fire start, Squib?' Jack asked when the group rejoined her, 'and why did you run away?'

Four pairs of eyes were staring at her. 'It was an accident,' Squib answered, 'and you know why I ran.'

'I'll eat my hat if it was an accident,' Adams stated loudly.

Jack frowned, opened his mouth to say something to Squib and then, deciding against it, linked Olive's arm firmly through his.

'How's my sister?' Jack asked. Squib backed away.

'May's well.'

'So then, what news?'

'Sarah Bernhardt died,' Thomas offered, 'and there was a

massive earthquake in Tokyo and Yokohama. Don't you get news-papers out here?'

'Occasionally.' Jack smiled encouragingly at Olive. 'How about some good news?'

'They've started building a new Parliament House in Canberra. Oh, and they say the last Cobb & Co coach will run in Queensland this year. So this is it, eh, Jack? Your own spot in the world.'

Jack gave his brother a flash of white teeth and then they were laughing again, punching each other lightly on the arm. 'You should see the sky out here, Thomas. Pinks and whites turning to blues in the morning. And the stars – the stars are wondrous.'

'So then, you came for the scenery?' Olive scraped at something sticky on the sole of her shoe.

'Olive, I tell you, there's nothing in Sydney that compares to this.' Jack took her hand.

'I can quite believe it.' Olive stared at a roughly built timber frame sitting under a tree. Strips of blanket led from a water-filled tray on top to hessian walls. 'What is that contraption?'

'My fridge,' Jack announced proudly, lifting the hessian to reveal a cut of salted mutton and a bowl of dripping. 'Come on, Olive, you must have some news for me?' Jack clucked her under the chin.

'She looks like she's in shock,' Adams pronounced. 'Tired probably.'

'Are you feeling better now?'

'Yes, Jack, I'm fine,' Olive answered quickly.

'Good. Well, I'm sorry the hut's gone, but never mind. We'll make do.' Jack squeezed her shoulders.

'You two love-birds will be right,' Adams agreed. 'I'm just sorry I had to bring this wild cat back with me. Handy kid, burning your place down, Jack.'

Squib walked off into a stand of thick trees to where a rough lean-to stood. It rested precariously against the trunk of a large gum tree.

'What about the house?' Olive turned on her heels, almost tripping over a fallen branch. 'You said there would be a house.'

Adams and Thomas looked cautiously at each other and walked away slightly, inspecting a fallen branch caught in one of the trees above.

'And there will be.' Taking Olive's hand Jack directed her to a log near the camp fire.

'I'd hardly want to sit here, Jack. Why, it's so hot a person could fall ill.'

'Sit where you like then,' Jack replied softly. 'However, for the time being we'll have to make do, Olive.'

Olive frowned. 'With what? You've been here five months.' She twisted a stray length of thread around a button at her wrist. 'You can't expect me to live here.'

'I've been here by myself,' Jack gently reminded her, 'for longer than I expected after you changed our plans.'

'Actually –' Olive sniffed, mopping at her brow with a lace handkerchief '– they were *your* plans, Jack, and a person can't be blamed for falling ill.'

Thomas gave a low whistle, and commented on the flash of green plumage in the tree above.

'Bush lorikeet,' Adams explained. 'Anyway, Miss Olive, your man Jack has his brother to help him now. It won't be long and you'll have a good solid house.'

'The grocer becomes a builder,' Thomas agreed. 'I'll give you a few months, brother, and then I'm back to Sydney. I promised May I'd return.'

'Has it changed much?' Jack asked.

'You wouldn't recognise the place. It's like a great machine has gone through and knocked down everything in its path. Many of the old faces have gone. May misses you. She thinks you should return.'

Squib noticed the look Olive gave Thomas. It was brief but

unmistakable. There was knowledge between them, and Squib doubted Jack would like it.

The dark edged its way into the stand of trees so quickly there was barely time to tidy their plates before they were enveloped by it. Olive watched the girl pick up each plate unasked and stack them to one side ready for washing in a bucket. Considering she depended on a sturdy branch for a crutch, she managed to move about quietly. As she slopped water the girl hummed an unknown tune, which set Olive on edge. Even the music was different out here. Jack explained the girl was a bit of a night owl, preferring to bed down for half the day and sit up during the night. The thought of Squib's half-wild ways didn't endear her to Olive, but there was no doubt she was adept at stoking the fire, fetching water and cleaning up. Considering there was only three or so years difference in age between them, Olive wondered at the suitability of Jack being in the middle of nowhere alone with a girl on the brink of womanhood; especially a girl who watched his every move, anticipating his every need.

'With luck you'll have a decent roof over your head by winter, Miss Olive,' Adams said, revealing a bottle of rum. 'He could have rebuilt the Mankells' place, but he said he wanted something new for you.' Adams took a swig of rum, the liquid patterning his beard in the firelight.

'Is there a house already here?' Thomas held out a grease-rimmed pannikin for a splash of the rum.

'Go easy on that,' Jack cautioned with a frown.

Thomas gave a mock salute. His elder brother had changed in the few short months since he left Sydney. The easy banter that once flowed between them had been replaced by an almost aloof attitude. He seemed older, more serious. Was this what independence did? Or had Jack merely absorbed the strange lone-liness of his new home.

'On the western side of the river there's a homestead. Needs a lot of work though,' Jack revealed. 'Besides, I want Olive and me to have something special.'

Squib pressed her lips tightly together and threw a scatter of bones into the darkness. She retreated to just outside the rim of the campfire.

Jack stuffed a wooden pipe with tobacco and he and Adams puffed away, their conversation interrupted by the ongoing relighting of the tangy tobacco and the slurping of rum.

'I can't take the girl with me, Jack. At least not this trip. Reckon you'll have to tie her up to keep her out of mischief.'

There was a scrabbling of leaves as Squib moved further away from the fire. She'd sooner shoot the man than have him touch her again.

Jack took a swig of rum, and wiped his mouth with his hand.

'My suggestion,' Adams continued, 'is to make use of the girl while you've got her. Let her pay for her keep.'

'I've been thinking. Perhaps the best thing to do is to put a notice in the Stringybark Point paper when you eventually get back to town. Let people know she's here.' A spray of embers rose into the air. Jack pushed a skinny log into the fire. 'I'm sure she's lonely for her kin. She doesn't sleep at night. Wanders around like a night owl or lies awake.'

'Not natural,' Adams replied. 'Not natural, are you, girl?' He scanned the blackness. 'Anyway, have a think about that notice. You might appreciate a bit of help.'

'Maybe if people treated me nicer rather than spending their time trying to be rid of me things would be better,' Squib replied. She hoped Jack felt bad.

'You go to sleep and wake up to see your house burnt and think how people should treat you,' Adams argued. 'I'd be tying her up of a night. That'll stop her shenanigans.'

Thomas finished his rum. Here he was sitting around a camp fire as Adams talked about tying up a girl to keep her out of trouble, and the expression hadn't altered on his brother's face. He wiped sweat from his brow.

'You better get cracking on the house, Jack. We don't want your lady here burning up for lack of shelter.' Adams took another swig of rum and winked at Olive. 'Reckon we better send word for a priest.'

Squib gathered saliva in her mouth and spat loudly in the grass.

It was meant to be a celebratory dinner, however rabbit stew and dirt-smeared damper wasn't exactly what Olive expected. She didn't know what she had expected on arriving in this deserted place but it had been more than this. For the hundredth time that evening she gathered her skirt tight against her legs and clamped her body rigid. She was sitting on a log in the middle of a paddock where any number of creepy-crawlies could accost her, and no one seemed to care. Picking as daintily as she could at the gristle between her teeth she accepted the swig of rum Adams poured into a pannikin. The liquid was firey hot.

'Steady old girl,' Thomas cautioned.

'Liquor isn't just for the satisfaction of menfolk,' Olive retorted. She needed the hot reassurance of the drink.

'Last time I was in Sydney women didn't smoke or drink in public.' Jack tapped out his pipe.

'And you didn't smoke a pipe, Jack,' Thomas replied.

'Everyone smokes a pipe out here, lad,' Adams answered. 'Your brother here only sees me once a month. There's no regular store for papers and such like.' Adams corked the bottle. 'Shut-eye time.'

When they eventually retired for the night, Olive stripped down to her underwear, slipping between the scratchy blankets in the lean-to. There were jersey silk pyjamas and cakes of Pears soap stacked under a tree with the rest of the too-few luxuries she'd carried from Sydney, however she was beyond exhaustion. Besides, what did it matter any more? Especially in these conditions. She placed the slush lamp, with Jack's dreadfully smelly concoction of rendered animal fat, carefully outside so that a soft light illuminated the small space. Then she waited. Outside, Adams and Thomas settled by the camp fire, the silences in their conversation increasing. Above her the bark roof hung stiflingly low. Having promised not to think of her old life, Olive pictured her snug bedroom with its calming yellow walls and comforting scents of hearth and home. She wondered what her family were doing. What were they thinking? After her lie regarding visiting the Gees was discovered, Olive felt sure that Henrietta would press elopement as the reason for Olive's disappearance. If that was the case, her family would try to avoid the slightest whiff of scandal, until her disappearance lengthened and they received no word from her. Eventually they would believe that the worst had occurred. Olive knew the time had come to write to them. At the very least she could allay their worst fears even if she chose not to reveal the details of her new home.

'You all right, Olive?' Jack squatted at the entrance to the lean-to. 'Thomas said this is only your third night sleeping outdoors.'

She sat upright. 'Are you coming to bed?' she whispered, patting the blanket with her hand.

'Umm, well, no. I've spoken to Adams about a minister and he says we'd have to travel to town in six weeks or so to be wed.'

'But are you coming to bed?' Olive tried to keep any sense of urgency from her voice.

'Well, no. It's just not right.'

'Right for whom?'

Jack cocked his head. 'We're not married.'

Olive let the blanket fall from her shoulders. 'We've been apart for months, Jack.'

'But you've not been well, and you still look a bit peaky.'

With shaking fingers Olive slipped the strap of the white silk camisole low over her shoulder. She was sure she heard Jack swallow. 'Now you want to wait another month?' She smiled, hoping it appeared more natural than it felt. 'I've been so lonely for you.'

Jack cleared his throat. 'We should be married, Olive.'

'What does it matter out here?' She gave a weak laugh.

'God lives here too.'

In the yellowing lamplight, Jack's eyes looked dark as he stared at her. Olive lowered the other camisole strap. If she didn't sleep with Jack now she was sure her resolve would weaken. 'I never took you for such a religious man.' Having visualised their coming together on the long trek north, Olive knew the future lay in her female attributes, though her mind was disgusted at the thought of what lay ahead. Olive was well aware of what a man could do to a woman, and such a relationship – even if love did exist – was no longer palatable.

'You know I was brought up with the good book.' Jack's voice never wavered.

Olive's fingers plucked at the flimsy material, the strap slipped free and she wriggled a little, baring white skin and petite breasts. Jack's eyes no longer met hers. They focused on her body, roaming her skin unashamedly, which was rarely exposed to light. In the strained silence Olive sensed him hesitate, and then, abruptly, he was gone. Outside someone belched. Olive buried her face in the coarse blanket and wept.

## ⋘ Chapter 30 ⋙

## Absolution Creek, 1965

Meg finished sweeping the veranda and gathered the fallen leaves in a dustpan. Willie wagtails and soldier birds hopped across the lawn in search of insects. Meg could hear the twin poddy lambs bleating beyond the garden, their tone suggesting starvation. Harold had arrived with them yesterday. The rest of the ewes weren't due to lamb for another few weeks, however somehow the mother of these two managed to get herself in trouble and then promptly die. The men were now feeding out corn every second day instead of twice weekly as had been Cora's stipulation. Sam explained that although the ewes looked as sleek as race horses not all the lambs were likely to survive. *Lambs*. While the twins were beyond excitement at their arrival, Meg mentally added them to her to-do list. Apparently they had to be fed three times a day!

She knocked on her aunt's bedroom door. Cora had spent a day shuffling about the homestead until her maimed leg forced her to bed. The self-diagnosis was one of arthritis and the pain had kept her normally active aunt bedridden for two days. Meg wasn't really surprised. A cold front had hung over Absolution Creek for a week and even Sam was complaining of aches in his past fighting injuries. She poked her head in the door. There were two mice running about the floor and a furry, bulbous spider had taken up position on the far wall. Meg looked at the gaping ceiling and the monstrous tree and wondered what other nasties lurked in her aunt's room.

'How's everything this morning?' Cora asked. 'It doesn't feel so cold.'

'It isn't. It's meant to be a few degrees warmer today.'

Cora leant back in the chair at her desk. 'Thank heavens.' She rubbed her leg. 'And the men?'

'They're replacing the tin on the woolshed.' Meg decided against mentioning the proposed work to the hayshed and the changed sheep-feeding routine. According to Sam these were unapproved jobs undertaken at Harold's instruction. Instead she retrieved a crumpled blouse and brown jumper from the floor. 'You look better in the face. Not so strained.' Meg dangled the items, a letter falling from the clothes to the floor.

'Yes, I am feeling better.' Cora held out her hand and took the letter quickly.

Meg draped the dirty clothes over her shoulder. Cora wasn't the type of woman to ever look pale, thanks to her olive skin. In some respects Meg was pleased that her aunt's leg was the cause of her illness. Initially she worried that she may have been partly responsible for her aunt's ill-health. Cora was more than obliging in answering Meg's questions regarding her family, specifically the problem between her aunt and mother and the differing accounts of her father's passing during the war. However, this led to Cora telling the story of a little girl named Squib. For some inexplicable reason Meg believed the story of this long-lost child had somehow affected her aunt. Quite frankly she'd been remote and melancholy ever since. Just how the girl Squib fitted into Meg's world bewildered her, however she was prepared to humour Cora in the hope that eventually she would learn something a little more pertinent. 'Can I get you anything else, Cora?'

'Yes, spring.'

Meg agreed. The cold ocean winds that swirled up from the bay, were nothing compared to the cold of the bush. Here it worked its way into you, burning your fingers and noses. The men complained of chill blains and Sam's ears and nose were on their third set of skin.

Dirty clothes in hand, Meg left her aunt staring at a trail of sugar ants on one of the bedroom walls. The letter sat in the middle of her desk.

The twins were sitting at the kitchen table. They too were feeling the cold. So far their morning highlight was limited to an early feeding of the two poddy lambs, and the expression on their faces suggested boredom was about to set in.

'Is Aunt Cora still sick, Mummy?'

'She's feeling better, Penny. I'm sure she'll be up and around very soon.'

'I like it when she's in her room.'

'Jill, don't say that about your aunty. We're lucky to be here.'

'Yeah, lucky to be here,' Penny mimicked, returning to her crayons.

Meg drew the curtains above the sink and removed biscuits from the oven. The smell was tempting and she ate the flaky mixture in two bites, setting down a biscuit apiece for the girls.

'Wait till they've cooled,' she warned, humming as she stirred the remaining mixture. She greased another baking tray and began to dollop piles of batter onto the tray with a tablespoon. She was dying for a cup of tea, but there was still a load of washing to be hung on the line, the house water supply to be checked and kindling to be collected for the fires before lunch. There would be time enough for tea when the sun was at its zenith. Sliding the tray into the gas oven she checked the temperature. The flame was a yellowish colour and an accompanying whiff of gas meant the cylinder was low. 'That's all I need.' She looked at the wood-burning Aga next to the 'new-fangled' gas oven, as her aunt called it, and frowned at the thought of having to use it for baking cakes. The gauges on the front of the Aga's door verged on the unreliable. Meg found it impossible to keep the fire burning at a constant temperature. It was either too hot or too cold.

With the girls nibbling cautiously on the warm biscuits, Meg braced the chilly morning and loaded the Hills hoist with an assortment of clothes before sitting the basket on the wooden table in the laundry block. Outside the back gate she turned left at the fruit tin, which had been secured on a post and formed their rain gauge. Meg walked the quarter mile down the dirt road to the house dam, Curly and Tripod close on her heels. The lambs quickly followed, chasing her as if she carried a bag of liquorice allsorts.

'Whoa, you little terrors.' Rocky and Dillon were runty little animals. Meg patted their soft fluffy heads as they butted her legs.

By the time they reached the dam only Rocky remained. He ambled up behind Meg and the dogs, until all four of them stood on the top of the bank to peer down at their dwindling water supply. There was a dark ring of wetness from the dropping level. The dam needed topping up. The only way was to pump water from the creek to the dam near the woolshed and then on to this dam. 'Well, we'll have to do something about this,' she said aloud, squatting to pat Rocky as Curly barked.

A white utility appeared at the paddock gate. A willy-willy of dust tailed the vehicle briefly as it stopped near the dam a couple of hundred feet from Meg. The driver lowered the window and she made out the outline of a man. He raised his hand in a momentary greeting. Meg raised her own haltingly, embarrassingly aware that she resembled Dr Doolittle. Her indecisiveness about whether she should walk down the dam's embankment and introduce herself was solved when the vehicle drove away, leaving an empty road and a silence she doubted she would ever become accustomed to.

Squinting against the morning light, Meg hugged her arms. The landscape was cold and barren this morning. It spanned out from the dam in a blur of wintry browns: coffee, tan, russet and auburn, each colour fed by rain, bronzed dry by the sun and then finally seared by the bite of daily frosts. Meg longed for spring. She visualised the greening of the butts, of the long grasses, and imagined a carpeting of the cold ground with fresh tender shoots. As she scraped at the dirt beneath her heel, an image of the glistening harbour of her old home came to her. She recalled her aunt's words on their arrival – how the loneliness could drive the weak to drink. For her the great void of humanity that was her new home had created a different vice: reflection.

The bush gave a person too much time to think, too much time to wonder about what might have been. Recently Meg found herself daydreaming about being single again, about finding a man who loved her. Of course, when she thought of her girls, reminding herself that she had chosen this life, guilt dissolved her thoughts – at least for a little while. Although it was impossible to clear her mind completely of her concerns, Meg was managing to concentrate on the daily tasks that filled the long hours.

Why on earth would her mother blame Cora for the loss of her husband when they'd never met? And why lie about his death? Maybe Sam was right. Meg was in the middle of a sibling argument and it was a nasty, blame-apportioning mess.

'Come on, dogs. You too, Rocky.'

They were almost back at the homestead when a piercing whistle bit through the air. Horse appeared at a trot from between the avenue of trees, the strapping on his rug tugging at his hind legs. A few minutes later Cora was limping to Horse's side, a bridle over her shoulder. Curly and Tripod were speedy defectors, racing to their mistress's side to watch impatiently as she threw the rug across the back fence, and slipped the bridle over twitching ears and into an open mouth. Cora swung up onto Horse's bare back.

Meg watched the older woman with admiration. It was disconcerting to admit that her aunt probably had more staying power than the rest of them. Meg figured Cora would keep breathing just to prove a point, even if the rest of her body packed it in. 'Is everything okay?'

Cora backed Horse up a few steps and flashed a grin from beneath her hat. 'Everything's perfect once I'm on Horse.' She slapped her weak leg. 'By the way,' she called over her shoulder as Horse broke into a trot, 'your biscuits are burnt and the dam will be filled by week's end.'

Meg ran alongside her. 'Great, thanks. I was wondering –'

'It was the vet.' Cora nodded briefly in the direction of the dust and trotted away.

Meg gazed into the distance, wishing they'd met.

The auger spat the corn into a peak. Using his hands Kendal spread the kernels across the top of the feeder. He indicated to Sam that the two-tonne feeder was almost full.

'Here's trouble,' Harold commented dryly, nodding towards Cora, who was riding across the paddock towards them. Together he and Sam took hold of the auger's frame and pushed it clear of the grain hopper. Sam blocked off the corn's flow before Harold switched off the engine.

'I thought she was crook.' Kendal jumped from the back of the truck, checking the chains that held the feeder to the truck's frame.

'Arthritis,' Harold explained. 'The cold weather comes and she's bedridden for a day or two.'

'My pa had a bad back,' Sam revealed. 'Once it went on him he'd be useless for a fortnight.'

Kendal rolled his eyes.

'Have you asked her yet how she hurt her leg?' Harold asked Sam.

Sam shook his head. 'Nope. Meg said it was an accident.'

'She fell off a dray and got trodden on real good by a horse when she was a kid,' Kendal explained. 'Damaged her eye too.' He turned to his uncle. 'She's only got partial sight in that eye, isn't that right?'

'Something like that,' Harold admitted. 'I don't know all the details. Anyway, she's going to go off about increasing the ewes feed too soon. I'm worried about keeping the old girls and their lambs alive and she's worried about a break in the fleece come shearing next year.'

'And?' Sam queried. Meg's aunt was all flying hair and hat from a distance.

'A break in the staple will mean a decrease in the price offered,' Kendal explained. 'Sheep need good constant fodder for consistency in their wool and the girls have had a rough trot this year.'

Cora crossed the paddock and came towards where the men stood.

'Good to see you up and about,' Harold greeted her.

'Thanks.'

'Miss Hamilton, I know what you're going to say,' Harold began, 'and I'd like to point out –'

'How are we going for corn?'

Sam took a step forward. 'We've got three silos left, Cora. About twenty-nine tonne.'

'Is that right?'

'Pretty much,' Harold agreed.

'Well, feed everything today and then I want the silos tarped.'

'What for?' Feeding sheep wasn't exactly something Kendal lived for. 'Half of them were fed yesterday.'

Curly arrived in a screech of dirt and promptly weed on the work-truck tyre. Tripod's arrival was quieter as he joined Curly to sit squarely by Cora, panting. Kendal took a step back from the pooling urine and grimaced.

'It's going to rain in a day or so,' Cora replied, ignoring the looks on their faces.

Sam gazed up into the cloudless sky. 'A bit cold for it, isn't it?'

'I've seen the signs.' There were ants crawling up the wall in her bedroom and another trail marching through Meg's biscuit mix. There were also telltale mounds of ants' nests, which had risen a couple of inches in height in readiness for water that would soon lie on the ground.

'Right then.' Harold tugged his jeans, and readjusted them about his waist. 'We better get to it.' He scratched at the scab on his forehead where the ram's horn recently struck him.

'Wait on,' Kendal argued. 'What signs? There's no rain predicted.'

Cora flicked the reins. 'Good to see you're familiarising yourself with things, Sam.'

'What are you grinning about?' Kendal asked Sam as Cora rode away, her two dogs following in tandem. 'And what's the go with this sign thingy?'

Harold selected a pre-rolled cigarette from his hat-band and lit it. When he puffed out the smoke he crouched in the dirt. Sam and Kendal followed suit. 'Out here everyone's got their own methods for predicting rain. The standard ones are: ants building up their nests, particularly those little sugar ants you see about the place; then there's those slater beetles – bugger me if they don't always head towards higher ground; and black cockatoos are a sure thing. Miss Hamilton always worked on three, preferably in a belah tree, but my own father said a pair was enough. Sign of a good season. Couple that with a full moon . . .'

'So what's she seen then?' Kendal wondered.

Harold stood. 'I've no idea, but if Cora Hamilton says it's going to rain, it will.'

## ≪ Chapter 31 ≫

## Stringybark Point Village,
## 1965

It was dark by the time Scrubber arrived at Stringybark Point. He trotted into town with his girls straggling up the rear, and Dog sitting on Samsara like a king. The stringybark trees still lined the road into town, still met at the three-way intersection like gabbling housewives. It was a spot where roads led to and from nothing. Cadging a paddock for his horses from a townie, Scrubber stumbled the remaining half-mile on foot. The street was quiet, the General Store and post office closed up for the night, and the children's playground dark with shadows. He never did take to Stringybark. Even Veronica thought it just plain unwholesome for a small village to have three pubs. Of course, now there was only one left, which was where he intended to camp for a night or two while he gathered his strength for the final leg of his journey.

The public bar was packed. Scrubber made a point of acting inconspicuous and slunk to the end of the dented wooden bar amid the stench of beer and the haze of cigarette smoke. He paid for his beer and rum chaser and savoured the taste of the grog, eyeballing any stares with a come-and-get-me antagonism. 'You got food?' he croaked to the barmaid, keeping his neck concealed. He was sure Veronica's damn scarf still reeked of strawberries.

'Sure, love. Chops and veg, snags and veg or a bit of cow.'

Scrubber nodded. 'With gravy and eggs?' She wasn't a bad sort, although one side of her head looked like a half-bag of spanners.

'We can do that.'

'Snags then and a bed?'

The barmaid selected a key from a numbered board. 'Upstairs, last on the left.'

The bar was greasy with fumes, and the timber walls scattered with black-and-white photographs. Scrubber ran his eye over the old photos of the town, over relics from days past. There were long yellowing tusks from a boar pig mounted on polished wood, a brown snake curled tightly in a glass jar and the remains of a rifle that had been smashed over someone's head. And then he spotted a newspaper clipping. 'Hey, girl, can I see that?'

The barmaid followed Scrubber's jabbing thumb to a cheaply framed newspaper clipping hanging over the till.

'No busting it, mind,' she warned him, lifting the picture off the wall.

Scrubber squinted through the haze of cigarette smoke at the print on the page. He spat on the glass frame, cleaning the grime off with his cuff. Sure enough it was Cora Hamilton. Said so right under her picture.

'Well I'll be damned.'

*Cora Hamilton of Absolution Creek, pictured with the Wangallon Station bred Montgomery 201. Miss Hamilton purchased the top sire at the Premier Merino Show and Sale from the Gordon family of Wangallon, amidst fevered bidding. Montgomery 201 is a direct descendant of Waverly No. 4, the big-framed, high-yielding national champion of 1922. Waverly No. 4 was immortalised on the 1923 shilling coin and has made regular appearances on our currency ever since. He was bred by the late Mr H. Purcell of the now government-resumed Waverly Station.*

'She lives here.' The barmaid leaned forward, giving him a fine view of cleavage a younger man would drink all night for. 'Not that we see her much. But that buy of hers certainly put Stringybark in the news.' She topped up his rum, and shoved the cork in the bottle. 'Course, we only got mileage out of it for a couple of days, but when a person lives in a town their whole life, well, it's good to see stuff like that.'

Scrubber tapped Cora's face through the glass. 'So you know her?'

'Me, know Miss Hamilton? My mother would say it wasn't proper, but I'd be real pleased to meet her. She's like a . . . like a famous person. You know they say she killed a man. There was some kind of kerfuffle in 1924. Course the locals here won't speak a word of it. They're afraid the relatives will walk out of the scrub one day and finish anyone who says a word against her.' She sidled a little closer. 'Do you know her?'

Scrubber nodded. 'Aye, I do.'

The barmaid smiled. 'How'd you know her then? Tell me.'

'I saw Waverly No. 4 too. Used to work out there for the Purcells.'

'Sure you did.'

That would be right, Scrubber thought. The few times a man had something worth telling, no one believed him.

Her face resumed its disinterested expression. 'You want anything else, old timer?'

'Got a pie? It's for me dog.'

The barmaid returned with a brown paper bag. 'Never heard of a man feeding his mutt with a pie.'

Scrubber snatched the bag from her, grease already darkening the paper. He opened the bar door and gave Dog the tucker, who took it politely between his teeth and swaggered off. His job for the day completed, Scrubber dropped enough coins on the bar for his food and board. His hands strayed to the pouch at his waist. He looked at the partition down the middle of the bar; through the mesh he could see blacks on the other side. It had been nearly forty years since he'd last eaten in a hotel and some things hadn't changed.

Scrubber and Veronica humped it out of Purcells' in the summer of 1924. There wasn't anything much to stay for after the boss cocky came down with an illness that saw him hole-bound within a week. The missus stayed on, Evans in control. Even old Dobbs walked. Didn't like the look of things, he muttered, leading an ancient horse out the boundary gate. Scrubber agreed. They left at daylight on foot, the air thickening with heat and haze. Notwithstanding the sporadic stories circulating the bush about Matt and his missus, Scrubber knew Waverly Station had been good to him. He was leaving with full pockets. Waverly No. 4 stamped his hoof as they walked past his paddock. The glory days were finished, although no one informed the ram as he trotted away.

They eventually found work about fifty miles downstream at a place called the Five Mile. Veronica cleaned and cooked at a boarding house, and he joined a local shearing team about the district. The steady work was a boon for the both of them and they got on well, what with him being away three weeks plus out of every four. Soon after they heard Waverly was slipping. Evans couldn't keep men on and the missus was too melancholy to stay out there. A month later everyone was talking about a big sale. The Gordons of Wangallon Station purchased Waverly Station, walk in, walk out. Scrubber reckoned old Purcell would've turned in his grave.

They were ten days into a month's job at a big shed not far from town when Matt Hamilton showed up. Scrubber, waiting at the table for the next fleece to be thrown, fairly busted himself rushing to the shed door to say g'day.

Matt grinned. 'I thought you'd be at Purcell's.' They shook hands. 'Obviously the scrub-cutting got to you, eh?'

'The boss dropped dead at Christmas, so I left. Been working the sheds around the Five Mile ever since. Even got meself a woman.'

A shadow crossed Matt's face. 'Well, I'm real pleased for you, mate.'

'And your kid Squib? Any word?'

Matt shook his head.

'Everyone was real sorry to hear what happened – me especially. She fixed my wrist.' He held his hand up for inspection. 'Still, there's every likelihood someone may have picked her up, don't you reckon? How long you been searching for? Sturt would be the one to talk to here. He knows everything.'

Matt lit a cigarette and took a long slow drag of it. 'It was raining and then the creek flooded and then we got word the trackers were on our trail.' His words tapered off.

'There're always signs, though,' Scrubber persevered, looking over his shoulder at the wool table. The other wool rollers were calling at him to hurry up. 'Muddy tracks, checking with people along the creek.'

'The thing is I never got to look for her. The trackers found us. Evans pointed the finger and, well –' Matt shifted his eyes about the cavernous shed '– Abigail's in the State Reformatory for Women in Sydney.'

'But there weren't no proof.'

'No there wasn't, but . . . how'd you know that?' Matt's eyes tightened.

'Heard it.' He thought of the kid lost in the bush, waiting for the father who never came. 'So, you just left her?'

'Look, by the time the business with Abigail was done I didn't know what to do next. I mean, I had the other kids to look after and I couldn't leave Abigail.' Matt wet his lips and looked at Scrubber. 'Squib was out there too long by herself.'

'So you think your girl could be . . .' Scrubber couldn't say the word. 'Someone could have found her.'

'Maybe.' Matt's eyes grew watery. 'I'd like to think that someone was caring for her.'

'And she's a real smart kid.'

'Sure. Sure she is.' Matt didn't sound too convinced. He stubbed out his smoke on the boards. 'I'm looking for a job, anything going?'

'Dunno.' Scrubber hadn't felt such disappointment in a person, ever. He left a kid like that, didn't even bother.

Matt stopped him as he tried to walk away. 'You gotta understand. If Squib is still alive then she's got a chance for a better life if she stays away from me.' Matt sighed.

'How'd you figure that?'

The boss of the board, Sturt, stalked towards them.

'I'm Matt Hamilton, formerly of Waverly Station.' He extended his arm to shake hands, but it remained there, mid-air. 'I was looking for a job. I was overseer and –'

'I know of you, Hamilton,' Sturt replied. 'Oh yes. Your missus was the one who robbed Mrs Purcell and you lost a kid, too, didn't you? What'd you do with it then, eh? What'd you do with the money? Or have you still got that fancy piece of jewellery?'

'My wife never took it.'

Sturt crossed his arms across a fatty chest. 'But you ran?'

'Not only because of that.' Matt scratched his thinning hair. He'd run because he'd thought it possible that Abigail did take the necklace. After all he'd never believed his first wife could have been a thief and look what she did. And he'd run because he was worried for his kids. And he'd run because of Evans' insinuation regarding the dead overseer, Martin. But he couldn't explain all that to Sturt or Scrubber. 'We ran cause I thought at first she might have.'

'And your missus is in gaol,' Sturt confirmed. 'Ain't no work for the likes of you here.' He turned on his heel. 'And *you're* lucky to be here, Scrubber, so get back to the table.'

Scrubber couldn't believe it. Matt hadn't even gone looking for his own kin. Some people would kill to have a semblance of a family. He knew he would. 'Waverly Station's been sold,' he called after Matt. 'Seems like every-thing's been buggered up.'

Matt Hamilton kept on walking out of the shed.

It was some time after Matt's brief appearance that Scrubber started to feel crook. It came on gradually, like a dose of the squirts after a hefty feed of emu egg. Veronica was good about it, mopping his brow and such, but it soon became pretty obvious that he wasn't suffering from any malady she could cure. He lay on the sagging mattress in the lean-to at the back of the boarding house, groaning as flecks of light striped the mattress through the ill-fitting timber walls.

'You'll be right, lovey. Reckon you ate something a bit off.' Veronica shovelled dirt over a puddle of water from the previous night's rain. The muddy liquid had drained in from outside and, having filled a quarter of their narrow space, was enticing a hoard of critters into their shady home. A hairy bush spider, young black snake and a couple of lizards had already been in for a visit and Veronica wasn't reckoning on welcoming anything bigger. With a final splash of dirt onto water she flattened the gooey concoction into a smooth paste, before tossing the shovel out the open door. Throwing armfuls of water over her face and neck from a bucket, she patted her neck dry. 'I know what you need.'

Into a bowl Veronica scooped two handfuls of flour, added a spray of sugar and then opened a paper bag of currants. She sprinkled the dried fruit on the rough table, picking out invading ants. Satisfied, she added a handful of the fruit to the mixture, and scraped the remainder into the bag. She added water before she began kneading the dough like a prize-fighter, her forearms bulging white sinews of muscle. 'How about I make you some johnny-cakes, eh lovey? I might even be able to nip a bit of honey from the kitchen after I've tidied the rooms up.' She rolled the dough into a ball and rested a dripping rag over the top. Wiping floury hands on her dress, she placed a cool palm on Scrubber's brow.

He clucked Veronica under her chin and patted her rounded backside. 'You're a good girl to me you are, real good.'

'Nonsense.' She dabbed at his brow, and moistened his lips with a bit of water. 'You saved me, you did, from working for that toff. Never did take to Mrs Purcell. No need for a woman to strut around like she's got a carrot up her behind. Not when everyone else is starving.'

'It weren't a bad job, though?'

'No, not too bad. Not until Mrs nose-in-the-air Abigail Hamilton arrived; her with her books and big ideas. Us housemaids was expecting them to ride out together one day – you know, like best friends. Beats me why the woman would go and steal that pearl necklace. I had it on good account that as her husband was overseer it wouldn't be long before Mrs lah-de-dah Abigail became Mrs Purcell's fulltime companion.' Veronica wrung out the wash cloth and wiped his arms. 'Come up in the world they would have then. How the mighty fall.'

Scrubber turned on his side and moaned.

Veronica padded away to return with a bowl of water. 'You gonna tell me what's wrong then, lovey?'

Her cooling hand stroked his brow. Scrubber sweated under the weight of her concern. How was it that the difference between right and wrong could creep up on a man unawares? Worse, with the doing of something now undoable and the Hamilton saga circulating through the bush like a water bag on a hot day, there wasn't even any benefit to his actions. Scrubber sat up; pushed away the wash cloth. He was about as clean as he'd ever be. 'I need you to do something, Veronica.'

'Really?' She hiked her skirt up.

'Not that. I need to know if anyone's taken in a kid – a girl.'

'Not that Hamilton girl.' She covered her knees again.

Scrubber nodded. 'The very same.'

Veronica threw the cloth in the tin wash bowl, splashing water onto the bed.

He grabbed her wrist. 'That girl did me a good turn. Her father did me a good turn.' He pulled her closer. 'I wanna return the favour.'

'All right, just as long as you don't fancy her.' Veronica moved the wash bowl. 'She ain't that much younger than me.'

'And *you* ain't that much younger than *me*, girl, but that don't mean I've taken a liking to her.'

'What you gonna do when you find her?'

Scrubber twisted his face up. Some things he knew, others he didn't.

## ≪ *Chapter 32* ≫

## *Absolution Creek, 1965*

Sam turned the collar up on his jacket and looked down between his riding boots at the trail of corn beneath them. Harold as usual was finding every pothole on the paddock, and the truck dipped and dived sideways, the feeder slipping half a foot in differing directions with the movement. With only one feeder on the property, Kendal was relegated to chopping wood for both houses and finding a roo with which to feed the dogs.

They met up with Kendal at the entrance to the 800-acre block. Cocky as usual, he wound down his window to ask if Sam was warm enough. There was a dead emu in the back of the old blue ute and a trail of blood painting the metal tray.

'Nearly finished?' he asked, a cigarette dangling from the corner of his mouth.

'Kendal, we don't normally shoot emus,' Harold said, chewing a mangled match. 'We'll run this bit out in here and then go back and get another quarter load. That should do us.'

Harold had been itching to get out of the cold as well so Sam knew there wouldn't be any mucking about. The work truck was missing the window on the passenger side and had lost its winding mechanism on the driver's.

'It's a bit rough in there.' Kendal pointed over his shoulder to the paddock beyond. A mob of ewes was already walking towards them. 'I better check that chain.' He made a show of ensuring they were secure before clapping Sam on the shoulder. 'By the looks of the light I'll only have time to burn the feathers of this bird here and chop enough wood for old Uncle Harold. You'll have to chop the wood for the big house when you knock off, Sam.'

'No worries.' Sam resumed his seat on the rear of the truck. 'I'll be sure to tell Cora you didn't have time to chop any wood for her.' He expected a grunt of annoyance. Instead Kendal gave him one of his lopsided grins.

The vehicles parted and Harold veered from the road, heading towards a clump of trees. Sam grabbed at the side of the tray, his fingers closing over the cold metal as the truck bumped across the ground, a handful of ewes following. They travelled a few hundred yards before Harold gave a wave from the cabin.

'Righto.'

The ewes were on the corn the moment Sam began to release it. From across the paddock eager sheep made their way towards the feed as a growing wind buffeted the kernels, scattering them across the ground. As the vehicle bounced across the paddock Sam didn't notice the feeder slipping with its decreasing contents. Harold drove the work truck through a catchment drain and hit a log in the long grass. The impact shunted the truck sideways, the off-skew feeder adding to the vehicle's momentum as it tipped onto its side. Tossed against the moving feeder, Sam flung himself clear of the rolling vehicle to land on the corn trail with a thud. For a moment he didn't move; couldn't move.

Harold yelled.

Sam quickly hoisted himself up onto the passenger side of the vehicle. Harold lay against the driver's door, his body partially wedged by the steering wheel. 'How on earth did you end up in that position?' he asked.

'Good driving, eh? Bet they don't drive like that in the Big Smoke?'

'Geez, you people are strange,' Sam replied. He reefed open the door. 'Anything broken?'

Harold gave a grimace. 'I'm pretty sure everything would be manipulating just fine if I could move.'

'Well, that tells me nothing. Rope?' he asked hopefully.

'Yeah, yeah, behind the seat.'

With the rope located and tied around part of the tray, Sam dropped the end to Harold. 'Just tie it onto the steering wheel. I'm gonna come down in there and pull you out. The rope's a bit of a –'

'Safety line.'

'Pretty much. I don't eat as much as you fellas do.'

'I know.' Harold shook his head. 'Saos.'

Wedging his foot between the seat and the hump of the drive axle, Sam reached Harold quickly, pulling him free of the wheel. Harold managed to stand on the driver's door.

'Now we're cooking.' Sam grinned as he jumped from the vehicle to pull Harold free. They both landed heavily on the ground. 'Well, at least you didn't fall on me.' Sam laughed.

'My head's killing me.'

Sam shrugged off his coat. 'Here, put this on and try and keep warm.' He helped Harold to a nearby wilga tree, noticing that the man's head wound was directly where the ram had struck him.

'It's a fair walk,' Harold reminded him.

'Do me good. See you soon, eh?' Sam gritted his teeth against the cold and began the five-mile trek home.

⊰◈⊱

Meg was at the sink peeling potatoes as the day dwindled to a close. She added water to the saucepan of vegetables and checked the eggs simmering on the stove top. The twins loved to plunge buttery toast into the rich yolk and an easy dinner suited Meg. The day had become quite topsy-turvey after Cora's weather forecast. Lunch was rushed; biscuits needed to be rebaked; Jill required disinfectant, bandaging and cuddles after a tumble outside; and firewood needed to be gathered and covered. The lady of the house had, of course, retired to her room.

With the house quiet, Meg opened the letter she'd received that morning and had been carrying around in her apron.

*My dear Meggie,*

*We have had our differences, you and I, however, regardless of your feelings toward me, please know that I write this with only the best of intentions.*

*Cora Hamilton cannot be trusted. It is because of her that I lost the only father I ever truly knew. And it is because of her that your father walked out on both you and me when you were a baby. I am sure by this stage that I don't have to spell out the reason why. Take a good look at Aunt Cora if you've not already guessed or been enlightened by another.*

*You should know that Cora is my stepsister, however we are only related by marriage. I guess I should have told you that before.*

*I am sorry you left home. That shouldn't have happened. But now you're up there take my advice. Believe nothing she says and accept nothing from her. She's a trouble-maker, always has been. Please return to Sydney. I only need word from you and I will evict one of the tenants.*

*Your mother, Jane*

Meg reread the letter and scrunched it into a ball. So it was true, Cora Hamilton wasn't even her real aunt. Now what was she supposed to do? Pack up and go home? Meg tossed the letter in the Aga, slamming the door shut. Through the window a figure walked across the paddock. Meg was startled to see Cora climb over the low hedge to walk swiftly towards the approaching man. As he drew nearer she could see it was Sam.

Meg was out the back door and racing towards her husband as Sam and Cora reached the work shed. Kendal was slouching against the blue utility, watching a mound of something burning on the ground. Meg could smell petrol and flesh and, whatever it was, it stank enough to entice Curly and Tripod to within a few feet of the burning mass.

'Sam, Sam?'

Meg felt her arm gripped tightly. 'Everything's all right. We tipped the truck and I had to leave Harold out in the paddock. I'll get him.' Her husband looked drawn, his features tight with cold and concern. He turned to Kendal. 'Checked the feeder chains, did we?'

Kendal stared at Sam, a blank expression on his face, the air thick with dislike. 'Is he okay?'

'Freezing, I'd imagine, in this weather.'

'You're bleeding.' There was a rip down the front of Sam's jeans, the area glossy with blood. Meg knelt to inspect the wound only to be brushed aside by Cora.

'It'll take more than that to kill him.' Cora slipped onto the bench seat of the ute.

'I'm fine,' Sam agreed, 'we've got to go.' He sat behind the steering wheel and turned the ignition.

'Me too.' Kendal left the burning mass.

'No.' Cora held up her palm. 'There's not enough room. We'll be back soon.'

As the ute disappeared through the house paddock gate the twins arrived. They walked up to the molten black mass of scorched flesh, gooey moisture and scattered feathers, and turned opened mouths and wide eyes towards their mother.

'It's, it's . . . What is it, Kendal?' Meg asked.

'An emu.' Kendal kicked at the carcass. 'Anyone would think he was *their* uncle.'

'What are you killing the bird for?' Jill asked. Tripod was by her side immediately, his wet nose nuzzling her bandaged knee beneath her stockings.

'For the dogs to eat.'

In the months since their arrival, Meg rarely found herself in Kendal's company. He was a raggedy-looking youth with a mango-shaped head and thick eyebrows, and there was just something about him Meg didn't like. 'Is it normal to kill emus?' she asked.

Kendal eyed her off slowly. 'Does it matter?'

Tripod gave Jill's hand a lick and joined Curly, who was already snuffling around the edge of the dead bird.

'The meat's good for them and so's the oil. Gives them a real shiny coat.' He ruffled Penny's hair, his hand slick with dried blood. 'It's like you having to eat your vegies.'

Penny screwed her nose up. 'Yuk!'

Curly set to chewing on the carcass, his growls of delight matching the twins' chorus of *yuk*. Kendal laughed.

'Come on, girls. Back to the house.' By now Meg knew the eggs would have boiled dry, probably burning the bottom out of the saucepan as well. It was proving to be a long day.

'You know, I told Sam to check the chain on the feeder properly. Make sure it didn't tip and cause an accident.'

Meg wrapped her cardigan more snugly about her.

'I have to tell you, it's a bit difficult having to carry Sam.' Kendal kicked at the burning carcass. 'He's a good bloke and all, and I know Harold would never say anything, but you know, being the one that's doing the work and not being paid, well it's a bit difficult.'

'I'm not really in a position to say anything, Kendal.'

'Sure you are. You're her niece. And you're one of us, so you know how things work. One day she might leave you the place and then you'll have the opportunity to put a few things right. You'll be able to make the decisions that Harold reckons should have been made years ago. He's a smart man, my uncle. Real handy to have on a property. Besides, a woman like you, you've got rights. Cora Hamilton, why she ain't got so many. Personally, I don't know how she's got away with it for so long.'

Meg wondered what her aunt had got away with. Having the audacity to manage the property when she was a woman? Or was she mismanaging it? Certainly the state of disrepair to the homestead was an obvious issue. Then there were her aunt's two days of bed rest resulting in immediate changes to her instructions. Obviously the men didn't agree with how she was running things as Harold had promptly ordered extra sheets of corrugated iron and lengths of timber, and booked a truck to deliver the goods when they arrived. There was also a dozer coming to push scrub along the creek in the hopes of eradicating some of the pig-nesting areas. Apparently Cora was yet to be informed of these developments.

Jill and Penny were arguing. They had made it partially back to the homestead when they had discovered some sun-weathered bones, which were now the subject of a furious debate about what animal they belonged to. Meg glanced in the direction of the girls, her mind spinning. First Kendal was blaming Sam, then he was talking about her aunt not belonging – not being one of them. It was bizarre. 'I have to go, Kendal.'

Kendal's filthy hands smeared the crisp white paper as he rolled a cigarette. He gave her a wink as she left.

# ⚔ Chapter 33 ⚓

## Absolution Creek, 1924

Jack wiped at the sweat on his brow and heaved one end of the timber onto his shoulder. Thomas strained at the opposite end. 'They tell me it's a privilege to take the heaviest end,' Jack joked as his brother finally hefted the length of wood up and onto one shoulder. They slid the timber onto the stack already filling the dray and, tugging at the horse reins, began walking their load back to the new house site. It had been a fortnight since Olive and Thomas's arrival, and with Jack worrying about his brother losing interest or altering the length of his stay, his first priority was to cut all the timber they required.

'Is everything all right with you, Thomas?' Jack gave the brown horse a whack on the rump to keep moving.

'Sure.'

'You've been a touch quiet. Olive too. You didn't have a blue or something?'

'Nope, of course not.' Thomas made a show of dusting his trousers.

'You'd tell me if something was up?' Jack persevered. It took nearly three days to meet Olive's eyes after what had occurred in the lean-to. Having never seen a near-naked woman before, Jack was at a loss as to what he should do. He knew what he wanted to do, but the wanting and the doing were two different things, and what he thought to be the good part was religiously aligned with marriage. At least that was what he'd been educated to believe. On the other hand there hadn't been a great deal spoken about nakedness in church, which is why he watched Olive undress. 'It's just that Olive seems different.'

'Does she?' Thomas picked at a piece of bark on one of the lengths of timber. 'Didn't notice.' He tried not to think about the day in the boarding house when Olive made him promise not to tell Jack what McCoy had done to her. 'Guess women can be a bit like that – changeable.'

'Changeable,' Jack repeated. Maybe it was the bush, or the many months apart, or the simple fact that his girl was used to better things. Whatever the reason, Olive wasn't Olive. She was skinnier for one thing, and quiet. So quiet that at times she seemed nothing like the girl who had kissed him so blatantly the day of his father's accident. 'Maybe she's homesick.' He thought of her body illuminated by the slush lamp.

'Probably. I mean it's a bit different for her. I don't know if I would have come all this way for you, Jack.' He batted his eyelids.

'Very funny.'

'You'll have to take her into town again, you know. Give her some civilising.'

'I don't have time for trips away, Thomas. Anyway, she saw Stringybark Point when you met up with Adams. She knows there are other women about.'

'Saw it!' Thomas laughed. 'She asked one of the shopkeepers where the main street was when we were standing in it.'

They approached the house site from an easterly direction. It was a pretty spot, with a thick line of trees on the western and southern approaches protecting it from the blazing summer sun and any nasty southerlies that might sneak their way in during winter. Having moved camp from the lean-to at Thomas's suggestion, the building of the house was progressing nicely. A couple of hundred yards away from the site, Olive and Squib rounded the corner of the partially built house. Squib, dressed in a cut-down version of one of Olive's dresses and a shady straw hat, carried two dead rabbits. They were arguing. The horse halted automatically at the pile of timber.

'You caught them. You skin them.' Olive brushed her skirt. 'Jack, if you persist in eating this game instead of providing some decent sheep meat then let the girl prepare it. I'm afraid I wasn't brought up to butcher animals.'

'She should learn,' Squib argued, dropping the rabbits in the dirt. 'I'm not her slave, so if *she* wants to eat *she* has to do her fair share.' Having finally thrown away the crutches a couple of days previously, she limped to a sandy spot on the ground and sat down.

'Don't talk to me like that, young lady.'

'Are you going to let the girl stay here?' Thomas asked Jack quietly as the argument raged.

Jack shrugged his shoulders. 'Adams will send the letter to the newspaper when he nears a town, although I had to push him to do it. Seems he thinks Squib would be better off here. Anyway, I gave a description, explained her story. So we'll see who shows.'

'You might have her for life.'

'Then I guess there'll be another mouth to feed. Besides, a bit of company won't do Olive any harm.'

Squib was sitting in the dirt with her back to the dropped rabbits. 'I'm not so sure about that.' Thomas looked at the skinny-hipped girl with the shoulder-length hair and berry-brown skin. 'You like her, don't you?' He'd seen Jack look at Squib sometimes. Not the way he did at Olive. Thomas couldn't explain it. It was the same, but different. In the city he didn't think that a man like Jack, not yet in his twenties, would take a second look at a girl like her, but it seemed to Thomas that out in the bush everything changed. Squib was smart and easy to look at and she knew things that made Thomas feel stupid, even though he was older. He realised then that plenty of men out here would probably like a girl like her. 'Well, Jack?'

'Yeah, I guess I do.'

Thomas hesitated. 'Not more than Olive?'

'Jack, will you *do* something,' Olive yelled in frustration. 'Either she goes or I go.'

'No one's going anywhere,' Jack answered calmly. 'Squib, show Olive how to skin the first rabbit, and then she can do the second under your instruction.'

'But, Jack –'

'No buts, Olive. We're in the bush now, so you'll have to learn how to live here. Actually, you should count yourself lucky that you have Squib to show you how to do things.'

Together Jack and Thomas began unloading the long trunks. They felt rather than heard Olive's approach.

'I would appreciate it, Jack, if you didn't talk to me that way in front of that girl. Your expectations are –'

Jack dropped the log on the ground. 'For heaven's sake, Olive. This isn't Sydney. Much as you'd obviously like to play ladies out here, in the bush there simply isn't a place for it.'

Olive looked to Thomas for assistance.

'Everyone's equal out here, Olive,' Jack continued, 'so everyone chips in and helps. Okay?'

'*Are* we equal, Jack?' Olive countered. 'Are you sure you're not favouring her?'

Jack lifted another length of timber.

'Look at me!' she continued. 'What were you thinking bringing me out here to this godforsaken place?' Olive gestured around them. The landscape was dull with browns and beige. 'And then to expect me to work like a slave and put up with a common street urchin in this dust-filled wonderland of yours. Absolution Creek is no place for a woman, Jack.' Olive walked away.

Jack tipped his hat back and scratched his forehead. 'I've never heard her speak like that before. That was something I'd expect her mother to say.'

'Well, that went well.' Thomas slid the last length of timber from the dray. 'You know she never sees you. You're gone from sun up to sun down.'

'I'm trying to make something for us here. I just don't get what Olive expects of me.'

Thomas thought of Olive's upbringing, of what she'd left behind. It was funny, although he was younger than his brother, he too had grown up since their father's passing and Jack's leaving of Sydney. Suddenly he was the head of the small household he shared with his sister, and he was beginning to understand why there was a rift between Jack and Olive.

'Jack –' he spread his arms wide '– you have this. This is your dream. But Olive has given up her entire life for you.'

'And you don't think that I haven't given up anything, Thomas? Do you know how hard it's been living up here for months on end, alone. Trying to learn how to manage a property with a handful of textbooks, worrying that any day I could be bitten by a snake, or drowned in the creek or attacked by blacks. Worse, I could be a failure and have to return to Sydney. Then where would I be? What would I do? Absolution Creek is my chance at a future. Olive knew that and she agreed to follow me, to be my wife.'

'Jack,' Thomas argued, 'this is an adventure for you. It's not for her.'

Squib appeared, patiently offering a water bag so that both men could slake their thirst. Once finished, Jack reached out and ruffled her hair. 'You'll show her how to skin those rabbits, won't you?'

'I guess,' Squib reluctantly agreed.

'Thanks.' Jack's smile was broad.

Thomas wiped his chin, and watched as Squib walked away. 'I think she's a bit old for that.'

'Maybe you're right.' Jack counted the logs piled in the three triangular heaps on the ground.

The three Aboriginal men came out of nowhere. 'You boss?'

Thomas automatically reached for Jack's rifle in the front of the dray, only to find his hand stilled by his brother.

'In case your aim is better than your judgement,' Jack said evenly before approaching their visitors. He was aware of Olive rushing to Thomas's side in fright, her leather shoes crackling the leaf litter. They'd grown close on the trip north. Maybe, Jack considered, a little too close. When Thomas finally left, Olive would miss him.

The Aboriginal men squatted beneath the shade of a belah tree. They were dressed in white man's clothes, with thick leather belts, carbine rifles and wide-brimmed hats. The spokesman of the group spat tobacco through a grey-black beard.

'You boss?'

'I am. Jack Manning.' He too squatted in the dirt.

'This house when the wet comes, whoosh.' The man flattened his palm against the ground and scraped the dirt clean.

Jack tilted his hat on the back of his head. 'A flood you mean.'

'Yes, boss.' The man drew a squiggly line in the dirt. 'Creek,' he said by way of explanation. Then, using the pad of his thumb, he marked out Jack's burnt hut and his new site. On either side of the creek he drew a wavering line. 'Last big wet.'

'Is that how far the water came up?' Jack asked. He was aware of Squib squatting beside him in the dirt, watching the men, them watching her.

'Yes.' The man nodded at Jack's partially built house. 'This bad site.' He pointed to a number of large trees. 'That there mark ten feet up, that's a water mark.'

'Jesus, Mary and Joseph. That's from flooding?' Based on the height not only would the land on this side of the creek nearly all go under in a big flood, his new house would only have its roof showing. 'Damn it.'

'You build on a ridge. That's the place for white fellas.'

'The Mankell house? That's on a ridge,' Jack said.

The spokesman moved his torso backwards and forwards. 'Maybe you be safe there, maybe.'

'Maybe?' Jack copied the Aboriginal man's pidgin English. 'It's not like I have a lot of options.'

'This area path for water.'

Squib sat on the ground. 'Do you know where my father is?'

The man looked at her. 'You safe here, little one.' His hand hovered inches from the top of her head. 'You safe here with this white fella.'

'Wait.' Jack rose to his feet with the men. 'I've got sheep. Will they be safe?'

'We hunt on your land?'

'Of course,' Jack answered.

'You look after black fella and we look after white fella.' He patted Squib on the head, and spat a wad of tobacco into the dirt. A mob of lorikeets flew over them. 'Never have sheep on this side when water come.'

'Thank you.' The words sounded tame to Jack.

'You call me Captain Bob. I work for Mr Joseph Campbell. Someone been killing his sheep so I'll be about a bit.' The men slipped into the scrub. Jack looked again at the water mark on the rough bark of the trees. He scratched the slight stubble on his chin and gave a groan.

That night they ate roasted rabbit and fried potatoes.

'So what do we do, Jack?' It was the third time Thomas had asked the question. Once again Jack shrugged his shoulders.

'Do what Captain Bob told us,' Squib muttered between sucks of bone marrow. 'My father always said they were here before us.'

Thomas threw a bone over his shoulder. 'Can't you ask a neighbour about this flooding business, Jack?'

Jack looked at his brother. 'It's a day's ride to the nearest one and they're nowhere near the creek.'

'A day?' In the dwindling light Olive looked incredulous. 'Why would you choose land so far away from people?' She'd barely eaten any dinner. Every time she tried to take a mouthful she saw an image of the rabbit she'd been forced to skin.

Jack threw his chewed rabbit bones over his shoulder. 'This is the bush, Olive.'

Squib tried not to smile as she gathered the dirty plates.

'If we cross the creek and head due west there's a good ridge a half day's ride or so on the other side. That's where the Mankells' old house is. It's a ways from the creek and it runs into pretty sandy ground, so I'd reckon you could make a good garden of it, Olive.'

'A garden? What do I know about gardening?' Olive flicked at an ant crawling over her lace-ups. 'I hate these dark nights, you can't see anything.'

Thomas stretched his legs out and faced Jack. 'You're not serious? Why, you've already got half a house built here. Now you're saying we should up and move just because an old black tells you so?'

'You saw those water marks. What do you expect me to do?'

'All that work,' Thomas complained.

Jack didn't bother reminding Thomas that he did most of it. 'You ever been in a flood, Thomas?' He looked at Squib. 'Or been washed down a creek?'

Squib swished the plates up and down in the bucket. Olive was grinding tiny black ants into the dirt with the sole of her shoe.

'Well, I haven't and I don't intend to.' Jack looked at the faces ringing the fire. The work days were long enough without battling opinions at the end of each one. He reached for his father's Bible. Thomas settled down for their nightly reading. It was a habit that helped fill the hour or so after their evening meal. Olive, on the other hand, gave an angry sigh and walked away. Her slight form stepped over the low foundations of the homestead. A silhouette appeared from within the canvassed corner as she lit a slush lamp. 'I'm beginning to believe it would have been better if Olive hadn't come.'

Squib snapped to attention at Jack's words.

'You don't spend enough time with her.' Thomas poured cold tea from his pannikin onto the fire. It sizzled loudly before evaporating into the embers.

'I have a property to manage.' Jack flicked through the pages of the Bible. 'I don't have time for hand-holding.'

'So I noticed.' Thomas rolled onto his side.

Squib lifted the slush lamp, the weak light illuminating the Bible's pages. Leaning over, she ran her finger across the passages. 'That's where you finished last night, Jack.'

'So it is.'

'Be a full moon tomorrow,' Squib said, nodding knowingly at the sky. 'It should be a fine day for travelling.'

'I think you're right, Squib,' Jack agreed. 'We'll start packing up at first light.'

Olive sat on the edge of the narrow bed and listened as Jack read aloud. There was some comfort in hearing his voice fill the silence around them. If the others had not been with them she may have sat by his side and shared in the reading. Later they could have talked about the day, spent some time together. Olive needed that.

She needed to know that the old Jack, the fun Jack, the caring Jack, had not been totally snatched up by the land he was now tied to. She needed to know that some semblance of the man she'd fallen in love with still existed. The greater part of her was desperate to tell Jack what had occurred in Sydney, however she no longer knew what his response would be. The pity of it was that she had changed too. She would turn seventeen soon and she felt like an old woman.

Through the canvas the light of the camp fire gave off a friendly glow. Olive could see Jack's outline. Thomas lay on Jack's left side, the girl close by on his right. The girl Squib was always close to Jack, and Thomas too was like an extra limb. She stared at the blisters on her palms, at her ragged nails. In spite of the number of times she had washed her hands she could still smell the dead rabbit. She wondered what her family were doing tonight. She had still not written to let them know she was all right. Now she wondered if she should. A change was occurring within her. It was not something she could articulate, for beyond the most obvious of symptoms there was little else to judge her condition apart from intuition. In acknowledging that she believed she was with child, the initial disgust Olive had felt at the possibility of such an event occurring had now been replaced with numbness. That was why she'd not contacted her family. She really didn't know what to do. It was bad enough that her parents would be furious on learning that she'd run away to be with Jack Manning without a word. But to learn that she was unmarried, pregnant. Olive already felt uneasy in this new world of Jack's. She couldn't bear to be shunned by the old world as well.

# ⋘ Chapter 34 ⋙

## Absolution Creek, 1965

'He was lucky, simple as that.'

Having picked up the telephone thinking the ring was for Absolution, Meg was surprised to hear two local matrons discussing Harold's accident. A doctor must have been called for and by all accounts Harold would be fine.

'Well, that woman wouldn't be able to run the place without Harold. Anyway, it's not seemly, a woman being in charge, regardless of whether she's black, white or brindle.'

The back door slammed, heralding Sam's return. Replacing the receiver, Meg quickly went back to the sink and set to work scrubbing the burnt-out saucepan. 'Is Harold okay?' she called out to Sam. It was two hours since Cora and Sam's departure. Two hours since Kendal's puzzling conversation and the battle to get the twins fed and ready for bed.

'He will be,' a male voice answered.

Meg turned to see a man aged somewhere in his forties leaning against the kitchen door. His lanky frame filled the space and his hair gleamed like a crow's wing. Sam and Cora bustled past.

'So, you must be Meg,' he said, striding towards her and shaking her hand.

Meg extricated her hand from the warm grasp as Cora introduced the stranger as James Campbell. He sat beside Sam, long legs stretched out across the linoleum flooring. 'We've met actually. You were having a conversation with two dogs and a poddy lamb, if I recall.'

'That was you?'

His chin dipped in acknowledgement. 'I cut through Absolution on occasion to visit clients. Anyway, Cora here said I should come for dinner, seeing as I *saved* her manager.'

'There's enough?' Cora clearly expected Meg to say yes.

'Of course.' Meg looked at her husband. 'How's your leg?'

'Fine.' Sam frowned.

Meg turned her attention to dinner. As it appeared no one was showering before eating, she retrieved the corned meat from the warming oven and was about to carve when James reached for the carving knife.

'It'll be precision perfect,' Cora reassured her. 'You can set the table, Sam.'

Meg backed away, moving to plate up carrots and potatoes and cut thick chunks of bread. 'You haven't said how Harold is.' Did she sound breathy? *Breathy*, how ridiculous she reprimanded herself. She'd met a man in her aunt's kitchen with her husband and suddenly she was a school girl again.

James opened a drawer and, selecting a serving fork, arranged wedge slices of the pink briny cut on their plates. 'He'll be right,' he answered, a piece of meat finding its way to his mouth. 'He has a nasty bump on his head, which will keep him horizontal for a bit.' He licked his lips. 'Tasty.'

Meg wasn't quite sure if it was the meat James was referring to.

'I'm sure Harold feels a whole heap more comfortable having received the expert attentions of a vet.' Sam prodded his injured leg.

'Large animals are my specialty.' James unsheathed his pocket-knife and prised open the blade. 'Sure you don't want me to have a look, Sam?'

Cora poured four shots of rum and clinked glasses with Sam as Meg sat the plates down. 'Here's to you, Sam. You got Harold out of the vehicle and walked back here in record time without getting lost.' She left the rum bottle sitting on the table.

'I'm sure Kendal thinks he would have done a better job.' Sam took a sip of the rum.

'He was only riled because he didn't come with us when we went to fetch Harold,' Cora answered.

James sculled his own drink and topped up everyone's glasses. 'Anyway, a darkened room and a noiseless environment is the only way Harold will lose the headache.' He smiled at Meg who had taken up residence at the head of the table. 'I'm looking forward to this. It's a long time since I ate a meal whipped up by such a pretty chef.'

Meg felt her cheeks warm. 'Well, that's what I seem to do here. It's four meals a day and –'

'And a bottle at night?' James looked directly at Sam. 'It's an old bush saying, Sam. Four meals a day and a bottle at night. Cheers.'

'Word gets around,' Sam answered soberly. If it killed him he wasn't having another drink in front of Campbell.

They chewed their way through the brine-flavoured meat and vegetables and then started on the bread. By the time the meal was over the new loaf was relegated to crumbs, the jam tin was nearly empty and the rum bottle remained enticingly centre stage. Meg watched her husband's eyes stray to the dark liquid throughout the evening.

'When I was at the Jeffersons' barbecue on the weekend everyone was talking about the next weather change coming through.'

Cora twirled the dregs of rum left in her glass. 'Really?'

'Yep.' James dabbed a finger at some crumbs on the table. 'Marjorie Williams says it will be a beauty.'

Meg did her best to join in the conversation, however she and Sam were relegated to the periphery of bush life. They knew none of the locals James talked about and were surprised to hear of the whole other life that existed beyond the boundary gate. There were barbecues by the river, tennis and cricket competitions, local picnic race meetings and the odd amateur theatrical group that travelled through the area from time to time. Although their time on Absolution was only just passing the two-month point, it seemed to Meg that their new life was being constrained by Cora's almost reclusive existence.

'The tennis comp starts again in late August. You should come up, join in a bit.'

James's invitation, Meg noticed, was directed at her.

'Sure,' Cora intoned. 'I meant to mention it to you, Meg. No doubt you could find a babysitter somewhere.'

'I don't mind a bit of tennis.' Sam licked jam from his fingers, his upper lip a smear of red.

'Really?' Meg wished she didn't sound quite so surprised.

James put the kettle on the Aga and rummaged for the tea caddy in the cupboard. 'Your aunt is a bit of a home body, but that doesn't mean you can't have a life. I'll let you know when there's something on and you can jump in the utility and drive yourself to Stringybark.'

'Meg can't drive,' Sam replied. 'She relies on me.'

*How to make a woman feel useless,* Meg decided, as she watched James negotiate his way around the kitchen. He had the build of a swimmer, with a tapered waist and a well-developed chest and shoulders. She quickly drew her eyes away as he located teaspoons, sugar and her baking tin of biscuits.

'Jackpot.' He promptly devoured two biscuits and sat the tin on the table.

Sam opened four wall cupboards. 'Okay, I give up. Where are the cups?'

James, Meg and Cora all pointed to the same cupboard. Sam raised an eyebrow. 'I see you've been here before, James.'

The kettle boiled and finally they were all sipping their tea.

'You haven't met our little ones,' Sam said over the rim of his cup, 'Penny and Jill.'

'Kids too?' James nodded approvingly at Meg. 'You'd never tell.'

Sam clanged his cup on the saucer.

'That's enough.' Cora lit her second cigarette in as many minutes. 'You've made your point.' She flicked the silver lighter shut. 'You'll have to excuse James, Sam, he doesn't get out much either and he's a bachelor since his dear mother died.' Cora couldn't believe it. James actually thought he could try to make her jealous by showering attention on Meg?

'Mummy's boy, eh?' Sam taunted.

James drained his tea cup, thanked Meg for dinner and excused himself. The kitchen was silent as his footsteps sounded in the hallway.

'Did I say something?' Sam gave a yawn.

'Turn the outside lights on for him, Meg.' Cora slumped back in her chair.

Attempting to ignore the tiny flutter in her stomach, Meg followed James outside. He was at the end of the path near the laundry, his hands busy with a cigarette. Meg flicked the light on the external laundry wall, a pool of white haloing James.

'You'll be right then?' It was freezing and her breath appeared as puffs of steam.

James was wearing a large jacket, the collar of which revealed a lining of tawny wool. Meg could almost feel the heat radiating from him.

317

He took a puff of his cigarette. 'I'm sorry, I've got something on my mind. I shouldn't have behaved like that. In my defence you are as pretty as a picture.'

For a moment she couldn't answer. Meg almost expected to see another woman standing behind her.

'Not used to compliments, eh?' Another drag on his cigarette. 'If you don't mind me saying it, there are plenty of fish in the sea for a woman like you.'

Having met the man all but an hour or so ago, Meg couldn't decide if she should be flattered or concerned. 'I do mind actually,' Meg replied.

'Sorry, it's just that I've had a bit of experience with messy relationships. Anyway, Cora told me you don't have the best of marriages, so I figured –'

'Well, you figured wrong and I don't appreciate my personal life being discussed!'

He cocked his head to one side. Despite his wide-brimmed hat Meg sensed he was faintly amused. 'Sorry. I may be a little rusty when it comes to helping a person.' He dropped his cigarette on the cement path, ground it dead and said loudly, '*Particularly pretty ones.*'

'I'm married, with children,' she replied stiffly, looking over her shoulder towards the house. James's last comment was loud enough for Cora and Sam to hear. Was that what he wanted?

'So why are you whispering?'

She stamped her feet against the cold. 'You're impossible.'

James scratched his cheek. In the stillness Meg heard the faint rasp of nail on stubble. 'There'll be a full moon in a couple of days. Cora's right, there will be rain.'

Meg's cheeks were numb, her fingers icy. 'It's too chilly for rain,' she snapped. 'I don't know how Cora thinks that could happen.'

'This is Absolution Creek.' He merged with the darkness. 'Anything can happen.'

A day later Meg was gathering kindling with the twins, the lambs sucking on the girls' skirts and butting them in their bottoms whenever they leant over. It had been an early start to the morning with a large truck carrying building material trundling in just after dawn. Cora had slammed doors from one end of the house to the other and Sam had been quiet and withdrawn. The late night had left Meg with a dull ache in her head, although remembering poor Harold stopped her feeling sorry for herself.

'Stop it.' Jill gave the lamb a gentle shove.

'He's only playing, sweetie.'

'Daddy has a sore leg like me.'

'Yes, he has, Jill.' As the girls continued to pick up twigs and pieces of bark, Meg thought of the thick bandage around her husband's thigh. The wound needed more than disinfectant and the salve concocted by Cora, but there was no way Sam was having his leg stitched up by a vet, and he refused any attempts to get him to an actual doctor. Meg could only hope it didn't get infected. At the thought of their local vet, Meg's cheeks warmed. Ridiculous, she berated herself. Hadn't she just turned her family's life inside out hoping for a fresh start? She was married with two gorgeous girls, and it angered her knowing Cora told a complete stranger that her marriage wasn't great. It reeked of her own mother's attitude towards Sam, but it also reminded Meg of their problems.

'Mummy, what's the matter?'

Meg ruffled Penny's hair. 'Nothing, just thinking. Why don't you girls go inside and get your woollen beanies and we'll go for a walk.' As the girls ran towards the house, Meg pushed the wheelbarrow over the uneven ground to the homestead fence. There were two rather long pieces of wood, partially split, lying in the grass and these she added to the barrow. How life changed. Only a few months ago her world revolved around stacking grocery shelves, caring for the twins and hoping World War III didn't break out between herself and Sam, or Sam and her mother, or all three of them. And then there was the question of money – the constant working to get it, her concern for her children, and Sam's unemployment and drinking problem. Everything had changed, was changing . . . She threw a bundle of twigs into the wheelbarrow. This move had been for everyone's benefit – at least that was what she had told herself. Was it time to admit that a change in geography hadn't altered her most basic problem? And now there was more clutter to fill her brain. Her mother's strongly worded letter and the revelation Cora and Jane were not blood sisters.

'How's Mrs Bell this morning?'

Meg turned to find James Campbell standing before her with Horse and a long-haired black and white border collie at his feet.

'I didn't hear you.' Meg thought of her unwashed face, glanced at her grubby woollen jumper. 'What are you doing here?'

'And here I was thinking you'd be offering me coffee and cake.'

There was ten feet between them. It felt like a mile and an inch. Realising she was biting her bottom lip, Meg busied herself with the barrow. 'The twins will be out soon.' The collie's enthusiastic scratching with his hind leg only amplified the awkward silence.

'Can you just let Cora know that Horse is fine.' He patted the animal's neck. 'I've checked the abscess that I syringed recently and given him a shot of penicillin. Okay?'

'Cora will be home soon if you need to see her.'

James handed Meg Horse's lead. 'If you can just pass the message on.'

Meg looked at the lead, at Horse, at James.

'There's just one thing, Meg, and you can tell me to butt out if you want –' he paused '– but you might want to learn how to drive. Out here if there's an accident or something, well, it's a pretty important skill to have.'

'Okay.'

He gave her a wink. 'And there's nothing more attractive to a bush man than a capable woman.'

Meg tugged on the lead, unwittingly forcing Horse to follow as James walked down the track towards the avenue of trees. What on earth was she meant to do now? She didn't know the first thing about horses. In the distance she saw Sam standing at the corner of the work shed, hands on hips, watching her, watching James.

Horse whinnied. Penny and Jill arrived in a flurry of hair-pulling to stop bewildered at the back gate.

'Mummy, you have Horse,' Jill announced.

Horse tugged his head sideways, lowering it to eye the twins. His nostrils twitched and flared in interest. Jill reached her hand out and was allowed a small pat before Penny's squeals and Meg's cautionary words caused the animal to smell her inexperience. Horse shifted the weight on his four legs, the leather lead jerking Meg's arm as he backed away, head lowered, his hoofs digging into the dirt. Meg held her ground and dug her own heels in. 'Just behave.' Horse blinked and walked forward to snuffle at her fingers. They were a few minutes into their battle of wills when James drove past the house. 'Great,' Meg muttered. She could just imagine the grin beneath that big hat. As she pondered how to rid herself of Cora's unwieldy animal, Horse reared backwards, yanked free of Meg's grasp and trotted away.

'Bye, Horse.' Penny and Jill waved enthusiastically.

In the middle of the house paddock Horse ran around in circles, kicking up his hind legs in delight.

Meg was outside playing hopscotch with the girls in the dirt, using an old bone as a marker, when Cora arrived back late morning in the ute. She parked the vehicle with a screech of brakes and slammed the door. She had been out to check on the truck that had arrived earlier and she wasn't impressed by what she had discovered. Meg cringed.

'Where's that husband of yours?' Cora shouted, her voice high-pitched.

'Here,' Sam replied tersely, appearing from the direction of the shed.

Excellent, Meg thought, backing away from their hostile tones.

Cora strode towards Sam. 'Do you mind telling me what you think you're doing allowing the purchasing of all that blasted material for the wool and haysheds?'

'Hey, don't yell at me, why don't you query your precious manager?'

'I would,' Cora's words were almost too controlled, 'however, thanks to you he's out for the count.'

'Well, that's not my fault. You want to do all of us a favour and get rid of Kendal. He's just a troublemaker and you know it.' Sam shoved his hands in his pockets and turned away.

'I'm talking to you.'

Sam turned immediately, his face inches from Cora's. 'Firstly, I'm not an employee, I'm your niece's husband, and secondly, I don't blame Harold for trying to fix things up around here. You're tighter than a fish's arsehole with money. Jeez, even your own house is falling down.' Sam spread his arms wide, encompassing the land about him. 'Quite frankly, Harold's ideas are just plain common sense. You fell on your feet when you were left this place, Cora, so why don't you look after it?'

'Really?'

'Yes,' Sam said firmly, 'really. So do us all a favour and stop being so pig-headed.'

Having retreated to the laundry with the twins, Meg was relieved when there was a momentary pause in the row. Her aunt and husband were like the two old bulls she saw occasionally through the kitchen window, grudgingly meeting at the water trough but spending the rest of the day in separate corners of the paddock. Meg was starting to wonder if Absolution was big enough for both of them. In the distance there was a low rumble. She automatically looked heavenward. A few minutes later a low loader with a dozer on the back roared past the house and out through the house paddock gate in the direction of the creek.

'Jesus, Mary and Joseph!' Cora yelled as she half-ran back towards the utility. 'I'm going to kill you men.' The ignition spluttered and died. 'Damn it all!'

'Well, kill James Campbell first,' Sam yelled back. 'I don't appreciate my wife being subjected to that oversexed vet of yours. Anyone would think he lives here too, he's around here that much.'

Sam walked inside. Meg followed him, shuffling the twins into the sunroom on her way past and meeting Sam on his return from the bedroom with three rum bottles under his arm.

In the kitchen he opened the bottles and proceeded to pour the contents down the sink. Tossing the now empty bottles aside he accidently knocked the radio to the floor, smashing it. 'Damn.' He waggled a finger at her. 'You're my wife and I expect you to stay that way. I may not be the best husband, but you've not always been the supportive partner. You stay away from Campbell or I'll clock him one, and then we'll have to leave and go back and live with your bloody mother.'

Meg knew her mouth was open but try as she might she couldn't seem to shut it. On his way out of the kitchen Sam grabbed Meg, pushed her against the cupboard and pressed his lips on hers. 'And . . . and don't forget it,' he finished, striding from the room.

Arms dangling by her side, Meg was brought back to reality by a movement outside the kitchen window. Horse was pulling furiously against a tree, the lead wedged firmly between two branches. 'Oh shit!' she exclaimed.

# ⋘ Chapter 35 ⋙

## Absolution Creek,
## 1924

The Mankell homestead had an air of disuse hanging over it. A hallway leading from the missing front door divided the two living rooms and led to a walkway and large kitchen. Jack swiped at dust-thickened cobwebs. Raw tongue-and-groove pine walls and matching timber floorboards were a feature of the two large rooms, which stood opposite each other across the hall. A mirror image of one another, with a long row of broken or missing casement windows and a picture rail, their most impressive feature was matching ceilings of pressed metal.

Jack stared at the closely interlocked pattern of flowery embossed steel and gave a low whistle. 'Well, will you look at that.' In the middle of each ceiling was a circular decorative piece nearly twenty-four inches in diameter. The cornices and skirting sheets were of a Grecian design. 'We've come up in the world. No shoddy timber ceilings in these rooms.'

'It would look better painted white.' Olive rubbed the door knob and oblong plate. 'Brass,' she explained, looking up to find Jack,

Thomas and Squib all staring at her. 'Well, embossed ceilings are meant to be painted not left raw like these.'

Two plain table lamps with fitted burners, partially burnt wicks and long glass chimneys were lying behind the door. 'Good as new.' Thomas held the lamps aloft. 'Not even a crack.'

Jack nodded. 'Looks like we'll have to invest in some benzine for special occasions.'

The dusty hall extended into a walkway and a large kitchen. Squib inspected overturned crates and the heavy wooden table.

'What happened to the floor?' Olive scuffed at the hardened dirt. 'Surely people don't live like this.' She squealed when a family of tiny field mice scampered from beneath a crumpled hessian bag on the dirt floor.

Squib folded the hessian bag, oblivious to a lizard clinging onto the woven material. 'It's tamped dirt, silly.'

Olive frowned, looking confused.

'This place must be pretty old.' Thomas prodded at a crumbling wall. 'This looks like grass.' He picked out a few tufts of straw. Dried dirt crumbled in his fingers. 'It's mud brick.'

Jack checked the fireplace. The brick innards looked usable and the flue in good condition. 'It's pretty modern, really.'

'We had a hole in one kitchen wall in our cottage and we'd drag logs in through it for the fire,' Squib explained. 'Sure will be a lot of wood carrying here.'

'Well, I think it's positively archaic,' Olive said snootily, wondering how she would cope cooking in such a basic kitchen. The most involvement she had ever had with meals was discussing menus on the rarest of occasions with her mother. Now she'd been relegated to skinning rabbits. At the thought of her parents, Olive's eyes moistened.

Another covered walkway led a good twenty yards from the large kitchen to a square building ringed by an open veranda. Squib stepped carefully around missing and broken boards to investigate.

There were four rooms, two on either side, with doors and a single broken shuttered window all opening out onto the veranda. A fifth room had been an obvious add-on to the opposite end of the building.

Jack fixed his elbow against the door and gave it a firm shove. 'A bathroom and fully functional at that.' A water pipe led from a bucket on the floor to a shower head. A hand pump positioned halfway up gave a creak of resistance under his hand.

Squib poked a finger in the plug hole of a white porcelain pedestal hand basin, wondering how Jack would ever fit into the galvanised hip bath.

'So how is the water heated?' Olive asked, noticing the hand basin didn't appear to be connected to any pipes.

Squib stifled a giggle. Wait until she notices the lavatory, she thought with amusement. The small building of corrugated iron was a good sixty yards from the rear of the house.

They wandered back out. Parts of the bark roof were missing in the bedrooms, although a square of material, perhaps once a makeshift ceiling, hung from a corner of one of the rooms. Inside there was a broken wooden rocker and a large brass bed with three legs propped up against the wall. 'Main bedroom,' Jack guessed.

'Fixable?' Thomas asked.

Jack shook the bed, and dropped it down in a haze of dust and cobwebs. He pressed the springs. 'Couple of candle crates for support and she'll be good as new.' He looked at Olive and smiled.

'But we don't know who's slept in it,' she complained.

'Probably just as well,' Thomas decided.

Next door a sapling had taken root, pressing its young body out through the window. 'Can I have this room?' Squib knelt on the dirt floor and began digging in a circle around the tree to form a trough. Jack squatted beside her, his hand measuring the circumference of the woody plant.

'By its size it looks as if it's been here for five or so years,' Jack surmised. 'Not that I'm an expert. See how it's growing towards the light.' Squib followed his hand as he drew an imaginary line towards the sunlight. The sapling was skewed sideways as if someone had given it a gigantic push in the direction of the open window. 'This bit of a depression here –' he scraped dirt from the cracked skirting board '– gave the tree a watering when it rained.'

'And it's still growing.' Squib plucked at a leaf, resting a hand on Jack's shoulder. 'It survived.'

'Well, it found a home,' Olive said rather impatiently.

'Can this be my room, Jack, and can I keep the tree?'

Jack looked down at the crooked tree and the lost girl standing beside it. He could feel Olive's eyes boring into the back of his head. 'Sure you can.'

'No expense spared here,' Thomas joked as they walked back through the house to the hallway. In the adjoining room a pigeon flew through a broken window, the damaged ceiling revealing blue sky and wispy cloud.

Squib was humming. 'Only a few floorboards need to be replaced here, Jack.'

'Looks like they ran out of money.' Jack examined the rotting boards. 'Half the roof shingle, half bark; timber floorboards here and tamped dirt elsewhere. And a kitchen in the middle of the house. They didn't give much thought to the chance of a fire.'

Squib gave three loud sneezes, rubbing her nose clean with the back of her hand.

'It was a soldier settler's block,' Jack explained. 'I suppose they couldn't make a go of it.'

'Or didn't want to.' Olive sniffed, sneezed and sniffed again. 'Still, they made some improvements. The rest we'll have to make do with, I suppose, until we can get the materials to spruce the place up a little.'

'Money permitting,' Jack warned. 'I don't want anyone getting too excited. The roof's our priority.'

'They must've planted the avenue of trees facing the west.' Thomas tapped at a loose wall board. 'That was a good idea. Well, time to unload the dray. If you sweep out your bedroom, Olive, we'll get your room set up first.'

Olive gave a grateful smile.

Squib let Thomas walk ahead, dawdling behind in the hallway, certain Olive would complain immediately. Squib knew Olive didn't want her to stay.

'It's not forever, Olive.'

'Then why did you say she could have that bedroom, keep the tree?'

'The tree will take care of itself. Come winter the wind will blast in and Squib will chop down the thing herself.'

'And the room?'

'What am I supposed to do? Make her sleep outside? Hope she runs away? She'd end up in an orphanage.'

'Firstly, she's not a child. She's a young woman. And don't tell me you haven't noticed, Jack Manning. Secondly, she's of an age where she could find gainful employment as a maid.'

Squib tip-toed along the hallway and flattened her back against a dusty wall.

Jack gave an indulgent sigh and took Olive's hands. 'Stop making everything so difficult.'

'Do you know how long it's been since you've held me, talked to me, Jack? It's like I don't exist out here. I feel like another task to be attended to at the end of your day.' It was the first time she'd cried in front of him since her arrival from Sydney. It had crept up on her gradually, this feeling of her life not being her own anymore. McCoy had ruined her both physically and emotionally, and now Jack's disinterest and the harshness of her new home ate at her daily.

Jack stroked Olive's tear-stained face, and took her by the shoulders. 'Once this place is tidied up a bit you won't know yourself. Everything will be much better. And once we're married –'

Squib cleared her throat and stepped into the kitchen. 'Jack, Thomas needs a hand.'

Olive's unblinking stare quite unnerved Squib, however she stood her ground as Jack left. 'You can help me get some firewood, Olive.' The older woman didn't move. 'Bush men expect their women to be a bit capable,' Squib reminded her, 'and you and I both know you've got some work to do.'

'Where have you been?' Jack sat by the camp fire, a notebook in one hand, a stubby pencil poised mid-thought. The fire was a good distance from the homestead. Squib figured he had lit it to ensure a little peace and quiet, for Olive's complaints began with the rising of the sun and didn't ease until the fireplace was cleaned and the house swept out.

'Walking. You know I don't like being cramped up inside. Everything worth seeing or hearing's out here.'

'You shouldn't have left her with all that mess, Squib.'

'I helped, Jack. Anyway, I'm not her slave. If she wants to live here then she has to do a bit too.' She drank thirstily from the waterbag.

'They're asleep.' He nodded towards the outline of the old homestead. 'I was going to wake them up so they could see the moon.' He glanced heavenward. 'Sometimes I wonder if the moon we see in the city is the same as this one. It's so much bigger here, much brighter.' He looked at her. 'Don't you get scared when you go off wandering?'

'What's there to be scared of?' Squib sat by his side.

Jack waved an arm vaguely westward. 'Sometimes I wonder what else is out there.'

329

'Silly,' Squib laughed. 'What are you writing?'

'*Drawing*,' he corrected. 'A fence. The one on the south-east boundary needs repairing. I've been so busy worrying about this house business that I've forgotten what I came here to do.'

'Tend sheep.'

'Yes, yes.' He smiled. 'I like them, you know, Squib. I didn't know if I would first off. The man who sent me here gave me all these books to read on sheep husbandry, and before I knew it I was buying the ewes at the saleyards and paying men to help walk them here.' He chewed on the stick. 'Now I'm worrying about fences. It's a whole new world to me.'

'Don't you own this land?' Squib never guessed that Absolution wasn't his.

'One day I will.'

Squib considered his words. 'Are you like an overseer?'

'I guess. Mr Farley, the owner, has no kin so I figure he'll probably leave Absolution to me on account I did him a favour once. So then, what do you really know about sheep?'

'My father says that sheep are only as dumb as the people that work them.' Squib thought about Mr Purcell and Waverly No. 4. 'You know there's a ram on the shilling coin.'

'Waverly No. 4? Of course.' Jack tucked the stubby pencil in his notebook.

'I had that coin once,' Squib revealed. 'My father worked for Mr Purcell of Waverly Station and I saw the ram, Jack. I use to walk down to the paddock and talk to him. Once I had a bit of stale apple in my pocket and he nibbled it straight out of the palm of my hand.'

'Go on with you, is that true?'

'True as the day I fell off the dray and lost my family.' Squib lowered her voice. 'I haven't told anyone cause people think the ram is pretty special and they don't believe me when I say I patted him.'

'I don't know if I believe you either.'

Squib elbowed him in the ribs.

'Ouch. I believe you. How else would you know so much about sheep?'

'You won't tell anyone, will you, especially Adams?'

In the firelight Squib's face was soft and golden. She looked both older and younger simultaneously.

'Of course not.'

'You'll be a good sheep man, Jack.'

When Squib woke a few hours later a light breeze ruffled her hair. She wiggled on her side hollowing out a hole. Jack's warm breath was moist against her skin. The moonlight traced the line of his body. Very slowly, Squib rolled onto his outstretched arm.

Olive lay on the bed, the window and door open to the elements. It was a hot night, and the full moon was unforgivingly bright. Above, a swathe of material covered the bark roof, although it provided little comfort as she knew the things that crawled and crept would hardly be dissuaded by a length of calico. The mosquito netting provided her with far more reassurance. It extended from a rod a couple of feet above the bedhead, its filmy edges tucked securely beneath the flock mattress. She daren't move lest she disturb the careful barrier, for once disrupted her night would be one of almost obsessive checking for insects and spiders. She wormed a little further down in the bed. Perspiration pooled on her stomach and thighs, yet she kept the neck-to-knee nightgown smoothed low over her legs. Having already forgone the sheet in the need for a modicum of comfort against the heat, her gown was the last vestige of decorum and self-discipline.

She lay flat, unmoving and uncomfortable, the night gown growing damper by the hour, her skin itchy. Of course Jack and the girl would be sprawled in the dirt outside, lulled by the earth they loved. At the thought of their mutual contentment Olive started grinding her teeth. Had she not done her best to be with Jack? Had she not given up everything to follow him to this place? Olive thought of her family, and of the privileged upbringing she had once taken for granted. Now she dreamt of carpeted floors, groceries delivered daily, and an iceman who ensured that her choice of beverage was never lukewarm. Everything was so primitive in this new life that she'd chosen that at times she could have screamed at her foolishness. Why had she followed Jack? Why had she not given more thought to where she was going? Why had she not appreciated her own family more? The answer haunted her. Her craving for independence and her love for Jack had propelled her into a life of oblivion.

Outside, an unknown night bird gave a lone cry. The sound pierced the tight constriction of her chest. Transported to the outskirts of Chatswood, Olive recalled the glistening leaves of the tree above, the close sentinel of woody plants that shielded her attacker and allowed his pleasuring. How beauty and horror could come together so easily astounded her. It was this single element that haunted her, yet also allowed her to focus beyond the brutal acts of her assailant.

There were methods of coping, withdrawal and anger being the uncontrollable emotions that struck her daily. Olive was taunted by the simple fact that if she had not followed Jack then she never would have been at Mrs Bennet's boarding house, and she never would have been attacked. If only she could talk to Jack, if only she could explain what happened. Yet how could she when Jack remained indifferent towards her? The man she had decided to spend the rest of her life with had changed almost overnight. He was perpetually busy and always distracted. Now when he looked at her there was impatience where there was once love. She was not suited to Jack's new life. They both knew it.

It had taken some weeks for Olive to comprehend this. And when she did, she saw it with terrible clarity. Jack was in some ways already married to the land he managed, and the girl was an extension of his love. A common bond held them fast, and though he would be loath to admit it, Jack saw in the fledgling woman the companion his new life required. Her mother would call them a pigeon pair. Had the thought not riled Olive she too would have addressed them as such, thereby relegating her own position in the household to little more than decoration. Decoration – what a ludicrous term. Her skin was lacklustre, her eyes dull, and her hair . . . Well, she doubted if it would ever be truly clean again.

Olive concentrated on her breathing. The fluttering of her chest steadily increased. When the attacks first began some weeks after her assault Olive believed her heart was failing, that she was dying. Yet the attacks kept coming, day and night, irregular in appearance yet constant in the frightening sensation of a racing heart and shortness of breath. Olive focused on the surface of the toilet table. She counted the objects upon it: her silver-backed hairbrush and comb, a stoppered glass bottle of Atkinson's Red Rose perfume. With difficulty she tugged at the mosquito netting, her hand reaching for the bottle of Lavender Salts on the bedside table. Distraction often assisted in calming such attacks, and she sniffed at the invigorating salts, falling heavily against the pillows. Above, the stretch of calico displayed unknown shadows. The rippling shapes reminded Olive of Sydney Harbour, and she imagined the water glittering across Rose Bay towards her home. The life she loved was gone, was sliding away on an outgoing tide. It was as if some mythical creature had sucked the essence out of her, leaving Olive only a meagre shell to inhabit, and a horribly altered world from which there was no escape. She didn't know if she could bear another day. Something had to change. Sadly, she acknowledged it was she who would have to adjust, for to exist in this land there was simply nothing else to be done.

If it were not for the child growing within her, Olive would have run. She would have returned to Sydney and accepted the punishment meted out by her parents. She imagined their joy on her return and then their anger and disappointment as her story unfolded. To have run away to the outer limits of society with a man unworthy of the Peters name would stun them into silence. Yet her family, although controlling and snobbish, knew their place in society, knew their path in life. And they were a loving family. They would eventually forgive her and life would go on.

Olive turned on her side. The bed creaked. She wasn't going anywhere. She could hardly return to Sydney society carrying a criminal's child; nor could she lie and tell her family that the baby was Jack's. They were not married after all. Either way, she would be a terrible disgrace. The embarrassment that such a situation would cause her family was untenable and Olive could not bear to cause them any more pain. The shame coursing through her would never abate. She would carry it for the rest of her life.

## ≪ *Chapter 36* ≫

## *Stringybark Point Hotel, 1965*

After two nights resting at the Stringybark Point Hotel, Scrubber began to feel better. The publican's wife was a right little boiler when it came to whipping up a feed of bacon and eggs for breakfast, and Scrubber quickly sported a pot belly. He was gobbling down four meals a day and a couple of fortifying beverages at night. His decision to relax for a bit came after the barmaid plonked the article about Cora on the bar. He would have recognised the girl anywhere. She still had that shoulder-length hair and smooth skin.

It was only later while lying on his sagging mattress, Dog hiccupping beside him, that Scrubber gave thought to the picture. Cora's youthful appearance he put down to the newspaper print. Even he would look partially human in black and white. No, it was the eyes that confused him – like they belonged to a stranger. And that girl hadn't ever been unfamiliar to him. He'd carried Cora around like a showy fob watch, like that ram on the shilling coin.

'Well, Dog, Cora Hamilton bought herself a fancy ram.' He gave a chuckle and tweaked Dog's nose. 'What do you think about that?' If the Purcells were alive they'd be livid. The stockman's daughter, the wildcat, having the audacity to purchase some of Waverly No. 4's blood. Scrubber was so chuffed about the way Cora's life was going that he decided another night wouldn't do him any harm.

So here he was sitting on the balcony in a cane-bottom chair, his yellowing toenails airing on the wooden railings. The boozy inhabitants below were long in bed, apart from a single station wagon with feet sticking out its rear window, and a reprobate passed out in the middle of the road. Scrubber, having already chucked an empty rum bottle at the prone figure, couldn't be sure if the person concerned was dead or not; either way there were good odds he'd be road kill by morning.

Dog trotted out onto the veranda, lifted his leg and peed through the railings to the street below.

'Deadly aim, old fella.' Dog waddled back to sit by his side.

Down the street lay the old police block vacated by fire in 1924. It had been a busy town back then, with three hotels, two shops, a post office; heck, there was even an undertaker dedicated to the passing citizens of Stringybark, and there were quite a few back then. Scrubber rubbed his bristled cheek, and prodded at a tooth only days away from being ejected from his jaw. It was hard this falling apart. What he wouldn't give for a few more years, just a few. Veronica once told him he should be lucky to make sixty – that sixty was a fair innings – and that people such as them that slaved for others were buggered by fifty. Well, he was over sixty and it was only a fair innings until you got there. He wanted more. The only blessed consolation was that this journey would end with him parked beneath a silver brigalow. Beautiful shaped trees they were, especially of a morning when the sun hit them just so. Would be nice, Scrubber decided, to be compost for such a thing, to know that in the end he'd contributed to something real pretty.

Across the road a single box tree swayed in the northerly wind. The tree was the only reminder of the old days. Planted near the hitching rail outside Green's Hotel and Board at the turn of the century, it had provided shade for the tethered horses of the patrons inside. Untying the pouch at his waist, Scrubber perched the leather bag on the railing.

'Not long to go now, mate. We'll be on our way tomorrow and then it's just a couple of days' travel. I'll make it too. I had my doubts, but now, well, I think we'll make it. Take a gander across the street, will you? They never did rebuild Greenie's place. She was a good little establishment too. Remember old George on the piano and candy-arsed Lorraine? Yeah, she was lickable – real tasty – not that I had a second go, not with canny-eyed Veronica in tow. Pretty sure it was Lickable Lorraine that got me so riled that Veronica ended up with child. Anyways, it's good to remember, ain't it? Good to remember the good and the bad . . .'

Veronica, always a ferreter when it came to gossip, brought news within a fortnight of a runaway child and a fire on a soldier settler's block. A blacksmith from down south picked up the tale from a grocer, who'd got it from the publican at Green's Hotel and Board, who'd heard it off a postal and supply rider by the name of Adams.

'Reputable is what the fella said,' Veronica intoned as she stuffed their few belongings into saddle bags. Circles of sweat patched her dress at the armholes and waist.

'You sure you want to come, woman?' Having tried every conceivable angle to dissuade Veronica, Scrubber was considering clocking her one on the back of the head. 'It'll be fierce hot.'

'I'll manage.' Veronica sniffed, stuffing a dirty hanky between damp breasts. 'Besides, there's a child involved.'

Scrubber saddled the horses, punching his fist into the belly of the old nag he'd brokered for Veronica. The mare was a bugger for holding wind and then letting it out once a man thought the girth strap was good and tight. A fine match he reckoned for his Veronica. 'Fine. Come then, but I'll be leaving you in town. It wouldn't be proper for you to go bush with me and Matt. It's men's business. We gotta find the people that took his girl.'

Veronica carried the three-legged stool outside and used it to mount up. 'You sure that Matt Hamilton will come?' she asked sweetly, before giving a moan as she flung her leg over the saddle. The horse gave a half-hearted pig-root. Scrubber smacked the mare lightly on the nose.

'If he's still out working at Mulligan's he'll get my message and he'll come. We'll meet at Green's Hotel and Board, seeing that's the only place I know of, thanks to you, Veronica.' Scrubber did one final check of their drafty room and then slashed a hole in the mattress, poking his stash deep inside. There wasn't much point going looking for trouble.

'Tell me again why we're doing this, lovey?' Veronica swayed danger-ously in the saddle. 'Why you've become a good Samaritan. Not meaning to be difficult, but it ain't really your character.'

Scrubber saddled up. 'Let's just say I owe them.'

They poked the horses out of the grounds of the boarding house. In spite of his complaining, Veronica paid the monies owed on their accom-modation, plus enough to hold the hut until their return. Scrubber guessed old V knew what she was doing. Having taken charge of such things since their hooking up, he dared not argue. Besides, it weren't so bad having someone else worrying about the basics for a while. He guessed that was why his parents married.

Veronica's hand stole into a saddle bag where salted mutton waited. 'I don't think my arse was meant to be five foot off the ground.' She stuffed the strips of meat into her mouth.

'It won't be if you keep eating.' Scrubber pulled on the reins, turned the mare onto the dirt road and jabbed at the horse's flanks. 'If you need to chew on something, chew on this.' He tossed her a wad of tobacco from his pouch and watched with surprise as she caught it. It would be a good week's ride across to Stringybark Point if Veronica didn't hold him up. Scrubber hoped Matt would only be a day or so behind them. 'Come on,

Veronica,' he called over his shoulder. 'You're gonna have to keep up. I don't want to have to leave youse by the side of the road.'

'And who else will wash your filthy smalls and service you regular like, if you get rid of me?' Veronica hollered.

While he was loath to admit it the woman had a point. 'Cook you a tasty feed of chops for tea,' he promised. 'Keep your eye out for my favourite feed.'

'A stray sheep on the side of the road?' Veronica fluttered her eyelids.

Scrubber nodded. 'That would be it.'

# ✠ *Chapter 37* ✠

## *Absolution Creek,*
## *1924*

Squib tailed the Aboriginal men, slipping between thick stands of belah and spiky dry grass, shadows hovering as the trees grew denser. Having noticed them in the distance while investigating the land around the homestead, she had been intrigued to see Captain Bob. Although previous ramblings had taken her over many parts of Jack's land, this area was completely foreign. When she heard the sound of trickling water, Squib gathered she'd been drawn in a half-circle back towards the creek.

Captain Bob squatted alone in a clearing within a clearing. A fire burnt at his feet, a spiral of white smoke heading directly skyward as a cross breeze rustled branches overhead. Squib hung on the edge of the tree-lined circle, her toes cushioned by short springy grass. Fallen timber, unseasonal clumps of wildflowers and grazing wallabies fringed this new world. The trees ringing the clearing were misshapen and odd, as if recovering from old wounds carefully inflicted.

'We have sacred places, our people,' Captain Bob whispered. It was as if his words were gathered by the branches and flung back and forth through the air. 'Some are ceremonial for corroborees. Other areas are used for our living needs. Some for the carving of women's cooking things and some for canoes.' He gestured to the trees surrounding them.

Squib noted that the woody plants were aged and knotted, many scarred with great pieces cut from their trunks. 'For canoes, for the flood you talked off?'

'For past floods and those to come.' Captain Bob nodded. 'We don't own the land, little one, the land owns us. The land is our mother. You know this, yes?'

A number of wallabies, crouching on their stubby front legs, ambled slowly from Squib's path as she walked across the clearing. The fire was hot and pungent.

'The Dreamtime all around us, little one. We exist in it and beyond it. Listen to your heart.' He gestured to a rock and a wallaby, then scooped dirt into his palm and let it trickle freely back to the ground. 'Feel what they feel. We share their spirit.'

A lady beetle settled on Squib's hand.

'This is not the time for the black man. The white fella's time has come and we must be like the animals when the cold comes. So build your nest, little one, and do not venture far, for the whites would see you taken from the man who would be your kin.'

Squib thought of her long dead mother, of her brother. A vision of Ben in a room crowded with boys drifted with the heady smoke. There were large wooden crosses on the pale walls and many of the children were crying. 'Ben? He's lost too?'

Captain Bob sprinkled the fire with water.

'And my father?'

'You will meet again, but it will not be as you imagined.'

Squib bit her lip. 'So I have to stay with Jack? I knew I did.'

'And now you have something for me, but remember the spirits cannot protect you from another man's judgement.'

Squib considered Captain Bob's words. Only one man knew the secret of her family. She looked Captain Bob directly in the eyes. 'The man who brings the mail, Adams, he's the one who is killing the sheep.'

Captain Bob displayed bright pink gums and partial stubs for teeth.

Squib looked at the dwindling fire. The hollowed dirt that protected it provided no fuel for the dying flames. She looked back to the place where Captain Bob sat. It was empty.

# ≪ *Chapter 38* ≫

# *Absolution Creek, 1965*

The twins were poking their fingers in the air vents on the dash.

'Now, I want you girls to stay very quiet. Remember what I told you?'

They nodded obediently, elbowing each other into submission, and wiggled back into the bench seat. Meg turned the ignition, and placed her foot on the clutch. She slowly moved the column gear stick into first and accelerated. The station wagon gave a series of hops forward and the twins slid off the seat, squealing excitedly as the vehicle stalled.

'What happened, Mummy?' Penny asked.

'Damn it all.' Meg mentally retraced her steps. At least Sam's station wagon was clear of the garage. She had managed to reverse it out of the narrow timber structure without any damage, although her stress levels weren't faring as well.

Penny elbowed Jill back against the seat. 'Stop it.'

'You're hurting me,' Jill complained, pinching her sister.

'That's it.' Meg turned to them. 'Out. Come on, hop out. It's hard enough trying to teach myself how to do this. I don't need you little scallywags distracting me.'

Penny and Jill stared at her in dismay, bottom lips drooping.

'That look might work on your father, but not me.'

The girls scrambled out of the vehicle. 'It's your fault.'

'No, it's *yours*.'

'Inside the back gate where I can see you, thank you, and I don't want you two moving from there until I return.'

'Yes, Mummy.'

Meg waited until the girls were safely within the homestead surrounds before trying again. It couldn't be that difficult. She'd watched Sam drive on numerous occasions. 'Clutch, gear, release clutch, accelerate.'

Once again the vehicle hopped a few paces forward. This time Meg was ready. Her feet moved swiftly to the brake and clutch, and she flicked the gear stick back into neutral before it stalled again. 'Progress.' She rubbed her hands together, checked to ensure she was still alone. The station outbuildings were quiet. No one was around and Meg didn't expect Cora or Sam to show for at least another hour. There had been fights aplenty since yesterday, what with the dozer, timber and iron arriving and Horse's entanglement in the tree. Meg expected Cora to be in full lecture mood by dinner. Until then the afternoon was hers.

This time the station wagon moved forward with a single jolt. Meg squared her shoulders, depressed the clutch and went up a gear. Swerving to miss the poddy lambs nibbling grass by the roadside, the vehicle whizzed along the dirt road past the dam and was soon heading out towards the silos. The gate was open and she steered the vehicle through it cautiously before trying her luck and going up into third gear. A satisfied smile crossed her face. Turning left she drove up onto the main road. It was a good few miles until the boundary gate and Meg practised going up and down gears, accelerating and decelerating. Soon she was driving like a pro, the window down, her elbow resting on the door frame. The wind was freezing and her cheeks turned numb quickly in response. Meg didn't care. She threw her head back and gave a yelp of pure joy.

Driving wasn't so hard. Wow, at the rate she was progressing a driver's licence would be hers next week. Meg visualised driving to Stringybark Point to do the shopping, maybe even going further afield for a bit of sightseeing. No more days filled with housework now; all she had to do was pack up the girls and go. Everyone else had a life so why couldn't she?

The boundary gate appeared before her like a brick wall.

'Damn.' Meg pressed the brake pedal to the floor, and the car skidded on the dirt. Trying to right the vehicle's path, she over-corrected and within seconds the car hit the gate, smashing it to pieces. Meg came to a stop a couple of hundred yards onwards, the engine running. She looked into the rear-vision mirror, her white knuckles clutching the steering wheel. The gate was ruined and the Absolution Creek sign lay in the dirt.

When her shock subsided a little, Meg inspected Sam's car. The old Holden was invincible. Wiping a saliva-moistened finger on the bonnet duco, a tiny fleck of white paint was the only sign of her recent altercation. Could be worse, she decided, although the thought of fronting her aunt with the news was more numbing than the actual accident. Picking up the property sign, Meg pushed the still-attached nail into the hole on the upright post then proceeded to stack the busted gate timber into a pile on the roadside. One section of the gate was actually more damaged than the other. Meg figured Sam could probably drag a piece of mesh or even a spare gate if there was one lying around to block the hole. That was something.

Meg was still perusing the damage and procrastinating about returning to the homestead when Ellen appeared from the direction of Absolution Creek.

'You right?' she asked a little offhandedly.

'All good here,' Meg replied, trying to sound flippant. 'Bit of a brake problem.'

Ellen surveyed the wrecked boundary gate from inside her vehicle. 'Oh dear.'

'Pretty much. How's Harold?'

Ellen bit her lip. 'Okay. I'd feel happier if he'd see a doctor. It's all very well having James Campbell checking on him. It's just . . . well, it's a head wound. The same spot where that ram hit him when he was knocked over in the yards.' Ellen shook her head. 'I know Cora thinks the world of James, but he is a vet.' She sniffed. 'Of course, Harold's just as bad. He keeps telling me it's just a flesh wound.'

'Ellen,' Meg began, feeling decidedly uncomfortable. 'What *is* the relationship between James and Cora?'

'They're friends. Although I think they care very deeply about each other. Why?'

'Just wondering.'

'He won't cause any problems,' Ellen advised her, 'if that's what you're worried about. Cora would never put a personal relationship above the welfare of the property. James has his own responsibilities and Cora has Absolution, and that seems to suit the both of them just fine.'

*Friends*, Meg thought. She liked the sound of that word.

Ellen placed her hands on the steering wheel as if she were about to drive off, and then dropped them back in her lap. 'I didn't expect you to stay. You being a city girl.'

'Oh?'

'I guess the proverbial pot of gold has a fair bit to do with it.'

'*Pot of gold*,' Meg repeated, although she was pretty sure Ellen alluded to Absolution Creek. A guilty sense of excitement rushed her thoughts. It was the first real confirmation that the property would one day be hers.

346

'Anyway, I just wanted to say that apart from your inheritance I admire you for hanging in there. That aunt of yours can be difficult, however people respect her, Meg, for what she's done, who she is. You shouldn't listen to gossip.'

'Gossip?'

'You go to town. You've got eyes and ears,' Ellen replied softly. 'I must go. I promised Harold I'd be home by dark.' Shifting the vehicle into first gear, Ellen drove away.

Ellen's words echoed in her head. It seemed Absolution would one day be hers. She'd said that Cora had a past Meg needed to understand, and that James and Cora were just friends. Remembering this, Meg felt both excited and intrigued, however her mind seized on the last point. Why was James hanging around Absolution if Cora was only a friend? Surely he had better things to do than be on-call for her aunt. Ellen's vehicle threw up swirls of dust as she drove away. Meg knew why. James Campbell was interested, there was something between them. She may have married when she was a teenager, but Meg knew when a man was keen on a girl. With a smile on her lips she drove home carefully and parked the station wagon in the garage. Somehow the boundary gate's destruction seemed unimportant.

## ❧ Chapter 39 ❧

## Absolution Creek, 1924

Olive heaved up a breakfast of eggs and toast. It was her second sickness of the day following weeks of nausea, and still she felt no better. Pushing the casement window ajar she breathed in mouthfuls of gritty air as sticky black flies buzzed about the room. She yearned for an orange to cleanse the bitter taste in her mouth, and silently pleaded for a day of rest. Sunday seemed so far away. It was only just past daylight yet the butter needed to be churned, the new vegetable plot dug, and a cooked midday meal was expected to be ready on the table, regardless of whether Jack remembered to return to the house to eat or not. Olive's immediate concerns were a lie down and at least a dozen Aspro tablets. She knocked back a handful, her fingers resting briefly on her slightly protruding stomach.

'You're with child, aren't you?' Squib poked a length of wood into the fireplace and dropped another log on the dirt floor before hooking a pot of water onto the swinging arm above the flames.

'Of course not.' Olive busied herself, shaking dirt and leaves free from Jack's and Thomas's clothes. After a full day standing over the boiling copper in the sun, the clothes she'd hung over a makeshift line between two trees had broken, dropping the clothes in the dirt. 'I'm not washing these *again*. They'll have to do.'

'You have all the signs.' Squib closed the window, her attention drawn to the black flies buzzing about Olive's sick bowl, which stuck out from beneath the curtain of the candle box cabinet. 'I've seen them before when Abigail had my sister, Beth: the sickness and the tiredness and that.' She pointed at Olive's stomach. 'How far gone are you?' Squib counted out six large potatoes from the hessian sack on the floor and began to peel them with a stocky knife. 'Whose is it?'

'I'm not *gone* anywhere.' Olive tugged at the ugly frock made by a dressmaker in the village last month. It was difficult to believe that the calendar was inching towards late May. She'd been on Absolution Creek for three-and-a-half months. With a final straightening of the dress seams, Olive squared her shoulders. 'It's the change in diet. I'm a city person. I'm not used to this kind of food.'

Squib dropped the potatoes into the boiler. She really couldn't understand why Olive didn't just pack up and leave. 'Why'd you come, then?' She fished out a piece of corned meat from the bucket on the wooden table. It had been sitting in brine for two days, but with the unseasonably warm weather it was time for it to be eaten. The minister hadn't passed through Stringybark Point on account of a fever hitting a family of eight. They'd drunk water from a river where a dead cow had been found. Olive and Jack were still not married.

'Why don't you go home with Thomas?' Jack's brother had determined to leave in July. It was the time of the year when the rainfall was at its lowest, making travel much easier, at least that was what Squib heard. She put the meat and a good portion of the brine into the cooking pot.

'How do you know how to cook that?' Olive was intent on changing the subject.

Squib wiped her hands on her blue serge dress. It was one of two sewn by the village dressmaker. A third in poo brown was a cast-off from Olive. 'I've got eyes. Besides, most of it is common sense. You don't always need a recipe book.'

Olive decided on a more companionable approach. 'Living out here,' she said, pouring a glass of lukewarm water, 'well, it's hard on a couple. I never see Jack. At least Thomas comes home for meals, but not Jack, he's out from dawn to dusk. Why, the man only needs a water bag for sustenance.'

'He's making a living. We're meant to be making a home.'

Olive took a sip of water to settle her stomach. 'Making a home? Apart from making pastry and scones, the only thing I've learnt is how to chop wood and sprinkle water on dirt floors and get my arms burnt red by the sun.'

Squib washed the paring knife in the ceramic basin, drying it on a towel tucked through a belt at her waist. 'This is our home and we have a responsibility to care for it – both the buildings and the land.'

Olive wanted to tell the girl that Absolution Creek wasn't her home, and that she should only speak when spoken to or else she'd be on the next packhorse to Stringybark Point. Instead she piled the washing to one side. The girl knew Olive's condition. Maybe there was some benefit in keeping her on. She was adept at cooking and cleaning and was probably born into service. Only yesterday, the girl mentioned an interest in purchasing some cheap spoilt fruit during the winter. Olive was dying for a little variety. 'Are you still planning on making jam?'

'Why?'

'I thought we could make some preserves as well.'

'Perhaps,' Squib answered tightly.

Olive ran a finger along the washed boards in the hallway. She had approached Jack for an entrance parlour yesterday complaining it was quite wrong to walk directly into a hallway. To her delight he agreed, although he quickly changed the structure to an open veranda, promising to build it during the winter.

A slight breeze stirred the swept path as Olive walked along the side of the house. They'd finished the roof last month and it was a comforting sight even if it did look like a patchwork quilt with its high-shingled roof interspersed with sheets of shiny new corrugated iron. Once the woolshed was completed, Jack promised to replace the kitchen fireplace with a built-in stove and stone chimney. The stove was already purchased, courtesy of Anthony Horden's mail-order catalogue.

The rear of the house block was where the chook run, clothes-line, vegetable plot, outhouse, wood shed and pile were located, the copper taking centre stage. Beyond was a tangle of low brush and wind-twisted pine trees. More than once Olive considered walking through the shadowy grove and not reappearing. At nearly five months gone, she was aware that one day she would wake up and no longer be able to conceal her ruination. To date, loose clothing and a general increase in her own weight had assisted, however time no longer favoured her. Olive stared into the ridge. She envisioned a cool glade of sun-stippled grass and it was quite an enticing thought to simply lie down as the characters did in a fairy tale, to be awoken to a fresh new world abundant with hope and love. It was a pity that she was such a coward.

Olive chose instead to rely on Jack's Christian charity. It was a decision long in the making, one compounded by the shock of the attack, which she now recognised had slightly unhinged her faculties. Looking back she saw a stretch of days filled with complaints, and she knew it was her attitude that caused Jack rarely to return home. When he did it was to campfire quietness and a child-woman who knew his every mood. Well, Jack Manning was *her* fiancé and, while their love had been eroded, Olive determined to salvage something from it. She had given up everything for him and it dawned on her that her pride refused to see her left with nothing. She thought of her father. He'd aspired to a better life and through hard work and perseverance achieved his goal. If he were here he'd be telling her to do the same thing.

'You wanted him, Olive,' he would tell her. 'It is your duty to help him achieve his dream. As your own mother supported me.'

Only one lifetime stretched out before them both and it was with the future in mind that Olive determined her hateful secret must be revealed.

Her confidence grew daily. It was like a bird in a nest, testing its wings before that first life-affirming flight. Soon Olive would sit Jack down and explain the ordeal she had suffered. In her heart she knew he cared and she believed she could be a good wife. She simply needed to forget her shame and share the misfortune that plagued her body. Once Jack understood, once he accepted Olive was the wounded party, she knew everything would be all right. Honesty and loyalty were now the virtues Olive aspired to.

The wood pile was dwindling again and the eggs needed to be collected. Then there was the vegetable plot. She looked at the oblong square, some twenty feet in length and width, and it seemed to glare back at her. After pegging it out a week ago, Jack had handed her a hoe and declared the job women's work. Ever since, Olive had fought the baked earth on a daily basis. So far she had an eighth of the area turned. The ground was so hard the hoe bounced when struck and it had taken a week to get the tilth to any depth. However, Olive persevered. Although broad beans, cabbage and carrots were of major importance, her desire to prove her worth was far stronger.

With a sigh she bound strips of cloth around her cracked hands and recommenced her prodding of the earth's crust. As usual her mind turned to Sydney and her family. With great determination she brought it back to the hoe, and concentrated on tilling the earth. Within minutes her lower back was paining. Sweat ran down her thighs. A gust of wind whipped up a flurry of dust, depositing her straw hat in a nearby stand of needlewood trees. She couldn't run after it, not this morning. An appropriate profanity was slow coming to her lips. The best of Thomas's complaints were Holy Ghost, while Jack and Squib were particularly fond of Jesus, Mary and Joseph. The pair used the phrase so frequently Olive feared the trilogy might pay them a visitation in complaint. She tucked a stray lock of hair into the bun she'd taken to wearing on the nape of her neck, and marvelled at city women with the time to have their hair styled.

'How are you going with it, Olive?'

She could have cried at the sound of his voice. Instead Olive pasted a smile on her face and turned to greet Thomas.

'You work too hard.' He dusted off her runaway hat and sat it carefully on her head. 'I'll do it.' His fingers closed around the hoe's wooden handles, brushing hers. 'Look at your hands.' The rough bandaging showed traces of blood. 'You shouldn't be doing this.'

Olive took a firmer hold of the hoe. 'Everyone has enough to do without carrying me. I'll manage.'

'But —'

'Leave off please, Thomas. You just have to let me muddle on in my own silly way.'

Thomas watched as she struggled with the unyielding ground. 'But I could help, Olive. You don't have to do this.'

'I do if we want some vegetables by August.' She was crying again. All she ever seemed to do these days was water the ground with her tears. Tightening her grip on the hoe, Olive struck force-fully at the dirt, each thudding contact with the ground jarring her arms and neck, burning her shoulder blades, tearing at her cracked palms. 'I can't eat salted mutton and damper forever. I'm dying for fresh fruit and trifle with cream, and crumbed cutlets with spaghetti.'

Thomas knew what he wanted to say, however the right words failed him. Some days he wished he were older. Some days he wished he could take Olive away from all of this. 'Have you . . . Have you spoken to Jack?' Thomas began awkwardly. 'Maybe . . .'

Olive continued striking at the plot. 'No. No, I haven't. It's not easy for me.'

His hand stayed her movements. 'It's not right keeping it from him. It'll eat you up inside.'

'He spent months up here alone waiting for me to arrive. He's been carving a place for us in this . . . *this* patch of nothing so that we, *we* can have something.'

'Olive, I know I gave you my word back at Mrs Bennett's boarding house, but –'

'Stop it, Thomas.' She pointed a broken nail at his chest. 'I *will* tell him. I've just been trying to find the right time. He's never here and when he is, he's either exhausted or with you, or –' Olive glanced towards the house '– *her.*' She steadied her breathing. Thomas thought her violated, not burdened with a criminal's child. There was more than one man who would be shocked.

'Jack's my brother, Olive. But . . .' Thomas swallowed. The words rushed from his mouth. 'If you want to leave I'll take you back to Sydney.' He looked at the ground and scratched his neck.

Olive touched Thomas's cheek, her heart softening. In another time she may well have been his woman, for Thomas was the kinder, gentler man Jack used to be. He leant towards her, awkward, tentative. She closed her eyes, totally willing to suffer for companionship, for human touch. *Oh God*, she whispered as Thomas's lips brushed hers. How far could a woman fall?

'Are you going to collect the eggs, Olive? They start breaking 'em up if you don't get 'em early.' Squib was standing at the corner of the house, her face flushed. Both Thomas and Olive dropped their hands and moved apart too quickly.

'We've nearly three dozen ready for sale. We're hoping to get some seedlings for this monstrosity,' Olive said too brightly as she nodded at the plot. 'Run and get the basket, will you, Squib?'

Squib remained rooted to the spot. 'I'm churning the butter.'

'You get the eggs,' Thomas directed Olive. 'Well, go on with you then, Squib. Jack will be expecting butter on his bread today.'

When Olive returned the vegetable plot was partially completed. The soil was dark and cloddy and Thomas was using the back of a shovel to bash the clumps up. Olive could have hugged him were it not for the eggs balanced precariously in her straw hat. 'Thank you.' The way he looked at her, the depth within his eyes; Jack's younger brother was growing up quickly. Slowly Olive backed away.

## ⚹ Chapter 40 ⚹

## Absolution Creek,
## 1965

Sam cut a piece of meat from his mutton chop, and mashed cauliflower and cheese sauce onto his fork. They were sitting in the dining room, their conversation polite but limited. It had been tense since yesterday's fiasco. Firstly, the owner of the dozer wanted payment for a day's lost work and transport costs when Cora cancelled Harold's job. The timber was unable to be returned, having been cut to specification, which meant there was little point sending the corrugated iron back to the rural merchandise shop. It appeared Harold was the only winner out of the whole debacle. Sam knew when to keep his head down, and tonight was one of those times. Cora was brief in her lecture regarding the unexpected costs, pointedly explaining that the yearly wool proceeds were the property's main income.

'It's a tight ship here,' Cora concluded, 'it has to be. There are certain challenges to running a property.'

'Yes, well, talking about challenges,' Meg began, 'I had a bit of a problem myself today.'

Cora and Sam stopped talking and eating respectively.

'I was teaching myself to drive the station wagon and the brakes went and I hit the boundary gate.'

The room was silent. Cora interlaced her fingers beneath her chin.

'Anyway, it's broken. Sorry.'

Cora stared at her.

'Broken quite badly,' Meg emphasised, attempting to fill the silence.

Sam's Adam's apple bobbed up and down. He looked from his wife to Cora.

'Sorry about that.' Meg knew she sounded quite lame. 'I figured that if I could drive I could get out and do a few things.'

'Like what?' Sam asked.

Cora began to chuckle.

Confused, Meg looked from Cora to her husband. 'Like have a life.'

Her aunt laughed. 'Good for you, girl. I was starting to believe you didn't have any get up and go.'

Meg was stunned. 'So you don't mind? You're not annoyed?'

'Why should I be? Gates are fixable.'

Sam didn't look too pleased. 'You already have a life.'

'Have a more fulfilling life, then,' Cora said in a placating tone, turning to Sam. 'A happy wife means a happy life.'

Meg grinned and cut a portion of meat. It was delicious.

'So, when's this rain coming?' Sam looked unimpressed.

'The full moon's tomorrow,' Cora began. 'There will be a northerly change tonight, I imagine, and if you go outside later you'll notice that there's a ring around the moon.'

Sam rolled his eyes. 'Another sign, I gather.'

'Actually yes, the old timers said it was moisture in the atmosphere.'

357

'Which old timers?' With the gate disaster a non-issue and a day's silent treatment her allotted punishment after Cora found Horse entangled in the tree limb, Meg figured she'd served her penance. 'Jack Manning?'

'Who's Jack Manning?' Sam splattered flecks of half-chewed peas onto the table.

Cora winced. 'The previous owner of Absoluton Creek,' she answered.

'How'd you get it, then?'

'Luck, fate. Either way I was very fortunate.'

'I'll say,' Sam agreed. 'Got out on the right side of the bed that day.'

'I saw Ellen this afternoon. She wants Harold to see a doctor.' Meg took a sip of water. For someone thought to have only suffered a bit of light concussion Harold's convalescence was taking a while.

Sam swallowed his last mouthful. 'How did you end up with the property? Was this Manning bloke a relation?'

'Harold's feeling better.' Cora tapped out a cigarette from the silver case. 'Although his headache hasn't eased so Ellen's taking him in to town to see the doctor. They'll stay in there for a few days. There's little point getting lumbered out here. Our black soil road turns to glue after a decent fall of rain.' She blew an impressive smoke ring into the air and watched it spiral upwards to the pressed metal ceiling. She gave Sam a rare smile. 'So, how's your leg?'

'Good.'

'Hmm . . . said with conviction. No swelling, no redness, no infection?'

'Nope.'

After a dessert of apple pie and ice cream Sam did the unimaginable and cleared the plates.

'The lad's almost ready to join the wait staff at the Australia Hotel,' Cora observed tartly. 'I'd say he has an agenda, however I actually think he's beginning to enjoy his new life.'

Sam's evening habit was to listen to the radio after dinner and enjoy more than a splash of rum in his black tea prior to bed, but not tonight. The rum was pooling out in the rubble pit after he'd poured it down the sink; the radio he'd knocked over was irreparable and then there was that out-of-character kiss in the kitchen. Meg thought of James. She wasn't in a rush to join Sam, and when Cora relaxed into a plush brocade chair near the open fire, beckoning Meg to join her, she quickly accepted.

The fire was warming and Meg closed her eyes briefly. She could hear her aunt pick up her reading glasses from the side table, and the pages of her latest novel, *For Whom the Bell Tolls,* rustling under her fingers.

She opened her eyes again. 'Good book?' Meg hadn't read any Hemingway. She was still ploughing through Donald Horne's *The Lucky Country,* her end-of-day exhaustion invariably leading to the re-reading of pages from the night before.

'War, honour, revenge, love.' Cora lifted horn-rimmed glasses. 'You should read it one day. You might learn something.'

'I don't know where you find the energy to read in the evening.'

Cora removed her glasses. 'Next year when the girls go away to school you'll have more time.'

'Go away to school?'

'Why, yes. There are no decent primary schools around here. I suggest one in Brisbane. Absolution Creek can contribute a little.'

A shower of sparks sprayed out on the tiled hearth as Meg poked the burning log. Her aunt might be in control of their work life but the twins' futures were not under her jurisdiction. She sat cross-legged before the fire.

Cora closed her book, fingering the tasselled bookmark. 'I'm sure you would have appreciated a better education, and obviously you want the best for your girls.'

'There was nothing wrong with my education.'

'No, of course there wasn't.'

Meg knew she was being handled, placated. What worried her was that her aunt spoke as if Meg's future was here on Absolution Creek. It was true she'd been excited when Ellen insinuated the property would be left to her, but Meg hadn't yet thought beyond that point. Her thoughts flitted back to their Sydney apartment, her regulated yet strangely comforting existence there and the life she now led. . .

'What are you thinking about?'

'Primrose Park.' Meg cleared her mind of images of a blue-green sea merging with a narrow strip of sand and parkland. 'You can see it from a side window in our flat. It's so beautiful with its expanse of green lawn and wavering trees.'

'I'm sure it is.'

Meg rested her chin on her knees. 'When I was a child I played along the foreshore. I even have a little hidey-hole filled with oddments from my childhood. It's on the side of a hill that leads to the water's edge. I used to wander down to the park every day. When you sit close to the little harbour, which spills up to the park's edge, you feel like you're nestled in a frill of trees ringed by plants and water and energy.'

Cora placed her novel on the side table. 'It's very different to here, then.'

'Oh yes. When there's a full moon in Sydney you don't feel as if you're at the beck and call of the elements. Out here the moon, the sun, the weather controls everything, from the length of the days the men work to the vegetables we grow, to the feed the stock eat. We don't seem to matter. People don't seem to matter. The men go out every day and still they are never done, never finished. I feel that the bush is encroaching on us. That we're in a continual battle with it.'

'Well, this house does sit in the middle of a paddock.'

Meg turned to her. 'It's more than that. I always feel as if the bush is the stronger of us, with its secrets and its long history and its ability to –'

'Survive?'

'Yes,' Meg agreed. 'Survive. In the city, at least where we live, you're never alone. It feels like a living, breathing entity, yet I'm not competing with the city to exist like we seem to out here. The place is a fairyland at night with its hillside dwellings, tiny boats on the water and the people and places, the things you can do. Why, I could fill up every evening from now to Christmas telling you about the grocer's shop where I work, my favourite shops and cafés . . .'

Cora lit another cigarette then snapped the lid of the lighter shut. 'And I wouldn't be interested in hearing about it, Meg. Distance makes people romanticise about the past, a place, and we both know that your beloved city didn't hold you enough to stop you from coming here.'

Meg wondered what circumstances moulded a person's character; whether her aunt's matter-of-fact attitude was an inherent part of her or a characteristic formed by life experience. She took the hearth brush from its stand and swept up ash and dirt, gathering it into a neat pile. There was still the kitchen table to be set for breakfast, the dough for their bread to be mixed and the dinner plates to wash, which would be sitting in the sink untouched.

'The way you feel about the city is how I feel about the bush, although I don't understand your love for such a manmade environment, and I'm sure that beyond your fond descriptions there are many people living in the city who don't feel like you do. There would be those who feel adrift amongst a sea of strangers, bereft and alone; those that look beyond the brick square feet that contain their lives and wish for something better, greater.'

'And have you found that something, Cora?' In the flickering light her aunt's profile was determined, youthful.

Cora lit another cigarette. She was in the habit of using a porcelain ashtray with a perforated edge, which was decorated with an interweaving narrow velvet ribbon. 'How are you and Sam getting on?'

'Good,' Meg answered carefully. 'Although James Campbell suggested you think otherwise.' The words came out in a rush.

Cora frowned. 'Did he now? James can be overly enthusiastic when it comes to women. He took it upon himself to make a couple of well-placed telephone calls regarding your husband.' Cora lowered her voice and glanced towards the door. 'Sam's been involved in some nasty altercations in Sydney and it's all around town he's a drinker.'

'I see,' Meg said flatly. 'Small-town gossiping. Life must be boring out here.'

Cora tapped her finger on the arm of her chair. 'You're the new blood in the district. People talk.'

'But we're family.'

'*You* are,' Cora reminded her, 'and you should have told me Sam's predicament was a good part of the reason for you coming here. I never wanted another male on the place. I've enough problems trying to keep Harold under control.'

'Well, maybe you should be paying a bit more attention to him. Sam seems to think he has some good ideas. And it sounds to me like it's just as well he organised all that work stuff without your knowing about it. The property needs it.'

Cora's mouth tightened. She took a long puff of her cigarette before stabbing it out in the ashtray. 'Really?'

'Yes,' Meg continued, 'and I also think Kendal would be a lot happier if he were paid for the work he did.'

'Do you?'

'Yes.'

'Well, you seem to have developed some strong opinions for someone whose life barely takes her twenty feet beyond the back gate. I didn't realise you were so knowledgeable on the workings of the property or understood the set of circumstances that sees Absolution lumbered with the likes of Harold's nephew and constrained by costs. I don't want to know who's been feeding you such tripe, but someone has been rolling the bullets and you most obligingly are firing them.' Cora lit another cigarette. 'Now that we've covered that topic let's move on to what I wanted to discuss with you.'

Meg tried to calm her breathing.

'I've noticed a change in both you and Sam. For the better,' Cora explained. 'You're both more settled, happy – especially Sam – which is to be expected, I guess, a couple of months down the track.'

'I sense there's a *but* coming.'

'I just want you to be sure about the direction your life is taking. Let me put it this way: I can put up with Sam if you can.'

Her aunt certainly didn't believe in prevaricating.

'And I want you to write to your mother. Again.'

Meg glanced about the room with its picture rail of watercolours.

'It's only fair to let her know what your intentions are, and that Absolution and not Sydney is your future. If you hold out the olive branch you'll have a far better chance of reconnecting with her and paving the way when it comes to approaching her for assistance with the twins' education.'

'Gee, maybe she can come and visit and we can all sit around and have a friendly chat like old times.'

'Meg, I'm being serious. And yes, it would be easier if she did visit.' Cora's need for a final confrontation with her stepsister had firmed in the months since Meg's arrival. The retelling of 'Squib's' story was the catalyst. Cora needed Jane to admit her part in the Hamilton family's demise. She needed Jane to admit to her face that she'd purposely let her fall from the back of the dray and that in her desperate need to have Matt Hamilton to herself, Cora's brother Ben had eventually died. Cora wanted Meg to hear it from Jane's mouth. All of it. It was simply wrong for Meg not to know about the past.

'Why has it taken so long for you and Mum to tell me that you were stepsisters?' Meg asked.

'So you *have* heard from her.' Cora twirled her reading glasses. 'I guess I figured your mother would do the honours, but then I suppose you would have asked questions and Jane wouldn't know how to reply.' Her eyes darkened. 'That's part of the reason you're here. I want your mother to admit what she did to me and my brother. I want you to know the truth.'

Meg was beginning to feel a little uneasy. 'About what?'

'You know what, Meg, about me. What she did to me.'

Meg's eyes were drawn to a particularly fetching watercolour of blue-green hills hanging above a marble-topped table. A crack ran from floor to ceiling behind the painting, a jagged reminder of the unstable foundations beneath them. She took a breath, saw the tears glistening in her aunt's eyes and visualised the young girl falling from the rear of the dray some forty years ago. Meg knew Cora's words to be true. It was the story of Cora 'Squib' Hamilton, her own mother's stepsister, the child who'd been lost as a young family ran from the law in the dead of night.

'Cora, I –'

'It's probably hard for you to hear but your mother was the catalyst that made me what I am today, good and bad. But I think we've talked enough tonight.'

'Are you all right? You look a little peaky?'

Cora closed her eyes for the briefest of moments. 'It's been a struggle all this remembering, Meg. That's all.'

Beneath the carpet the timber floorboards creaked as Cora left the dining room. Meg sat the mesh guard across the fireplace, banging it into place. A small chip appeared in the mahogany surround and she rubbed a finger over the indentation, glancing over her shoulder before walking around the room to turn the lamps off. Through the casement windows the moon illuminated the garden. The fence and trees were thrown into relief by the white light. Meg could almost see the dam bank from this angle. It was a crisp, clear night, a night for the lonely. Meg shivered. She knew her aunt didn't ride out at

night to be with a dead lover, but all the same, some nights at Absolution Creek anything did seem possible.

'So, what was the old girl on about tonight?' Sam was sitting up in
bed reading a book.

'You're reading?' Meg couldn't even begin to explain her aunt's
life. Hers had been a gradual realisation that Cora and Squib were
one and the same, and that the nasty stepsister was in fact her own
mother. Tonight had confirmed Meg's suspicions.

Sam folded down a corner of the page and closed the slim
volume. 'Don't sound so surprised, I do know how to read.'

'Sorry, it's just that I've never seen you read a book before.'

Sam grinned. 'Well, you know it's really not that big of a step
to go from reading the form guide to –' he showed her the book's
cover '– *The Farmer's Handyman*, or whatever it is. Thought I'd
better do some research before I embarked on fixing Lady Cora's
feeder tomorrow.' He gave a cough. 'And the gate.'

Meg screwed her nose up. 'Sorry about that.'

'Hey, no problems here. I guess the old girl had to rub off on you
eventually. Just don't go getting too independent.'

'Cora said the girls would have to be sent away to school next
year, probably Brisbane.'

Sam's eyes widened. 'Well, that's a bit of a windfall. We never
could have afforded a boarding-school education for them.'

'She didn't offer to pay for all of their education, Sam. In fact,
she suggested I ask my mother.' Meg changed into her flannelette nightgown and began putting the day's folded washing away in
the tall chest of drawers. 'Apparently there are no decent schools
around here.' It took some time for her to notice that although the
room was as cold as usual, there was no lingering scent of cigarette
smoke, no laden ashtray on the bedside table.

Sam gave a grimace. 'I hadn't thought about schools.'

'If the girls left I don't know what I'd do.'

'We'll keep you busy.'

Sure, Meg decided, cooking meals and cleaning the house. Next door one of the girls gave a dreamy whimper. The little mites were exhausted by the end of every day and, while their childish arguments continued, there certainly wasn't the bickering that had seemed to rule their daily existence in Sydney. They were happily thriving in their new environment. As of today, surprisingly, so was Sam.

'I might not want to be separated from them.'

Sam patted the bed. 'Well, let's just wait and see what happens. So, who is this Jack Manning, anyway?'

Meg hunched her shoulders. She didn't want to go into this with Sam tonight. The conversation would weave through her dreams and Meg couldn't bear to be haunted by little Squib, not when the grown-up version lay a wall's width away. Nor did she want to know any more about her own mother's part in Cora's childhood, for Meg had a terrible feeling that Squib never did find her father. Outside, a dog barked. Meg tucked the remainder of the clothes in the drawers. A pair of pantyhose caught her eye. They were in her sock drawer and appeared to have been stretched out of all proportion. Huge ladders ran down each leg.

'Ah, sorry about that,' Sam said sheepishly. 'They help with the chaffing.'

Meg's forehead creased.

'You know,' he persevered, 'when you're riding.'

'Of course they do,' Meg said, giggling. She was relieved to have her thoughts broken. 'Let me know what colour you prefer and I'll buy you some.' She slid between the sheets. 'You like it here, don't you?'

Sam rested the book on his chest. 'You'll drive me to smoking in bed again if we keep having these normal conversations. But yeah,

I do like it here. Outside you can see where you've been once a job's done. And the thing is, I might be a learner, but I'm prepared to listen to Harold. I've got a lot to catch up on.' Dropping the book on the floor he took her in his arms. 'I might be a bit grumpy over the next few weeks. I've never gone cold turkey before.'

'We'll survive.' Meg snuggled into him, relishing the closeness. Tonight all she wanted was to be held. Too much separated them for anything else, and Sam would take sex as a sign that everything was fine – that an end to his drinking would rectify all their problems. Meg knew better.

He tugged at her nightgown. 'Let's get rid of this passion killer.' Reluctantly she allowed his wandering hand to unclothe her. The man had rights after all. He was her husband and the father of their children.

Through the window the moon cast puppet-like shadows against the drawn curtains. The flickering shapes danced haphazardly, coerced into movement by moonlight and a rising wind. There was a sudden lull, a clatter of leaves on the roof and then the wind picked up again, the shapes changing direction. The northerly that Cora predicted had arrived. With the gradual unfolding of her family's past and the abrupt transformation of her husband, Meg knew much had altered for her as well. Sam's cheek was against hers, his breath steady, rhythmic. She too had grown and changed, and for some of those closest to her, they may not consider the change to be for the better.

# ✎ Chapter 41 ✎

## Absolution Creek,
## 1924

Squib left the house at daybreak, saddling the brown mare at the yet-to-be-repaired stables. Thomas and Jack rode southwards and then split up; Jack heading east and Thomas west. Once Thomas cleared her vision Squib cross-whipped the mare into a gallop. They were a couple of hundred ewes short and, despite Jack and Thomas searching for nearly six hours yesterday, they were yet to find the missing sheep. Jack was part way to the creek when she finally caught up with him. He was looking down at a pile of bones and what remained of a sun-dried hide.

'Dead horse.' Squib reined in the mare. It was an unusual spot for an animal to die. There was no shade in the immediate area, only an expanse of coarse grass.

'I thought I saw you tailing me. What are you doing out here at this hour?'

Squib cocked her head sideways, a thick plait falling over her shoulder. 'One of yours?'

'Yeah, she got bit by a snake a few months back and dropped

dead.' Jack's horse shifted its legs restlessly. 'This one was my pack-horse, but I reckon she's taken to me now.'

'You should have skinned her, Jack, and sold it to a Hide and Tallow shop.'

'Really?'

'Well, what do you think they make those fancy horsehair boots out of or that fancy lounge suite Olive's been hankering for? Horse hide fetches a pretty penny you know.' Squib looked again at the wasted coin lying on the ground.

'I never thought about that,' Jack admitted.

'You know, if the sheep are still on Absolution they'll be feeding into this northerly wind. That's what they tend to do.'

Jack scratched at his brow, the action tilting his hat. 'Yeah, yeah, I remember. It's just I've got this feeling they've been stolen.'

'Stolen? Well, let's have another look, eh, before we call in the troopers.'

Jack gave her a lopsided grin as they spurred their horses onwards.

'I love the way the sky is streaked with cloud some mornings,' Squib commented, 'with those little wispy bits that sort of merge with the pinks and reds.'

Jack's horse grew level with Squib's. Ahead, the pale smudge of red faded as the sun clambered over the horizon. 'Me too. Not everyone sees beauty out here.'

'That,' Squib said softly, 'is because they don't look.'

The wind changed within half an hour and soon they were riding due east into a glittering sun. Squib pulled the brim of her hat a touch lower and narrowed her eyes. 'They must have crossed the *crick*.'

Jack waited near the creek's edge. 'I think it'll be up to the horses' bellies. What do you reckon? Hey, Squib, what's the matter? You're white as a sheet.'

Squib backed her horse up. The last time she'd crossed the creek was in the dray when they moved their belongings from one

369

side to the other, en route to the Mankell house. The waterway had been a trickle then.

Squib closed her eyes and grabbed Jack's arm. 'I can't do it. I can't follow you over, not with all that . . .' She mouthed the word *water*.

'The water?' Jack asked, a little confused. 'Oh, the water on account of . . .'

Squib backed her horse up a little more. 'I'm, I'm . . .'

Jack trotted his horse to her side. 'Get down.'

'Why?'

Jack waited as Squib did what she was told. 'Now, you hop up behind me and hang on tight and I'll lead your horse over. Okay?'

Squib bit her lip.

'Get up,' Jack ordered, extending his arm.

Squib took it and scrambled upwards. Jack smelt of tobacco and the soap he used for shaving, and she sucked in the scents, her arms wrapped tightly around his waist, her cheek planted firmly against the width of his back.

'Hang on tight.' Securing her horse's reins he gave his mount a flick.

'I can't do this, Jack.'

'Sure you can. You're my Squib, you can do anything.'

The tang of vegetation filled her nostrils as the squelch of mud and the slosh of water competed with the measured breaths of the horses. Jack's reassuring voice urged the mare onwards. Squib felt the push of the mare against the restraining forces of mud and water and tightened her grip around Jack's waist.

'Squib, are you okay?'

She opened one eye, barely able to concentrate on anything beyond the heat of his body.

He patted her bare leg. 'Come on now, you're safe. Hop down.' Jack's voice was almost gruff.

Squib reluctantly did as she was told and soon they were

ducking branches and following a sheep trail out into the paddock. They rode quietly, Squib still raw with the feeling of Jack's body.

'There they are, Squib.' Jack pointed to where a mob of ewes grazed into the wind. 'Looks like they're all there. I reckon they must have crossed further up where the creek's narrower.'

'Probably.' Squib wondered if Jack intended to return the way they came. At the thought of being so close to him again she felt quite light-headed.

'I reckon we should be able to find where they crossed and go back that way ourselves. I'm sure you don't want to go through that rigmarole again.'

Jack trotted ahead, whistling a mismatch of tunes. A series of sheep trails wound through the grasses. They interlaced across the grassy plain, converging and separating like wayward footpaths. Choosing a creek-bound track they finally crossed the dry bed. Squib tailed Jack homewards, not daring to ride abreast for fear that he would sense or, worse, see reflected on her face, the strength of her wanting. They all saw her as a child yet her mother was pregnant at her exact age, married to her father and making a home.

*See me, Jack, want me*, Squib whispered as the distance between their horses grew.

Why couldn't Jack see they were meant to be together, especially now, especially after what she'd seen pass between Thomas and Olive. But that was the problem, she realised, Jack didn't know, he hadn't seen.

## ≪ *Chapter 42* ≫

## *Absolution Creek,*
## *1965*

Horse padded softly through the countryside. Cora's father once told her to follow the sheep trails if ever she were lost in the bush; that they would eventually lead her to water, to safety. She guessed that was what she was doing now: following a trail highlighted by the moon's glow to the one person who could help her. Horse whickered softly. Ahead the landscape spread out flat and quiet. Every sound was magnified in the expanse around them: the creak of leather, Horse's teeth chewing at the bit, her coat flapping about her. Belah trees framed their progress as they crossed from Absolution Creek to the country belonging to another.

This property was well tended. Fences were taut, gates swung properly, unlike some of those on Absolution Creek, and outbuildings were solid and in good repair. The paddocks, however, were clipped short from over-stocking. The owner obviously worked on the adage of the more stock the better, but Cora knew that the paddocks would be slow to grass up after rains and quick to turn to dust during a dry period. She leant down from the saddle to undo a gate, swinging Horse around to ensure the chain was secured good and tight. She didn't need any more arguments or accusations, not when she was travelling under cover of darkness to ask for help.

Having ventured this way on horseback only once, she halted beneath the face of the moon to get her bearings. She hadn't been feeling very well since the altercation in the yards with the ram, and the letter received from the solicitor did little to help her constitution.

'Come on, Horse.' She flicked the reins lightly. It was only a couple of hours until dawn and Cora wanted the whole business to be concluded so that she could be home as quickly as possible. Having never once asked for help during her life, this whole quest was proving more loathsome the closer she edged to her final destination. 'Come on, Horse, get a move on.' He pricked his ears and moved into a trot. An owl flew upwards from the grass, startling the horse and upsetting Cora's seat in the saddle.

Ahead, a line of willowy shapes emerged. Cora shushed Horse quiet, and stilled their progress. Even if she wanted to move she doubted her ability to do so. Her heartbeat grew louder as the travellers came into view. She could see eight Aboriginal men, widely spaced. Each man carried a hunting spear and they looked neither right nor left as they crossed the ancient landscape on foot. Horse made a loud snorting sound, and backed up a few paces before falling silent again. The men tailed off into the smudgy silhouette of trees, the last one turning to face her. He rested on his spear, one foot placed in the crook of his knee. He was perched, almost defiantly, for long seconds, then he too was gone, melting into the night.

Immediately Cora was a young girl again sitting under a tree with a mangy dog, the land illuminated by moonlight. There were eight of them then, too. Whether imagination or reality, the moment returned with absolute clarity, and Cora found herself unnerved by the memory. Soon afterwards they had left the Purcells' property in the dead of night. Now here she was, and with all the time between then and now she'd seen them again.

Horse shook his head and reluctantly recommenced their journey. 'I know how you feel, old boy.' Cora patted his neck and gave him a brief scratch between the ears. A shiver ran down her spine. She was of a mind to turn back, for surely the appearance of the Aboriginal men was a warning. 'I've come too far now.'

Horse picked his way carefully through an area thick with gums, finally locating the dirt road leading to the Campbell homestead. James was fifth generation, and the scent of old money was as tangy as the leaves Horse crushed beneath his hoofs. The homestead was encased in a veranda. It had once been open, then gauzed in, and was now partially enclosed with cheap weatherboard. It ruined the look of the house and had been a cross James's mother bore with shame, yet the homestead was prized for its furnishings and lavish garden, and James did his best to ensure the property's upkeep: this despite the deaths of two Campbells in the fifties and the resultant death duties imposed by the government.

It was still dark when Cora dismounted at the main entrance, freeing Horse to wander the parkland-like surrounds and neatly clipped English maze. Even with the recent passing of the family matriarch, Cora remained uncomfortable standing on Campbell soil. James's forefathers had not been kind to the Indigenous peoples who roamed this land in the early days, although Captain Bob was a respected employee until he defected to Absolution Creek. Cora rapped sharply on the veranda door, stepped inside and lifted the heavy brass knocker on the main door. She knocked loudly. It was a few minutes before she was answered.

'Cora?'

James was dressed for a day's work. She could smell coffee and soap.

'I'm sorry, James. I needed to see you.'

'Is everything all right?' He peered out into a steel-grey sky and ushered her inside. 'You didn't ride here?'

They were in a long hallway with leadlight doors and exposed timber beams. 'You know me.'

He wrapped an arm around her shoulders. 'And you couldn't use the phone or wait until daylight?'

'And have everyone in the district know my business?'

'Fair enough.'

They walked through a darkly furnished parlour, followed by a less formal sitting room. The rooms smelt musty. Dust and disuse hung in the corners of the aged rooms.

'I've missed you.'

Cora gave an imitation of a smile. She cared too much to hurt him with false expectation. Towards the rear of the house they turned down an external walkway that led into a kitchen twice the size of hers. There was an ancient wood stove, a newer Aga and a large gas oven and cooktop, commercial in size. A breakfast of eggs and bacon was congealing on the scrubbed wooden table.

'Coffee?'

'Yes please.'

Cora sat in one of the high-backed wooden chairs and snuck a piece of buttered toast from James's plate. The room was stuffy and hot thanks to a raging fire in the Aga, and condensation was forming on the windows above the double sink. Everything was spotless. Even the china cabinet with its willowy blue and white breakfast setting shone. 'I'm sorry I've come unannounced.'

'Lucky you caught me. I've a big day on.' He handed her a mug. 'I've got to get Mitchell's horse back to him this morning and then I'm heading to Stringybark Point to do a shop before I get scurvy.'

Cora didn't smile.

Instead she took a sip of coffee and played with an orange in the large fruit bowl near her elbow. 'I've got a problem.'

James sat beside her and took her hand in his. 'Apart from me?'

375

'I'm serious.' Releasing her hand, Cora retrieved a letter from her pocket. James read it through, once, twice.

'So the little bugger's suing you and he wants thirty-five thousand pounds?' Turning his fork over, James shovelled fried egg into his mouth. 'Who would have thought he had the brains to think this up.'

'It was fifty thousand initially.'

'Well, I'd take him to court.' James refolded the creamy paper.

'I've got a fifty per cent chance of losing,' Cora complained. 'He was drunk when the accident happened, however we showered him and by the time Harold drove him the one hundred-plus miles to the hospital he'd sobered up.'

'Your word against his, eh?'

'His collarbone was broken badly so Jarrod's case is based around an inability to work.'

'I'm no expert but I would have thought the odds were in your favour. You don't look convinced?' James took another mouthful of cold egg, pushing his plate to one side.

Cora sighed. 'The horse float had a defective brake.'

'So you're thinking you should pay him out?'

'Yes, but I can't.'

'Why not? You've got nil expenses and it's not like you spend any money on improvements.'

Cora took the letter back. 'Well, thanks for summing up my management style.'

'Hey, I'm on your side. I just don't get it.'

Practically everything inside the homestead had been there since the early 1800s. It was fine for James to be judgemental – he'd never been poor. Not really poor. 'I wouldn't ask unless I was desperate.' She paused. 'I was wondering if you'd lend me the money. I could pay it back over, say, ten years, with interest.'

James pushed his cold breakfast plate to one side. 'Cora, ten years? What's going on over there?'

'Nothing. Sorry, I shouldn't have asked.' She rose to leave.

'Look, sit down.' James led her back to her seat. He took a breath. 'You've got sheds that need repairs and a house that's falling down around you.' He rubbed his eyes. 'Even Ellen's concerned.'

'She never liked me.'

'Probably not, however you never have been and never will be like anyone else. You're an enigma, with a childhood story that's probably done the rounds of every kitchen, shearing shed and pub in a six-hundred-mile radius since 1923. I know some of it. I know what you lost and how you got Absolution, and I can only imagine how hard it's been for you to hold onto the property.'

'I've got Jack Manning to thank for it.'

'Cora, I appreciate what he did for you, but I'll never respect him because of the hold he has over you. He ruined you for every man that followed. He ruined you for me.'

She'd never realised that James vaguely understood her attachment to Jack. Cora stared at the table wishing for words of explanation that would probably never come.

'Well?' James's voice carried more than a hint of anger.

'I'm here to talk about *this*.' She waved the letter in his face, unwilling to be led into yet another argument.

James thumped his hand on the table, and the knife and fork clattered. 'They're not mutually exclusive, Cora. I know you care, so what the hell's the problem? Why won't you marry me?' His amber eyes were dark.

For the first time Cora found herself on the brink of telling James why it was so impossible to commit to him fully. But how to find the words when she herself had an image of a cage and a tiny door, which now seemed permanently wired shut. She was scared of losing James. That was why she couldn't commit to him, although her fear would hardly make sense to the man sitting opposite. She had lost the two men she loved most in her life as a girl, and she was scared that if she opened herself up to that type of desire again something would happen and she would lose James as well.

James was still staring at her, waiting. Cora gave a weak smile. Did he want her to come right out and say it? Did James really want to know that she was still in love with Jack Manning?

'Cora?'

This wasn't a conversation Cora wanted to have. She felt foolish and vulnerable. It was such an old wound and the depth of it meant it would probably never heal. Instead she drank her coffee, stared out the kitchen window as light flickered across the land beyond. Maybe she would be better off packing Meg and her brood back to Sydney and just walking away from Absolution. She sure as hell wasn't going to borrow from James if it meant she had to tell him the truth. She could just imagine his reaction.

*James, I know you've heard the story that I killed a man. It's true. James, I don't own Absolution and the lease runs out in a matter of years. I'm sorry. I misled you about the ownership because I don't want anyone to know. I don't want anyone to know because the government could take the land away from me if they wanted to. Absolution's all I have.*

'I can't do this, James. I'm sorry. I can only tell you that there are certain arrangements in place that restrict my –' she gave a glib smile '– borrowing potential.'

'Then I can't lend you the money. I want you in my life. I do.' He ran his fingers through shower-wet hair. 'Jeez, Cora, between this vendetta you have for your sister and your inability to commit, well, let's face it, there isn't any room for me in your life. It's taken me a while to understand but I don't think you're capable of loving anyone, or at least not me. So I guess what I'm saying is that if I can't have you then I'm at least entitled to the truth. Come back when you're ready to share your problem with me.'

'Point taken.' Cora pushed out her chair. 'You might stay away from Meg too. It was wrong of you to flirt with her that night in the kitchen on the off-chance it would make me jealous. She's got her own relationship problems without being subjected to our debacle.'

'Fair enough.'

Cora left him sitting at the table. She noticed that dust sheets covered most of the furniture. Weak sunlight filtered through the house as she halted at the portrait of Eloise Campbell in the dining room. Wife to a respected squatter, mother to three children, and doyenne of local society, she had been immortalised in oil. Eloise was probably turning in her grave at Cora's presence in her beloved homestead. It shouldn't have come as a surprise that James lived under her thumb while she was alive, but Cora expected more of him; she expected more of everyone. Maybe that was why she was so hard on herself.

Outside, Horse came to Cora immediately, his hoofs clip-clopping across gritty pavers. Mounting up they turned down the dirt track and began trotting homeward. Cora kept her gaze on the road ahead. In the east, thick thunder knobs knotted the horizon, lightning glazing the grey-blue cloud. Frustration and sadness welled within her. She didn't expect to ever return to the Campbell homestead and the reality of her loss bit deeply. It was always the same: fate always meant she would lose those she loved the most, and she did love James Campbell. Now she would never know if she could love him more than Jack.

James sipped steaming coffee, his gaze alternating between the portrait of his mother and the newspaper. Having intended to be on his way by now, he was hunkered down in the dining room trying to make sense of what Cora *hadn't* said. James adjusted the kerosene lamp on the side table. The blackout had begun a few minutes after Cora's departure and now here he was in the room he'd been firmly barred from entering as a child. He still took delight from sitting in the blue velvet armchair, his feet sinking into the top of a matching foot stool. A long low window offered an unrestricted view of the grassy plains, beyond which clouds were gathering. They perched above the western tree line, lightning barrelling across the far horizon. Eloise Campbell stared at her son from the opposite wall. Every time a disagreement occurred with Cora, James would stew about it in the company of his mother.

His mother was correct in nearly every aspect when it came to declaring Cora Hamilton's lack of suitability as a potential Mrs Campbell. They were different, he and Cora. In everything from upbringing to social status to wealth they were diametrically opposed. Except for one thing: he loved Cora, and his mother knew it. Notwithstanding the district gossips who took sides as if they were barracking for opposing rugby teams, James knew that in her heart Eloise Campbell was a romantic. When she was alive his mother knew James rode out at dusk to return in the dark of night, knew he would cut through Absolution in the excuse that it was a good shortcut to some of his veterinary clients. She ignored these trysts and indeed often spoke of Cora as a capable woman.

James remained convinced that if they had ever met in person, Eloise Campbell and Cora Hamilton would have been ready friends, for despite their social differences they were strong-willed women who had given their lives to a demanding environment. In the end, despite the endless rumours regarding Cora's past, there was only one thing that barred Cora from acceptance, which meant the only way his woman would have gained entrance to the Campbell homestead during his mother's lifetime would have been if she were passing around canapes at one of her gatherings.

How disappointing, then, to discover that his beloved mother's passing did not alter his relationship with Cora. James was starting to believe the relationship was a dead end. In fact, the thought of finishing things for good made perfect sense, except that he kept going back to her. Kept on hoping that Cora would give in and see what their life together could be. There would be no children now. He was reconciled to that, and in truth the loss of fatherhood was nothing compared to not having Cora; annoying, bossy, argumentative, intelligent, capable, Cora.

James shook his head. 'You're a worry, mate. She's going to drive you to drink.' Adjusting the kerosene lamp, he flicked absently through the pages of the *Stringybark Point Gazette* before dropping it on the floor. Now he had another problem: having given her an ultimatum, the woman was so stubborn that he could be assured Cora wouldn't be picking up the telephone any time soon. James turned on the radio. He'd missed the district's forecast so he listened to the announcer as rainfall totals for the catchment area east of them were read out. There had been substantial falls along a good forty-mile stretch of the river and the storm cell was heading west.

'West,' James repeated, his large fingers twiddling with the tuning dial. Static drowned out the announcer's voice. Outside, cloud was mounting in the west heading east towards Campbell station. James didn't like the look of it. The telephone gave a brief ring and he was up and out of his chair, walking through the sitting rooms to the kitchen.

'Yeah, James here.'

'James, gidday. Pat here from Wells Farm, east of Stringybark Point.'

'Yeah, Pat, how you going up there? I've just heard the weather report.'

'Average, real average. WellsTown was evacuated yesterday due to flash flooding and it's heading your way.'

James bit his lip. 'How bad?'

'Well, no one can get down to the river to check heights. I'd say the water would have to be in the top end of the Stringybark Point Creek by now. Listen, I've tried to let a few people know downstream of here, mate, but my missus is already up on the roof. I've gotta go.'

'You got help coming, Pat?'

'We'll be right. You're gonna have to try and get onto some of your neighbours –'

The line dropped out. James gave three short rings and waited, tried again and waited. No one was answering at Absolution, and James doubted Cora would even be back at the homestead yet. Now what was he going to do? He didn't particularly relish leaving his own place at this time, however a horse needed to be trucked back to the owner and that job had to come first. He could only hope that everyone was on the ball at Absolution Creek and knew what was coming their way.

The whir of an engine was soon followed by the appearance of the work truck and a Massey Ferguson tractor. The vehicles trailed through the house paddock gate to stop outside the machinery shed. Leaving the laundry and the partially hung basket of washing, Meg walked down to the shed, the lambs in pursuit. With the previous afternoon taken up with hand-filling sacks of grain to finish feeding, the repairing of the feeder was the first job of the morning. The vehicles were parked in a row outside the shed. A chain hanging from a stoutly limbed tree lifted the feeder into the air, where it dangled momentarily before being lowered to the ground and into the work shed.

The work truck appeared relatively unscathed to Meg, apart from a dent on the driver's side door. However, the feeder was a twisted mess of steel. She was listening to Sam and Kendal arguing about the damage to it when Cora appeared on Horse, riding in from the west. Emerging near the stables she was greeted by Curly and Tripod, a welcoming party of excited barking and mad circling that failed to bring a smile. One look at her face and Meg knew that this was a woman you wouldn't want to get on the wrong side of. Sam and Kendal stood back as Cora dismounted, squatting to inspect a long tear in the metal side.

'You always have to check to make sure it's real secure,' Kendal stated.

Cora gave Kendal a thousand-yard stare and circumnavigated the damaged feeder once more.

'Well, you were the one that checked it before we went into the blasted paddock,' Sam retaliated.

'This isn't about apportioning blame.' Having satisfied herself with her inspection, Cora dug her hands into the pockets of her jacket. 'Accidents happen.'

'Yeah right,' Kendal scowled. 'Anyway, it's buggered now. We'll need a new one. Reckon the cost of it should come out of your wages.'

Sam kept his eyes on Cora.

'Well, Sam's a mechanic by trade, so he's going to have a try at fixing it.'

'It's really a boilermaker and welder's job,' Sam explained, 'but I've done a bit of both.'

Meg gave him an encouraging wink.

'You'll fix it,' Cora replied. She turned to walk away.

'Hey, Miss Hamilton,' Kendal called after her. 'What's on job-wise?'

'Leave her,' Meg suggested, her fingers pulling on his oilskin jacket.

Kendal's cheeks pinked up instantly at her touch. 'Trying to figure that woman out is like trying to pick at a broken nose.'

'Well, something's riled her.' Sam squatted down, ran his fingers over the buckled feeder.

Cora stared above and beyond them, turning in a tight circle as she surveyed her holding, hands on hips, hair whipping about her face. A couple of hundred yards away a brown snake slithered across the dirt to where her two dogs lolled in the grass. Cora rushed for a shovel that was leaning against the shed and raced to where Curly was barking. Tripod emerged with the snake partially twisted about his front leg. He barked and whined, finally jumping clear of the slithering reptile.

'That's a bit unseasonal,' Kendal commented as Cora jabbed the sharp edge of the shovel into the brown snake until only nerves kept it writhing in the dirt.

'Damn it.' A few feet away Tripod was walking very slowly, almost dazed. Cora handed Kendal the shovel and moved quickly to his side. 'You'll be right, little mate.' Flicking open her pocketknife she took hold of his ear and cut the top off it. Blood gushed freely from the wound. Kendal speared the shovel through the air. It landed a few feet from the shed, clattering to earth on a piece of tin.

'Will that save him?' Meg asked, incredulous.

Cora enticed Tripod to walk around a little, his back leg shuffling in the dirt, his muscles spasming. 'Maybe. Bleeding him is about the only way to get the venom out that I know of.' When he fell over she lifted him into her arms, whispering words of endearment and petting him.

Meg kept a discreet distance behind her aunt as they walked back along the one-sided avenue of trees. 'Cora.' Meg finally increased her stride to match her aunt's.

'I don't have time for anything at the moment, Meg.' Cora looked out towards the west where a thick line of purple clouds was moving steadily towards them.

'Is everything all right?'

'Apart from Tripod?' She patted the dog's soft hair. 'No. I'm expecting big rain. Not that it probably matters anymore.'

'I don't understand.'

Cora gave a condescending smile. 'I know you don't. Anyway, it appears personal agendas have lost their importance. I think time's finally run out for me.'

# ⊰ Chapter 43 ⊱

## Stringybark Point Hotel, 1965

Rain wasn't something Scrubber calculated into this trip. Of course the inevitable happened when a fella strayed from his plans. The extra day at the hotel meant he'd woken to a cloud-burst that would have made a man in his grave sit up at the noise of it. He leant over the balcony railings, half-expecting to see the prone body from a few nights prior squashed on the road like a pegged-out fox pelt. The main street was empty; the pub below was quiet. Everyone had retreated to the holes they'd climbed out of. He thought of his girls, cold and wet in the paddock, as the rain bounced off the bitumen and pooled on the dirt verge along the kerb. They'd seen worse.

He took up position in the cane-bottom chair, Dog asleep beside him, the animal's four legs tilted skywards. Damned if that animal couldn't sleep standing up. Even now the collie was oblivious to the drops of rain dripping on his nose from above. *Well, maybe not,* Scrubber mumbled, as Dog opened his near-toothless mouth so that the rain settled on his tongue. Wherever they went it had always been five star for Dog. The mutt just had that ability of getting the best out of every situation. Scrubber hoped Cora would take the dog on after he was gone. Not as a favour, for he'd no right to ask anybody for such a thing, but maybe because he was an old dog who'd done good and was in need of a home. Veronica would have liked that.

Scrubber stretched back, patting the tobacco pouch at his waist. His money was near gone and with no banks about it was back to bush tucker and the stars for a roof. It was the way things should be, he reconciled. A bushman didn't spend his last days holed up inside waiting for that thing to whisk him off to the nether world. No, a man wanted to suck up the tangy scent of the scrub, to sniff at the blue haze of summer, to curse at the September winds and growl as cold froze his fingers in the saddle. He wanted to go surrounded by what he loved more than anything: the bush. She was a hard woman: contrary, stubborn, frightening and sometimes downright petulant. Yet in spite of his own demons, the bush had given him a home of sorts and in return he loved her.

The publican told him it was around one hundred miles to Absolution Creek, but a cross-country shortcut would have him there in under two days. The travelling would be easier too if he stayed off the puggy wet roads.

'Well, Dog, we're off.'

Dog stretched, yawned and slowly made it into a sitting position.

'I think you'll have to ride with Samsara again on account of your age and the weather.' The dog cocked his head to one side, gave a single bark. 'Shush,' Scrubber reprimanded, 'you're not even meant to be here.'

Dog gave a low whine and sauntered away.

'No need to get your knickers twisted. Always did have an attitude,' he mumbled. Scrubber patted the tobacco pouch. 'Well, old mate, we're off again. Hope you're well rested cause this last trek will be the best and the worst of it.' He looked across the street to where Green's Hotel and Board once stood. Beginnings and endings were always difficult to forget.

If it weren't for the fact he didn't mind the old gal, Scrubber would have left Veronica on the roadside some hundred miles back. There was also the niggling doubt that he'd ever find another woman, so he suffered her complaints about the horse, the saddle, the state of the roads, the weather too cold and too hot, camping rough, sleeping little and eating poor. Whew, it was some journey. How a woman could squander her energy on such things he'd never understand.

On approach, Stringybark Point looked like any other bush village: a mangle of low-slung houses, three hotels staring each other off across the dusty main street, a couple of stores and the usual post office and police station. The buildings resembled a skew-whiff set of stairs, worn and uneven against a pale blue sky. Scrubber flicked the reins on his horse, and whistled to Veronica to get a move on. They clip-clopped into a town dozing quietly beneath gums and box trees. A dusty road was interspersed with hitching rails, horse troughs and a single gas lamp. A couple of mangy dogs, half-breeds, wandered ahead of them. A child balled somewhere down the street to the right. At the hitching rail outside Green's Hotel and Board, Scrubber left a complaining Veronica under the shade of a tree while he went about the business of stabling the horses. A gush of smelly water drained down from a pipe into the open gutter. Scrubber sniffed manure, dirt and soap; someone's bath water.

'Stay out of trouble,' he advised her as Veronica practically fell from her ride.

'Legs have gone numb,' she said by way of explanation when he shook his head.

The first Scrubber saw of Lickable Lorraine he was out stabling the horses at the back of the hotel. The woman was sitting at the rear of the hotel's kitchen peeling potatoes, skirts hiked over her knees and a large bowl gripped between enviable thighs. Her child-rearing breasts, glossy dark hair and green eyes made up for a miserable mouth and poor eyesight that no doubt accounted for her squint. It was love at first sight.

'Youse new here?' She ran a peeling knife, blade flat, across her thigh.

He puffed his chest out – not bad, he thought, for a man in his early twenties – and tried to think of something canny. 'Yep.' With the horses bedded down there was no reason he couldn't partake of a bit of conversation. Scrubber admired a particularly impressive calf muscle.

'Welcome. I'm Lorraine. Cook and chief bottle-washer at this here establishment. You staying long?'

Scrubber watched the knife move smoothly across pale skin. 'Could be. Got a bit of business to attend to. You know if a Matt Hamilton's arrived in town?'

'Name's familiar, I'll ask around.' Lorraine sat the bowl on the ground. 'I like a bit of business meself.' She ran her fingers along the neckline of her blouse, rubbed slowly at her fleshy cleavage.

Scrubber licked his lips. He wasn't one for knocking back a bit of scratch and sniff. 'I've a woman.' The rear of the hotel was empty. A single piece of timber banged in the breeze.

'I won't tell if you've got coin.' Lorraine walked towards him with a swagger that would have shamed a dandy.

Stocky hands manoeuvred across Scrubber's chest. The earthy scent of potatoes mingled with tobacco and something like lemons. With Veronica waiting out the front, Scrubber calculated how much time he had. In truth he didn't need much. Grabbing the woman he hurried her toward the stables and into an empty stall. He ripped at her blouse, and held the fleshiness of her in his hands. With one arm pinned along a wooden beam, he thought of the ways he could take her.

'Eh?' Lorraine complained. 'You're a young one, aren't you, to be so pushy.'

'Don't bother about my age,' Scrubber replied, 'everything works.' He prised her legs apart with his knee, lifting it high against her as he fumbled with the buttons on his trousers, his leg moving against the flesh of her.

'Coin first.'

Scrubber shook his head. 'I never pay for something before I've got the goods.' In reply he used his fingers for a bit of exploration. It was enough of an enticement to get him good and ready. He shoved Lorraine's capable hands downwards; let the woman do a bit of work. No point rushing things – after all, he wouldn't be coming back for seconds. He didn't intend paying for firsts.

'Cheeky,' Lorraine laughed. 'We'll get on you and I.'

Scrubber grasped at her hips.

'Lovey, lovey, you out here?' Veronica stood at the rear of the hotel, a towel over her shoulder. 'I've got us a room. Are you there? I'm going to the wash house.'

Stifling Lorraine's giggle, Scrubber pushed her roughly into an adjoining stall.

'Here,' Scrubber answered, quickly righting his clothes as he watched the width of Lorraine's arse disappear.

Veronica side-stepped horse manure and empty feed buckets, pausing to let past a dark-bearded traveller who was leading his horse to the stables. 'What you doing in there?'

'Finishing up,' Scrubber explained, trying to right his clothes. 'I had to move the horses over.' He scratched at his crotch. It was a pity to waste it. 'Come in here, girl.'

Veronica gave a tight frown.

'Come on, don't be shy. I've got a present for you.'

Scrubber looked across the crowded bar. A fella by the name of George was playing the piano in the corner. A couple of the patrons – tall bush-bearded types with meaty hands and no voices – were trying to accompany him. There was a lot of glass swaying and liquid sloshing and yells of 'more, more'. Nearby a young fella with dead man's eyes took to shaking and yelling.

'Pipe down, Sergeant,' the publican hollered. 'We ain't on the Somme now. Take your war outside.' The lad fell silent.

Scrubber scrutinised the grainy bar. He never had been much for crowded places. He was on his second drink when something made him look up.

A bit dim he may be, however a man knew when his name was coming up in conversation. After a tea of soup, roast beef and custard in the dining room, all for the fine price of a shilling, Scrubber left his girl in the Ladies Bar, and it was there Lorraine made a point of becoming fast friends with Veronica. He watched their heads bobbing and laughing in shared confidence, worrying that by now loose lips would have told Lorraine their life story. Sure enough, Lorraine poked her head through the door from the Ladies Bar to talk to a heavy-set man with a black beard. The man pinched Lorraine's cheek and dropped some coins into her palm. In return she gave him a dreamy look. They held each other's gaze for longer than Scrubber reckoned to be decent. He didn't like the look of the man. Bog Irish, he reckoned; lower than. He should know – his own family being of a similar slant.

Minding his own business was at the top of Scrubber's list while he waited for Hamilton to show. He didn't want any trouble at this stage, whether it be with Veronica or anyone else, so he'd turned down Lorraine on their second chance meeting; turned her down on account of the fact that a money earner such as she would have a man for a keeper. Now here was Lorraine, her fleshy mouth spilling who knew what into another man's ear.

Through the swirl of tobacco smoke old black beard nodded at Lorraine's words and followed her pointed finger. Lorraine left the bar with a come-get-me pout. Scrubber would've pulled his head in like an echidna if he thought it would have saved him from a fight. No doubt he'd have to pay up for services only partially rendered by Lickable Lorraine. Through a sliding door to his left was a parlour and if it weren't for the fact that a group of cockies were in there having a quiet nip he would have slunk in and out the other door. Pity he weren't a nob.

'You a friend of Hamilton's, then?'

The bearded man was in his face without even a how'd you do.

Scrubber slurped on his rum. 'What's it to you?'

The man called to the publican behind the bar. 'Eh, Greenie, you got the paper – the one with the lost kid in it?'

Scrubber pricked his ears.

'I'm Adams. I've seen the girl over at Absolution Creek. Real tearaway she is.'

'You've seen her? You've seen Squib?' Scrubber downed his rum.

Adams patted him on the shoulder, elbowed a patron off a stool and pushed himself closer to Scrubber. 'Sure thing. You kin, then?'

'No, just helping the kid's father. He's been worried sick.'

Adams opened the paper. 'Yep, says here the girl's name's Hamilton. So she'd be Squib Hamilton. The father worked at Purcell's place, Waverly.' He held up the paper for Scrubber to read.

'Never did take to learning.'

Adams folded the paper. 'No matter, mate. At least we know the kid's safe.'

Scrubber couldn't believe his luck. Not half a day at Stringybark Point and he'd found the girl. Despite his intention he nodded.

'Well then, that's the first confirmation we've had. And the girl's step-mother, she's the one in gaol for thieving the jewellery?'

'Stepmother?'

Adams gave him a hard stare. 'It was all over the papers. You sure you're friends with the father?'

Scrubber hesitated. 'Yes.' He tapped his rum glass on the counter. 'Who's the kid with?'

'Some soft city-slicker. Safe, oh yes, safe as houses.' Adams pushed the newspaper towards the publican who, with a nod, put it under the bar. 'So, this Squib's mother, she was a half-caste?'

'No.' Scrubber stretched out his answer. Abigail Hamilton wasn't black. He avoided the man's eyes. 'You might have the wrong person.'

'Not likely. '

Scrubber tapped his glass on the counter again, grateful when the publican finally reappeared to top it up. 'You can't believe most of what's written up in them papers, you know.'

'Hey, Adams, you out of the clink then?' a stranger enquired, sticking dirt-brown fingers into three tumblers of rum.

'Mistaken identity,' Adams replied, a shower of spittle festooning the square of bar towel and Scrubber's glass.

'You mean no proof,' a flat-headed sherry drinker intoned.

The publican wiped down the bar, a long fingernail scraping the cracked surface as he went. 'Keep your calm, Adams, they're only playing with you.' He topped up Scrubber's rum. 'Accused of stock theft our Adams was. Most unfortunate.'

Adams sculled his drink. 'Those Campbells will get their comeupperance and *others*.' He spoke real low. 'You being a stranger here, I'd keep my head down. There are always things that happen in the bush that's best kept local, if you get my drift.'

Scrubber swirled his rum and swallowed the dregs. The warnings were already about and his time in Stringybark Point was only nearing four hours. Adams returned to his seat at the far end of the bar. Scrubber got up and walked in the opposite direction. He hoped Matt Hamilton made an appearance real soon, for it seemed he wasn't the only man with an interest in his daughter.

# ❊ Chapter 44 ❊

## Absolution Creek, 1924

Squib tried to wiggle her toes against the tight brown leather. It was as if her feet were tethered to the ground. She felt like a captured, frantic animal desperate to break free. Were it not for the fact the sturdy lace-ups were a present from Jack she would have thrown them away. Instead, she bit her lip, finding solace in the memory of her nightly freedom. The shoes were Jack's second gift. Although he'd not purchased the material for her new blouse and skirt, he'd given her the money for it on their last trip to town, much to Olive's annoyance. Olive talked of carpets and a clothes mangler, a lounge-room suite and china cabinet, and queried the need for Squib's clothing as if Squib were not even in the room. In return Jack asked whom Olive was expecting to visit.

An old girth strap shortened and religiously polished for a week cinched in Squib's waist, and her hair was now restrained by a single thick plait. Squib recalled her father gathering wild daisies for her mother, of buying a length of ribbon when there was coin for such luxuries; Jack cared for her – a woman knew such things.

If her father arrived tomorrow Squib doubted she could leave Jack. In fact she was sure it would kill her.

Through the gaping stable wall a shaft of sunlight spun gold through Jack's hair as he lifted a swinging plank of wood and positioned it back in place. The movement dimmed the light and it was some seconds before Squib grew accustomed to the darkened space and could see Jack's outstretched hand searching for the hammer. Squib was by his side immediately, hammer in hand, smile ready. Her fingers grazed his and he smiled softly, where once he would have ruffled her hair. He hammered the final board in the last of the stalls into place, striking the nails dead centre.

'I just need to repair the gate and do a bit to the roof and these will be as good as new.' Jack gathered his tools.

'It's a fine job, Jack.' They walked out into a morning noisy with birdsong. Topknot pigeons and willie wagtails were competing for branch space in a nearby brigalow tree.

'I'll accept a compliment from you any day.' Resting the tools on an upturned tin, Jack sat on a knobbly log and patted the space beside him. 'Noisy little fellas.'

Squib sat down and placed her leather-encased feet squarely in the dirt. 'Woolshed next?'

'It's not too bad.' He gave her a nudge. 'Might get you to run your eye over it, though, you being a bit of a sheep woman.'

Squib nudged him back and felt her cheeks heat up. 'One of the timber planks is broken where you roll the bales out and there's another needs replacing on the board itself. One of the pens has a broken latch on the gate and there's an overhead beam, non-bearing, that has a crack in it.'

Jack let out a sound that was half-cough, half-surprise.

'Well,' Squib said, shrugging, 'you asked.'

'And I'm glad I did. We might ride over there this afternoon.'

'Okay.' Squib smoothed her skirt as she'd seen Olive do.

'Do you know where Thomas has got to? I thought we might ride out and check the ewes.'

'I'll come.' It was days since Jack had doubled her on his horse across the creek. During that time Squib waved Jack off to work in the morning and welcomed him home at night while Olive either slept or tidied herself before their evening meal. That single event had altered things between them. Although neither of them spoke of it Squib knew they'd crossed their own creek that day.

'Won't Olive need some help in the house?'

'If I wasn't here she'd have to do it herself,' Squib argued.

Jack turned to her. 'That's not the point.'

'Isn't it?' Squib asked, genuinely surprised. 'I'm not staff.'

'Have I ever treated you that way?'

'Sometimes, a bit.' Squib kicked at the dirt, becoming overly interested in a line of ants heading to a nest a few hundred feet away from where they sat. 'No, not really. The others do, though.'

Jack brushed dirt from his trousers. 'And I'm sorry for that. Olive's used to a different life.'

'My father would call that a poor excuse.'

'Smart man, your father. I wouldn't mind meeting him one of these days.'

'It would be real good if that happened,' Squib agreed. 'So can I come?'

'No. I want you to find Thomas for me and then help Olive.'

'Well,' Squib answered carefully, 'he's probably with Olive. They spend a lot of time together.' Squib knew her father would not be happy if he could hear her now, however what was she to do? Captain Bob had told her that she would be safe with Jack, yet Olive's dislike of her was a danger.

'I hadn't noticed.' Jack took a few steps backwards and looked up at the stable roof. A piece of corrugated iron was flapping in the breeze. 'I better fix that.'

Squib took a breath. 'Well, maybe you should *notice* – Olive and Thomas, I mean.'

Jack turned to her. 'Meaning?'

'I'm not a child, Jack. I see things.'

The pallor of Jack's face resembled the blue-grey of the iron above him. 'What have you seen?'

It was enough. Squib patted him on the arm and, lifting her skirts, walked away.

'Hey, Squib, Cora, come back!'

She kept on walking. Jack Manning only used her real name when he was being *serious* Jack, and on those occasions she rarely answered him. There was, she realised, some advantage to belonging to no one. Yet she knew one day Jack would say those words again and it would be proof of his need for her, of his wanting. She crossed the short distance from the stables to the dirt track and looked eastwards. Part of her wished they'd not moved from Jack's original house site with its tall sheltering trees. She had a sense things would have been better on that side of the creek – happier, safer. Now she couldn't even revisit the site without Jack by her side, for the creek lay like an impenetrable barrier between the past and present and Squib knew her fear of water would remain with her for life.

This then was her home – this place that once belonged to another. This place with its roughly built homestead and wind-twisted trees. The soil varied from hard ridge areas to rich black soil such that Mr Purcell would have dreamt about, yet trees layered some paddocks like the hairs on Jack's hand and to make a go of things he would have a hard time thinning them so that grass could grow. This place contained both a multitude of possibilities and nothing. It could be the best and worst of things to come.

Squib wasn't sure what made her turn northwards. The wind blew from that quarter and she faced the strong breeze as a gnawing sensation grew in her stomach. Without knowing why, she ran to the stables. With Jack gone she peered out from behind a tree, the hairs prickling on her arms. The screech of hens carried on the air. She heard a door slamming and then raised voices. Two men on horseback dismounted at Jack's campfire at the front of the homestead. Squib pressed her shoulders against the bark, craning her neck to look again at the strangers. A tall man and a squat one with a beard. 'Adams,' she breathed. His build and facial hair were unmistakable. She recalled Captain Bob's words: that the spirits would not protect her, that there would be a reckoning. Swiftly untying the tight leather shoes, Squib hid them under an old canvas bag in the stables along with her hat, then she did the only thing she could. She ran as fast as her maimed leg allowed.

# ≪ Chapter 45 ≫

## Absolution Creek, 1965

Cora sat at the base of the great tree in her bedroom, her shoulder blades pressed tightly against the bark. By her side lay Tripod. The blood from his ear had congealed nicely, although his breathing remained erratic, his nose warm. Running her hand lightly across his back, she tucked in the old blanket around him. She hoped he would recover. It was asking too much of her at this moment to lose him as well. On the long, lonely return journey from Campbell Station Cora had dwelt sadly on what she was riding away from. She'd been so careful after Jack with her emotions; careful of not getting too close in relationships. Then she'd met James and he'd opened her eyes to something Cora had long since forgotten. Hope. She shouldn't have fallen in love with him. Once again she was alone.

Relationships were impossible, Cora decided as she rubbed her scalp against the knobbly bark. Fate turned against her with the first and pride had destroyed the second.

Cora wondered how she would manage to pay out Jarrod

Michaels and not default on the lease payment. If the worst happened, where would she go?

Outside the wind lifted. A scatter of leaves skidded down the corrugated-iron roof. A soft spray of rain patterned the open veranda and louvred glass. Although still winter, the rain would certainly help the parched oat crop. It had been struggling since a late March planting, surviving on intermittent showers that appeared unheralded and passed over the countryside. Every cleansing shower, however slight, left in its wake an optimism that one day soon it would rain, relieving both the land and those upon it from the burden of an unfathomable future. Cora carried this faith like a woman carried the thought of her lover. It was a seed planted by her beloved father, tended by Jack Manning and carefully cultivated by her own considerate hands once the management of Absolution Creek passed to her.

This mantle of responsibility was so much more than the daily running of the property. It was an understanding of the land, of the living matter within and on the earth's surface, whose survival was linked to the vagaries of the weather. Rain was life-giving out here. Nothing could survive without its presence. The more Cora thought of the coming rain, the more restless she became. Laying her hands against the bark of the great leopardwood, she recalled those who had walked the land before her, the old people of the bush. Through the woody plant she could feel their energy, their comprehension of all things beyond that made and controlled by man.

In her mind's eye they walked the earth again. Eight men, warriors all; stalking the moon-drenched night as Cora rode for help that wasn't forthcoming. She should have known better. She should never have gone to see James. It was always the same. You could never depend on anyone except yourself. Yet those men last night hadn't shown themselves for James's sake – they were beyond the loves of mere mortals.

A remembrance came to her then. It was over forty years ago. She could see the clearing, and Captain Bob and the two men with him who appeared like wraiths out of the scrub. It was his finger that captured her attention. She'd followed its line of sight, the bent finger pointing to evidence even Jack Manning could not ignore. And there it was: the telltale ring of darkness that stained the large trees around them. The marks so high neither man nor animal could survive such a deluge.

For a second it was as if the world went black. Cora took a steadying breath, recalling the words spoken to her during the dead of night at Waverly Station.

*When the people of the night sky come together in battle you will understand, for this will be the sign. This will herald the ending to the beginning of it all.*

Everything depended on the rainfall east and north of Absolution. There had already been one flood here of shocking proportions, and Cora, having seen the evidence, knew the result could be catastrophic. Even now she could picture Jack looking at the watermarks on the trees, shaking his head in concern. Why hadn't she realised before how much rain was coming? Why had her gift failed her? Certainly in the past her intuition did not always present itself accurately, yet nor did it abandon her so that action became impossible.

Running her hands against the bark of the tree, Cora's fingers touched an unusual bulge. Hidden in the shadowy corner of the bedroom a crystallised bubble of the tree's life force welled up through the bark. The oozing sap was the tree's attempt at healing whatever ailed it, and as Cora prodded the timber she understood that this life as she knew it was about to change.

# ⋘ *Chapter 46* ⋙

## *Absolution Creek,*
## *1924*

Jack squared up opposite Adams on the dirt path at the back door. It was clear the postal and supply rider wasn't here on a social call, for the man accompanying him carried a carbine rifle, and an air of expectancy showed in his dusty face.

'Where's the runaway? The Hamilton girl?' Adams spat on the ground, his companion's shifty gaze alert and untrusting.

'What do you want with her?'

'She accused me of stealing Campbell's sheep, she did.' Adams hooked thumbs through his braces and stuck his chest out so that a lard-hard belly folded over his belt.

Jack recalled his father's words about men who wore both belts and braces: no confidence, he'd said; men such as that always figured on being more than what they were. 'And?'

'And?' Specks of saliva gathered in the corners of Adams's mouth. 'Well, firstly there weren't no proof and no witnesses came forward, since the lie was told to a black fella, Captain Bob, that works for the Campbells. But that didn't stop them from throwing me in gaol for a week,' Adams complained, turning to his companion. 'Isn't that right, Will?'

'It's the truth, so strike me down if I lie.'

'So why are you here? It seems to me the matter's been solved.' Jack edged closer to Adams and his shifty company. 'You don't strike me as the type of man that would take umbrage with a female.'

'I'm here cause of this.' Adams produced a newspaper from his pocket. The print was creased and stained and he went to some effort to flatten the paper, brushing it against a meaty thigh.

Jack took the paper suspiciously and glanced down to where Adams's ragged thumbnail pointed. 'Move your finger.' Thomas and Olive looked over Jack's shoulder. Adams tipped his hat on Olive's arrival. 'Well, what of it? That's the notice you and I talked about regarding the girl. Has someone come forward?'

Will took a step forwards and rested the stock of his rifle on the dirt path. 'There was this theft, you see, by one Abigail Hamilton. She stole jewellery from a Mrs Purcell of Waverly Station.'

'I knew it!' Olive interrupted.

Jack held up his hand to silence Olive. A furious sigh was her response.

'She was the missus of a big-time sheep stud owner over to the east in the slopes,' Adams continued, 'the one with the ram on the shilling coin.'

Olive huffed. 'The audacity.'

'I know of them.' Jack could still see the shilling coin spinning across Mr Farley's desk.

The man called Will cleared his throat. 'Anyway, the story you tell about finding the kid after she fell off a dray and was washed down the creek . . . well, it matches the yarn going about the place, about the Hamiltons running from the law in the middle of the night, about a kid being lost, a girl. That is the girl's name, isn't it? Hamilton?'

Jack wasn't following. 'So you have found her kin?'

'What we found, thanks to a traveller by the name of Scrubber –' Adams displayed yellowing teeth '– is the girl holed up here with you is most likely of darkie blood. Her real mother was a half-caste.'

Olive lifted a hand to her mouth. 'Never! In this house?'

'I'm sorry to say it, missus,' Adams commiserated, 'but yes.'

'You're sure?' Thomas stepped from the threshold to join his brother.

Olive lifted her chin. 'I told you to send her to an orphanage, Jack.'

'Be quiet, Olive, this is man's business. Now,' Jack continued more amenably, 'if she is who you say she is – and that would have to be proved – what if I'm happy for her to stay here?'

'Jack!' Thomas placed a hand on Olive's shoulder to quiet her.

'Don't let your enthusiasm to be rid of the girl get in the way of the truth, Olive,' Jack reprimanded. He sensed her fury in her steely voice and erratic breathing.

Adams cleared his throat.

'The law says any child –'

'She's not a child,' Jack corrected.

'Any child,' Adams repeated firmly, 'with mixed blood has to be sent away. It's for their own good.'

'An orphanage,' Jack replied, 'their own good, really?'

'It's the law,' Adams said as if he had a shiny badge of authority pinned to his chest. 'So where is she?' He turned in an ungainly half-circle.

Jack gestured vaguely about them. 'Who knows? The girl's never been one for normality. You said that yourself once.'

'She's not in the house,' Olive said. 'She was with you, Jack.'

'Some hours ago,' he countered mildly, making a show of shading his eyes to stare off into the shimmering bush.

'Well, we'll be having a look about and if we don't find her this time we will eventually.' Adams tossed Jack a canvas bag. 'There's your mail, *friend*.'

'Thanks.' Jack caught the mail bag, then waited as the two men walked back to their horses.

'I knew that girl was trouble,' Olive snapped, 'and here are you, Jack Manning, kowtowing to her and giving me lectures about getting on with her.'

'That's enough.' Jack bustled Olive and Thomas inside. 'For starters, Squib doesn't look black to me. Does she look Aboriginal to you?'

Thomas gave a non-committal shrug.

Olive lifted her chin. 'I wouldn't know what she is, Jack.' Turning to walk the length of the hallway she paused to stamp her heel on a black beetle. 'I've never mixed with natives before. Now, who is for tea?' she asked sweetly.

## ⋘ *Chapter 47* ⋙

## *Absolution Creek,*
## *1965*

Cora tucked a spare sweater into the saddle bag and hung a water bag and stock whip from the pommel. Horse, attuned to the slightest variation in Cora's mood, waited patiently as she swung up and into the saddle. He settled beneath her slight weight, lifting a hoof in turn as if measuring her balance. In the distance the homestead appeared almost bereft. It sat squat and ungainly amid motionless trees, a messy line of add-on roofs of various heights running into the squat forms of the power house, meat house, laundry block and garage. Only the leopardwood tree relieved the asymmetrical lines of the homestead, its great branches rising up and over the structure like a chivalrous gentleman holding a rain coat. Cora hoped the old girl withstood the coming storm. Although she did her best to wad up the opening between the iron and the tree's trunk, netting and builders putty were no match for the elements, nor the continual movement that stretched and tugged at the old building as the earth moved. Heavy rain made doors catch and foundations slip and resettle;

prolonged dry weather saw cracks appear in walls and ceilings. Cora knew instinctively her home was failing her. It was sinking into the ground from which it had come.

A single whistle brought Curly running and, with Sam and Kendal saddled up, they set off three abreast, a disgruntled group of riders heading east to the creek. Once or twice Curly turned to bark in the direction of the homestead. Cora whistled at him softly. They both missed Tripod but he was yet to make a full recovery.

'So what's the rush, Cora?' Sam finally asked when half an hour of silence turned a pleasant ride uncomfortable. Lunch wasn't even considered.

'I'm pretty sure the rain will come in this afternoon and we only need a couple of inches to make the creek crossing impassable.'

'Montgomery?' Sam asked. 'He might get caught over there, right?' Everything up here was about the weather. It was either too hot or too cold, or there was too much or too little rain, or it fell at the wrong time.

'Ten points,' Kendal grunted. 'We're mustering the block over the creek.'

'I just have a feeling we might be in for a bit more rain than we bargained for,' Cora explained, 'and I don't want Montgomery caught with the rest of the rams on the other side.'

'You see, old mate,' Kendal said, 'there's been a sign.'

Yeah, Cora thought, there has been. Eight black fellas walking across the countryside in the dead of night and the last time I saw them I fell off the back of a wagon and lost my family. 'You could say that.'

'Hell of a way to run a property.'

'Well, Kendal, as I have one and you don't, clearly it's working.'

Sam was almost inclined to turn around and head back to the work shed. He was no mediator, and Cora and Kendal's jibing was enough to drive a man back to the bottle. He rubbed a hand over his wounded leg, wishing he'd remembered to put his pantyhose on, wishing he'd had that extra chop at breakfast. He just knew it was going to be one of those days. The sun was diminishing in strength as they wound through the trees in an easterly direction. When they reached the denser trees near the creek its rays barely penetrated the thick canopy above. Kangaroos, wallabies, even a pig and some suckers crossed their path, the latter dodging between him and Kendal with a series of snorts and screeches that set Sam's mount to bucking, and Curly on a brief chase.

'Hang on there, ringer,' Kendal called laconically over his shoulder.

Sam dug his thighs and heels in, and finally his mare steadied up. Dolly was a spritely old girl and, Cora assured him, steady of foot.

It was damn cold in the shade and the path they rode along was non-existent. Cora led them through trees packed so tightly that Sam was certain his clothes would be torn from him. As it was his face was whipped by prickly belah branches and he spent every second ducking, weaving and contorting his body around branches. Eventually they entered a clearing.

'That's some track.' Sam wiped a cobweb from his face and flicked at a greyish spider cadging a ride on his thigh. He didn't really go much on the plate-sized variety Cora bred.

'It's a good place to cross and as we're now on the south-east boundary it'll make the mustering easier.' Cora clucked Horse down a slight bank and then trotted him quickly across a narrow trickle of water.

'She hates water,' Kendal whispered as they followed. 'It's actually quicker to follow the track and cross a good mile or so to the west.'

'Well, we're here now,' Sam said.

'Must be nice being so amenable, Sam,' Kendal commented as they rode up the far bank to where Cora waited. 'Must have something to do with being paid.'

'Yeah,' Sam agreed. 'It does.'

Cora dismounted and drew a mud map of the paddock in the dirt with her finger. 'This is us.' She made a cross on the squiggly creek line. 'You two split up. Sam, I want you to follow the fence until you get to the next corner, here –' she tapped the dirt '– then come a good five hundred yards into the paddock and muster in a weaving motion in a northerly direction. Got it?'

'Yep,' Sam answered. Cora sounded pretty serious.

'Kendal –'

'I know the drill, Boss. Halfway down the paddock to start mustering.'

'If you lose each other just follow the creek. Sam, the plan here is to get the rams over the waterway. I'm going after Montgomery.' Cora remounted and cantered Horse off into the scrub, Curly tight on her heels.

'What's the go with chasing one ram?' Sam wondered aloud as Horse's hooves and the crackle of brush echoed through the timber.

'He's not just one ram.' Kendal mounted up. 'He's a bit like the Colt by Old Regret. He's worth a thousand pound.'

Sam followed the boundary fence, skirting wide-girthed trees and the odd gravel-edged ant hill. He eased back into the saddle, relaxing the reins. This was the life. Absolution provided a man with a bit of everything: arguments, honest work, intrigue and a spot of adventure. Who would have thought that Sam Bell, the citified mechanic with a hankering for the bottle and a good fistfight, would be riding a horse over seven hundred miles from Sydney? Sam gave a chuckle. If his Sydney mates saw him now they'd be cock-eyed in disbelief. Well, lap it up, boys, he murmured. He was home and hosed. Sam Bell was on the road to the good life. No grog, no fights, and a wife who knew what side her bread was buttered on. Yes, siree. One day Meg would own Absolution Creek, Sam was sure of it, and no over-sexed vet would be getting his hands on the place. In a few years they'd be riding the high life. All that was required on his part was to be a bit amenable to everyone.

It was some time before Sam realised he'd not travelled the designated five hundred yards into the paddock. He edged Dolly away from the fence and instead of retracing their tracks began to do a half-hearted sweep across the land. He watched birds swooping in and out of a mimosa bush and paused as two young foxes scampered through the grass, snapping at each other inter-mittently. Sam's leg began to pain as he steered his horse reluctantly away, rain splattering his face. The sky was peppered with swirling blue-tinged cloud and he spurred his horse, suddenly conscious of the task at hand.

Dolly refused to break into a trot, preferring to walk a zigzag path through the trees. The rain came across from the west in soft waves, and kangaroos hopped by to camp under branches shiny with water as Sam rode past. It was soon apparent he was lost. Every tree looked the same, every angle of the paddock similar in aspect: a flat horizon of stock-clipped pasture interspersed with variegated patches of tall wavering grasses and clumps of trees. With no sun for guidance, Sam turned the collar up on his jacket and let Dolly have her head. The old girl walked steadily across the paddock, oblivious to the rain now pelting down. As the soil was becoming soggier Sam guessed they were heading west from where the rain originated.

'Good on ya, Dolly.' Now he knew why Cora talked to her animals as if they were human.

They reached the creek as a crack of thunder sounded overhead. Sam wasn't a softie, but with no rams in sight, a wet afternoon holed up under a tree seemed a waste – particularly when he could have a go at the feeder that waited under cover back at the work

409

shed. Dolly led him along the waterway where thick lignum grew, the air dense with moisture. Ten minutes later they were across the earth-covered pipe crossing and walking back towards the homestead. Sam gave a satisfied nod, patted Dolly on the neck and rode happily home.

Sam flicked up the visor on his welding mask and turned the gas off on the cylinder. The sharp splatter of rain hitting corrugated-iron sounded like a thousand marbles being scattered on the roof above him. He stood upright, wincing at the pain in his thigh. Meg was right: the cut could have done with a few stitches, however he wasn't letting any vet stick a cow-sized needle in him. Heck, he probably would have ended up being sown together with bailing twine, while Cora's vet tried his best to entice Meg with his lopsided grin. Stitched up or not, the painful gash certainly didn't like the long ride over the creek. He was pleased to be home.

The work shed quickly became an island as the rain thundered down, the wind carrying sheets of moisture into the building. Sam watched the downpour obliterate Harold's house in the distance, blur tree and sky so that it became impossible to tell what was land and air. It would be a struggle to get back to the house in all the mud the way his leg was feeling, particularly as the wind was becoming stronger. For the briefest of seconds he imagined being lifted into the sky and hurled into the scrub, never to be found. Removing his thick welding gloves, Sam examined his handiwork. The feeder was usable again. Sure, it looked a bit battered and pockmarked from where he'd bashed it into some semblance of its former shape before welding it, however it had actually come up better than anticipated. He began stacking the sharp metal cut-offs against a 44-gallon drum, and rested the heavy mallet he'd used to bash the feeder into shape on the edge of the pile. His thoughts turned to Meg. After all what else did a bush man do on a wet afternoon? Even though he couldn't promise he'd be at his peak, he'd give it a good go.

'So you managed to get home.' Kendal trudged into the shed, soaked through, Bouncer by his side. The dog looked like it could do with a feed.

'Well, I didn't see any rams. You?' Sam wiped his hands on a greasy rag. Rivers of rainwater were beginning to flow into the shed.

'I got them. They were hanging in the north-west corner. Is Cora with you?'

Sam shook his head. 'Didn't see her.' Bouncer was snuffling at Kendal's ankles. 'I thought that dog –'

'A dog has one bad day and Cora wants them put down. Won't have anything disobedient on a sheep run, *she* reckons. As if she'd know anything about that.'

Sam turned back to the feeder.

'Not a bad job, for a city bloke.' Kendal gave the feeder a brief once over.

'And like you could have done better.' Sam placed the gloves on the workbench and began tidying the tools he'd used.

'Meaning?' Kendal rolled himself a smoke, drips of rain falling from his hat brim.

'Your mother know you're smoking?' Sam hoped for a break in the rain; bad leg or not he just knew he was inches from an argument.

'What's it like then, having a wife related to Cora Hamilton?'

'Well, it gave me a paying job.' Sam wasn't really sure what Kendal was angling at. 'What's really up your nose, Kendal? Lobbing in here unwanted and discovering you weren't going to be paid or working for a woman? Cause it sure doesn't bother your uncle. He mightn't agree with everything Cora says but I notice he's still here.'

'Working for a woman doesn't sit well. It's not in the natural order of things.'

Sam slid welding rods into a packet and sat them on the work bench. The shed was getting wet and muddy; a gap in the iron overhead ran water along timber girders to spill in a curtain. 'It seems to me neither you nor your uncle have anywhere else to go and you resent that.'

'She couldn't run the place without Harold. *He's* doing *her* the favour.'

'Really?'

Kendal took a drag. 'I suppose if you can't tell what she is, it doesn't really matter, but folks know. You ever wondered why no one's rung up and asked you around for a meal or a beer?'

The kid was angling for a punch in the nose and with the trouble Sam's leg was giving him it was going to happen sooner rather than later.

Kendal took two steps forward and poked his finger against Sam's chest. 'Well?'

Sam gave Kendal a shove. 'Back off.' The dog growled.

'If youse went to the flicks there'd be special seating, you know.' Kendal took a final drag of his smoke, flicking it onto the now waterlogged ground. 'But you'd be in one section and the blacks would be in another and Cora Hamilton, well, she wouldn't be welcome in either.'

'What on earth are you talking about?' Sam looked at the youth standing opposite him in the cold and wet of the shed. Kendal was all rangy limbs and attitude, but there was something about his words that bit into Sam's brain.

'She's a darkie. You know, touch of the tar brush and all that. Cora Hamilton probably shouldn't even be holding this land; which means youse shouldn't be here and your citified wife shouldn't end up owning it.'

Sam lunged out with a swift uppercut. It was the same swing

he'd used in the mechanic's workshop in Sydney. He followed his fist with the full weight of his body, a smile of satisfaction lacing anger as he envisioned the boy laid out in the mud of the shed. Sam's knuckles struck flesh and there was the resounding crack that only came with the shattering of a nose. Kendal gave a yelp like a wounded animal and stumbled backwards. For a moment Sam doubted the kid would fall and he readied himself for another punch, a quick felling jab to the kidneys. Sure enough, Kendal kicked out with his boot, striking Sam in his wounded thigh. Sam collapsed immediately, landing on his backside in the mud, aware Kendal had also fallen to the ground.

The dog hovered about Kendal, snuffling and whining like a tired child. 'Oh be quiet,' Sam chastised, struggling upright, using the feeder for support. Blood was soaking through his jeans and they were soggy with mud. He began to wonder if now he would need stitches, thanks to Harold's hoodlum nephew. 'Great, we'll both end up dying of blasted pneumonia.' He winced as he put equal weight on his injured leg. 'Hey, Kendal, wake up.' The boy appeared to be out cold. His face was a grey colour, blood oozing from his nose and a split on his top lip. Sam rubbed his bruised knuckles into the palm of his hand. For a kid, the boy sure had a hard skull. *Wait till Lady Cora hears about this*, he thought with amusement. It was just damn lucky Harold wasn't here.

He walked to where Kendal lay, cautious of any underhand tactics. He'd been in plenty of fights in his youth when a 'sleeper' had jumped up unexpectedly to land a sneaky right-hander; or worse, lift a leg for an attack on the crown jewels. He skirted Kendal and kicked him ever so lightly in the thigh. The boy didn't stir. Sam leant down warily and tapped the boy on the cheek. It was then that he noticed the blood seeping out from beneath Kendal's body. The boy had fallen onto the pile of steel cut-offs. Sam took a step back, his face turning pale.

## ⊰ Chapter 48 ⊱

## *Absolution Creek,*
## *1924*

Adams spent an hour or so riding about the property, leaving with a none-too-pleased expression on his face. Jack watched as the pair rode past the homestead, the one called Will pointing at the leopardwood sapling growing out from the side of the house. A steely light settled over the countryside as Jack made a point of walking to the middle of the dirt track, sweat masking his face in the noon heat. Adams looked through the dust, coat-tail flapping, and laughed. For the briefest of moments Jack visualised lifting a rifle, aiming it at the solid target of Adams's back and dropping the man in the dirt of the road. Instead he trudged through the back yard, with its timber fence, wood shed, copper and outdoor toilet, hopeful Squib was hidden somewhere nearby. At the vegetable plot Thomas and Olive could be heard indoors, their voices murmur-soft. Only able to imagine their conversation, Jack gave the wind-twisted trees and scrubby bush a final scan. He knew Squib's absence was premeditated and he thanked the saints his girl's intuition was strong.

The kitchen grew silent as he entered. Olive held a skein of wool. Thomas concentrated on a penny-dreadful novel. The pretence at normality angered Jack. Where were they when he battled alone in the scrub? Where were they when he and Squib mustered sheep on foot and checked for maggots in the dusty haze that was Absolution Creek?

'Well?' Thomas asked. 'They didn't find her, did they?'

'No,' Jack confirmed. His thoughts alternated between what he wanted to do and what the law allowed. Maybe Adams was wrong. Maybe the girl they searched for came from a different family. Jack wiped sweaty palms on his trousers. His father's Bible sat in the centre of the table. Of course she didn't, the similarities were too great: the fall from the dray, the surname, and then there was Squib's own revelation of having once lived on Waverly Station.

'We have little choice in the matter.' Thomas sat the book to one side and cut a wedge of bread from the loaf in the centre of the table. 'We have to assist the authorities.'

'And no doubt you two reached that decision unanimously,' Jack challenged. Olive didn't meet his gaze. 'There's always a choice. What I can't fathom is why Adams would go out of his way to chase after the girl.'

Thomas considered his brother's question. 'Well, apart from the law, are you thinking revenge for that sheep-thieving business?'

'Revenge is for fools and madmen,' Olive interrupted. 'Besides, the law's the law, they're merely doing their duty.'

'Jesus, Mary and Joseph, Olive, you've been after the girl since the moment you arrived. Why? It's not like you could have managed without her. You weren't used to washing or cooking or doing things a bit rough. Why, the first few weeks all you did was complain while Squib did most of the work.'

'So I suppose I don't do anything around here then, Jack.' Olive stopped darning Jack's woollen socks and stuck her finger through the hole in them, waggling it around for his benefit.

'I'm not saying that. I'm asking you to appreciate that Squib has done a lot to ease your way into our new life.'

'She knows no better.'

Jack banged his fist on the table. 'That comment's beneath you, Olive.'

'And I'm sick of having to put up with her attitude. The girl would be a housemaid in my father's home.'

'Well, we're not in Sydney any more,' Jack replied curtly.

She eyed him back. 'And you're not telling me anything I don't know.' She tossed the socks into a basket on the dirt floor.

Jack knew his choices were limited. Squib would either have to be hidden until the trouble with Adams blew over or he'd have to find some other tactic to ensure her security. Either way he could not rely on his brother or fiancée for assistance.

'You look a little peaky, Olive,' Thomas said. 'Can I get you anything?'

'I'm sure she's fine, Thomas,' Jack answered. 'I was looking for you this morning.'

'I was helping your fiancée as you never seem to be around.'

'I see.' Jack didn't though, not really. What was he missing that Squib had seen? Olive looked reasonably healthy thanks to the extra weight she now carried and while Thomas was overly attentive towards her at times, there was nothing to suggest there was anything other than friendship between them.

Jack upended the mail bag, grateful for the distraction. A newspaper and a number of letters slid onto the table. He wasn't an argumentative man and he guessed it possible that Olive's feelings for Squib were reciprocated, leading to the girl's destructive comments. Women sure could be difficult.

'The minister's due in Stringybark Point next week,' Thomas read from the newspaper, his voice sober.

'Thank heavens.' Olive's comment was barely audible.

'Well then.' Having waited for this moment for weeks, Jack discovered the burst of joy he'd anticipated was sorely lacking.

Olive was staring at him, her expression strangely hopeful. 'All good things come to those who wait.' His words sounded flat. What was he doing with this woman who was so at odds with this new world? What on earth was he doing?

'I'm glad.' Olive squeezed Jack's hand.

'Really, I thought you hated it here.'

'Oh Jack, it's been hard I'll admit, but we can make things work.' She gave a wistful smile. 'We'll have to make a trip of it. Town for the weekend it is.'

Thomas coughed. 'Of course, I'm happy for you both.'

Jack wondered if God would smile on him now, if marriage to Olive would clear him of disobeying his father's dying wish. For surely that's what this union meant. It was a joining beyond love. It was a chance for redemption. Having patiently waited to consummate his love for Olive, he'd grown tired from the wanting – tired and angry – yet perseverance was undoubtedly the key to salvation. Obviously they were meant to be together. Jack made a point of checking the mail, his thoughts spiralling downwards. There was an abyss opening around him and he knew to step inside was to lose the one thing that gave his life meaning: Squib. Yet she was but a girl and he nearing twenty. The thought was ludicrous.

Thomas rustled the paper. 'What news then, Jack?'

The thought of a shady tree appealed to Jack while he sorted out his feelings. He knew what he wanted, but could he break another promise?

'Jack?' Thomas pointed to the mail. 'Are you going to hoard it all day?'

'Ah, right you are, Thomas.' Jack sifted through the envelopes, opening them one at a time. One letter advised that a writing desk he'd ordered was due to arrive at Stringybark Point in a week; another, from May, was filled with Sydney gossip. A third envelope, with familiar writing, had been posted in Sydney. 'This is from you, Olive,' Jack said with surprise, waving the creamy envelope in the air. 'It's certainly got held up in the post. Well, look, you addressed it Absolution instead of Absolution Creek.'

Olive blinked. 'From me? But I didn't write any . . .' She watched as Jack opened it, her mind travelling back to Mrs Bennett's boarding house and the morning of her attack. *A letter, a letter?* Olive felt faint; the room spun. *The letter.* She *had* written a letter to Jack. A letter saying she would not be following him to Absolution Creek; a letter saying she would not give up her life for his. How on earth could she have forgotten it? She clutched at the collar of her dress. Not only had Mills McCoy ruined her, he'd stolen part of her memory as well. Bile rose in her throat. Her hand grasped the edge of the table for support.

Jack read the few scant lines, disbelief mingling with anger. 'You weren't going to come?' he asked, stunned. 'You weren't coming?'

Olive opened her mouth, turned to Thomas.

'Let me see.' Thomas read the few brief lines and noted the date, written in Olive's hand. 'This was the day of . . .'

'The day of what, Thomas?' Jack snatched the letter back.

'Nothing,' Olive replied quickly.

'Nothing?' Jack yelled. 'Nothing! What's going on? You haven't been yourself ever since you arrived and –'

'Leave her alone, Jack.' Thomas placed a hand on Olive's arm.

'Leave her alone?' Jack swiped the mail off the table, knocking the bread knife onto the floor. He read aloud from the letter:

*Sadly, I have come to realise such a place is not for me . . . Both our worlds have changed . . . Forgive me . . . I lack the courage to venture into the unknown, to live an isolated existence far away from family and friends.*

'That's nothing, is it, Thomas?' Jack's jaw tightened. 'What on earth's going on? Why are you here if you didn't want to come in the first place?'

'Leave her alone, Jack.'

'No, I won't. I deserve an answer.'

'Obviously she changed her mind,' Thomas replied.

'Is that what happened?' Jack thought of Olive's complaints over the preceding months. 'Did you get cold feet?'

Her eyes brimmed with tears.

'Please let her be, Jack.' Thomas took the letter from his brother's hands; replaced it in the envelope.

'I have a right to know, Olive.' He squeezed her fingers.

'I'm with child,' she answered simply. 'If you'd bothered to come near me over the last weeks, to hold me more than once or twice, to sit down and be interested in my day, in what I was doing . . .'

Jack's body went limp. It was as if the world had stilled.

'Mother Mary.' Thomas paled. 'You never said . . .'

Olive ignored Thomas and looked at Jack. 'You've shown me nothing except the affection of friendship. If you'd given me the briefest of touches, been interested in more than what lies beyond these walls I would have shared my pain with you, but no. Jack Manning finally falls on his feet and he's too obsessed with his precious new life to spare a moment, however brief, for the woman he supposedly loves; the woman who gave up everything to follow him to this godforsaken world.' Olive burst into tears.

'But how?' Jack looked at Olive. 'Who?' he asked Thomas. 'Why? I thought you loved me.'

'It's no one's fault.' Olive gave a wan smile. 'I never did realise that you were quite so God-fearing. I thought a man's wanting would come before marriage, especially out here.'

'Who's the man?' Jack's throat tore. 'The father? Did you expect me to raise a . . . a bastard?'

Olive looked him square in the eyes. 'At first, yes. I didn't know how to tell you so I expected you to think the child was yours.' She gave a choked sob. 'Otherwise, without you, I'd be ruined.'

Her words fairly winded him. 'I see.' Jack thought of that first night in the lean-to. Her wanton behaviour that had seemed so out of character was borne of a desire to cover up her disgrace.

'Then I realised I had to tell you,' Olive continued, 'that I had to trust in your love for me.'

'I'm so sorry, Olive,' Thomas said softly.

Jack almost forgot Thomas was present. He saw it then: his brother's love for Olive. Squib's words became clear. Jack visualised Olive and Thomas together on the lonely trip north: the time together in the train carriage, the rough sleep-outs; the months in Sydney after his leaving. Slowly, painfully, Jack began to understand what occurred, what was still occurring between his only brother and the woman meant to be his wife. Like a sleepwalker Jack stared out the casement window. Outside, the wind picked up. It rushed through the twisted trees, sending dirt and leaves in waves across the ground. Squib's accusation returned to burn an image in his mind.

'I love Olive,' Thomas revealed. 'I can't help it, but that's the truth of it.'

Jack turned from the window, a wedge of steel lodged in his gut. Olive's lips formed a small *o*.

Crossing the floor in two strides, Jack punched Thomas in the face. The boy dropped to the ground. 'You're no longer welcome in this house.'

Olive rushed to Thomas's side. 'Jack, how can you do that? It's not *his* fault.'

'Really. Last I heard it took two.'

Thomas shook Olive off. 'You've got it all wrong, Jack. Let Olive explain what –'

'At this point in time, Thomas, I wouldn't care if you told me she'd been accosted in the paddock by a bushranger. The end result is the same. She lied.'

Olive collapsed against the cupboard. Plates and cups fell, scattering white shards onto the dark soil of the floor.

'And she has kept on lying. I may well have lived my life bringing up another man's child.' Jack took a steadying breath, sure his heart would never return to normality. 'I want both of you out of here by nightfall.'

'Our God – the one we learnt about at Father's knee – is not a brutal God, Jack.' Thomas supported Olive about the waist, a final piece of crockery crashing from the top shelf onto the floor.

'Leave.'

Olive blanched. 'Where am I to go, Jack?'

'Anywhere, nowhere, back to your beloved Sydney. I don't really care.' Jack turned to his brother. 'Take two horses.'

'Olive can't ride,' Thomas pointed out.

Jack's words cut the air. 'That's not my problem.' He recalled the girl in the white silk clouche hat and the infectious smile, and felt only pain.

'You once told me, Jack, that God lived here too. Well, quite frankly he doesn't, he couldn't. Nothing could live out here, *nothing*.' Olive's words cut the air like a flint match.

Jack gave her a single withering gaze. 'Tidy the mess before you leave.' He pointed to the broken crockery and then walked out into the midday sun.

'You've become as mean-spirited as this land you love.' Olive's desperate voice carried along the hallway.

'Jack, please listen to Olive's story. I'm sure that once –'

'What for? You were brought up under the guidance of the church, Thomas. You should have known better.' Jack strode away from the house. Olive had lain with another – his own brother – and they'd both been prepared to lie about it for the rest of their lives. That was why she wrote the letter, Jack decided. The child was Thomas's. Olive must have been with child before she left Sydney and decided that his younger brother would not be able to provide for her.

'I do know better, Jack. I know what forgiveness means.' Thomas was standing on the top step, his fingers entwined with Olive's as Jack disappeared through the trees. 'I'm not the father of this child.' His words went unanswered. He turned to Olive. 'He didn't hear me.'

'He's right, it makes little difference, Thomas. In the beginning I did intend to pass this child off as his and that was wrong. I'm only sorry that you've been involved in my undoing.'

'Why didn't you tell him about the attack? Why didn't you tell me . . .' His voice trailed off as his eyes travelled to Olive's abdomen.

'I've provided your brother with the excuse he needed.' She sniffed into a handkerchief. 'We both know he's in love with another and it's a devotion that goes beyond right or wrong.' Olive tilted her face towards the sun; relief and sadness, freedom and uncertainty surged through her veins. 'We should pack only what we need and leave immediately.'

Thomas took her hand. 'We should wait for him to come back and set things right.'

'No, we should leave,' Olive said firmly.

'You're sure?'

'Yes.' Olive smiled. 'I am. There's no place for me here at Absolution Creek.'

# ❊ Chapter 49 ❊

# Absolution Creek, 1965

'Where have you been?' Meg emptied a saucepan down the sink and sat it back on the kitchen table. A steady stream of water was dripping from the ceiling in a number of places and it was all she could do to keep up with the rain infiltrating the other rooms in the house. 'Surely it couldn't have taken that long to fetch the rams in.'

Sam looked at her blankly. He was wet and muddy.

'I had to take most of the paintings down in the dining room. One of the walls has rivulets of water pouring along the length of it. I think I've used every saucepan, towel and bucket in the house and I can't stop it.' She mopped up water on the kitchen table with a towel, squeezing the dirt-flecked moisture into the sink.

'Where's Cora?'

'Who knows? The sunroom's flooding from the drain pipe outside. The poddy lambs escaped from the garage after I fed them and the gutters are overflowing and –'

'Forget about the house, Meg,' Sam said, raising his voice. 'Where's Cora?'

'Okay. You don't have to yell. I haven't seen her since you all rode out this morning.' Meg glanced at the kitchen clock. It was now 3 pm. 'Is something wrong?'

'You could say that,' he answered tightly. 'Damn it all.' He slumped in the nearest chair and then stood again, fidgeting with his shirt collar, his belt, the high back of the wooden chair.

'The girls are in their room.' Meg glanced towards the door leading to the walkway. 'Tell me what's happened.'

'Kendal's been injured.'

Meg's heart skipped a beat. 'Injured? How? Is it bad? Where is he?'

'He fell in the shed. I swear it was an accident, Meg. He's hurt bad, real bad.'

Meg grappled with the implication of Sam's words. 'So where is he?'

'Still out there. I think he's dead.'

Meg leant against the sink for support. 'Oh, Sam.'

Cora tugged at the brim of her hat. The rain continued to pelt down and she could feel the water beginning to seep through the seams of the oilskin jacket. She'd been walking for hours and was still a good trek away from the main creek crossing. If only she'd left the homestead an hour earlier then maybe she would have found Montgomery before he'd decided to seek refuge under a stand of wilga trees. It took an hour to locate him. He had retreated a couple of miles to the south-east, as far from the creek as possible, and was nowhere near his usual patch of ground. It was a canny move on the ram's part, but Cora couldn't risk leaving him there alone with no access for weeks if they did get a good run down the creek. She was surprised Sam didn't see Montgomery when he rode that way, but what did she expect? All these young blokes were tussock jumpers. They rode from tussock to tussock and saw nothing in between.

Horse gave a low whicker and nudged her shoulder. Cora knew what he was thinking: it was time to dump the ram and head home; every man for himself. She patted him on the nose and put up with his hair nibbling. Walking was the better option at the moment, for Montgomery and Horse had never been friendly and their meeting under the wilga tree earlier had led to an almost nose-to-nose standoff. Only a brief break in the rain and Cora's dogged 'on foot' persistence managed to get Montgomery moving, and it had been a battle to keep up any pace since. The ram walked ahead slowly, his legs matted with mud, his wool sodden. Every so often he would stop, look over his shoulder at Cora and Horse, and then resume his onward progression. At the rate they were going it would be dark by the time they reached the crossing.

Cora pushed and ducked under belah branches heavy with rain. When they passed through the clearing where Jack's original hut once stood – the one she had accidently burnt to the ground – Cora slowed. There had been no substantial flood here since before Jack Manning had walked this very ground. Here he'd cut scrub in a ring around the hut, fished at the creek, read letters from the woman he loved, who in return lied and lost him. They all lost him in the end and Cora still carried the scars.

Montgomery gave a series of grunts and trotted ahead, disappearing into a thick stand of trees. Cora resettled herself on Horse's back, and followed the ram between the woody plants. The dense overhead canopy sheltered them a little from the rain, and it was here that Montgomery dug in his heels and stopped. Horse waited patiently as Montgomery considered both directions, his stately head turning first left then right.

'We don't really have time for a debate on this, Montgomery,' Cora scolded. Horse whinnied in agreement.

The rain continued to fall steadily and with nothing to eat since the single piece of toast at James's place at daylight, Cora knew she would have to draw on her resolve to get Montgomery to safety. 'Don't think about James,' she chastised, 'or Jack for that matter. Think about getting home.'

Finally Montgomery trundled onwards. Horse followed suit and they left the tree-arched pathway for open grassland and pouring rain.

# ≼ Chapter 50 ≽

# En Route to Absolution Creek, 1965

Scrubber never had seen such a dirty storm. It hounded him from the east, like a money-lender ferreting away, until by the time sunlight streamed into his eyes the angry squall was almost upon him. The rain had started real soft, similar to a woman pawing at his skin offering plenty, lulling a man into a false sense of security. Then the swirling breeze arrived, teasing, playful, raising dried leaves in swirling ribbons of brown, before shape-shifting into a fierce wind that lifted anything not tied down. Rubbing grit from his eyes, Scrubber elected to keep plodding onwards. The girls were pleased to be on their way again and Dog was back sitting astride Samsara, all little Lord Fauntleroy, nose in the air.

'Well, mate –' Scrubber patted the pouch at his waist '– how are you travelling?'

Hindsight wasn't something Scrubber ever had time for, never-theless, with the wind howling and the wet stuff from above increasing in intensity, he knew he should have fetched some timber and sourced a dry camp before the storm hit and darkness spread across the plains.

'I know what you're thinking. At my age a man should be prepared.'

The trouble was he never was one for minding a bit of wetness: that tangy splat of rain on a man's face; the smell of dry dirt turning damp, branches heavy with moisture. Being cooped up in a hotel room only made Scrubber's desire to keep moving greater. Once out in space and air he wanted to suck it all in. Hadn't he been riding for the last three months trying to keep the east at his back, attempting to stall the inevitable while fulfilling the one thing that had been eating into him all these years? Course he had an excuse. Two actually. Veronica and then his own sickness.

'Bugger.' The rain lashed his face as Scrubber trotted his entourage towards the outline of some trees. The trunks were thick enough and close enough to provide a smattering of cover, and it was here Scrubber dismounted. 'Get off, Dog.' The mangy animal snarled, eyes glowing in the dark. Scrubber grabbed him by the scruff of the neck and threw him off, and then set about unsaddling the horses and his gear. He piled everything up in the direction of the incoming rain at the base of the thickest tree. Spiky leaves brushed his skin. He let the horses find their own cover and layered the ground with a couple of saddle blankets. Throwing the swag about his shoulders, he huddled close to the timber. Dog nosed his way into Scrubber's cocoon, positioning himself under his bent knees.

It wasn't too bad, Scrubber mused, opting for a positive slant as he peered out at the driving rain. He bit his lip as a sliver of pain ran through his belly, a razor slicing him raw. 'Not now,' he groaned. Hadn't he been holed up in a hotel for two days without even the hint of an ache? The surge rippled and dissipated then bit again, fiercer, stronger. Scrubber concentrated on a blade of grass, watching the rain belting it back and forth. His vision blurred and refocused until an image of Squib wavered before him. Then the world went dark.

# ⊰ Chapter 51 ⊱

# Absolution Creek, 1965

A trail of mud signalled their progress as Meg and Sam dragged Kendal through the homestead. Behind them the twins watched as Meg flipped back the bedcovers. Kendal flopped lifelessly onto the sheet. Meg grasped her side, pinching at a painful stitch.

'Is Kendal hurt, Mummy?' Penny had two fingers shoved in her mouth and Jill peeped over her sister's shoulder.

Kendal was still alive, his breathing shallow. Sam pulled the boy's muddy boots off. 'Now what?'

Meg's breath started to return to normal. 'Turn him on his side.' She grappled for nail scissors on the bedside table and began snipping at Kendal's clothing.

'We'll be here all day,' Sam complained, removing Kendal's pocketknife from the boy's belt and slicing through the material. The wound was on his shoulder: a deep gash that appeared to have bled itself out. 'I reckon he knocked his head, that's why he's out to it.' Sam stripped Kendal to the waist. 'Penny, fetch a blanket from your room for me.'

Meg probed the nasty gash. The blood was already congealing. 'I think you're right.' There wasn't enough blood in the dirt at the work shed to suggest he was going to die from blood loss. Meg closed her eyes briefly in relief. They were lucky. Sam was very lucky. 'When he wakes we'll have a problem, won't we?' This was Sam's third fight that Meg knew of, and although she expected Kendal to recover he'd definitely press charges. Her husband was looking at gaol time.

'One problem at a time,' Sam countered.

Meg propped pillows beneath Kendal's head and then selected a clean shirt, which she pressed against his injury. 'I don't know what else we can do for him.' She pulled the bed covers to his chin and glanced out the door at the curtain of rain, which continued to obliterate the countryside. 'Would we get him to Stringybark Point?'

Sam scratched his neck. Penny and Jill reappeared in the bedroom doorway, a blanket draped between them, their eyes agog. 'Thanks. Now you two run along and check the leaks in the house for your mother and we'll get Kendal settled.'

'Will Kendal be okay, Daddy?'

'Sure he will, Jill.' Sam unwrapped the end of the blanket from around his daughter's leg.

Penny looked doubtful. 'If Aunt Cora was here she'd know what to do.'

Sam turned to his wife. 'Out of the mouths of babes, eh?'

'Off you go,' Meg ordered, scooting the girls out and shutting the door behind them.

'I could bundle him into a vehicle and give it a go,' Sam said, staring at Kendal. 'The problem is I don't know how bad the road will be. If I get bogged Kendal really will have a problem.'

'Yeah, he probably is better off here. If that wound gets jolted around it might start bleeding again.' Meg rested her hand on Kendal's brow. He was hot to the touch.

'He had it in for me from the very beginning,' Sam began. 'Not that I can blame him – not being paid and all. Still, for a kid he sure has an attitude.'

'Why's he even here?' Meg smoothed Kendal's hair. 'He's not being paid and it's not like he's the friendliest of people.' She waited unsuccessfully for Sam to make a comment. 'What were you fighting about?'

There didn't seem much point in avoiding the truth. 'He said something about Cora not belonging to the black or the white section at the Stringybark Point flicks. That she wasn't entitled to the land and therefore you weren't, either. A fella wouldn't make a comment like that unless some truth lay at the heart of it. Anyway, right or wrong I decked him one. A smart bloke would have noticed all the animosity from the beginning. Kendal's dislike for your aunt, and Harold continually trying to overrule the woman he works for. Combine that with your mother's attitude towards her sister . . . well, it all equals trouble.'

'I don't see how that adds up to anything,' Meg responded.

'Maybe it's a bit like trying to join missing dots, but I can see by the look on your face that you had some suspicions. You knew, didn't you?' he asked hesitantly, praying Kendal's accusations weren't about to be confirmed. 'You knew your aunt was of Aboriginal blood.'

They were facing each other across their bed, Kendal's prone body between them. Meg wrung her hands. 'I'm not sure.'

'Well, I'm not sure that I'd admit to it, either.' Sam considered the ramifications; thought of his little girls whom he loved and the Sydney-based mother-in-law who considered herself too high and mighty for the likes of Sam Bell. 'I need to ask this, Meg. Is your mother . . .'

Meg's cheeks flushed a bright pink. 'No, of course not.' She sat heavily on the edge of the bed. 'At least, I don't think so.'

'So you don't know for sure?'

Meg lowered her voice. 'No, Sam Bell, I don't know for sure. However, apparently Mum and Cora are stepsisters by marriage only, so I'm figuring she isn't.'

'Stepsisters, eh? And you didn't feel the need to share any of this with me earlier?'

'No, yes. Damn it, I don't know, Sam. I've had a lot to think about over the last few weeks and our relationship hasn't exactly been great.'

Sam looked both surprised and disappointed. 'Funny, from where I stood I thought things were improving.'

He rummaged in the chest of drawers for a dry shirt, jeans and a jumper. 'Well, let's forget about us for the moment. This business with Cora is a lot for a person to take in.' He stripped off, quickly changing into the fresh clothes. 'So now we know why your mother and Cora don't get on. What a mess.' He flipped his shirt collar up and over his jumper and then prodded at the wet and bloody bandage on his thigh. 'You know, I'm not sure if a darkie can even hold land in their name.'

'Would you mind not calling my aunt that, please?'

Sam pulled on the clean jeans. 'Sorry, but you know we do have to consider our own reputations, Meg, and our future. There isn't much point staying on here if there's nothing in it for us.'

'I thought you liked it here.'

'Let's not change the subject. How long have you known?'

'Well, I don't. At least . . . well, Cora's been telling me the story of a little girl called Squib who lost her family in the twenties. I guess I didn't really pick up on the fact that Cora was Squib until she told me. Not that Cora mentioned anything about . . .' Meg faltered. 'Anyway, if you're asking me if I know for sure, no I don't. However, I've had a few conversations with Kendal as well and when we went to Stringybark Point shopping last month, Cora just seemed to be treated differently. People sort of didn't talk about her as if she was one of us.'

'Would you have come to Absolution if you'd known?'

Meg's fingers plied the blanket beneath her. 'We don't know how much or little of that blood she has in her.' Of course, a telephone call to her mother would answer all their questions.

'Does it matter?' Sam opened the door. A wave of moist cold air swept through the room. 'Obviously there was enough to make her decide not to tell you.'

Meg didn't answer.

'Well, now she's gone and got herself lost out in this blasted weather. It's already near dark with this heavy cloud cover.'

'Are you going out to look for her?' Meg asked, giving Kendal a final glance before joining Sam on the veranda.

Sam frowned. 'No.'

Cora reached the creek crossing just as darkness began to settle in. Edged by trees, the low bank was frilled by great knobbly roots. Finally, a cleared space showed the track that headed west, away from danger. The outline of the mounded dirt across the pipe was visible, the cement edge white against the dark soil. Montgomery took a tentative sniff at its muddy approach, raised his head into the driving rain and backed up like a horse.

'Go on then, Montgomery, don't baulk now,' Cora called, her voice doing battle with the noise of rain slashing the waterway into a miniature stormy sea. The ram turned, sniffed the air and took a step back towards where they'd come from. Curly growled. Cora wheeled Horse to the right, blocking the ram from escape. 'Come on. Just walk over the damn thing. Walk, Montgomery.'

The ram changed direction.

'For a prize animal you sure are dumb.' The ram glowered in the gathering dark. Streaks of lightning illuminated the blue-black sky and lit up the land about them between snatches of rolling thunder.

Cora didn't like the look of the sky. In all her years on Absolution Creek she could not recall seeing such lightning in a wet or a dry storm. Something made her glance over her shoulder. The flash that followed was like a floodlight revealing a thick storm swirling westward, while the one nearly upon her was heading towards the east.

The rain whipped at her face and she tugged on slippery reins. 'In a few more minutes it'll be pitch black, Montgomery. None of us will be able to see a thing.'

Horse whinnied in agreement. Curly barked. Cora unfurled her stock whip from the saddle and flicked it towards the ram. She raised the plaited leather above her head and snapped the crack at the end in mid-air. The sharp clap pierced the air and Montgomery moved backwards towards the crossing. Cora lifted the whip again. Horse moved forward automatically and Montgomery faltered under the noisy barrage. Again and again Cora cracked the whip as the ram took a few steps closer to the crossing. It was tough going. Each time Cora flashed the leather she listened to the resounding crack as it competed with both rain and thunder. Finally, Montgomery bolted over the crossing to the edge of the track where grass gave his hoofs greater purchase than the muddy road.

Cora wound up the whip, and thrust her arm through it and over her shoulder. 'Thank heavens.' She ran her hand down Horse's neck and gritted her teeth. She could do this. She had to do it. The only way to get home was to cross the blasted creek. 'Now it's our turn.' They were halfway across the mounded dirt when a lightning flash struck the ground only feet away. Horse reared instinctively and slipped. Cora felt the saddle slide out from beneath her, her hands flailing.

She was lying in mud, her head pounding from the impact. Gradually, another noise replaced the pain in her head. It was the sound of rain hitting mud inches from her ear. Splats of dirty water mixed with raindrops on her skin. The rain was growing heavier.

Pain raced up Cora's leg. Horse was lying on her weak leg, Curly whining next to her.

'Horse? Horse old mate, get up.' Cora clawed her way up from the mud, her fingers twisting against the saddle. Yanking at the solid weight she tried to move her leg left to right, quickly realising it was pinned from the thigh down. Horse's breathing was ragged.

'Horse, Horse, wake up!' When the next flash of lightning illuminated the sky the scale of the animal's injury became apparent. A great gash revealed blood and bone. His head had hit the edge of the cement pipe. 'No, not my Horse,' Cora whimpered. 'Not my friend.' Reaching out she grasped a handful of wet mane. 'I love you, Horse. I love you.' She wanted to look into those trusting brown eyes one more time, just once, but she couldn't. Horse faced away from her towards an unknown paddock. With shaking hands she unhooked the holster and drew her pistol. She pulled at a gloved finger with her teeth and freed her hand, and was soon loading a single bullet into the chamber with trembling fingers.

*Hold your breath, Squib,* her father would say. *Pull the trigger nice and slow and then let the air out.*

Cora did as she'd been taught, her hand perfectly still. When the thunder cracked and lightning followed, the round hit the highlighted target neatly. 'Good Horse.' She patted him quietly as he gave a final kick. 'Good Horse.'

Cora holstered the pistol, placed her free foot against Horse's back and pushed as hard as she could. 'Come on, come on,' she yelled through gritted teeth. 'You can do this.' Twisting and turning made little difference, her leg didn't budge an inch. Eventually exhaustion began to radiate through her limbs. Cora fell back in the mud, the rain lashing her face, the swish of water only feet below. She tried not to think of the creek, of where she lay, of her beloved Horse pinning her down. Nonetheless fear stalked her; it moved stealthily across the sodden ground to sit heavily on her chest.

'Go home, Curly,' Cora commanded. 'Go fetch help.'

The dog looked at her, walked a few steps and then halted.

'Go!'

Curly gave Horse a sniff and then disappeared into the rain.

Above her the sky raged. It was as if two weather tribes fought each other on the backs of clouds, lightning as spears, thunder their war cry. Cora lay and waited for the inevitable. The perfect storm that Captain Bob once spoke of – the one that would send her into oblivion – had finally come to Absolution Creek.

# ❧ Chapter 52 ❧

## Absolution Creek, 1924

Jack waited two days for Squib to return. During her absence he stayed well clear of the homestead, relying on distance to ease a thickening disappointment. He lived on nothing but water and aged bread, and spent long hours by the creek, bare feet splayed in the water. Occasionally he would flick through his father's Bible in an attempt to find the slightest thread of understanding, a modicum of solace, but an answer eluded him.

Olive's admission continued to flatten every aspect of Jack's world. Combined with Thomas's disloyalty, it was difficult to think clearly. His inability to see their true characters reflected, he believed, on his own limited view of the world, and in that knowledge Jack recognised a degree of selfishness he was previously unaware of. Yet the anger needling his mind was greater than his compassion. This land, which he cared for and was so proud of, even the homestead, meant nothing to Olive. He meant nothing to her. Clearly her arrival at Absolution Creek was borne out of desperation.

At the water's edge Jack recalled the life he'd sought on leaving Sydney. His dream remained simple: to have a place of his own in the world and to share it with loved ones. Was it so hard to have both? Where once the Bible sat by a horsehair chair in the kitchen of their grocer's store, it now rested on the warm sand of the creek's bank, the gold lettering now partially faded, and leather cover worn with use. Would it not have been better, Jack wondered, to have given in to temptation that first night of Olive's arrival; to have lived the rest of his life blissfully ignorant of his fiancée's deceit? Such a question could never be answered. It did, however, lend credence to his increasing lack of faith. What was the point of living a life good and true if others did not? Why be burdened with guilt at ignoring his father's deathbed promise if one's penance was never enough?

Jack thought of Squib running through the bush, accepting and grateful of any kindness shown her. The girl who'd survived the very worst of obstacles still found pleasure in her life, found pleasure by Jack's side, and was grateful for what she had. Jack was not immune to her easy smile and interest in all things rural. Out of the mismatch of inhabitants that once resided within Absolution Creek's homestead, Squib was the only person with whom he could share his aspirations, who was actively interested in what he was trying to achieve. Should the girl have been ignorant of bush life Jack suspected Squib would have done her best to learn. As it was he remembered with more than fondness the nights they'd sat by the camp fire, good-naturedly quarrelling about one of Mr Farley's animal husbandry books.

The snap of a branch diverted Jack's thoughts. On the far side of the creek a mob of ewes padded quietly to the water. They jostled for position briefly before lining up like soldiers to drink as one. Their white muzzles dipped into the liquid and then rose to swallow a mouthful before dipping again, their woolly backs pressed close together.

Jack strode up the bank to where his horse waited, intent on repaying the support received from a girl on the edge of woman-hood. There were ways of stopping men like Adams and no doubt methods of thwarting well-intentioned governments if the coin was sufficiently thick. What swirled in Jack's mind was against every-thing he'd been instructed to believe in, and if his parents were alive they would undoubtedly condemn his actions. Perhaps that was the reason he left his father's Bible on the sandy creek bank, for as Jack rode away he was only aware of the goodness nestled in the girl named Squib and a burning need to save her.

Squib awoke to a vision of the sapling in the corner of her room. Light was beginning to stream through the window and a cool breeze rustled the leaves of the leopardwood tree. On the floor tiny star flowers stained the timber boards in patches. The unseasonal flowers blew slowly across the boards in miniature circles to melt against her bare feet as Squib splashed water on her face and tidied her hair in a long plait. A single clean blouse lay over a chair with the too-few items that filled her kerosene-box wardrobe, and she dressed swiftly, aware of how quiet the house was. At this hour even Olive should have been up and the homestead scented with the remains of fried eggs. Normally Squib would have already had the men's breakfast things washed and tidied away and be sitting down to tea and toast by the time her ladyship appeared. The still-ness unnerved her.

Having spent nearly one-and-a-half days holed up out on a pine-covered ridge since Adams's unscheduled arrival, Squib returned footsore and exhausted to her bedroom at midnight. She'd not noticed anything out of sorts then. She'd skirted around the house and entered her room via the veranda to ensure she'd not woken anyone. Now with hunger making her ill, Squib walked hesitantly to the kitchen. Instead of the usual stove-warmed space, the area was pleasantly cool for late summer. Shards of broken plates and cups were scattered across the kitchen floor, along with pages from a newspaper and a couple of scattered envelopes. Windows were open as well as the front door, and blowflies crawled over the kitchen table. Squib shivered; something was terribly wrong.

The rest of the homestead was equally uninhabited. The two living rooms, both only partially furnished, were empty. In Olive's bedroom, clothes were strewn about, the dresser drawers open and clearly rummaged through. Thomas's room was equally dishevelled. With growing nervousness Squib opened Jack's bedroom door. His barely used space was neat, the wardrobe closed, drawers intact. Squib sat on Jack's bed, trying to decipher what had occurred in the house during her absence. If all Jack's things were still here – if he hadn't packed anything while the others had – then that meant that Olive and Thomas had gone. But why would they go? A small gasp escaped her lips as understanding took hold, then an overwhelming feeling of joy settled in her chest. Lifting Jack's rarely used pillow, Squib buried her face in it. There was the faintest scent of soap and the unmistakable smell of Jack: a mix of leaves and soil. With a squeal Squib hugged the pillow to her chest. Everything pointed to the same conclusion. Olive's secret was now revealed. Learning that she was with child and in love with another, Jack had thrown both his brother and the woman meant to be his wife out of his home and off Absolution Creek.

Squib went back to the kitchen and with renewed energy tidied the broken plates, threw away the mouldy bread and stoked up the stove with wood. Once the kettle was warming she picked up the mail and stacked it neatly to one side. The newspaper she folded carefully. Jack always read it at least four times and once he was finished with it Squib usually spent an evening cutting it up into neat squares to hang on the rusty nail in the dunny. The letter was sitting beneath the bread knife.

*Dear Squib,*

*Much has occurred in your absence and I hope this letter finds you safe. To be brief, Olive and Thomas have left for a better life. We both know Olive was never happy here so I've come to see their leaving as being for the best.*

*I want to add that you have been nothing but fair and willing since the day I found you by the creek and if at times I or others have treated you poorly I want you to know how sorry I am. To make some amends and to protect you from the likes of Adams I'm leaving for Stringybark Point to have papers drawn up to make you my ward.*

*Please know that no matter what happens there will always be a place for you at Absolution Creek and I hope you will stay on. Keep safe.*

*Jack*

Squib re-read the letter. 'Jack's ward,' she mouthed softly. She didn't want to be Jack's ward. She screwed the letter up tightly in her fist. Clearly Jack didn't understand that she cared for him. That out of everybody she had ever known in the world he was the one that she *now* loved the best. There was no one else. Her father had abandoned her.

Squib knew they were meant to be together on Absolution Creek. She'd dreamt about their lives together, had seen their future. Even with Olive's presence, Squib understood she would always be by Jack's side. Not perhaps as a woman hoped to be with a man, however she would settle for second best if the choice was that or nothing, for Squib couldn't live without Jack Manning in her world.

Now, though, Olive was out of the picture. There was no barrier to her happiness. Squib knew she would have to saddle up and ride after Jack. She would have to find him and remind him that, with Olive and Thomas gone, only a handful of years lay between them and that she was prepared to wait. She would wait forever if she knew one day he'd be by her side.

Squib shut the flue on the stove, closed the window and with a handful of currants and a water bag for provisions ran outside. She would ride all day and night to find Jack. She had to. Squib didn't want to be Jack Manning's ward. One day she hoped to be his wife.

## ⪻ Chapter 53 ⪼

## En Route to Absolution Creek, 1965

Scrubber awoke on the ground, rain filling the whorls of his ear, mud masking his cheek. He righted himself against the wet earth and fumbled for the pouch. Unlacing the leather, he dropped it down his shirtfront, patting it securely. The pain hit again, stabbing him between breaths.

*Surely that wasn't his boy over there, was it? Crouching in the grass? How long was it since Brendan had been home for a visit? Ten, twenty years? He must call Veronica, tell the old girl their boy was home.*

When he opened his eyes Dog was standing opposite. He looked like an oversized water rat, and had Scrubber's hat gripped between his teeth. 'I'll be right, mate.' Scrubber claimed his hat as Dog snuck under his arm. 'Don't worry, I ain't leaving you or the girls out here alone in this weather.' He knew he needed to get some perspective on the situation, to talk his way out of the pain. A man could be in worse predicaments, after all. And no matter what lay ahead of him it would never be as bad as what his boy Brendan went through during the war: living like rats in that bloody desert, with scant supplies and fouled water. All to stop some bloody General by the name of Rommel stampeding over the rest of the world. Well, they could have it. Brendan was dead of disease by 1943, buried in someone else's crappy country. That's what buggered Veronica. That's when she started to eat and couldn't stop.

A few feet away a couple of kangaroos bounded to a stop under a tree. Dog gave a low growl. 'Plenty of room for everybody,' Scrubber pacified. The rain was coming thick and fast. Through the scattered trees a flash of lightning highlighted a ridge of storms in the west. Dog howled. Scrubber patted him to quietness. 'Yeah, it don't look real good and it's not very far away.' He'd never seen two storms converging from opposite directions. He thought back to the publican's suggested route. They were travelling in a direct line to the west, which meant the creek that eventually wound through Absolution should be somewhere on his right, perhaps only half a mile or so away. After he reached the creek he'd continue to head south, cutting through a few neighbours' paddocks until he reached a mounded crossing. That was the way towards Absolution homestead. The problem was he was reckoning on things getting pretty damp. A ripple of lightning flashed overhead, revealing the trees Scrubber sought refuge under.

'Belah.' He clucked his tongue. 'Should have known it.' Another flash of light silhouetted a myriad of belah saplings. The trees were a prime indication of heavily flooded country. 'I think we'll pack up camp and move on, Dog. Ain't got much choice. I know my limitations. A couple of nights holed up out here and I'll be buggered.' He whistled to his girls and began collecting his gear. 'Come on, Samsara, your turn.' The easterly storm consumed his thoughts, reminding him of the day they'd left the granite country. That sneaky thing out there lay only days behind. Time had nearly caught up with him.

Cora opened her eyes to the sting of rain and a coldness that ate at her bones. The shivering had started some time ago, and although it initially helped to warm her now it made no difference. It was her leg that hurt the most. Horse's dead weight was like a rock sinking into flesh and bone. The only positive element to Cora's predicament was the heat of Horse's body, which succeeded in providing some warmth. When the rain eased a touch, she hooked her fingers around the saddle, quickly retrieving her dry sweater from the saddlebag. Stripping off she re-dressed with the dry sweater next to her skin.

Why had no one come looking for her? Even if Sam didn't understand the vagaries of the weather, Kendal did. He may not like her much but the kid did have a bit of decency in him. Unless – Cora gave a choke of understanding – unless what she'd battled all her life was finally winning. She knew what everyone thought: Cora Hamilton didn't have a right to be on Absolution; didn't have a right to hold land or employ white people like she was one of them, or poke her head above the trees by purchasing Montgomery 201. In fact, Cora Hamilton didn't have any rights at all, for she was of Aboriginal descent, living in a country that believed Aboriginal children would be better off being cared for by Church Missions or the like, and such prejudice was an act of parliament.

Cora wrapped her fingers more securely under Horse's saddle. How easy for all involved simply to forget, to let the rain wash away the stain she made on their lives. It was only fate that saved her instead of her dear brother, Ben, only the enigma of her earlier life that allowed her to exist on Absolution Creek in her own right, on her own terms. Yet such a life was couched in solitude and reflection, and while people were wary of her, Cora was not immune to their glances and snickers. What was worse, there was every reason to be afraid. For it was true – if she lost Absolution – she would have nowhere to go.

Not that it probably mattered now.

Cora listened to the creek growing in strength, heard the telltale whoosh of water. She thought of the pistol at her waist and wondered if she had within her the strength to cause her own death. Her heart fluttered. It fell and rose, became sporadic in its beat. All her life the memory of being swept down the creek to Absolution had tainted her dreams. Now it seemed all too likely that the force that had carried her to Jack Manning, to safety, was returning to take her away again.

If she was lucky the water would come quickly, dragging her under with Horse, her useless leg flailing in the current. If it came slowly . . . at the thought Cora nearly passed out from the terror.

Dog started howling at dawn and didn't draw breath until Scrubber cuffed him on the side of the head. It was hard going for everyone and he never had taken to whingers. They'd already lost one horse during the night. Petal, always the least interesting of the girls to Scrubber's mind, simply stopped walking around midnight and wouldn't budge. Not in the mood to fight a woman's contrariness, he slipped the bridal from her obstinate head, counting on Petal to trot on. It didn't happen. The last Scrubber saw of the bay mare she was standing in the downpour and was quickly enveloped by darkness.

Tapping Samsara's flanks, Scrubber angled through a stand of stringybarks and across fallen timber until they were back trailing the creek through the drizzle. Great watery lakes filled every hollow and swamp to spread across the landscape. In places it drained down the eroded banks back into the creek, which although fast moving was yet to overrun the sandy waterway – a good sign at least.

Scrubber slid down into calf-deep water and let Dog off Veronica's back for a stretch and a pee. He didn't figure the storm being finished yet. The wind had dropped and there was still no birdsong. He chewed on a piece of bread from the loaf purchased at the hotel, washed it down with water, and then offered some to Dog. The mutt gulped at it, begged a bit more and then drank from Scrubber's sodden hat.

'Now are you right?' Stupid question, Scrubber decided. The water was part-way up Dog's body and he didn't complain when he was sitting atop Samsara again. 'Righto, Veronica, we're on the homeward bound. It's up to you. Now be careful where you're walking, girl, there's hollows and such like about and we don't want you going down.' The mare didn't look that certain, though she took his weight without complaint when he bustled up quickly to escape a black snake gliding across the water's surface. The snake headed straight for Samsara.

'Damn and blast.' Scrubber reached for his rifle as Samsara reared upwards in fright. Dog slipped off and into the water. Deciding the rifle would be of little use, Scrubber slid from the saddle and splashed through the water as the snake veered off in Dog's direction. 'I don't bloody think so,' Scrubber roared, wading forward. The snake, momentarily confused by the rippling surface, halted. Scrubber lunged and grabbed the slithering creature near its head, then smashed it against the trunk of a tree. Blood splattered the rough bark. The snake plopped lifeless into the water.

'Let's go,' he panted heavily, as a familiar pain ripped through a body beginning to fold. Staggering back to the horses, Scrubber lifted Dog up onto Samsara's back and mounted Veronica. Dog let out a stringy bark.

'Save the thanks for later,' Scrubber mumbled. 'We haven't got there yet.'

## ≪ *Chapter 54* ≫

## *Absolution Creek,*
## *1965*

Meg tucked the blankets around Kendal. His forehead was hot, his skin flushed. Hollows of black underlined his eyes and with the slightest of movements a moan would escape his lips. Bex powders were the only medicine Meg could offer and she doubted their effectiveness. Kendal, awake intermittently throughout the night, complained of nausea, shivering and pain. All Meg could do was apologise, finally offering the last of Cora's hidden rum to help ward off his misery. At least now he was asleep. Closing the door Meg checked on the twins. They too spent part of the night awake. Jazzed up by the leaking house, the fierce storm and Kendal's misfortune, sleep finally came amid tears and tantrums. They lay top-to-toe in one of the single beds, a vision of fanning hair and small hands and feet. Meg left them to their dreams.

The veranda was soaked from the rain. Out near the dam an inland sea appeared to have engulfed them overnight. Water surrounded them. It gurgled down the drainpipes, overflowed gutters and was still spilling into the house as it trickled through holes and gaps in the iron roof to track strutting and beams. Finally it seeped through the joins in the pressed metal ceilings or crept down walls. Meg peered through the clingy wet gauze. There was no sound except that of water: dripping, trickling, seeping, flowing water. Although the rain was now only a drizzle, the clouds were still thick with moisture. She guessed she would have to go back to the kitchen, to Sam. It was all she could do not to cry, both for the state of her marriage and her lost aunt. Why hadn't she pushed Sam to try to do more to find Cora last night, instead of slinking away in shame?

In the kitchen Sam fiddled with the radio, a screwdriver in one hand, a scatter of broken parts on the table. Meg checked on Tripod. Much to Sam's annoyance she'd bundled Cora's dog up, settling him in a dry corner of the kitchen. Apart from the occasional whine, Tripod made little noise, however he was still alive.

'Any luck?' Meg asked brightly. One of them needed to attempt a reconciliation.

'What do you think?' Sam didn't look up from his task.

'Hey, I didn't break it,' Meg snapped. They'd slept in separate rooms last night. She with the twins and Sam on a mattress in the kitchen. 'There's more rain coming.'

'You think?'

Meg rinsed her empty coffee cup in the sink, her teeth grinding. 'Lose the attitude, Sam.'

He flung the screwdriver across the room. 'And why the hell should I? That first week we were here I told you this was the wrong decision.'

'A few nights ago you were telling me how much you were enjoying working here.'

Sam glowered.

'Well, you were. Don't blame me for the mess we're in now. I wasn't the one who had the fight with Kendal or refused to go and look for Cora.'

'We should have packed up and headed back to Sydney. Talk about being deceived. You've got a ripping family, Meg.'

'And like you had anything better to offer. No job, the drinking and fighting, leaning on me all the time and then abusing me when my attempts at trying to better our position in life aren't perfect.'

Sam piled the radio parts on the table. 'Well, I can understand why you would want to do that at least.'

'That's an unkind thing to say.'

Sam shifted in his chair and threw an arm over the back of it. 'I've been outside,' he said quietly. 'There's water everywhere. We've got about two days' wood left for the fire if we're careful. Food?'

Meg tucked sleep-ruffled hair behind her ears. 'We can make do for a week. There's a heap of tinned goods in the pantry.'

'Kendal?'

'He'll survive. What about Cora?'

'I don't see there's much that I can do for her. Have you seen the water out there? A horse might be fine out in it but I haven't had the experience.'

*And the one who has*, Meg thought with annoyance, *is laid up in bed, thanks to you.* She picked up the telephone.

'I've tried the operator, I can't get anyone.' Sam filled the kettle and placed it on the Aga.

'The storm's damaged the lines, I guess, but I wonder . . .' Meg rummaged through the books on the bench until she located a district telephone book. She twirled the handle on the telephone. 'James, James Campbell.' A shrill noise carried down the line. 'Well, this part of the line isn't damaged.'

'Campbell Station, James here.'

Meg briefly described the situation, including Kendal's 'accident'.

'And you're telling me she's been out since yesterday and no one bothered to go after her?' James was clearly distraught.

'Well, um, I didn't know until it was near dark and then Kendal hurt himself and –'

'Forget it, Meg. So where exactly did she go?'

'Where did Cora go?' Meg repeated to Sam.

'Over the creek to the back paddock to get that bloody ram,' Sam said loudly.

'I heard him,' James confirmed.

'What should we do?' There was a moment's silence, the void filled with the crackle of the telephone line.

'Nothing. You've done enough. I'll try and get my hands on a chopper, not that it'll be easy. There's been a major disaster east of Stringybark Point. Meg, you guys have got to prepare yourself.'

'For what?' She thought of Cora, of the weather, of Kendal lying injured in their bedroom.

'There's flood water coming your way. Absolution Creek is one of the wettest spots in the district. You may be isolated for some time I'm afraid. Turn your radio on and –' The line dropped out.

'James said there's a flood coming our way.' Meg replaced the receiver. 'The line's dead.' A crack of thunder sounded. 'He said we'd be isolated.' Lightning sliced the sky, illuminating the kitchen as a loud bang shook the house. 'That hit something.' Meg shuddered. There was a screech from the other end of the house. The twins were awake.

'What's he doing about Cora?'

'He said something about a chopper.'

'Well then, we can relax.' Sam made more coffee. 'You might as well settle in and stop stalking about the house. There's nothing we can do.'

'I'm so worried about Cora. What if something happens to her out there? What if she dies?'

'She won't die. I bet she's holed up somewhere, high and dry. A woman like her can't spend her life out here in the sticks without knowing a survival trick or two.'

'Imagine what James Campbell thinks, us leaving Cora out there all night.'

Sam swirled sugar into his tea. 'Who cares what he thinks?'

'I do.'

Sam blew on the surface of the steaming beverage. 'I know you do.' The kitchen light flickered and then went out. 'Great.'

## ≪ *Chapter 55* ≫

## *Absolution Creek,*
## *1965*

'Come on, Samsara.' Scrubber tugged fruitlessly at the lead as thunder crackled. The old girl adamantly refused to budge and a good ten minutes of wheedling and cajoling made no difference. He slipped down from Veronica's back and quickly discovered he was in a hole. The water was up to his chest.

'Damn and blast, if a man wasn't wet enough already.' Still, he could have fallen on a log and twisted an ankle or worse. Scrubber trudged against the weight of the water, away from the insects massing on floating bits of timber and on the trunks of trees. Branches were weighed down with bird life, and crawling with centipedes and ants that would fall onto him if he brushed a laden tree limb. Reaching higher ground, he proceeded to offload Samsara. He lifted Dog onto Veronica's back and dumped everything else, including the saddle, in knee-deep water. Finally the bridle was off.

'Well, you've played your part. I'm figuring it's everyone for themselves.' Scrubber gave the mare a pat on the nose as Samsara twitched her ears, her brown eyes unblinking. Dog whined. 'Yeah well, life's like that,' Scrubber replied sullenly, heaving his backside into the saddle. Samsara turned and walked away in the opposite direction. 'Always was the smartest in the pack.' He dipped his head against the driving rain.

They'd been moving all morning, barely stopping over the last twenty-five hours. The creek gurgled alongside them, spilling its banks in lower places to join the water already lying across the sodden landscape. Scrubber was beginning to doubt if he'd be able to navigate the creek at the crossing the publican talked about. Reaching another 'give and take' he dismounted, and pushed and pulled at the wooden upright. So far they'd managed to get through three of these fences that stretched across the winding creek forming a boundary between neighbours. With the ground saturated, the posts bowed under his strength, at least at enough of an angle for him to carefully walk Veronica over the wires. This post was a little more difficult, and it was with a feeling of utter exhaustion that Scrubber managed to get over the fence to the other side. The pain was building again, rippling through him, reminding him that time was shortening.

'Could be worse. I could be tucked up like the rest of the terminals in a white-walled room, hey, Dog?'

Dog didn't answer – he was too busy sniffing the wind.

The water came slowly at first, lapping at the edges of her clothes, swirling and prodding at Horse so that Cora's body moved ever so slightly. With the rain's return Cora sensed a change in the creek's movement. The water became muddier in colour. Branches, bottles and a child's toy bobbed on one side of the crossing, caught by the mound. Soon a surge of dirty flood water mounted the crossing. The pressure of the water grew quickly, pushing at Horse's lifeless body, slowly dislodging it. With the movement a shocking pain crept through Cora's trapped leg and she screamed in agony. Then the water was upon her, over her, under her, pushing at her in every direction.

Cora tried to grasp the saddle, her head bobbing briefly above the water before slippery hands tugged her down into murky depths. The current yanked her free of Horse and, gasping for air, she gave herself up to the unknown. She pictured Jack Manning, longing to cradle his head as she had all those years ago, to feel the warmth of his touch.

There he was. Cora could see Jack standing before her, his reflection distorted by the water. Joy welled within and she floated in the dream of him, her fingertips quivering with expectation as she swam through a silvery tunnel. Engulfed by an intense stillness Cora fixed her eyes on Jack, on the stream of light silhouetting his body, on the smile that was only for her. Cora sensed she was only a heartbeat away from being reunited with the man she'd always loved, so why was he suddenly turning from her? Telling her it wasn't time? Telling her to go back?

Lungs bursting, Cora splashed her way to the surface. She thrust her arms towards a log and made a grab for it. The pressure and jolt that followed knocked the remaining breath from her body and she spun sideways, her arms pinned down.

Cora woke lying on the creek's bank. Disorientated, she spluttered up muddy water, half-expecting to see Jack Manning by her side. Instead, a grey-headed man was untying a rope from around her chest. A mangy collie was prodding at her bad leg with a paw, and a horse was snuffling her hair. The man gave a chuckle and then collapsed onto the ground beside her.

'I should have known you'd be in some sort of scrape.' His voice was barely audible, his words a mess of tangled letters and hoarse wheezing. 'Recognise you anywhere, I would.'

He patted her arm. The dog licked her cheek. Cora sat up slowly, wincing at the pain in her leg. 'Do I know –?' There was a filthy scarf loose about his neck, and where the smoothness of a throat should have been, a crinkly neck with a hole in the middle of it. Cora thought she'd seen a ghost.

The dog barked. The man gave him a rough pat.

'She knows me, Dog. I knew Squib Hamilton would never forget old Scrubber, her mate from Waverly Station days.' With a grimace he managed to stand and, extending a hand, helped her up. 'We'll get you up on old V and save that leg of yours, eh? I'm sure glad you didn't turn out to be one of those useless women types.' The woman was still staring at him. 'Cause we've got to get you to higher ground. Lucky for you, Squib –' he tipped a sodden hat, gave a long wracking cough that shook his bony frame '– I can help. I'm in my prime.'

## ≪ Chapter 56 ≫

## Stringybark Point, 1924

*It wasn't really a lie,* Jack kept thinking as the papers were drawn up. Grateful that Mr Grey only asked the most essential of questions, Jack remained convinced the immaculately three-piece-suited gentleman knew he was not being truthful.

'I'm not altogether comfortable burdening a young woman with property. We know how fragile the fairer sex are.' Mr Grey perused Mr Farley's title deeds and the agreed letter of contract signed last year for a second time. 'However, considering the terms of the contract and your assurances that the staff in place at Absolution Creek are capable of carrying on in your absence, I'm happy to oblige.'

They were sitting in an office not dissimilar to Mr Farley's, although the quality of the furniture was unmistakable. The polished desk was covered in green leather, and two substantial bookcases bulged with the letter of the law. A mahogany sideboard carried an amber-filled glass decanter with two crystal tumblers. Jack doubted he'd ever told so many lies. Absolution Creek's workforce now included two station workers and a lady's companion for his orphaned niece.

'You will have to inform your niece, however, that this is not a permanent arrangement. In the event of your own premature demise, Mr Manning, one must hope that the young lady finds a suitable husband. Mr Farley's generous terms only last for ten years.'

'But can be renegotiated, and Mr Farley has no kin,' Jack reminded Mr Grey.

'Indeed it can. However, everyone has kin somewhere, Mr Manning: a second cousin, an uncle. Notwithstanding the appearance of such a relative, the contract only stands as long as the agreed twice-yearly payments can be made. Should the unfortunate position arise where the management onus falls on your niece, I would imagine a payment default to be a very real possibility,' Mr Grey stated with gravity.

Jack signed his name on the document. The timbered walls of the office were hung with pictures of men clustered in groups, and it was on these portraits that Jack concentrated. Mr Grey leant back in his chair, the wooden seat squeaking in complaint.

'Race Club Committee, Rugby Club Committee, Memorial Hall Committee. It's a pity Absolution Creek is so far from town. We could use a man such as yourself in Stringybark Point.'

Jack twirled his hat in his hand. It had been a long dusty ride and he wasn't up for conversation, especially when guilt hung like a cloud about his head. 'It's a touch busy for my liking.'

Mr Grey patted an overly long moustache. 'A touch busy – and you a Sydney lad. Well, the troopers are out of town this week following up on a lead, so I guess the town is a might rowdier than usual. So, you don't miss Sydney?'

'Never did take to the North Shore,' Jack admitted.

'Even with that marvel being built?' The solicitor interlaced winter-white fingers.

'Especially because of the bridge,' Jack answered. 'I think people forget folk lost their homes so that others could prosper.'

The solicitor coughed into a folded pocket handkerchief. 'Hardly patriotic, my lad.'

'The truth rarely is.'

Mr Grey's magnanimous attitude dissipated. 'Well, I see you've firm opinions, Mr Manning. Of course, at your age I was more inclined to less provocative conversation.'

'The world's changing, Mr Grey.'

The solicitor folded the documents, slipping them into an envelope. A twist of pink string held the letters intact. 'Yes, well. Everything's in order. I should tell you that there are any number of stories doing the rounds here in Stringybark Point with regards to children of mixed blood. If you see or hear of any you'll do your duty.'

Jack's fingers were on the outstretched end of the envelope. 'Of course.'

'Good.' Mr Grey released his grasp. 'Good day to you, then.'

Jack high-tailed it as fast as he could from the solicitor's office. Obviously Adams had been blabbing, and although Mr Grey's parting comment gave cause for unease, Jack sensed the man's words were more a gentle warning. He kept his head down and walked along the path leading to the intersection where three hotels stood facing each other. While a room and a feed were his immediate concerns, Jack knew it more important to stay out of sight. Adams still roamed the area and Jack doubted a bit of paper would content his one-time friend.

There were only a handful of tasks to attend to. One was to buy a new horse and stock up on some basic household stores – maybe even a length of ribbon for Squib – and another was to purchase bullets for his Winchester Carbine. Later he would visit the Bank of New South Wales and note Squib as a signatory on his checking account. After that, all that remained was for Jack to come to terms with his intentions.

There was a peculiar feeling Scrubber got in the pit of his belly when things didn't go to plan. It was like being winded by a well-driven punch. Combine that with a feeling of illness and he wasn't surprised to be sicking up last night's mutton. He wiped a shaking hand across his mouth, flicking away a stream of dribble. A man was doubly blessed when his woman wasn't about to see such weakness. Scrubber edged the night pot under the bed with his boot and walked out onto the veranda. The balcony at Green's Hotel and Board gave a splendid view of Stringybark Point's main street, such as it was – in particular its comings and goings.

The *goings* showed itself in the form of Adams and an associate who had ridden out nearly four days ago. The publican hinted they were off on business under the advisement of the local constabulary. Mullins, the dead-eyed returned soldier, added that Adams didn't mind a little revenge when it could be condoned under cover of the law. The eventual *comings* presented itself in the form of Adams again. He rode in late yesterday with extra baggage: a filthy mood that led to a fight. Scrubber quickly chose self-eviction from the bar, though his swift exit was based on nothing more than a hunch. After twelve hours of his self-imposed exile, there was still no sign of Matt Hamilton.

So here Scrubber was, rubbing a hole through the boards with the heel of his horsehair boot, waiting for Veronica to show with a bit of bread and milk to ease his stomach. The street below was busy with drays and riders. There was even a T-Model Ford parked on the opposite side of the street. Three children were prodding and poking at the shiny automobile, one scooting underneath to gawk at the mechanical innards. Out of boredom he counted the hitching rails – there were six of them, and eight water troughs interspersed along the dusty street. There was also an assortment of chickens, which clucked across the road, their wings akimbo, as a scraggly looking child corralled them onwards. A number of women were walking towards the grocer's, baskets over their arms. They lingered under the town's single lamp to chat with a mother who wielded a black pram with a screeching child within.

Beneath the balcony a dray came to a halt outside the entrance to the hotel. Two white Clydesdales stomped their hoofs impatiently as the back board was dropped and a couple of men alighted to heft a carcass swathed in bloody canvas. Dinner, Scrubber assumed. He was not in the least interested in food of any type and would be pleased when this ordeal was over. There was far too much noise and action at Stringybark. The entire town streamed with people during the day and quite often the public bars were open long after the regulated closing hour of 6 pm. And over all this clamour was the lumberyard a couple of blocks away, from which came the ear-splitting sounds of chopping, and the rumble of the steam engine that drove the great saw.

'Where have you been then, woman?' Scrubber asked.

Veronica sat the glass of milk and hunk of bread on the rattan table and fell tiredly into a chair. 'There's a couple that arrived a day ago, a man and woman. Rode all the way, they did, from some property out west.' Veronica gestured north and Scrubber rolled his eyes. 'Anyway, they called the doctor on account of her collapsing and being with child, but the woman was so affronted by the doctor that she told him to leave off and go help a sheep, which she felt sure he was more aptly trained for.'

Scrubber always did take to high-spirited women.

'They've taken rooms here. Oh, and so has *he*.'

'Who's he?' Scrubber wasn't quite up for one of Veronica's strung-out chinwags.

'Your Matt Hamilton, of course. The girl's father.'

Scrubber gobbled up the bread and gulped down the milk. 'Why didn't you say so? Well then, I'll be needing that clean shirt I've been saving. Have you patched my jacket and –'

Veronica's hand stilled his words. 'Everything's laid out on your bed, lovey, just as you wanted. The shirt's near almost white, it's been washed so well, and your coat is all patched up, the stains spotted with soap and water.'

He brushed her chin. 'You're a good girl to me, V.'

Veronica gave a dimpled smile. 'Can I come then? I've tidied my things too.'

'No,' Scrubber replied firmly, closing the balcony doors in her face.

Scrubber shook Matt's hand. 'I was wondering when you'd show. How long have you been in town for?' There was the stench of something raw and acidic.

'A day.' Matt began rolling a cigarette. He gummed a paper to his lip and rubbed moist leaves of tobacco between his palms.

'A day? Do you know how long I've been holed up here for?' Scrubber knew one tight punch would loosen Hamilton's attitude. The man acted as if he were doing *him* a favour.

Matt rolled the tobacco in the paper and patted his pockets for a light. 'Damn it.'

Scrubber tossed him the box of matches sitting by the candle. 'Well?'

'Well what?' Matt caught the box one-handed, and struck three of the flinty heads before success. He sucked on the cigarette. 'I'm here, aren't I? Against my better judgement, I might add. Lost my job to meet up with you, and all for what? To tell you in person that I don't want to see my Squib in a bloody institution.'

'An institution?' Scrubber repeated.

'Do I have to spell it out for you? Squib and Ben's mother was a half-caste. Abigail is my second wife.'

Scrubber leaned heavily on the washstand, the action rattling the ceramic pitcher sitting in the wash bowl. 'Squib's got darkie blood in her?'

Matt took a long drag of his smoke. 'Yes.'

'Well then, that accounts for Adams,' Scrubber answered thoughtfully.

'What are you talking about?' Matt asked.

'A man here by the name of Adams is interested in her. The fella who found Squib has her safe at a property called Absolution Creek. This Adams, though –' Scrubber scratched his cheek '– he's after Squib. Somehow he knows she's got darkie blood. There was this notice in the local paper and the owner of Absolution gave Squib's name and everything ...'

Matt stomped his cigarette out on the timber floor. 'Bugger him. Is this Adams a trooper?'

'Postal and Supply rider.'

'And part-time snitch,' Matt said tightly. 'No doubt on the bank roll of the government.'

Scrubber knew what the smell was. Matt had partaken of the bottle last night, and by the stench the result wasn't pretty. 'What do you want to do?'

Matt shook his head. 'You know I only came here to tell you to forget this scheme of yours. My stepdaughter, Jane, put my Ben into the authorities after Abigail went to gaol – that's why I couldn't risk finding Squib. I knew she'd be taken as well.' He prised open the tobacco tin and plucked at the loose strands. 'So much for family love.'

'So that's why you stayed away,' Scrubber replied. 'I wondered.'

Matt nodded and rolled another smoke. 'I know you did and I appreciate you trying to find Squib, but you understand now, don't you, I had to lose her to save her.'

'Well, now we're going to have to find her,' Scrubber said firmly. 'Cause if we don't, Adams will. Why are you looking at me like that?'

Matt gave the slightest tilt of his chin. 'Guess I figured once you knew the truth you'd walk away. Most whites don't have much time for the mixed bloods.'

'Purcell did,' Scrubber reminded him.

Matt snorted. 'Old man Purcell was only ever interested in a good worker. As long as a man kept his nose clean he'd look the other way. And he knew enough toffs in government to ensure his business and his staff were left alone. My family was safe while we were there, especially as Squib and Ben looked like me and not their mother. Evans was the one with the problem. Always hated me, he did, especially when I made overseer. It was him that stole that necklace, I reckon. Ain't nobody else could have done it.'

Scrubber kept quiet.

'Set me up real good and proper. Ruined my life, that Evans. Anyway, you've done enough, mate, and a person can get into a mile of trouble . . .'

'Yeah, I know.' Scrubber gave a toothy grin. 'But I've always been a bit of an aider and abetter.'

'Why are you helping us?' Matt asked. 'I mean, really, it's not your problem.'

Scrubber walked across the timber floorboards. He could have died in the bush if Matt hadn't found him. He could have gone through life with a crippled hand if it wasn't for Squib. Through the door leading out onto the balcony the street was quietening in the midday heat. Abigail Hamilton was in gaol; Squib was living with a stranger; the boy Ben was gone and Matt was out of work, again. 'I've got my reasons,' he answered. 'Now we need a plan.'

'Any ideas?'

Scrubber rubbed his hands together, and felt a rush of adrenalin in his gut. 'How good are you with a rifle?'

Stringybark Point, 1924

They packed up their belongings at first light. Scrubber silenced Veronica's questions with a peck on the cheek and enough coin to keep her fed for two days. If the worst happened, he told her, he wanted her to return to the boarding house. Not one for tears usually, Veronica fell to blubbering like a waif. In hindsight, Scrubber decided, it would have been easier to lie. He held her, patting her head until she told him to leave off – that she 'weren't no dog'. He grinned then. Such ministrations usually did the trick.

He sat her down on their lumpy flock mattress, and decided to fib to her about what he'd left behind at the boarding house. After all, he would have a God's holy time trying to keep his woman's grubby paws off it. Instead, he simply said it was their nest egg for when they were past working; a trinket saved for hard times. Having cautioned her good and proper like a husband should, lifting his hand for emphasis, he would have lain her down and lifted her skirts to seal the business between them, if it weren't for the pressing needs of the day. He left with a sharp slap to her arse instead.

With the directions to Absolution Creek marked out in Scrubber's mind like a moveable mud map, courtesy of the publican, Matt and he saddled up at the stables before leading their horses onto the road. The air was already laced with dirt as Matt tightened the girth strap on his tawny Clydesdale. A flock of swallows swooped low across the road from one hotel to the other.

'Bought him for a song.' Matt brushed the gelding's whiskered muzzle. 'He's a little long in the tooth but I figured he'd get me here and to wherever I'm going next.'

From the eaves of the hotel a clump of dried mud crumbled to the ground. 'Blasted swallows,' Scrubber complained, his hand reaching automatically for his rifle. An amused look crossed Matt's crinkled face, and Scrubber decided not to follow his natural inclination to blow away a few of their nests. Diagonally across the road another traveller was saddling up a fractious mare. The bay sidestepped the approaching saddle, but the next attempt was

465

successful and the man flew lightly up onto the mare's back. The horse gave a couple of pigroots, its hind legs kicking up swirls of dust, before the rider quickly took charge of his mount with a single tug on the reins. He was repaid with a rearing horse, hoofs striking the air. Scrubber figured the horse could do with a good flogging. In contrast, a sturdy horse more inclined towards packing goods than being ridden waited patiently nearby.

'Righto.' Matt swung up onto his horse, leaning forward to drag his leg over the hefty animal's back. 'Which way?'

For a moment Scrubber dawdled. The intersection was quiet. It wasn't like him to be indecisive, not when Squib was so close, but at the far end of the street a horse-drawn carriage appeared. In the opposite direction two men rode abreast up the centre of the road, one of the riders firmly holding a struggling bundle in front of him on his horse.

Scrubber knew instinctively something was wrong.

# ∞ Chapter 57 ∞

## Absolution Creek, 1965

'What will we do now, Mummy?' Having devoured two Sao biscuits Penny smeared Vegemite fingers on the kitchen table. 'I'm bored.' Large drops of rain dripped from the overhead light into a saucepan on the table.

Jill nodded furiously. 'I'm bored, I'm bored, I'm bored.'

'So am I.' Meg gathered empty milk glasses and plates and sat them on the kitchen sink. Through the window the rain moved across the paddock towards them. Appearing as a sheet of whiteness in the far west it gradually crept towards the homestead. The storm arrived in a splatter of egg-sized droplets, which increased in intensity until the only noise within the kitchen was the pounding of rain on the iron roof. It was the third such rainstorm in the last hour. Meg pursed her lips and thought of Cora.

'Mummy?' Penny called above the din. 'Mummy?'

'Go and check the house for me, will you?' It was the fourth time this morning Penny and Jill had been sent to check the rain-sodden rooms. Meg was beyond it. The old house was a disaster zone; every room weeped water. In the dining room it ran down the walls, slowly turning the floor dark with moisture. If it kept on raining the house would soon become uninhabitable. A portion of Cora's bedroom ceiling had already fallen in, and pieces of ancient bark, which looked like part of an earlier roof, lay strewn on the floor.

The slamming of the back door and the slosh of water on the porch announced Sam's return. He stomped down the hallway. 'I can't do anything about the power. This whole place could go up if I get that old generator going.' He indicated the overhead light and the steady drip. 'But Curly's back, covered in mud and exhausted. I fed him and left him in the laundry. It's dry enough in there.'

'That's not a good sign.'

'She must have fallen from her horse,' Sam decided. 'It was a pretty cold night last night, so let's hope she's hunkered down somewhere.'

'Cora's bedroom ceiling is beginning to fall in.' Meg filled the kettle and sat it on the Aga. She had to keep busy, otherwise her thoughts kept returning to Cora's lifeless body lying somewhere out in the drenched paddocks.

'Well, it was bound to happen,' Sam replied with more than a trace of annoyance. 'Damn ridiculous living like that, a great tree sticking out of the roof. You can imagine how much water has leaked into the house over the years.'

'Sam, this house is going to be unliveable if it keeps raining. I don't want to desert Cora but I have to consider the girls and Kendal. We need to get out of here.'

Sam ran his fingers through his hair. 'Well, we can't do much at the moment. The only thing we can do is to wait until we hear from James. At least he knows we're stuck here so that's something.'

'I guess.' Meg sounded unconvinced.

'What will you do? Go back to Sydney?' Sam gave Meg a questioning look as he leant against the sink.

A month ago Meg would have waited for Sam to make the decision. 'Yes.'

'I thought you liked it here?'

'I thought you did,' Meg countered, not that it mattered any more. Managing to stay with someone out of need and for the sake of children was one thing, but once disappointment mingled with a lack of respect . . . 'I would have stayed if I thought it might make a difference.'

'To us?' Sam confirmed. 'Well, before all this happened things might well have worked out for us, Meg.'

'But not now,' Meg agreed.

'We stayed together because we once needed each other, not because we wanted each other. There's a pretty big difference.'

'What you're saying, Sam, is that now is as good a time as any to jump ship.' Meg wanted to come right out and say it – accuse him of being a bigot. The whole thing was laughable. It wasn't as if Sam Bell had the right to be bigoted about anyone. He hunched his shoulders and yawned. 'That's how I feel too, Sam,' she retaliated. 'Disinterested.' Having fought and complained for the duration of over five years of marriage, Meg was at the point where she couldn't endure it any more. She didn't love Sam and probably never had. Maybe he was right. Maybe she did marry him to both spite and escape from her mother, for there had been a time when all she wanted to do was crawl out from under her shadow. 'And my having an Indigenous-blooded aunt doesn't help.' There, she'd said it.

'No,' Sam admitted, 'it doesn't. I don't want my children growing up in her home, Meg. They might be slighted and taunted because of their association with Cora.'

Meg threw a handful of tea leaves into a pot and added the boiling water. 'That wouldn't happen.'

'Really? You were the one who told me Cora was treated differently in Stringybark Point. Anyway, I'm not surprised. For years this country's lived under the mantle of a White Australia Policy.'

'Hey, that was for immigrants; to ensure our culture was protected during the early years of development.'

'And you don't think that attitude extended to Aboriginals? There were acts passed, you know. Aboriginal children were taken from their homes. Cripes, there's still those cordoned-off areas at the flicks and the separate drinking bit at the Stringybark Point pub for Cora's kind.'

Meg tasted bile in her mouth.

'You know, you've got to wonder how this Jack Manning managed to leave Absolution Creek to Cora and how a part-Aboriginal woman managed to hold onto it.' Sam sat down. 'I give Cora credit for what she's done. But I think you should prepare yourself for the fact that you probably won't be inheriting Absolution Creek, Meg. How could you? If Cora's holding onto it illegally, then she certainly can't pass it on to anyone.'

Meg poured tea for them both, her hands shaking. Beyond the kitchen the twins were racing up and down the covered walkway, their feet splashing against the sodden boards. So there it was, Meg thought miserably, the real reason Sam was leaving. They weren't even arguing. After all the years she and Sam had been together they were past even that. 'What will you do?'

Sam cradled the cup between his hands and blew at the steam. 'Head north. I might find work on another property. I figure Kendal could be a problem if I hang around and he decides to point the bone at me.'

'In some ways this move was good for you, Sam.' Meg didn't mean to sound condescending.

'I still care, you know,' Sam admitted, 'just not enough. I'll send money for the kids.'

Meg sipped her tea. She wouldn't count on that.

'Anyway, I suppose you better try calling Campbell again. Check and see what's happening with the search for Cora. Maybe another chopper can get us all out of here. Combine Kendal's injury with the twins and I'd imagine the authorities would consider us to be a bit more of a priority for an air lift; especially with this old house starting to disintegrate around us. And you should probably tell Campbell to get a message to your mother. She should know what's happened to her stepsister.'

In the corner of the kitchen Tripod gave a noisy yawn and managed to stand.

'You better add two dogs to the passenger list,' Sam suggested. 'I don't want to end up getting speared over a three-legged mutt.'

Meg ignored the racist reference. 'You think Cora's still alive?'

Sam gave a look that verged on disappointment. 'I reckon it would take a whole lot more than a bit of water to wipe Cora Hamilton off the map.'

# ≪ *Chapter 58* ≫

## *Absolution Creek,*
## *1965*

Scrubber tugged on the reins. 'Blasted horse, it's not like we've been travelling for days.' Ankle-deep in mud, Veronica gave a whinny but refused to move. Scrubber slid his hand up tight to the bit and gave the bridle a jerk. Ahead was a substantial tree that forked in the middle, splitting the trunk into two solid limbs. Behind them lay a mile of hard going. Scrubber knew when a battle was done.

'This is it.' He sounded almost jovial. Swallowing the pain eating at his guts he unlaced the rope and helped Squib, now grown up and all five foot six of surly womanhood, to slide down from the saddle. For someone near drowned she was surprisingly alert and full of unanswerable questions. *What are you doing here? Where did you come from? Where have you been all these years?*

'Have you caught your breath yet?' she asked, as they reached the tree and leant against it for support.

Scrubber knew the days of catching his breath were about as improbable as ever eating a cooked meal again. He tossed Cora his swag, water lapping at their feet. 'There's a dry shirt in there,

Squib. Put it on before you turn into a stalagmite, and take the blanket with you when you get yourself up that tree.' He figured the girl's leg was near buggered. Nonetheless, true to the lass he remembered, she didn't speak of it.

'My name's Cora, Scrubber. Squib doesn't exist any more.'

'Rubbish.'

Cora looked from the old man opposite up into the wavering branches. 'I don't think I can make it.'

'I'm figuring that would be right.' Scrubber pulled at the itchy scarf about his neck. 'A man travels for months, and right at the end when he's close to the finishing of something long in the making, the very person involved bales up.' Dog, soggy-haired from their trudging, gave a bark in agreement.

'What's that meant to mean?'

Scrubber spat a wad of bile into the soggy grass, and turned his back as Cora changed her clothes. 'Are you going to get up the damn tree or not?'

Cora tucked the shirt into her wet moleskins, discarding her soaked jumper. 'Where are you going?'

'Not up there. I'm staying right here with my horse and my dog. Ain't that right, Dog?'

'Dog,' Cora repeated. 'You called him Dog?'

Scrubber looked at the mangy animal's hind leg kicking out in a cycling scratch, and remembered another animal long ago who didn't have it so lucky. 'Yeah, after that mangy yellow dog of yours at Waverly Station.'

'Oh, Scrubber.'

He couldn't recall the last time a woman hugged him, especially one with mud-matted hair and more energy than a frog in a sock. 'No time for blubbering now. I won't look too smart if we're washed away on account of sentiment.'

'You should get up the tree too,' Cora urged. 'It's not fair to expect the animals to stay there with you when they have a chance to get away from the flood water.'

The girl had a point. 'Just let me get my affairs in order.' He patted Dog on the head, wished him well. 'You've been a miserable animal at times, but a man needs a companion and you weren't bad; no, not too bad at all.' Removing the bridle from Veronica he sat Dog on the saddle. 'Now, don't be giving each other a hard time and no backchat, Veronica. You always were a shocker for that.' Scrubber took a lingering last look at his mates. Two sets of plaintive eyes stared back. 'Stay out of trouble.' Bloody ridiculous, he thought, a man his age tearing up on account of a couple of four-legged creatures. He slapped Veronica hard on the rump. 'Well, get going.' They eyeballed him back. 'Be done with you then.' Veronica didn't move. Dog gave a growl.

Cora was already in the fork of the trunk and angling herself like a koala towards an outer branch. 'Can't you get any higher than that?' Scrubber hollered, his fingers pressed hard on his neck in an attempt to garner a bit of volume. A thick line of ants were fast covering the bark. When Cora didn't answer he climbed right on up after her, rope over one shoulder, water bag on the other; the tobacco pouch tucked down his shirt. It wasn't really what Scrubber planned. During the long ride from the hills he'd pictured a hearty welcome and a home-cooked dinner and then the explanation for his visit. After that he'd planned on going out to check on the horses and then he'd just amble away, real silent like, job done. Instead here he was, grunting and huffing and clawing his way up towards Matt's daughter.

'You made it.' Cora winced as she tried to keep her balance on the thick-set limb.

Scrubber gave a grainy cough. 'Was there a doubt?' Unravelling the rope he looped it over the branch above them and tied it around Cora's waist as the rain grew heavier.

'What about you?'

'I haven't got a buggered leg. Now shift over.' Scrubber split the blanket in half, made a neat hole in each piece and offered Cora the instant poncho. 'Over your head with it, girl, and back on with the oilskin jacket.' Once settled they sat there for some minutes surveying their new aspect: a curtain of rain. The noise came soon after, the sound of the bush moving as the crafty menagerie within it evacuated. 'You gonna tell me why you were out in this weather?'

'My rams,' Cora explained. 'They had to be moved to the other side of the creek for safety.'

'I saw you purchased yourself a tidy-looking individual, Waverly No. 4 blood, eh? Well, that grin tells me everything.' Scrubber squirmed about on the branch. For a man with no padding this wasn't the best of seats.

'Who'd have thought, eh, Scrubber?'

'Yeah girl,' Scrubber agreed, 'who'd have thought.'

In a distant tree line a mob of kangaroos bounded away in single file, the grey of their soggy pelts merging in and out of a rain-dulled landscape.

'Well, here we are again,' Scrubber joked. 'Just like old times.' They were six feet up. Safe enough, he calculated, at this distance from the creek. 'Nothing like a predicament to bring people together.'

'You and I know all about that. I often think about what Veronica said that day, about how she hoped I was worth it.'

Scrubber patted her sodden thigh. 'Well, considering the turn out you garnered on the day, I reckon that question was already answered.'

'I haven't thought about that day for a long time, Scrubber.'

The girl sounded wistful. They both knew she was lying.

# ≪ *Chapter 59* ≫

## *Stringybark Point,*
## *1924*

J ack wasn't expecting to see anyone at this hour. Tightening the reins to steady the mare he had purchased the night before, he frowned at the men across the road. He'd just as soon eat paper than slip arse-first onto the ground with two wiry bushmen for an audience, so he spoke to his ride low and soft, promising good feed and fresh water in exchange for decorum. One of the men rode a great Clydesdale, the other, perched atop a slight mare, was busy giving directions. Jack reached out for the packhorse's halter. He'd been a good horse, however Thomas and Olive's departure came with the loss of two fine animals and at least one needed to be replaced. Although the purchase was not in his budget, Squib's advice regarding the Tallow and Hide shop offered an eventual means for a bit of coin.

At the thought of Squib, Jack patted the documents sitting safely inside the saddle bag. Part of him wanted to be back at Absolution Creek, to be drinking sugary tea around the camp fire as he explained to her with a wink that she was now his kin. The look in those brown eyes of hers would be priceless. There would be questions and quarrelling, and then her innate good humour would present itself with a smile and a sticky elbow to his ribs.

The rest of him, that part buried by church teachings and Bible readings and wooden crosses, conjured a vision far more revealing. In it a young woman reached out and he took the warmth of her hands between his. It had been there all along this wanting. Finding Squib all wetted up like a drowned animal was the beginning of Jack's fondness. After that his partiality towards the girl slowly blossomed as she left the bedraggled despair of being lost, and joined in with the world again, his world. What Jack didn't know was the strength of Squib's feelings for him, although he sensed a mutual attraction. Not that it mattered.

In another world Jack may have fought to keep his maleness in check. In another time he could have waited until she turned sixteen. That seemed proper. The problem lay in the current attitudes of the people who considered themselves educated. Squib was too young to marry and too old to live at Absolution Creek unless she had the protection of his name.

Jack checked his carbine. The lever-action rifle would remain loaded until Squib was safe. It was what lay sandwiched between action and goal that worried him. He'd dreamt of it last night, of killing Adams, and the sensation of going against his beliefs fairly winded him. Not because of guilt, nor the Ten Commandments. The truth of the doing was that Jack didn't really care what action was required, as long as Squib was safe. It was three days since she'd run away. Three days since she'd sat beside him outside the stables. Jack was ready to head home. He yearned to be back on Absolution's rich soil, to breathe in the tangy scents, to meander along her cool waterways and ride through grasses wind-dried and crackling. At least that's what he told his brain; his heart knew otherwise.

The steady clop-clop of a horse and the grind of wood on dirt broke Jack's thoughts. The black horse-drawn carriage was quite a flash affair. The contraption halted outside Green's Hotel and Board beneath the shady box tree and Jack, having not seen such transportation since he'd left Sydney, began walking his horse across the unmade road to get a closer look.

A woman stepped out of the doorway of the hotel, a small travel bag in each of her hands, and greeted the driver. She wore a clouche hat and was as dainty in form as Olive. He couldn't see her face, but at the resemblance Jack experienced a slight twinge of regret.

Across from Jack the two riders ceased their talking and turned to look, clearly intrigued by the carriage too. The rider on the slighter horse trotted over for a keener inspection. There was something about him; the way he held his shoulders, tight and bunched, ungainly . . .

Jack spurred his flighty mare into a trot.

The scream was so loud Jack almost fell from his ride. The mare bucked and backed up and bucked some more. Digging his heels in he jerked the reins. The horse wrenched back, chewing on the bit, finally coming to a reluctant standstill.

'It's him! Get him away from me, Thomas! Get him away!'

Recognising the voice, as much as the fear in it, Jack flew from his mount, rifle in hand and crossed the dirt street to where his brother Thomas was attempting to stop Olive from sinking onto the ground. His brother was as white as a sheet. Olive was visibly trembling. Jack locked eyes with the man they were staring at.

'Mary, Jesus and Joseph! Mills McCoy!' Jack exclaimed, recognising the fighter's busted nose as the man dismounted.

'What's going on here, Scrubber?' the man on the Clydesdale queried.

'Mistaken identity,' Scrubber suggested, unconvincingly, looking at the assembled group as if ghosts.

'*He* was the one that did it, Jack!' Olive wept, slipping free of Thomas's grasp to slide down a wooden pillar into the gutter.

'He did it. Not Thomas. I never would have done this to you on purpose, Jack, never.'

Jack looked from Olive to Thomas. The man on the Clydesdale jumped from his horse.

'Are you sure it's him, Olive?' Thomas pointed at Scrubber. 'Are you *sure* he was the one who attacked you?'

Olive nodded. 'He was the gardener that worked at the boarding house,' she confirmed between sobs. 'He was the one who attacked me.'

Jack pointed at Mills McCoy. 'He did it?'

Thomas shook his head in confusion. 'That's Mills McCoy. The Mills McCoy from Sydney?'

'Mills 'Scrubber' McCoy.' Scrubber crouched and drew a knife from his belt. 'Well fancy,' he growled, 'what's a city lad doing here?'

'I could ask the same of you!' Jack threw his rifle to Thomas, and rushed the Irishman. With a low tackle he swept him against the hotel wall. Bone and flesh thudded against the timber boards, a spray of dust billowing out from the pine wood. Jack's fingers were on Scrubber's wrist holding the knife, his free hand on the Irishman's throat. 'Is it true what my brother speaks of? Did you violate her?' The man kept his lips clamped shut. Through the hotel window, the publican drew the curtains.

The burly hand of McCoy's companion was on Jack's shoulder. 'Leave off, mate, whoever you are.'

'You leave off,' Thomas growled, edging at the man with Jack's rifle.

For a moment Jack was back in Sydney again fighting off McCoy's thugs. He could smell the tang of the salt-crusted sea; there was blood in his mouth as the coin he'd laboured for was thieved. Jack tightened his grip. Sweat smothered the Irishman's brow and dripped down his nose. Slowly Scrubber pushed his knife fist against the weight of Jack's grip.

Jack strained against his opponent. He rammed his hand harder against the Irishman's windpipe, knowing what was coming yet unable to stop the path ahead. He saw Olive, alone and frightened, ruined for eternity. Jack felt sinew and muscle depress slowly under his grasp. He could hear Thomas asking the stranger's name, what his business was. The man's voice was tight.

'Matt Hamilton. Scrubber and I are here to find my daughter, Squib.' For the briefest moment Jack loosened his grip on Scrubber's knife-wielding hand. 'You're here for Squib?'

'Yeah,' Scrubber croaked. 'She belongs with her father, not you.'

Jack thought of the girl he loved. His brief dream of a life with her dissolved in seconds. Squib was too young. Matt Hamilton would never allow them to be together. He thought of Squib. If she did care for him, she would feel torn between her father and him. Hadn't she suffered enough? And once she left, what would become of his life?

He loosened his grip on the Irishman's knife hand.

In the split second that followed, McCoy's knife was in Jack's side. Jack kept his fingers pressed hard against the man's neck as the sharp pain rippled through his body. The busted face of the Irishman turned puce and he stopped breathing. When Jack stepped away the Irishman slid down the wall to land with a thud on the dirt.

'Are you all right, Jack?' Thomas asked, keeping his rifle on Matt.

'Sure,' Jack replied shakily. Turning towards his brother he too fell to the ground.

Thomas dropped his rifle and was by Jack's side instantly. With only the slightest hesitation he pulled the knife free of Jack's body. He undid his brother's waistcoat and pressed his hand against the glossy redness staining the shirt.

Jack looked at Thomas. Behind his kneeling brother, Matt Hamilton stood by Olive's side. 'You should have told me,' Jack gasped, 'about Olive.'

'Would it have made any difference?' Blood seeped between Thomas's fingers.

'Only for you and me,' Jack winced. 'It's bad, isn't it?'

'No,' Thomas lied, 'not too bad. Anyway, it's not too late. You know the truth of things now.'

'I should have known better,' Jack admitted. 'Looks like you'll be carrying on the family name, eh?' Jack gave a pained smile. 'Do one thing for me, Thomas. Tell Squib –'

'I need a tube, something I can get air in with!' Matt yelled.

A few feet away Mills 'Scrubber' McCoy was thrashing about like a landed fish. Jack watched as Squib's father, pocketknife in hand, flicked open the blade, made a rough incision in Scrubber's throat and jammed it into the dying man's windpipe.

'Well, he's dead now,' Thomas uttered, clearly stunned.

Jack felt in his coat pocket for his wooden pipe, and flicked it across the dirt. Matt gave him a surprised glance and then broke the end of it before rotating it into the Irishman's throat.

Scrubber spluttered as a gurgling noise rumbled up from deep within.

'He's breathing.' Matt rested back on his heels. From upstairs in the hotel came the sound of footsteps.

'You're a regular Florence Nightingale,' a gruff voice said. The butt of a rifle knocked Thomas sideways.

Jack looked up to where Adams towered over him, and then back at the ground where Thomas was lying, out cold. Olive was crying.

Adams laughed. 'Now back up,' he growled, pointing his rifle at Olive and Matt, indicating that they should flatten themselves against the hotel wall. As they did as they were told, something caught Matt's eye. 'That's my daughter!'

Squib was being held by Will, the man who had accompanied Adams out to Absolution Creek. A filthy rag was clamped between her teeth as she struggled like a wild cat.

Jack couldn't believe it. He'd imagined he would lose Squib to her father, not Adams. Now, when Squib needed him the most, he lay on the ground mortally wounded.

'So you're the infamous Matt Hamilton.' Adams gave a bow. 'Well, well. This is a pretty picture. I really have to give Scrubber there my congratulations.' He pointed the rifle at Matt's chest.

'Damn it, man,' Matt yelled, 'let her go!'

'Now that you've had your quarrel, I'm here to tell you that there won't be no problems if you mind your own bees wax.' Adams gestured for Squib to be brought forward, patting her mussed hair, oblivious to a number of well-aimed shin kicks. 'The kid must have ridden half the night I reckon. We found her camped not five mile out of town.' Squib continued to wrestle with her captor, rips to her dress proof of a fair struggle. 'Saved us a lot of travelling, she did. Now I'm sorry but the government says that these here minors have to be removed for their own safety.'

At that moment a young woman stuck her head out of the hotel door. 'Scrubber, my lovey, what have they done to you?' The girl rushed to his side, cradling his head. His throat was covered in blood. 'You mob of heathens.' She rested Scrubber's head on the ground, stepped over his body and was in Adams's face in a heart-beat. 'That would be right: I should have known a man like you would be involved. Bog Irish, that's what my Scrubber calls you. Piece of trash.' She spat on the ground. 'And what are you doing with that girl tied up and gagged?' She swung around. 'You should all be ashamed of yourselves. You either dumped her or hunted her, and it's only my man who thought to save her.' She glared at Squib. 'I hope you're worth it.'

Adams pushed her away and she returned to Scrubber's side, sobbing quietly as she cradled his head in her lap.

Thomas came to and rubbed his head. 'Jack needs a doctor.'

'Dark blood.' Adams pointed to the stain seeping across Jack's shirt. 'He's finished.'

Squib bit the man holding her and rushed forward.

She was stopped mid-flight by Adams's burly arm.

'Leave her alone,' Jack managed to whisper, clutching at his bloody side. He gave Squib a wan smile. 'Everything will be all right now, Squib. See, your father's here.'

Squib's eyes flicked towards Matt, then to Scrubber and back to Jack.

'Now, this is an interesting conundrum,' Adams said, removing the gag from the girl's mouth and casually lifting his arms to show he no longer barred Squib's path. 'She doesn't know which of you to go to.'

Matt called Squib's name. She inclined her head weakly towards him and then fell to her knees by Jack's side.

'Squib!' Matt exclaimed. 'How do you even know that man?'

Squib took Jack's hand, holding it against her cheek. 'He's the one who's been looking after me all this time. I waited and waited for you, Father, but you never came.' She laid her fingers on Jack's chest; his breathing was shallow, raspy. 'Why didn't you come?' she sobbed.

'I wanted to.' Matt took a step forward.

Scrubber remained partially stunned on the ground. 'My Scrubber cared for you, girly,' Veronica sobbed. 'He's the one that spurred your father on. Like a dog after a bone he was chasing you, and for what?' Veronica prostrated herself across Scrubber's body.

'For what indeed,' Adams agreed. 'For a half-caste gone feral.'

Squib blanched.

'You'll always be my Squib.' Jack coughed. Interlacing his fingers with hers he pulled her closer. 'I've left everything to you. Absolution Creek is yours to manage now,' he whispered.

'Jack, don't.'

He laid a bloody finger on her lips. 'While you have Absolution you have a home, Squib. Take care of her and she'll take care of you.'

'But I don't belong anywhere except with you. Please, Jack, let them fetch a doctor.'

Jack cradled Squib's face and brushed at a tear tracing the curve of her cheek. 'While you're on Absolution I'll be there beside you. Always.' It was then he saw it, the wanting. It was as he imagined her heart to be, layered with sunlight. 'I'm sorry to be going, now I know –' he wheezed '– now I know that you love me more.' He smiled under the pressure of her lips and, slowly retrieving the knife from the ground, slid it across his bloody wounding into Squib's hand. He folded her fingers over the bone handle. 'Live a good life.' Jack held her eyes as Adams walked forward. 'Stay on Absolution and be safe, Squib, be safe.' Then he gave a nod of consent.

Squib's fingers curled tightly around the knife. She held Jack's gaze.

'Do it,' he encouraged. 'You're surrounded by people who will protect you.'

'That's enough.' Adams dragged Squib up, twisted her around roughly. 'You've given me a pretty chase.'

Gritting her teeth, Squib speared the knife into the lard of Adams's belly. When her knuckles hit flesh she twisted the blade. Adams staggered backwards, looked at the protruding knife in stunned silence and lifted his rifle.

A single shot rang out.

## ⊰ *Chapter 60* ⊱

## *Absolution Creek,*
## *1965*

The flood water appeared like a shimmering mirage in the distance. It slipped quietly over the countryside, driven on by the strength of the surging water behind it. Cora slapped at ants and beetles as they swarmed to safety. Kangaroos and wallabies splashed in the distance as they trailed those that had already bounded towards higher ground.

Below them the water lapped at the trunk of the tree, while next to her Scrubber slept. His head had sunk onto his chest, and his breathing was ragged. Seeing him after all these years, having him next to her again, was a comfort; the memories he rekindled were not.

*After her father shot and killed the man Will, the day blurred into a series of distorted events. A doctor was called and she waited by Jack's side, hissing like a wildcat at anyone who came near as her hope, like Jack, slowly faded.*

*As Jack lay dying in the shade of the balcony, the town solicitor, the grocer and the publican tied Matt's hands roughly* behind him. They announced it was intentional murder and that the stranger would hang for the shooting.

'That one with the gash to his throat, Scrubber,' the publican said, his face sweaty with excitement, 'he was attacked by that man.' He pointed at Jack.

'Who stabbed this Jack Manning fellow, then?' the solicitor asked.

Olive and Thomas remained silent. Their eyes wide with shock.

'Who stabbed my Jack?' Squib screamed.

'I did it,' Matt announced, accepting the blame. He looked briefly at his daughter. 'I shot the man called Will and stabbed Adams; and that man there, the one called Jack Manning –' he glanced at Scrubber and gave a barely perceptible nod '– I stabbed him too.'

'Fath–'

'Don't say a word, Squib,' Jack warned quietly. 'Everyone's trying to protect you.'

'But?'

Jack held her wrist. 'If you acknowledge Matt as your father all of this will have been for naught. It won't save him and you'll be taken away for sure.'

Squib bit her lip until blood flowed from the fleshy skin. Her gaze met her father's. Was it true? Had her father really stabbed Jack? She gripped Jack's hand tightly as they walked Matt down the dirt street to the lock-up, her eyes blurring with tears.

'Scrubber, you make sure that nice young girl comes and sees me, won't you?' Matt called out.

Squib's eyes met Scrubber's as the doctor sat a black bag in the dirt beside Jack. He prodded the wound and dabbed a finger in the dark blood. 'I'm sorry.'

'Sorry?' Squib accused. 'What do you mean sorry?'

*'I can't help you, my dear.'* The doctor closed Jack's eyes.
*'Only God can ease your sufferings.'*
Squib gave a choked sob.

Cora bit her knuckle to stifle a cry. It wouldn't do to start bawling now, especially with Scrubber sitting next to her like a cockatoo, his head tucked under a wing. What would she say to her old friend? That she still lived in the past? That her previous life with Jack haunted her days and nights? That Jack was the reason she still rode out at midnight, hoping to be near the spirit of him and the land he loved? A habit of sleeplessness had been replaced by a desperate longing for a man she could never have, for Cora didn't see Jack as dead, merely physically missing from her world. That was why she continued her own nightly haunting of Absolution Creek. She searched for a world only darkness could conjure.

Below, the water continued to rise. The worst of the flooding would be closest to the creek's banks, the heights scaling the woody plants Captain Bob once pointed to years earlier. Cora began to hope the deluge might not be as bad as first thought. If the rain was limited to the river and creek system, a brief inundation along the lower country might be the worst of it.

A whirring noise sounded in the distance, waking Scrubber. Cora listened hopefully to the din as it grew in intensity, while grimly aware of the difficulty a helicopter would have attempting to spy them through the tree's canopy. 'It's a helicopter searching for us,' she told Scrubber. 'They'll be back.' Her words were not as comforting as she'd hoped.

Scrubber lifted his arm and made a fist. The wrist bone was skew-whiff, as if it hadn't quite fathomed how to hang onto the arm that joined it. 'Near good as new, the job you did on it. You were good to me, you know, and your pa, too: getting me that job at Purcell's, treating me as if I was like everybody else. Yeah, your pa was a good man.'

'It was a long time ago, Scrubber.' Cora thought of her father. It had taken years for her to forgive Matt for Jack's death. Even now, she was not sure if she ever completely would. In a tree opposite, bedraggled birds perched on soggy branches. The water rose quickly.

Scrubber gave a noise that resembled a laugh. 'Sure was. And here I am, the last one standing out of the three of us; never thought I'd make old bones. Even V's gone.'

'I'm sorry.'

'Well, old V thought she was pleasantly plump but she ended up real fat. Diabetes got her. I had to wait, you see, before I could come visit on account of V.'

Cora shifted on the branch. Veronica, a late addition to those tragic events of 1924, had been a friend, albeit briefly. 'You never did tell me how you knew Jack Manning.'

'Couldn't talk for six months, remember?' Scrubber winced as pain shot through his stomach. It was taking all his concentration to stay upright. 'We had a bit of a kerfuffle over a woman once. I knew Jack from my Sydney days.'

'You and Jack were in Sydney together?'

'Careful –' he steadied her '– don't go falling off. Yeah, tight world we live in, eh, love? We both left on account of the bridge.'

'I never knew. So, the fight you two were involved in, which I heard Veronica talk about later . . .?'

'Had nothing to do with you.' Scrubber didn't want to talk about Jack Manning. A man couldn't make amends for everything. He could only thank his stars that Matt Hamilton was so concerned about his girl's future that *he* took the blame for Jack's death. Mills 'Scrubber' McCoy was the only one left at the end of that fateful day.

'And Thomas and Olive?' Cora queried.

'Knew of them,' Scrubber answered smoothly, 'never properly

introduced.' Well, he thought that wasn't really a lie. 'They sure high-tailed it out of town after the fire.'

'Yeah, they did leave quickly,' Cora agreed. 'They never came back to Absolution Creek.'

'Well, I'm not surprised, girly. They were hardly the bush type.'

It gradually became obvious Olive wanted nothing to do with the events that occurred that morning beneath the balcony of Green's Hotel and Board. She had been ill for two days from the shock of Jack's death and, Scrubber figured, the knowledge that her attacker lay injured within the same building. Initially, Scrubber expected to be arrested. He figured a man couldn't be lucky enough to escape two crimes. Yet just in case, he had a plan. In his defence he intended to plead mistaken identity. Jack was dead, after all, and Veronica and Squib had joined the bloody fray outside the hotel after Olive's initial accusation, so they knew nothing of his past. As for Thomas – well, the lad only had Olive's word to go by. Coppers required hard evidence. As the second day unfolded and the police didn't come knocking at his door, Scrubber realised there were more important things afoot for Olive Peters. Veronica, at their door stickybeaking, brought Scrubber the news: Olive, who had already telegraphed her parents and told them she was coming home with her *husband*, Thomas, didn't want to be associated with any scandal. Well that piece of information nearly blew Scrubber away. Olive and Jack's brother, man and wife? Squib had only just finished telling him that Olive had left Sydney to join Jack. There had been more going on out at Absolution Creek than met the eye. Only one thing bothered Scrubber, and he didn't understand why. Olive apparently was with child.

*'It's what Jack would expect,' Thomas argued. 'Squib should come back to Sydney with us.' They were sitting outside their shared room on the hotel balcony, Jack's saddle bag on the timber floorboards between them. 'I just can't believe all this*

*has happened. My own brother, dead.' He hung his head in his hands. 'He never should have come north. The bush changed him.'*

*'I can't talk about Jack, Thomas. Every time I think of him all I see is Jack lying in a pool of blood. I don't want to remember him that way. I can't remember him that way.' Olive handed the papers back to Thomas. 'Anyway, we were talking about Squib.' She glared at Squib who sat on the floorboards a good ten feet away. Olive had lost weight over the last few days despite the pregnancy, and her right hand now trembled uncontrollably. 'None of this is any of our concern, Thomas.' Her voice wavered slightly. 'Firstly, Jack doesn't own Absolution Creek, otherwise we could sell it. Secondly, Mr Grey has confirmed the legality of this transfer. Jack left the management of the property to her.' Olive gave Squib a brief incredulous glance while dabbing at her forehead with a handkerchief. 'Of course, it's ridiculous. The contract will have to be terminated and Mr Farley will have to find another fool to run his back-water piece of real estate.'*

*'That's exactly why Squib should return to Sydney with us,' Thomas argued.*

*'To be reminded of this horrid ordeal on a daily basis? My, but you have a strange sense of humour, Thomas.'*

*'You've changed, Olive. Where's your sense of kindness? Please don't be like this.'*

*Olive leant over the railings and peered into a gathering darkness. 'I lost it on the way to Absolution Creek.'*

*'Well, Squib's coming anyway, regardless of whether you agree with me or not.'*

*'How like your brother you are. You cajole your women with flattering words and a gentle kindness, but in the end it is only your decision that counts,' she replied wearily. 'Bring her then.' Olive straightened her shoulders. 'The upper classes are always*

*looking for staff. But we'll be dropping her in the suburbs. She can't come with us.'*

*'Olive!'*

*'We can't risk it. You and I are returning to Sydney as a married couple. I'm with child. That's enough of a disgrace for my family without the added possibility of that girl revealing the truth. Do you really want to add our presence at a murder to our list of disasters?'*

*'Murders,' Thomas corrected quietly. He watched as Squib walked back indoors, leaving them alone.*

*Olive wiped her eyes. 'As for the other. . . matter, the one involving that McCoy person . . . well, I don't want it discussed ever again.' She blew her nose into the sodden handkerchief. 'If we're not careful we will be nation-wide news.'*

*Squib found Veronica by Scrubber's side. She quickly told them of Thomas's suggestion.*

*'Well, of course you don't want to go to a place like Syd-e-ney with the likes of them.' Veronica nodded in agreement as she poked at the angry flesh of Scrubber's windpipe. Having been holed up in their room for three days while Scrubber recovered, Veronica was keen to move on as soon as her man felt marginally better. Squib couldn't blame her.*

*Squib sat by his bedside. 'The thing is, V, they're sending father to prison or worse.'*

*Veronica nodded and patted irritably at lank hair.*

*'I should follow him to Sydney. At least be there –' Squib swallowed '– if the worst happens.'*

*'They'll take you then, girly, for sure.' Veronica looked at Scrubber for support. 'Then what will have been the point of all this?'*

*The words hung in the airless room. Squib could still smell blood. She expected the raw stench of it would haunt her for the rest of her life.*

'Why not go see your father tonight before they take him in the morning?' Veronica took Scrubber's hand. 'Do as your father asked of my Scrubber. Do you think you can go to the gaol with her, lovey, for a little visitation with Matt? Squib here can pretend she's doing the speaking for you?'

'I don't know if I can,' Squib said softly. 'He killed . . . he killed Jack.'

Scrubber turned his face to the wall.

Veronica squeezed Squib's hand. 'You'll go and you'll make your peace, Squib Hamilton. Your father came to rescue you, and you'll not thank him by deserting him.'

They were given five minutes. Scrubber sank into a chair in the shadows, a single candle barely illuminating the lock-up. In spite of the emotions tearing at her belly, Squib's hands linked with her father's and they stood brow to brow, the cold of the metal bars unable to dull the warmth that flowed between them.

'He was good to you, this Jack Manning?'

Sweat and urine saturated the stifling cell. 'Yes, Father, very good.' Squib was torn. She didn't want to let go of her father, ever. Yet at the same time she wanted to hit him so hard that it hurt. Matt looked over his daughter's shoulder to where Scrubber sat. 'I'm sorry. You, you –'

'I loved him,' Squib blubbered.

'I'm sorry,' Matt repeated. He waited until his child calmed down a little. 'You understand now why I didn't come for you?'

'Because I'm a half-caste,' Squib whispered between choked sobs.

'Don't ever use that word. You're a beautiful child born out of pure love. When I first saw your mother she was singing. She had the most beautiful voice, Squib. It was a voice that made people stop and stare. It was a voice that made you believe that you could do anything. I was at a Mission up north at the time and if she'd not agreed to run away with me, I swear I would have gathered her up and thrown her across my nag, then and there.'

'Really?'

Matt grinned. 'Really. Your mother was part-Aboriginal, and a finer woman I never knew. However, the world's a strange place, Squib. People are afraid of those that are different and this land still has wounds from when white fought black.'

'What happened to Ben?' Squib asked softly.

Her father gave a low moan. 'How did you know?'

'I dreamed of him.' Her father looked old to her. It was as if a lifetime had passed since they were last together. It showed in the grey edging his hairline, and the sunken depths about his eyes.

Matt nodded. 'Your mother had such abilities.' He paused as if considering his next words. 'The authorities took him.'

'Where?'

Matt's gaze fell to the dirt floor. In the silence Scrubber's laboured breathing sounded very loud. 'An orphanage.' His eyes met his daughter's.

Squib mouthed the word, her lips trembling. 'Was it Jane?'

'Yes, it was Jane,' Matt admitted. 'Don't think too unkindly of her, Squib. She never knew a father's love. She was jealous.'

Squib thought of her own doings with her stepsister, specifically the fall from the back of the dray.

'She's now a maid for the Gordons at Wangallon Station,' Matt explained.

'And Beth?'

'I had to give her up.' Matt brightened. 'But she's with a good family, Squib. They're from Tamworth way, with means. The father's a lawyer. I couldn't keep her, not the way things were, and, as it turns out –' he looked about the dingy cell '– it was the right thing to do. You always were a good kid, Squib.' He squeezed her hand.

'Father?'

'Yes.'

Squib tightened her grip on his hand. 'I'll always remember those nights when the moon was fat with light.'

'Me too, Squib, me too.' He kissed her forehead through the bars. 'Now go over there and wait for a minute, will you? I need to have a little chat with Scrubber before you go. Hey Scrubber?'

'But I'll never see you again.' Squib couldn't help the tears forming in her eyes.

'Sure you will, Squib.' He smiled. 'Sure you will.'

Reluctantly Squib drew away from her father. Scrubber walked across to the cell, his feet dragging.

'Can't say I ever expected to be on this side of the law.' Matt gave him a smile. 'What they said about you back there – what they said about that woman, Olive – is it true?'

Scrubber hunched his shoulders.

Matt rubbed his chin. 'Wrong place at the wrong time?' he asked almost hopefully.

Scrubber wheezed.

Matt shook his head. 'You'll take care of Squib for me? You and Veronica? I'm trusting you, Scrubber. There isn't anyone else.' He took Scrubber's silence as agreement. 'They tell me I'll be hanged by my neck till I'm good and dead.' He gave a sour grin. 'The only good part is with Abigail being in the State Reformatory in Sydney the Constable reckons I'll get to see her; one last visitation before I have my own judgement with the Almighty.'

Scrubber shuffled his feet.

*'Now I realise you've already done more than a man can ask, however I need one more thing of you.' He waited for Scrubber to nod. 'Good.' Matt lowered his voice. 'Wherever they bury me, let Squib know so she can come and visit one day. I'd . . . well, I'd just like that. It's important for your kin to know where you lie. Will you promise me that?' Matt angled his arm through the metal bars and they shook on it. 'Good. Now go.'*

Scrubber looked at the water flowing a couple of feet below the branch where they sat. The girl was still asleep, an occasional low moan escaping her lips. Scrubber's own discomfort refused to lessen and he knew that time had finally run out. But by jove he'd given that thing way out in the east a good run; that thing waiting to snatch him up and cart him away to the nether world. Not a man could fault him for lack of determination. Scrubber put a hand down his shirtfront. The pouch was still there, if a little damp.

Thinking back to that visit to the gaol cell some forty years ago, Scrubber wished he'd not been so out of sorts. If he'd been of sound mind and not beset by a throbbing ache that refused to ease, he may have paid more attention to the shadowy form of a person lurking behind the police station. At the time he was more concerned with his own wounding and the soft comfort of a hotel bed. So he'd hunkered down by a paling fence not ten yards from the police station, his stomach aching from a lack of food as it couldn't pass down his gullet. When Squib was finally thrown out of the lock-up it took all of Scrubber's strength to coerce the sobbing girl back to the hotel. It was too much for him, this doing of good deeds. Nothing ever went to plan.

At some time during that night he awoke to a flare of light. At first he thought the brilliance reflected into the hotel room was due to the rum and laudanum Veronica made him swallow to ease his sleep. Light flickered across the tongue-and-groove wall boards and it took some time for the haze swirling in his head to clear. The commotion in the street cleared his thoughts.

The fire was lit during the night. By dawn the timber lock-up and the station were totally destroyed, a burning pile of timber the only sign left of the law in Stringybark Point, for two constables along with Matt Hamilton were burnt to death and lay buried in the charred heap.

*The rumours circulated quickly: Lickable Lorraine pointed the finger at Mills 'Scrubber' McCoy; Veronica pointed the finger at Lickable Lorraine. Half the townsfolk reckoned Lorraine was just the woman to seek revenge for Adams's death, and when she punched Veronica in the nose, even the publican – the fount of all knowledge – considered Lickable Lorraine's involvement possible. Within hours, however, the sting of gossip floated back in Scrubber's direction. He was the stranger involved in the previous fight; Lorraine was local. They didn't have much choice.*

*'But you can't go back out there to Absolution Creek,' Veronica complained to Squib as she stuffed their items into cracked saddle bags, 'and we can't stay.' She looked at Scrubber for confirmation, her nose bruised and swollen. 'It's too risky. It's likely they'll hang Scrubber in the street, the town's that riled up. There are six people dead, including them coppers.'*

*Squib walked out onto the balcony. It was mid-morning. She could barely think straight. Jack was in a grave on the edge of town and her father had been burned to ash. It was almost beyond comprehension.*

*'I want to get some of the ash, as a remembrance, so I have something of my father.'*

'Did you hear what I said?' Veronica yanked Squib back inside their room and shut the wooden door with a firm click. 'No one's hanging around Stringybark Point, my girl.' She glanced at Scrubber. 'Not even Thomas stayed.'

'What?' Squib asked.

Veronica folded her arms across her chest. 'Him and that woman left at daylight. So you don't have to worry any more about being dragged off to Syd-e-ney.'

Squib swallowed. 'Without me?'

Veronica touched her swollen nose. 'They weren't hanging around to see what happens next.'

'What do I do, then? Where do I go?' Squib wrung her hands together. 'Jack's dead,' she sniffed, 'my father's . . .'

'High-tail it out of here with us, I say. Otherwise, girly, all these men –' she glanced at Scrubber '– all of their efforts will have been for nothing.'

Squib's head spun. 'What about Absolution Creek? Jack left it to me.' She recalled his last words, that he would always be by her side there.

'A young girl alone in the scrub,' Veronica pleaded. 'Why, there are wild men and natives and any number of calamities that could befall you. Come with us. Make a life with us.'

Squib shook her head, her thoughts clearing. 'They'd come after us for sure. There will be people wanting an end to all of this, wanting to make an example.'

Veronica paused from stuffing the hotel towels into a canvas bag. 'She's right, Scrubber. If we all stay together it could be risky.' She gave Squib a hug. 'Go back to your Absolution Creek. We'll stay at the Five Mile for a month.' Veronica smoothed Squib's hair. 'Join us there when things calm down.'

❖

'You awake then, Squib?' Scrubber poked at her shoulder. If he was freezing he could only guess at how Cora felt. Her skin was grey.

'Sure. I'm awake. I'm perched in a tree six foot up off the ground with flood water swirling below me. I'd hardly be asleep.'

Scrubber gave a croaky huff. 'No point getting annoyed with me. Do you remember that morning when you left Stringybark Point?' He retrieved the pouch.

'Yes.'

'Well, I did what you wanted. I went down to the lock-up and scraped up some of the ash.'

Cora turned to him. 'You did what?'

'On account of the fact you would have done it and on account of the fact that your father wanted me to let you know where they buried him, if he'd made it to Sydney. Well, he didn't even get a proper grave. Anyway, the lock-up was at the rear, remember. The bars were still standing the next day.' Scrubber set the pouch in her hand. 'I reckon most of what's in there is him.' Scrubber scratched his chin. 'I think.'

'This is –'

'Yep, that would be your father, Matt Hamilton, all six foot plus of him. Or near-abouts. Built like a brick outhouse, he was, with a face women loved.'

Cora hugged the pouch to her chest.

'He weren't a bad travelling companion, although Dog complained about favouritism from time to time on account of me looking after your father first of a night when we made camp. Anyway, it took me some time to get back to you but a man always keeps his promises.'

'Oh, Scrubber, I can't believe it.'

Scrubber gave a chuckle. 'I guess a man like me with no family worth speaking of . . . well, sometimes he just fixes his mind on a person until they become kin.' The countryside was submerged under an inland sea. Sticks, grass and a dead kangaroo floated past a stand of box trees.

Cora cradled the cracked leather pouch. 'You must be the best person in the whole world, Scrubber. Our family was lucky the day Father met you.' She squeezed his gnarly hand, her eyes brimming.

In an instant Scrubber felt the knife slip between Jack's ribs; recalled the Hamilton family leaving Waverly Station in the dead of night.

'To think you'd travel all this way, after all these years.' Cora sniffed. 'This means the world to me, to be able to bury my father.'

He could have told her he was dying, that he'd run out of excuses, that he wanted to go to his maker with a clean conscience. That was what he'd thought on leaving the hilly country. Now he wanted more, and wanting more meant he couldn't tell Cora the truth about the past.

'Well, you always were Matt's favourite.'

'Did he tell you that?'

'Sure he did, girly. Took after him, Matt reckoned.' Scrubber cleared his throat. 'Anyway, you bury him proper like and look to the future.'

'The future,' Cora repeated. 'I've always found it pretty hard to escape the past.'

'Well, you can't have a life with dead people,' Scrubber replied sagely. 'A person's got to let go and move on.' Rich words, he mused, when he'd been incapable of doing the same.

'Maybe I'll try doing that, Scrubber. Now you're here, once we get out of this, we'll be able to sit down and talk about the old days. There are so many things I want to ask you, so many things I need to know.' Cora's teeth chattered with coldness. She tucked the pouch down her shirt front.

'Sure thing, girly.' Scrubber thought of the people left in the world who knew him. After all the miles travelled and the years spent brewing, in the end only Squib's good opinion mattered. It mattered far more than forgiveness. How could he tell her the truth?

## ⊰ Chapter 61 ⊱

## Absolution Creek, 1965

The helicopter continued to hover over the Absolution Creek homestead. Meg peered out the side of the machine straight down into Cora's bedroom. Most of the ceiling had collapsed in on itself and the walkway appeared to have sunk a good foot into the ground. Only the leopardwood tree remained rooted securely to the earth, its branches sprawling starkly over the homestead's gaping roof as Sam was winched into the air. Tripod was in Sam's arms as the cable reeled them upwards and he gave a bark of acknowledgement when they reached the opening of the hovering chopper. The twins were securely buckled in either side of Meg and Kendal, Curly sitting safely between Meg's legs.

James freed the dog from Sam's grip and handed Tripod across to Meg. He replaced the headphones over his ears as Sam stepped out of the rescue harness. 'Can we do another run over the creek?'

The pilot tapped the fuel gauge. 'A brief one, James. I can't risk running low and I still have to drop this lot off at your place before I head back to Stringybark Point.'

The helicopter dipped its nose as it lifted and then flew eastwards. The land surrounding the house was covered in water. Here and there patches of grass broke the shallow coverage as they flew towards the dam. 'This is local water from the rain, not flood water,' James informed them, pointing to the white of the dam's bank. Thirty or so rams were bunched atop it, along with a couple of kangaroos and two poddy lambs. 'There's Montgomery!' James called loudly to Meg and Sam. 'Cora got him out.' Absolution Creek's prize ram lifted his rain-matted head and sniffed the air as the helicopter flew overhead.

The land shimmered under the rays of the afternoon sun. The cloud was breaking in the west and in the fledgling light it became easier to see the path of the flood. The main water extended to the east a good five or so kilometres from the homestead; the remainder of the tree-dotted countryside was simply rain-drenched. Sheep were feeding out through the soggy landscape and cattle were huddled on the odd dry ridge. As they neared the creek James leant further out of the side of the helicopter. The road leading in the direction of the creek crossing was easily spotted from the air and soon they were flying to the line of trees marking the waterway.

'Can you set me down?'

The pilot gave James a thumbs-down. 'That's a negative. I can't drop you alone, James, you know that. Anyway, this flood water looks to be draining away fairly well. The current will be too strong.'

James looked at Sam. Meg nudged her husband.

'Always did want to jump out of a chopper,' Sam said unenthusiastically.

'I've got a volunteer,' James yelled over the noise of the rotor blade. 'How about heading to the south-east boundary? It should be drier there and then we can walk back towards the water.'

The pilot handed James a hand-held two-way radio. 'I'll be back in one hour. You've only got a small window; it'll be dark soon.'

Meg told Sam to take care and then crawled carefully to James's side as her husband calmed the twins. 'James –' she gripped his arm '– be careful.'

He turned towards the water-devoured land. 'Look –' James pointed to the south-east where a saddled horse stood forlornly in water '– it looks like there's a dog sitting on top of that animal.'

The pilot nodded. 'I'll be damned.'

'You sure you want to do this?' Sam queried. 'Dropping into flood water isn't high on my to-do list.'

'This is it, James.' The pilot gave a thumbs-up.

James whipped the headphones off. 'This is Cora we're talking about, Sam.'

'Fine,' Sam responded dully.

The helicopter found a spot well clear of the worst of the water and hovered close to the ground. 'If you don't want to help then bugger off, but I'm going to find her.' He jumped out the door of the chopper and landed in knee-deep water.

Sam turned to Meg. 'I know you liked him, but it looks like you lucked out.'

Meg watched as Sam jumped from the helicopter, slipped and fell over on the soggy ground. She never had been religious, but on the odd occasion Meg almost believed there was a god, and today, at least, he had a sense of humour.

Around mid-afternoon, when exhaustion finally claimed Matt's daughter, Scrubber raised his face to the clearing drizzle. In the west the sun was poking through the clouds. Opposite to where he perched, the bark of a gum tree showed a slight drop in the water's level. Overhead a helicopter whirred towards them.

Despite the paleness of her skin and bedraggled hair she was still his Squib; the young girl he'd harmed by default. Scrubber took a long drink of her, this girl who was the last remnant of Matt Hamilton. At last he knew he could let go. He'd dreamt of a silver brigalow, a shady canopy that sheltered a grassy patch of solitude, and now the tree beckoned. Scrubber had travelled west in search of absolution. Absolution for his attack on Olive, absolution for his part in the demise of Matt Hamilton's family and absolution for killing Jack Manning. In the end he hadn't even bothered to discover if Squib was okay after they all left Stringybark Point, and hadn't Matt asked him to look after his girl? Sure, they stayed the month at the Five Mile. Then he and Veronica fled east.

In the end, Scrubber realised, forgiveness wouldn't be forth-coming. For his sins to be wiped clean he needed to admit them and if he did so Cora 'Squib' Hamilton's world would be ripped apart again. What was the point of opening old wounds when he could simply leave with something far more valuable – her respect, maybe even her affection. At the thought his eyes moistened.

Slipping quietly from the branch, Scrubber splashed into the water. The cool current carried him aloft and he floated away on a dream of his earlier life. These imagined recollections centred around his time at Waverly Station and in his final fancying of how life may have unfolded. Scrubber accepted his fate. When the water took hold he was sure a silver brigalow waited just ahead and he closed his eyes in anticipation.

Seconds later leathery fingers released their grasp on a string of pearls. The luminous necklace disappeared quickly into the murky current.

A few minutes later a leathery hand rose and then very slowly Scrubber sank from sight.

<hr />

There was movement and noise. Cora would have answered the voices were she not so unsure of where she was. The lower part of her body was numb, while the upper half stung with constriction. Flashes of churning water, a horse and a mangy dog were interspersed with the images of the main street of Stringybark Point and Scrubber. Jack Manning lay dead in her arms, blood seeping into dirt and dust. Cora sobbed for the man she'd loved and lost, yet when she imagined him again it was a young girl, Squib, who was with Jack. The distance grew between the scene and Cora's imagining. Like a cloud, the picture detached itself and floated away. Cora cried out at the loss of it. She wasn't ready to let go.

'Let go, Cora, I've got you.'

There was a rush of air, a jolt of pain and then warmth.

'I'll have to carry her, Sam. She can't stand. Radio the chopper and tell them we've got her.'

James lifted Cora into his arms. 'It's the old injury, James,' she whispered, barely conscious of where she was.

'My dear girl,' he replied, striding through the water, 'all wounds heal.'

## ⤺ Chapter 62 ⤻

## Campbell Station,
## 1965

Cora opened her eyes. Sunlight streamed through lemony silk curtains to reveal mahogany wood and cream walls. She knew she was in a bedroom, however she had expected to see a different environment; one of white and chrome. That sterile room came with an irritating nurse with a tendency towards waking her throughout the night. Rubbing sleep from the corners of her eyes Cora struggled up in the bed. This was the Lemon guest room at Campbell Station. Clearly her delusions were lessening, but her memory still suffered from infuriating gaps. Snatches of the hospital, of a helicopter, of James carrying her, were interspersed with flood water and the strangest of dreams. Cora was almost certain Scrubber McCoy had been by her side, had in fact rescued her from the swollen creek. But that couldn't possibly be true, and even the fractious night nurse agreed: no one else had been rescued from that part of Absolution Creek. Flipping back the bed covers, Cora stared at her plastered leg. She sure had done a proper job on herself this time.

'How are you feeling?' Meg, her arms stuffed with books and magazines, dumped her hoard on the bedside table. 'You've been out of it for quite a few days.'

'My waist is sore.'

Meg patted her hand. 'You were strung up in a tree, Cora, when James and Sam found you. Damn smart thing to do. The doctor said that you probably would have fallen out of it otherwise. You were pretty weak.' She poured water into a glass.

Cora wanted to ask about Scrubber but she didn't want to sound like a crazy person.

'This was with your belongings at the hospital.' Meg handed over an old leather pouch.

Cora clutched it in amazement. Scrubber wasn't a hallucination! He'd saved her.

'Is everything okay, Cora?'

'Yes, fine. Thanks. Is everyone else okay?' She accepted the water gratefully, taking a noisy gulp. Images of Scrubber sitting in the tree next to her flitted through her brain.

'Well, Kendal had a bit of an accident, however he'll be fine, and Sam's left.'

'Left you and the girls?' Cora sat the glass on the table, but kept the pouch tightly in her hand.

'It's a mutual decision. And I'm leaving as well. I'm going back to Sydney tomorrow, with Mum.'

Cora shook her head. 'Jane's here?' Seeing her stepsister while laid up like an invalid wasn't exactly how Cora pictured their first meeting after all these years.

'Yes.' Meg looked a little uncomfortable. 'I know it's not the best timing for it.' She glanced at Cora as if expecting agreement. 'It's just that I've been staying here with James for a week now and although he's been very kind I think it's best if the girls and I leave.'

Meg's cheeks were a mottled pink.

'Oh.' Cora didn't understand.

Meg made a fuss of straightening the magazines. 'He's a good man, Cora, and he's certainly not hanging around Absolution to check on the livestock.' She looked at her aunt almost severely. 'You know he slept at the hospital while you were there?'

'No, I didn't know. I've been hallucinating a little.' Cora tilted her head sideways. 'You like him,' she stated. 'Have you and he . . . well, have you –'

Meg's cheeks turned scarlet. 'No.'

Cora closed her eyes briefly in relief. 'Anyway, why is Jane here and why don't you go back to Absolution Creek while I'm recuperating?'

'We thought you'd drowned, Cora. Mum was already on her way here when James found you. Anyway, I have to get back to Sydney somehow.' Meg took Cora's hand in hers. 'Cora, the house is ruined. There isn't anything to go back to. What hasn't fallen down will have to be destroyed and then totally rebuilt.'

'Then I have nothing.'

Meg gave a wan smile. 'You have the land.'

'But I don't own Absolution Creek. I was only the manager, and if I default on just one payment the contract is terminated and then I have nothing. I'll never be able to repair the flood damage let alone build another house.' Cora ran her fingers through messy hair.

Meg frowned. 'I don't understand. I thought you owned the property. I thought I'd inherit it. That's half the reason why I made the decision to move. I couldn't think of any other purpose for you to have contacted me. It's not like you needed a carer.'

Cora manoeuvred to the edge of the bed and carefully lifted her plastered leg to rest both feet on the floor. 'Are you sure that you don't understand, Meg? Think back to the little girl, Squib.'

Meg tilted her head to one side. 'What?'

'An eye for an eye.' Cora softened her voice. 'Your mother took everything from me and so I wanted the only thing left of her. I

507

wanted to make her mad. I wanted to come back into her life and change hers, however insignificantly. I wanted you to understand what *she* did. I told you that the night we sat by the fire.'

Meg gave a burst of laughter. 'Me? I'm not sure if my moving out of Mum's place had the effect you were after.'

'Maybe not, but now you know the truth. She never would have revealed it.' Cora gave a satisfied smile. 'Little wins are sweet.'

Meg frowned. 'A little similar to your Aboriginal ancestry – a small fact you omitted to mention.'

'*Et tu*, Brutus?' Cora's niece was silent. 'Maybe now you can understand the importance of Absolution Creek. It protected me. It gave me the one thing white people couldn't touch – self-respect.'

'Yes, you always did have the uncanny knack of falling on your feet.' Jane Hamilton stood in the doorway, her grey hair drawn back into a severe bun. It had been forty years since they'd seen each other, and Cora found herself facing premature old age.

'Jane.' Cora gave a curt nod. Meg tried to excuse herself and was halted by her mother's hand.

'You took Meg as revenge for Ben. You took her to remind me that you still existed.' Jane drew the curtains open on a low hedge. Birds darted through the greenery. 'You needn't have bothered. Your type always survives.' Jane fumbled with a cigarette, lit it and exhaled the smoke loudly. 'Meg thought you were looking for an heir for Absolution Creek. I'm sure that's why she agreed to this hairbrained arrangement of yours. I knew better, but I must admit I didn't expect you to still be out here in this god-forsaken country and I never guessed you didn't own Absolution.' Jane took another puff. 'Canny girl like you – you're losing your touch, *Squib*.' Jane drawled her stepsister's childhood name.

'Ben died in an orphanage; hanged himself from a rafter three months after you reported him to the authorities.' Cora's eyes were steely. 'When he died he was a week away from being sent out to work, but he'd been bullied relentlessly. It took me eight years to discover the truth. Eight years of writing to numerous institutions, pleading for information. How do you feel knowing that you killed Ben? He never did any harm to you.'

'Don't be so melodramatic. Anyway, it was government policy.' Jane leant on the windowsill. 'Not much has changed since then.'

Meg was horrified. 'Mum!'

'Besides, Father died trying to save you,' Jane countered.

Cora clutched at the leather pouch. 'He wasn't *your* father.'

Jane took a step towards her and then, as if realising for the first time that her own daughter was present, halted abruptly. Meg's mouth was hanging open.

'*My* father's death was mapped out from the moment you watched me fall from the dray. Your scheming and your jealousy caused his death.'

Meg squirmed in the tub chair.

Jane opened the casement window a little, tossed the cigarette out and looked over her shoulder. 'I never realised what a tough little nugget you were. You were everything to Matt, you know. None of us ever got a look in – well, except my mother and Ben. Despite what you think, Abigail was a good person. She didn't steal that necklace.'

'She went to gaol for the crime, Jane,' Cora replied pointedly. 'Anyway, I guess Abigail had her favourites too. I can't recall you ever being tired from overwork.'

Jane sniffed. 'By the time I'd saved enough money out at Wangallon Station to travel to Sydney, my mother was dead. They couldn't keep her at the Reformatory for long without proof of the theft. Anyway, the streets aren't kind to single women and my mother was never streetwise.' Jane looked at Cora. 'I imagine you would have survived a whole lot better.'

Cora exhaled at the barb in Jane's words. 'You know I wanted to see you, to have it out with you. I realise now what a ridiculous idea it was. We have nothing in common, we have no shared values and you never did possess a shred of common decency. Nothing's changed.'

Jane lifted a thinning eyebrow. 'You were expecting an apology? In your own way, if only by default, you also ruined my life.'

'This should be good,' Cora muttered.

'I tried locating Beth over the years, but I never could find any records of her adoption. After Meg was born I had this need to share my past with my husband.' Jane stared at her stepsister. 'You seem to think you were the only wounded party in all of this. Anyway, the mistake I made was telling Meg's father of *your* birth right. He left that night and never came home.' Jane laughed. 'Damned by association. I gather he thought I was of a similar –' she stared down her nose '– strain. After that, well, I really did wish you the worst.'

'You said he'd died in the war,' Meg disputed.

Cora was speechless. She wanted to say that she was sorry. Sorry for the attitude that some white Australians held towards their Aboriginal counterparts. The problem was, of course, that Jane had fallen foul of her own racism. Like had married like.

'So the reason I have no relations on my father's side is because they don't want to know us?' Meg faltered. 'I can't believe it.' She left the room with a slam of the door.

'I doubt she would have stayed on even without this flood debacle.' Jane's fingers scrabbled at the neckline of the woollen dress.

'It doesn't matter.' Cora reached for the wooden crutches leaning against the wall. They were a bit fancier than the branches she'd used all those years ago. 'I wanted Meg to know the truth of things. Now she does. More importantly, now she really knows you.' Cora ignored the hard stare Jane gave her. 'Well, she's grown up in your absence. She's not a wallflower any more. She returns to you minus one husband, thankfully.'

Jane gave a single nod of assent. 'That's one thing we do agree on.'

'Look after those grandchildren of yours. They're good kids.'

Jane walked slowly to the door. Cora accepted this was a meeting that should never have occurred. Jane Hamilton wasn't capable of apologising, which was perhaps fortunate since Cora would never have forgiven her. The pity of it was that her stepsister needed forgiveness desperately. Jane's past acts were eating her alive. 'Have a good life.'

Jane's hand paused on the doorknob. For the briefest of seconds Cora was almost positive she mouthed the words *and you,* but she would never be sure.

Cora was sitting out on the veranda. For some minutes she'd been watching streaky clouds form and reform into varying shapes and sizes. It was a rather cathartic process, and while she yearned to be walking around normally she certainly wasn't minding the enforced rest. The garden smelt fresh, and the low hedges and flower beds gave her a heightened anticipation for the coming of spring. Cora felt as if she'd been given a second chance. Winter had been gruelling this year – in fact, too much of everything in her life had been hard. Meg and Jane had left a good week earlier for Sydney and although there were promises from Meg of keeping in touch, Cora's expectations weren't high. Meg Bell was just starting her life all over again and Cora had reminded her that the past she now knew wasn't hers. She needed to move on. Through the gauze, Curly and Tripod raced across the winter lawn, snapping and biting intermittently. They were behaving like pups again today and Cora found their enthusiasm infectious.

'How's the patient?' James kissed Cora on the cheek. He held a mug of coffee in each hand and a packet of biscuits under one arm. 'Talking to yourself again?' He glanced at the cracked tobacco pouch resting on the wooden ledge.

'Not today,' she admitted as James deposited the coffee and biscuits on Eloise Campbell's morning tea trolley. 'I keep thinking about Scrubber. That he's snagged in the creek or caught in a fence line somewhere.'

'He saved you, Cora. Let him be.'

'I know he did.' Cora looked at the pouch. 'Somehow, remembering those last few days all those years ago, well, he also set me free.'

'Good.' James disappeared into the house to return with a mottled green urn. 'It's the best I could do at short notice.'

'It's beautiful.' James handed Cora the tobacco pouch and she squeezed the leather into the narrow ceramic neck. 'Thank you.'

'You sure you don't want it buried or something?' James placed the lid on the urn, sitting it on the trolley.

'No, at least not for a while. I have a few things I want to talk to Dad about first.'

If James thought Cora a little morbid he was respectful enough to remain quiet. He drew a cane chair next to hers. To the east of Campbell Station lay Absolution Creek; by her side was James. 'Even if I could go back to Absolution Creek I wouldn't. Not now.' Cora pointed to a letter on the cane table. 'That's a directive to Grey's Solicitors stating that I've ended the contract of management between myself and the Farley Family Trust. They also get to handle Jarrod's lawsuit as the accident happened on their land, although obviously there will still be some paperwork to attend to at my end.'

James took her hands between his. 'You're sure?'

'Yes.' She smiled. 'I'm sure. Absolution protected me from the world, but it also stopped me from living my life. I just hope you can understand why it was so important to me to ensure everyone think the property belonged to me. It's all I've ever had, James. I was so young when Jack and Father died that I lost sight of reality and I was scared. For ten years I ran Absolution Creek with the help of Captain Bob and four other members of the tribe. By the time I took over the running of the property completely, everyone around here was either afraid of me or wishing me ill.'

'They respected you.'

'They put up with me: the girl who possibly murdered a man in Stringybark Point. A part-Aboriginal woman running a property.' Cora laughed. 'If I'd been you I would have stayed the hell away.'

'But I didn't.'

'No, you're in the dictionary under P for perseverance.' He kissed her then and as the warmth of James's arms embraced her Cora finally said goodbye to Jack, at least in this life.

'Harold rang,' James informed her. 'He's looking for a job.'

'No, really?'

James nodded. 'Apparently Ellen won't budge from the district now she's a member of the Women's Club.'

'What did you say?'

'That I'd think about it. Kendal's out of hospital too and looking for Sam.'

Cora laughed. 'He won't find him. Meg said he was heading north.'

'Well, good luck to him. I suppose you'll want to bring that famous ram of yours over here.'

'Of course, and Scrubber's horse and ancient dog.' Cora reached for the crutches.

'Isn't it about time you took my hand?' James asked.

'Yes,' Cora agreed, balancing carefully as James drew her into his arms. 'It probably is.'

# ≪ *Acknowledgements* ≫

My inspiration for *Absolution Creek* stemmed from a story my grandfather told my father in the 1940s. In the late 1800s a child was found wandering across the Garah Plains, an area some fifty kilometres to the south-east of where we live. Whether the child wandered from a campsite or fell from the rear of a dray was never established. At a time when roads were mere tracks, the bush scrubby and remote, and travelling arduous, such an incident is not difficult to believe.

Mr Purcell's stud ram in the story, Waverly No. 4, is based on arguably Australia's most famous stud ram, Uardry 0.1. Uardry 0.1 was bred by the historic Uardry Merino Stud. The ram was immortalised on the Australian shilling coin from 1938 to 1966. He featured again on the 50 cent coin in 1991 and, most recently, in 2011 on the $1 coin.

Much of the period detail in *Absolution Creek* comes from the Alexander family archives, in particular a 1923 Anthony Hordern's mail-order catalogue, which sold everything from groceries,

# Acknowledgements

furniture and saddlery items, to pressed metal ceilings! Similarly, while searching through 1950s *Agricultural Gazettes* and animal husbandry books from the 1920s, I found an old *Sydney Morning Herald* celebrating the opening of the Sydney Harbour Bridge. With the displacement of whole communities a largely forgotten aspect of this engineering marvel, I decided on Sydney as the beginning for the story. This seemed especially relevant to me as *Absolution Creek* will be published in 2012 during the 80th anniversary of the bridge's opening.

Thank you, as always, to my family and friends who have supported me throughout the writing of this novel. In particular I must thank my father, Ian, for his anecdotes and enthusiasm; my mother, Marita, who pulled me through a rough patch (I deleted 30,000 words mid-novel) with sage advice and love; my ever-supportive sister, Brooke; and David, who by now is used to my occasional tendency to call him by a character's name!

A book's production is very much a team effort. To Random House and the wonderful team within – most especially, publisher Beverly Cousins, editor Sophie Ambrose, marketing strategist Tobie Mann and PR stalwart Karen Reid – thank you for your continued assistance and professionalism. Thank you also to my literary agent, Tara Wynne, for her friendship and advice. To Todd Decker, book-trailer producer extraordinaire, and Scott Bridle (who would have thought I'd have a world-class aerial musterer/photographer only a few hundred kilometres away), thank you.

This year I would like to shine a spotlight on the Queensland–New South Wales border town of Goondiwindi, which from the very beginning has been so supportive of my writing endeavours. Thank you for your enthusiasm, support and friendship – in particular, Bev Cranny from the Nook & Cranny Bookshop, and Heather Scanlon.

The year 2011 was a tough one for writing, with mother nature throwing her weight around in the form of two floods that top and tailed it and a dry spell mid-year. Yet, as always, when I think of the problems we face in the bush today, I'm reminded of what men and women endured in the outback in the past. I hope my work shines a spotlight on those that came before us. During 2012 I'm proud to be associated with two great initiatives: the National Year of Reading and the Australian Year of the Farmer. As a writer and a farmer, I'm a great believer in nourishing both the mind and the body!

Lastly, to the many booksellers here and abroad, and my friends and readers, old and new: thank you. Without you all there would be no *Absolution Creek*.

# ❧ *About the Author* ❧

In the course of her career Nicole Alexander has worked both in Australia and Singapore in financial services, fashion, corporate publishing and agriculture. A fourth-generation grazier, Nicole returned to her family's property in the 1990s. She is currently the business manager there and has a hands-on role in the running of the property. Nicole has a Master of Letters in creative writing, and her poetry, travel and genealogy articles have been published in Australia, America and Singapore.

Visit www.nicolealexander.com.au

# ❈ Reading Group Questions ❈

1. What symbolic purpose does the tree in the homestead at Absolution Creek have?
2. Scrubber is an antihero in the novel. At the end of the story, he feels he's made amends despite deciding not to tell Cora the truth about his role in her past. Do you think he deserves to feel redeemed?
3. Which other main character could be said to experience a redemptive journey during the novel?
4. Squib's life is altered by a chain of devastating events. Is it fair that she blames Jane for much of it?
5. Do you feel Jack is selfish in his almost obsessive attitude towards Absolution Creek at the expense of his relationship with Olive? Or is Olive too quick to blame Jack for her new life?
6. Olive decides not to tell her family or Jack about the attack and the chance that she could be pregnant. What do you think of her decision?

7. What is the common bond that brings Jack and Squib together? Do you think Jack would have fallen for her if they had met in Sydney?
8. Who is your favourite character and why?
9. Do you think the use of an interweaving narrative – switching between two different eras – assists in making the story more engaging?
10. Squib/Cora spends years trying to find her place in the world. How important are the themes of identity and displacement in the book?